SAMANTHA RANSIER

Ask For Ellis!

A Tale from the Midnight Raven

S.R.

MIDNIGHT
RAVEN
PUBLISHING

First published by Midnight Raven Publishing 2024

You are so worthy of having your story heard. Thank you for being here <3

First edition

ISBN: 978-1-0687872-2-5

Illustration by Mew.Munn

This book was professionally typeset on Reedsy.
Find out more at reedsy.com

Contents

Trigger Warnings

Welcome back, Friend!

Thank you so much for joining me once again for another instalment of Tales From the Midnight Raven. If you haven't read Murderess of the Midnight Raven, you won't miss anything major. However, if you do, you'll have a deeper understanding of the underlying plot as a whole. The books in this series are not chronological, they run along the same timeline, so you can read them in any order or independently. If you love Ask For Ellis, I really recommend reading the other books in the series as you will gain a deeper understanding of the heroes, villains, and victims!

My name is Sam, and I am a massive proponent in the protection of people's mental health. Because of that, I like to be explicitly honest with my trigger list to not only protect my readers, but anyone who may stumble up on this little series of mine.

Ask For Ellis is a Male x Male romance between a fiery English Drag Queen running from a tragic past, and a strong but silent Single Father running from an abusive ex-wife. This novel focuses on awareness for Bi-Sexuality and true self expression, including self discovery.

The previous book in this series featured quite a lot of heavy topics surrounding prostitution and pimping. This novel continues along this vein, so if you aren't prepared for themes of sexual promiscuity and exploration that are morally ambiguous, please take care of yourself and put this book back down on the shelf!

Ask For Ellis hosts the following triggers:

- Sex, explicit and open door scenes which include anal and oral sex
- Unconventional and amoral sexual themes that will most definitely be perceived as morally grey/black
- Features of alcohol addiction
- Features of abuse of the physical and emotional kind, as well as mentions of sexual abuse (not depicted in great detail)
- Sex Work/ Prostitution/ Contractual Sex
- Extreme Rep for Mental Health including dramatized episodes of psychosis, psychotic depression, reckless behaviour, and a near miss attempt of suicide.
- Blood, Gore, and mentions of murder, suicide, and death.
- Mentions of infidelity.
- Contractual servitude.
- Cute gay shit that will make you squeal or cringe
- Elements of homophobic ideology (don't worry, he gets punched in the face)

As I always say, if any of these themes trigger or make you uncomfortable, I fully respect returning this book to the shelf. You are MY top priority and I have a duty of care to ensure that I am not needlessly harming anyone who reads my work. Please take your time and be gentle with yourself during particularly triggering scenes. Remember that you are worthy of helping and support.

Not that I NEED to state this, but I will anyway. The themes in this book represent mental health in their truest and rawest forms to the best of my extent as someone who has studied and worked in mental health for years. Of course, this is ABSOLUTELY not a representation of mental health as a whole. The events within these pages are dramatized and will absolutely NOT represent every individual who is living with similar mental health disorders. Psychosis and Depression are very real, and people with these are by no means villains. It is important to separate our fact from fiction and I will 100% say that some of the content will misrepresent at least fractions of these very real experiences. My work is not diagnostic criteria, my work is not a blanket with which we will define mental illness. This is simply representation.

If you or anyone you know is struggling with their mental health, is in an abusive relationship, or is a victim of human trafficking or modern slavery, please reach out to your local resources. Here in the UK, you can reach out to The Samaritans, MIND, and your local GP service if you are struggling. If you need further support or resources, please feel free to message me on Instagram (that is where I respond the fastest) and I can help as best as I can.

Thank you for being here with me. I hope you love Ellis and Brooke as much as I do

Love you forever!
Sam

This is dedicated to

Those of you who picked up a makeup brush and painted away the pain.

Daycare

BROOKE

They say that you never truly experience love until you look into the eyes of your own child for the first time.

Rae Everly Morris was born on August 5th, 2024.

She is my everything.

I knew the moment that I held her, she was going to change my life for good...

Unfortunately, I didn't realize at the time that the change it would enact upon me would be quite as severe as it was. My wife, Kelly, decided that she was going to run off with her co-worker a few weeks after Rae's birth.

She left me with a newborn baby, a filthy house that never

2

seemed to stay clean, and twelve years worth of love and joy... just dashed to pieces like they never happened. Heartbreak is painful, and I was jaded to say the absolute least. But Rae... she was my priority.

As I sat in my La-Z-Boy, I couldn't help but feel this overwhelming dread for the day to come. It was Rae's first day at daycare, and my first day away from her since she came home with me from the hospital six weeks ago. My boss had been nagging me to come back into the office for weeks now, but nobody ever quite understands the struggle of a single man with a newborn... none of my friends are necessarily the baby-sitting type, and no amount of paternity leave actually covers the costs of childcare.

Beside me, the static on Rae's monitor broke as the sound of her gentle whimpers pulled through the silent lounge where I sat, nursing a cup of coffee that was probably far too strong for my heart. I placed the mug on the coffee table before me and found my way up the stairs to the tiny bedroom where Rae now cried for me.

"Good morning," I whispered in a soft, bright tone as I dipped into the crib to receive the tiny girl from her cot.

She cried, her sweet pink cheeks glowing as she thrashed her tiny legs about in the air.

"Oh, goodness," The words drifted off my tongue in a doting manner, "Are we hungry? Shall we get you a bottle?" I asked, pulling her to rest against my chest with her head on my shoulder. Her tiny hands grasped the fabric of my shirt with all the might her tiny body could muster, and my heart burst with love for her.

I turned to pull a onesie from one of her drawers, then carried my daughter and her clothing down the stairs to the kitchen where I could prepare her bottle. Rae cried the entire time, but the impatient whines didn't bother me. In fact, her persistence drove my everyday life. Maybe if I was a little bit more like my Rae... I wouldn't have been so easy to walk out on.

With a fresh, warm bottle in my hand, I tipped a drop onto my wrist to check the temperature of her drink, then carried her back through to the lounge where I sat down in my La-Z-Boy again and laid her down across my arm.

"Right, you little mouse," I muttered sweetly, placing the nipple at her lips. She opened her mouth, her tiny hands flexing as she sweetly placed them on either side of the bottle.

She gulped down the contents of the bottle with a thirst that mimicked that of a man who'd not seen water for days. Sweet, soft grunts sounded from her occasionally. I held her close to me as she finished the bottle, taking in every single second of this while I could... savouring this feeling.

Beside me, the alarm warning me that I had twenty minutes before I needed to leave went off, startling Rae into a little jump. Her eyes narrowed and she began to whimper, her hands falling from the now-empty bottle. I scooped her against my shoulder and pat her back, whispering sweetly to her as I silenced the alarm.

I continued to pat her back, waiting for her to burp, and when she finally did, I pulled her down and laid her in my lap, "Shall we get ready to go, Mouse?" I asked softly, stroking her cheek gently.

She stared up at me with those beautiful, sweet green eyes. It was so clear that she had absolutely no clue what I was saying to her, but she was damn good at pretending like she was even remotely interested in me. I chuckled lightly and changed her into her onesie, a simple pink one piece that said "Daddy's Princess" in bubble letters across the chest.

Another alarm went off. Ten minutes. I grumbled slightly and laid Rae down in a bouncer as I scrambled to gather the rest of her things for daycare: extra bottles and formula, diapers, emergency clothing— it seemed like everything they'd need for her. She was quite an easy baby, to be fair.

The final alert pinged through on my phone and I stared at it for a moment, dreading the day to come. Finally, I swiped the alarm away and scooped Rae into my arms, covering her belly in kisses.

She squealed, her tiny hands batting at my face in gentle swoops. Her laugh was my favourite sound. I pulled her close, throwing her diaper bag over one shoulder and scooping my laptop bag over the other, carrying my keys in my mouth as I left through the front door, pulling it closed and locking it as I emerged.

It was far too bright and sunny. The world seemed so at ease, and as I carried my life in my arms towards my ratty old station wagon, my heart ached with the idea of what was to come.

I strapped Rae into her car seat as I had hundreds of times before, then climbed into the front seat and pulled my beaten-up car down the street towards the daycare centre.

The ladies in the reception were lovely, helping me to get everything set up quickly. They added my thumbprint to their database to unlock the door that would allow me entry through to the nursery. High tech, and moderately spooky.

Rae's teacher was an extremely bright, beautiful young woman with the brightest brown eyes and tightly coiled black hair that formed an afro at the top of her head. A rainbow-coloured bow glittered from its place at the front of her scalp, matching the bright colours of her dress. She was tall with curves that flowed through her whole body and gave her the most beautiful shape. When she saw Rae, her eyes lit up.

"A new baby!" She squealed sweetly, her face was animated, as though she had studied the best facial expressions for children. Rae took to her in an instant, her own green eyes widening as she squealed bashfully in response.

The teacher smiled, turning her head to meet my eyes as she waved. A closed-eye salutations that brought a smile to my own face.

"My name is Nora! I know we met during the tour that you did not too long ago, but I'll be your little one's teacher," Nora explained sweetly, then turned her attention back to Rae. "You must be Rae! I've been so excited to finally meet you. We are going to have so much fun today," She practically sang the words.

I found myself instantly drawn into Nora's warmth and kindness. The way the world seemed to glow around her, and the way my little girl instantly reached for her when Nora extended her arms to reach for her.

The warmth of my daughter's presence was soon replaced by the coolness of the air as Nora pulled Rae to rest sweetly against her large chest. She then glanced back at me, "Has she eaten this morning?" She asked.

"Yes!" I said happily, "She has eaten, and I've packed more of her formula. I've changed her diaper as well," I explained, then lifted the pink diaper bag from my shoulder, "Is there a cubby that I can store this in for her?"

Nora gleamed a white smile at me, bouncing Rae sweetly in her arms. "Yes, of course! Rae's cubby is right there," She motions to a small shelf with six other storage squares. Five of them were full except for one directly at the end where Rae's name was hung on bright blue-coloured paper.

I placed her bag in the cubby, then turned to Nora, hesitation in my stead as I became keenly aware that Nora would be keeping hold of my daughter. My heart raced, and I lifted my hand to rub my neck. "Right… erm…" I looked to the door, then back to Rae. "I guess I will… go?"

The nursery teacher smiled kindly, "Mr. Morris, I know that this is a very hard thing to, but I promise you with everything in my soul that Rae is going to be okay here."

I don't think that Rae's welfare was necessarily the main point of my concern, to be totally honest. There was no doubt in my mind that she would be safe here. I smiled at Nora and nodded quickly, "You're right," I said softly, then wiggled my fingers lightly at Rae before turning to leave.

"Oh, Mr. Morris!" Nora called, halting me in my steps as I turned back to see her holding Rae. She closed her eyes and tilted her head to the side as she smiled at me again, "You can check on her throughout the day on our app! You'll have all of the information in your email."

Something washed over me, maybe a sense of relief?

Whatever it was, it brought the anxiety that was currently coursing through my veins to a temporary halt and I nodded thankfully to her.

As I sank into my ratty old car, I felt that anxiety return. Was it sadness? Rae hadn't even cried as Nora swept her away from me… is it horrible of me to wish that she had?

I sighed, leaning my head forward to rest against the steering wheel of this piece of shit that I'd inherited from my uncle. Probably about the only good thing to come out of the past year other than Rae.

But I can only wallow in self-pity for so long before I have to pull myself out of the funk and get on moving again, so I did. I cranked the engine, turned on some music, and made my way into the city for my first day back at work.

* * *

Working as a paramedic dispatcher isn't all that bad. For one thing, I get to spend most of my day listening to some pretty interesting calls. If I am lucky I can save a few lives.

But the waiting time in between the calls always feels the loneliest. I sit in a room with about fifty other people who hardly know me, and the ones who do hardly speak to me... except for Jill and Brian.

They were my friends for ages before Kelly left me, but since everything went down with her running off, neither of them have really reached out. It is kind of awkward to say the least, because their desks are really close to mine, and my own anxiety prevents me from engaging with them.

I didn't expect either of them to wanted to speak to me now, but as I finished up my last call before my break, I turned to see both of them standing at the entrance to my boring grey cubicle with wide grins plastered on their faces.

"Hey," I said softly, offering a soft wave.

Brian waved in return and Jill stepped into the cubicle to perch herself at the end of my desk. She crossed her arms in front of her chest, "I know it has been forever since we spoke to you," she began, then glanced at Brian for a few seconds, "We just didn't want to overwhelm you while you were struggling with these really intense things... felt selfish to bring up happy news just yet."

Her stare hovered on Brian, intensifying until the realization suddenly hit him that she wanted him to disclose the rest of the statement. "Oh!" He chuckled softly, "What she means is... we are engaged!"

Confusion found itself stitched between my eyebrows as I glanced between my two old friends. "Engaged?" I asked.

Jill returned her gaze to me, her eyes softening, "We knew that with everything going on with Kelly... it might upset you if we were to tell you about it."

I softened my expression, then pulled my hand to rest across my forehead, leaning back in my chair, "Fuck... I thought you guys hated me," I admitted in a strained tone.

"What?" Brian frowned, "No, Brooke... shit," He brought his hand to his face, "I was worried you would think that."

"We just didn't want you to think we were being dicks," Jill reassured softly, then placed her hand on my desk next to where she sat. "Will you join us for lunch?"

The sound of my stomach grumbling denied me any chance of escape, and I glanced between these two people who... I think are my friends. Brian seemed quite keen on the idea, "There is a great diner down the road. We can grab something quick!"

I chuckled and shook my head, "Okay, fine."

They didn't lie, the diner was quite literally two doors down from our office building. *The Broadway Diner*; A quaint little hole-in-the-wall diner, with plenty of old American charm to boot.

Jill led me to a booth while Brian searched the jukebox by the door. She rolled her eyes, "Every time we come in here, he has to play the same song. They must get so sick of us." She twirled a strand of her deep brown hair around her finger as the opening notes to *My Way* by Frank Sinatra pulled through the speakers overhead and Brian sauntered back to the table.

Before any of us could speak, a server approached our table with a gentle twirl as he stopped before us. He had short black hair that was just long enough for the slightest wave of a natural curl to show. Brown eyes were framed by lovely long eyelashes. He wore a maroon coloured uniform with a black half-apron that tied at his hips.

To his breast, a golden name badge was pinned with the name Ellis.

"Welcome back, welcome back!" Ellis beamed, his voice lilting into a soft song as he brandished a pen and notepad. His energy was bright and cheerful, and he had a very distinct accent. Some sort of Northern British inflexion in each of his words.

Jill grinned, "Hi, Ellis!" She said sweetly, "We were just about to ask for you!"

The server grinned mischievously, batting his eyelashes at the pair as he turned his attention to me. "You're new!" His accent extended the vowel of his "e" to incorporate a "y" sound.

A wave of insignificance passed over me, and a warmth rose to my cheeks, but Brian stepped in to save the day.

"This is Brooke, he is our co-worker. Just got back off paternity leave, so we wanted to take him to lunch," Brian laughed, adjusting his black-framed glasses on the bridge of his nose.

This seemed to satiate the beast at the end of the table, and Ellis's brown eyes closed after an uncomfortably long time of lingering on me. "I see, welcome back then, Brooke!" He cooed.

I nodded once, glancing down at the menu in front of me.

"May we have our usual, Ellis?" Jill asked, summoning forth an affirmative nod from the man in maroon.

"Okie dokie, absolutely. And for you, Brooke?"

It felt weird, this was the most human interaction that I'd had in what felt like months. I cleared my throat, "Um, I think I'll just have a BLT and a glass of orange juice, please," I said softly.

Ellis scribbled down the order on the notepad in his hand, then tucked his pencil into his ear and smiled, "I'll have that out in a jiffy!" He sang, then turned gracefully on his heels to disappear into the kitchen.

Jill giggled sweetly, "I think it would be a lie if we said we came here for anything other than to see Ellis," She hummed, leaning back into her seat where Brian had looped his arm behind her.

"So, Brooke... how are things?" Brian asked, pulling Jill close. They looked happy.

I hummed, running my hands over the soft black material of my trousers as I thought about the appropriate response. "Rae is holding her bottles by herself now," I managed, the picture of her flashing into my mind. It softened the sharp features of my face and I lifted a hand to my brown hair, pulling it through the long strands of curls that took far too much maintenance.

A soft expression befell Jill's soft features and she nodded, "I'd love to meet her, your pictures of her on Facebook make my heart melt," she said in a genuine tone.

Jill leaned forward to place her elbow on the table, resting her chin on the new platform.

Brian's arm slipped down from the back of the seat behind her, his hand now positioned on her hip. "How is it without Kelly?"

Her name brought pain forward. Pain that I didn't quite want to process at this moment in time. I turned my head away to shield my eyes from their view and focused on the people who walked past the long window in front of the diner. "It sucks, really."

"Do you think you'd want to try dating again anytime soon?" Brian asked.

I chuckled, leaning back against the plush red seat. "I don't even know where to start with that," I admitted coyly.

Jill glanced at Brian, her face twisting into a genuine mischief before returning to my own gaze with a bright grin. "We have a friend. She is super nice, I think you'll like her. She is a teacher!"

"A teacher?" I tilted my head, then quickly clued onto the fact that they were trying to set me up with somebody. I looked down at my hands as they anxiously picked at the skin around my nails unconsciously. "I don't know… Rae is still so little and I don't have anyone to watch he-" I was swiftly cut off.

"I'll watch her!" Jill interjected, her eyes bright, "I mean, if that is okay with you. I'd love to watch her for an evening."

Brian chuckled, "We can get you the date, all you have to do is show up here tonight, eight o'clock. How does that sound?"

My brows furrowed as I glanced down at my hands again. This was a lot to take in for one day, did I even want to be subjected to this?

The soft swoosh of the kitchen door at my back swung

open and Ellis returned to our table with a tray perched on his fingertips, balanced perfectly. "Everything is ready for you!" He hummed out, placing dishes and drinks before each of us, "Is there anything else I can get for you?" He asked.

"No, Ellis!" Jill sang, "Thank you."

The man turned on his heels and swiftly stepped back towards another table, where he performed the exact greeting we had received on our arrival. Pitch and all matched to the exact tune.

I turned back to focus my attention on the sandwich before me, reaching to take a swig of my orange juice. It took me a moment to realize that Jill and Brian were on the edge of their seats as they awaited a response. My stomach growled again, so I scooped the sandwich into my hands and took a juicy, delicious bite. You could say the serotonin boost this gave me was enough to actively switch on the crazy part of my brain, because the next thing I said shocked me just as much as it shocked Brian and Jill.

"Sure... why not?" I said after swallowing the bite I had just taken.

Jill's eyes brightened and she cheered, pumping her fists into the air as Brian finally started in on his breakfast burrito.

We made pleasant conversation for the rest of the meal, and as our break wound to a close, Ellis slid back over to us with a smile painted across his face. "Are we ready for the bill, my darlings?" He asked, the black folders already situated in the pocket of his apron.

"Yes please," Brian said, extending his hand. He paid for his and Jill's food, while I placed the cash I had brought along in my own folder.

"Keep the change," I said softly. It was only $2.00, but it

was all I could manage with my current finances.

Ellis smiled thankfully and retrieved the black folders, "Thank you for coming, when you pop in again, ask for Ellis!" He sank the folders into his apron and then skipped happily off to see his next set of customers.

Later on that day, my head was a mess with thoughts as I stepped through the front door of the nursery and pressed the pad of my thumb to the fingerprint scanner. The screen lit up green and my picture and details flickered onto the screen, along with Rae's room number. The door buzzed, and I pulled it open to allow myself to walk through.

I turned down the hallway that led to Rae's room, a little white door with windows on either side. The name *Acorns* painted in an orange colour above the door. I peered through the window to see Rae laying on the floor beneath a canopy of dangling toys. Nora was nearby, snuggling another baby.

As I knocked, Nora glanced up, her eyes brightening as she saw me and waved for me to come in. I pushed the door open, then walked over to where Rae was playing.

"Rae-rae! Your daddy is here!" Nora says sweetly.

I knelt to scoop her up, and Rae's eyes brightened as she snuggled into my chest.

"Hello, my beautiful girl!" I hummed, "Have we had a good day?"

"Oh, we had the best day!" Nora hummed, pushing herself to stand slowly and placing the other baby in Rae's place. Once she had stood fully, she adjusted the cloth that had found its way in the wrong place, then met my gaze, "She is an absolute darling, Mr. Morris,"

My heart swelled with pride as I cuddled Rae, moving her

so that she could still see Nora. "Were you a good girl today? That's amazing to hear," I said softly.

Nora nodded and waved to Rae, "Bye-bye now Rae-rae! I'll see you tomorrow!" She said in an animated tone.

I chuckled as Rae let out a squeal, her hand extending in an attempt to mimic Nora's action. With that, I retrieved her diaper bag and turned to leave.

When I arrived back at home, Jill's car was parked outside. She got out as soon as I was parked and rushed to my door excitedly.

"Sorry for being so early, I just wanted to get acquainted with her before you left," she explained as I emerged from the car.

Apprehension began to grow, as I understood that this meant I was about to be leaving Rae with someone she'd never met... for the second time today. I nodded softly, "Would you mind unlocking the door? I'll bring her inside so you can meet her after the transition," I said, offering my co-worker the keys to the house.

She gladly accepted this deal, snatching the keys before running to unlock the door. I took this time to remove Rae's car seat from the base and pulled her out of the car, making sure to grab her diaper bag before I followed Jill into the house.

She had made herself comfortable on the couch in the lounge, her shoes placed neatly by the front door. I closed the door, removed my own shoes, and then stepped through to the living room, where I placed Rae's seat on the ground in front of Jill.

"Oh, Brooke!" She swooned, pinching the buttons that would lower the handle for the carrier. "She is so beautiful."

My cheeks warmed slightly, and I nodded, "She is, isn't she."

Jill dipped to unhook Rae from her straps and pulled her from the carrier, nestling my daughter in her arms sweetly. "Hello, you!"

Rae babbled cutely, reaching her hand out to grab onto Jill's hair as it fell before her. Jill only laughed, gently pulling the strands from her grasp.

The sense of uncertainty that I'd felt when I first heard the idea of Jill watching Rae for the night began to fade, and a smile pulled at the corners of my lips. I glanced down at my watch on my wrist, sighing as I realised how close the time of me leaving actually was.

"You can go get ready, I've got her." Jill bounced Rae gently on her knee, a toy from somewhere in the room had materialised in her hand and she was sufficiently distracting Rae. "I have babysat all of my friends' kids. I know what to do."

I glanced to the staircase, then back at Rae. For a moment, I felt like I couldn't lift my feet from where they were, planted into the ground like a tree. Already rooted in place. I don't really want to go. I would much rather have had my wife there. None of this would be necessary if...

"Go on, Brooke," Jill coaxed, a subtle laugh hanging off the end of her voice as she returned her attention to the girl in her arms.

With that, I felt my feet lift one by one until I had somehow managed to materialize myself within the safety of my bedroom.

This room was small. Four white walls with no decoration. Just a chest of drawers and a king-sized bed that sat at half capacity on the nights that Rae didn't sleep with me. In the corner, a box full of Kelly's belongings: clothing, pictures, and jewellery, sat untouched.

I pulled on a simple black dress shirt and a pair of navy slacks, then searched through the floor of my closet until I found the slick black dress shoes that hadn't seen my feet since mine and Kelly's wedding three years ago.

The memory flashed through my brain and I winced, forcing it away from my consciousness just long enough for me to pull the dress shoes on. Then, I stepped back to look at myself in the mirror atop the chest of drawers. My green eyes stood out against the black of my shirt. My hair still had just enough curl to it that I was confident in being perceived as somewhat put together... I looked nice. Nice enough at least.

As I stepped back down to the lounge, Jill wolf-whistled, "Looking suave, Brooke," She teased, "You're gonna have a good time," she assured me.

Rae babbled sweetly, and I knelt down in front of Jill to pull my daughter close for a quick goodbye... one that I definitely would have prolonged if at all possible.

Eventually, though, I had to pull from the embrace and return my daughter to her sitter for the night. For a day that was full of firsts... nothing could have prepared me for what was to come.

Or... who was to come.

The Date

BROOKE

The night air in Atlanta was significantly cooler than it had been hours earlier. This was a good thing, really, as the nerves currently wrecking my system were triggering an ungodly amount of sweat to collect under my arms. I will be forever grateful for the sweat-concealing properties of black fabric.

I secured my shit-wagon in the parking bay reserved for the call dispatchers, hoping that the marshal would see my pass and simply leave it instead of investigating to see that I wasn't actually on shift. I didn't really want to pay a fine on top of everything else I was struggling with at the moment.

The diner was a quick five-minute walk from the entrance of the lot, and I made quick time of the jaunt. At this time in the evening, there weren't nearly as many patrons within the diner. Just a few students and the occasional graveyard shift worker looking for a quick bite before work.

There was a soft chime sound over my head as I pushed through the glass doors with large silver piping as the handle. My eyes lifted to briefly acknowledge the tiny bell attached to the frame. The whole aesthetic of this place reminded me of those neon diners where your food would be delivered to you by waiters on rollerblades.

I scanned the available seats until I found the booth that I had filled earlier in the day was empty, and as a man of habit, I chose here to sit. I was almost half an hour early, but my nerves were all over the place.

A swoosh sounded from the kitchen door behind me as a server emerged... clearly not on rollerblades, and the energy in the dining area seemed to brighten instantly. The sound of light footsteps approached the silver-rimmed table I now accompanied and a familiar face materialised with a saccharine smile.

It was Ellis.

"Welcome back!" He cheered lightly, placing a hand on his hip.

I glanced up to notice the softest painting of a gold, shimmering eyeshadow on each of his eyes. Something that I must not have noticed earlier in the day, but the softness of nightfall outside afforded the shimmer it's due.

His pencil was docked delicately over his ear, and I could see the notepad he used secured to his apron with a clip.

"Hello," I said softly.

Ellis closed his eyes, then pinched his chin as contemplation pulled across his face, "You had the BLT and orange juice today!" He eventually hummed in a nasal tone, one of recollection.

"Yeah," I muttered anxiously, summoning a bright smile to Ellis's face as he opened his eyes once more. I noticed his lashes contained an occasional false lash that resembled streamers. They caught in the light as he batted his eyelashes.

"Would you like the same again, mate?" He queried. Something about his accent just made the interaction feel uncanny.

I looked down at the menu before myself, realizing that I noticed only had no clue what I wanted... but I didn't even know if I was truly hungry. With a bashful grin, I turned my attention back at Ellis. "Actually, I'm waiting for somebody," I explained.

His eyes brightened, "Oh?" He dramatically pulled his hand to rest on his chest, "A date?"

My cheeks warmed with the warmth of a blush, "Yeah," I replied flatly.

Ellis grinned with mischief burning behind his brown eyes as he ran his hand through his black hair, "Well, I will leave you to your lonesome until the goddess arrives then, eh?" He said assertively. "Can I at least grab you a drink?"

"Coke," I said, "A Coke would be nice, please."

He tapped his finger on the edge of the table, "Coming right up!" He sang, then floated away towards the kitchen once more.

Ellis was a nice guy. Maybe a bit too nice. His act felt superficial at best, but it could be due, in part, to my already stressful day. I couldn't help but be a bit annoyed when people were too happy around me. It was a feeling I craved but knew I'd not achieve.

Hardly a moment later, Ellis returned to my table with a cold glass of Coke. The condensation had already started to settle on the glass as he placed it next to me with the straw. Ellis retrieved his hand and wiped the moisture across his apron. "If you need anything, ask for Ellis!" He grinned, firing a finger gun in my direction before pottering off to check on a group of college students a few tables down.

Time seemed to move at an achingly slow pace, and I found myself mindlessly sipping away at the caramel-coloured drink beneath me. Before I knew it, I went to pull a sip through my straw, only to receive nothing but a sucking sound from emptiness beneath the clumps of ice. I glanced down at the glass, which now housed only the remnants of my anxiety-guzzling, and sighed softly.

Then I felt a presence at my side, a shadow which slightly eclipsed the light from a nearby ceiling lamp. It was accompanied by the gentle thud of glass on wood, then the soft sound of a glide. I glanced to my right to see a full glass of Coke and the slightly shiny trail from its slide across the table.

I looked up to see Ellis standing there with a friendly smile.

"I saw you were getting low. I drink when I'm anxious too… just not this kind of drink," He laughed softly. For half a second, the laugh felt genuine.

My eyes fell back to the new, full glass; then back to Ellis. "Thank you," I said softly, pulling the straw from the empty glass and plunging it into the new one. Ellis whisked the empty glass away, spinning gracefully on his heels towards the kitchen.

The bell by the front door chimed, and a woman with golden-toned skin and slick black hair entered. She was wearing a simple black dress that reached a few inches above her knees, and a pair of circular-framed glasses.

This woman paused as she entered, looking around the room as though she was searching for something.

Ellis stopped briefly at the entrance to the kitchen, "Welcome in, Darling!" He sang, "Find a seat and I'll be with you in a moment."

The woman seemed to nod, then her eyes fell upon me. She smiled. It was a cute smile, warm. My stomach bubbled with apprehension as she approached. "Are you Brooke?" She asked softly.

I had half a mind to lie to her. To tell her that I was just some random guy… but I didn't. Instead, I stood and extended my hand to her, "Hi! Yes, that is me. You must be…" My brain shut off as I tried to remember the name of the woman. I swore Jill told me…

"Hannah," she said sweetly, extending her own hand to shake mine.

Relief fell over my face, and I motioned to the opposite side of the booth for her to sit, which she did without protest.

I returned to my seat and placed my phone to the side of my menu, face up. "Sorry, I just want to keep an eye on my notifications… this is the first time I have left my daughter with someone else for an evening," I explained.

Hannah's brown, almond-shaped eyes brightened, "You have a daughter?"

My heart began to race slightly, and a smile instantly rose to my lips, "I do, yes. She's only a month and a half old." I picked up my phone and scrolled through images until I found one of Rae sleeping peacefully in her cot. Hannah smiled brightly, and she shifted adorably in her seat.

"She's like a little doll," she exclaimed, "So little, you must be absolutely petrified."

She understood; that was a good thing. I breathed out a sigh of relief and nodded, "Absolutely," I said truthfully, "I was so anxious that I nearly didn't come at all."

That was the wrong thing to say. I knew that because the second the words left my lips, one of Hannah's eyebrows lifted in a silent judgment. I instantly went into defensive mode, placing my phone back on the table as my brain scrambled for a way to rectify this fumble.

Just then, the kitchen door swung open behind me, and Ellis slid majestically to save the day. "Oh! This must be that beautiful woman you were telling me about!"

Okay, I take it back. I liked Ellis.

I nodded quickly, "Yes, this is Hannah!" I said, motioning to the woman before me. Hannah turned to Ellis and smiled respectfully, offering him a wave.

Ellis waved back kindly, "Can I get you started with a drink, girlie?" He asked.

Hannah thought for a moment before settling on a glass of lemonade. She then opened the menu immediately, "May I also have the Caesar Salad? With extra roast chicken please!"

He retrieved the notepad from his apron and jot down her order, then glanced at me expectantly. I floundered as I scooped the menu up. I had been sitting here for half an hour and still had no clue what I wanted.

"I'll just have a stack of pancakes with scrambled eggs," I said softly.

Ellis jotted this down, then smiled and retrieved the menus from our hands before skipping off to the kitchen once again.

Now alone once more with Hannah, I could feel that this wasn't going as planned. She still seemed put off by

24

my comment earlier, so I tried to start a new, different conversation.

"So, what is it you do for work?" I asked.

Her ears seemed to perk up a bit at this, and she straightened her shoulders. "I am a high school Geography teacher," she explained.

"Geography is cool," I chuckled, pulling down another large, nervous gulp of my Coke. "Have you always lived in the Atlanta area?"

She raised an eyebrow and crossed her arms over her chest, "I was born and raised here," she explained.

I couldn't quite comprehend what I had said wrong here, but I had said it nonetheless. The anxiety was growing stronger over my shoulders, and Hannah did not seem to enjoy my company. I filled the time in the only was I knew how… asking more questions.

"So…" I glanced down at the table. It was shiny and sticky from years of haphazard wipe downs. "How long have you been teaching here?"

"Four years," she said plainly, "I worked as a nurse's aide before then. What is it that you do?"

"Oh, I work in dispatch with Jill and Brian," I explained. Her eyes flickered with some sort of recognition and she nodded.

"That makes sense, they're both a bit odd, aren't they? Must be a thing for dispatchers." She said flatly, and the dig struck me straight to my core. This was not going well at all… and at this point, I didn't really want it to.

My phone buzzed; the screen lighting up with an incoming call. My eyes flicked immediately to the screen, only for my heart to stop instantly. It was Kelly.

I frowned, feeling a rush of annoyance as it flooded my veins, then I pressed the power button to silence the call.

Hannah glanced down at my phone but they didn't stay there for long. After a few seconds, her eyes fell on me, "What if that is important?" she asked.

"This is also quite important," I offered, but as that call ended, the screen lit up once more.

"I really think you should take that," Hannah said sternly. Her voice told me that it was more of a demand than a suggestion.

I pulled my straw to my lips, gulping down a sip of my drink before snatching my phone from the table and taking myself out to the front of the diner. As I swiped the icon across to answer the call, my heart beat hard in my chest.

"Hello?" I asked softly.

"Where the *fuck* are you, Brooke?" Kelly's voice peeled through the other end of the phone with a nasty snarl.

My eyes widened as I felt the shock strike through me like lightning. I gathered myself, glancing back inside to see that Ellis had returned to the table with our food. He was speaking with Hannah. I closed my eyes and sighed, "I don't have to tell you that, Kelly," I said flatly, resting my head back so that I could stare up at the light-polluted night sky above.

"Who the fuck is that bitch in there with my daughter?" Kelly shouted through the other end of the line.

A chill sapped the soul from my bones as the feeling of security fled my body. "What do you mean?"

"I came to grab my things and there is a fucking WHORE holding my daughter! Who is she, Brooke?" She shouted.

My body instantly began to tremble, and I pulled my phone from my ear so that I could message Jill. My fingers stumbled clumsily over the keyboard as I typed out the message.

"Answer me!" Kelly shouted.

By now, I was keenly aware that the door to the diner had opened, and Hannah was leaving with a box of her food in hand. She didn't even spare me a second glance as she turned the corner and made a beeline for her car. I felt my world crumbling around me, and glanced back to see Ellis staring out the window from my table. I waved to him apologetically and he nodded, seeming to understand. He skipped away towards another table.

"Listen Kelly, I'm out right now... That woman is a friend of mine, please just drop it-" I tried to reason with her but she cut me off.

"You left my daughter with some floozy so you can go around getting drunk, didn't you?" Kelly spat into the phone.

My heart raced and I clenched my fist into a tight ball, "Fucking hell, Kelly... I haven't left the house in months, and the one time I try to do something for myself, you blow up my phone being a bitch!" I shouted... probably much louder than I should have. I felt eyes on me from within the diner, and my heart sank even further.

"You dick," Kelly grumbled, and I could hear the distinct sounds of her sniffling on the other end of the phone. My chest ached. I hated it when she cried.

"Kelly..." I muttered, clutching the small metal device tight in my grip. I shuddered, forcing a heavy sigh from my chest, "Please just go home... I'll come home now."

Before I could say another word, she ended the call.

Anger bubbled inside of my chest, and I groaned. There was this splitting headache that was slowly crawling its way up the back of my skull and all I wanted was for everything to stop. I pulled in a deep breath, then shoved my phone into my pocket as I turned to re-enter the diner.

My food sat alone at my table. Hannah was gone, and the only pleasant part of this whole ordeal was that Ellis had refilled my drink while I was outside. I groaned as I sank into the booth, placing my hands over my face to conceal the genuine exhaustion that had found itself ripping at my senses.

"That went well," A soft voice pulled through the mostly empty dining area. I looked up to see Ellis standing at the end of the table, his arms crossed in front of himself as he stared down at me with a soft expression on his glamorously painted face.

Annoyance gathered between my brows as I quickly turned away from Ellis to stare at my pancakes.

"They're getting cold. Cold pancakes are shit," Ellis said with a cheeky grin, sinking into the seat across from me.

I glanced up, only lifting my eyes and keeping my head low. He sat there across from me with a sardonic grin on his face. I felt the urge to knock his teeth out, but the frustration that ebbed through my bones ached enough to significantly drain the last of the energy I had. I stared at the pancakes below.

He was right.

Cold pancakes are shit…

Ellis sighed, turning to glance at the only other table in the restaurant. A couple of teenagers chatting mindlessly in the corner. He rested back against the seat where he had decided to intrude upon my mental breakdown, closing his eyes as if he was savouring the few seconds of peace.

The bile I could taste in my mouth made the thought of doing any sort of eating seem like actual torture, but I picked up my fork to poke at the fluffy surface of the pancakes. "Long shift?" I asked in a soft mumble, mostly inaudible.

The man before me opened his golden eyelids to look at me, his face brightening considerably as the persona reanimated on his face, "I pulled a cheeky double," He said in a light, bouncy tone. "My second one so far this week!"

I lifted an eyebrow, "I don't know how you do it."

Ellis chuckled, "Trust me, Darling... there are far worse things I could be doing right this moment," He straightened his slender fingers to reveal a set of pink acrylics. His eyes fell on each of the almond-shaped nails as he inspected their quality.

His response was vague but appreciated. I guess there were far worse things I could be doing as well.

The lukewarm metal fork in my hand plunged into the soft dough of the stack of pancakes before me, and I sliced through to the bottom, repeating the motion to create a perfectly triangular stack of four. The teenagers from the other occupied table skipped past my table, waving excitedly at Ellis as they left. He offered them a bright, closed-eyed smile with a wave, then sank back as they disappeared through the door.

"Your date left," Ellis said in a much softer tone, his attention still far in the distance as he leaned lazily across the booth, one arm draped over the back.

I placed the forkful of pancakes back against the plate and sighed, "I saw."

He turned his eyes to fall on me, "She left you the bill."

Something in his gaze bordered on pity. It made me nauseous. I rolled my eyes with a heavy sigh and nodded.

My phone buzzed as a barrage of messages flooded my

phone. Some from Jill asking me what happened on the date… Hannah had obviously spoken with her. Others were drunk messages from Kelly. The first time she had spoken to me for weeks, and she was back to the mental gymnastics that I dreaded.

Frustration ached in my head and I pressed my elbows to the table, resting my forehead against the heels of my palms as a heavy sigh left my chest.

"It is rough, mate," Ellis said kindly, "You'll find a girl that'll stick. Don't you worry."

I glanced up at Ellis again. His eyes were settled on the clock in the distance. It struck me that I had far overstayed my welcome, and the diner had closed ten minutes ago. I pulled out my wallet and placed a $20 bill on the table, sliding it over to Ellis. "Sorry, I'll go now," I said in a resigned grumble.

Ellis glanced down at the bill and his eyes saddened slightly, "I'm sorry, mate," He said, placing the check on the table. $23.50 was the total. "She ordered extra chicken…"

Panic flooded my mind as I opened my wallet, but there was nothing more I could give. After a moment of deliberation and stress, Ellis reached across the table to pull my wallet closed, "I've got you this time. You've had it hard enough tonight already." He pulled the $20 close to himself and closed the black envelope. "You get on home to your daughter," He said.

The shame that coursed through my veins in that moment almost toppled every other emotion I was feeling, and I hung my head. Ellis reached to grab my plate, effortlessly sliding the food into a clamshell box and then placing it in front of me.

"I'll pay you back," I said quickly, "As soon as I get home,

I'll-"

"It is fine, mate. Just get home safe," Ellis' eyes glimmered with some sort of genuine kindness, and he slid from his place in the booth. He slipped the black folder into his apron and cleared my table of dishes, then turned to the other empty table and cleared it away.

I pushed myself from the booth, clutching the takeaway container in my hands as I stared down at it, the warmth still heating the tips of my fingers. "Thank you, Ellis," I said softly.

The maroon-clad server brightened considerably, nodding with a wink, "Don't forget, next time you're in... ask for Ellis!" He disappeared into the kitchen, and as he did I could see that he was the only person still here. The kitchen lights were mostly off and Ellis had stayed without judgement to accommodate me.

I understood, now, why people like him were so important. The kind people who would shamelessly help a disgruntled, broken man with nothing left in this world but his daughter. As I pushed through the front door, the neon sign which declared the diner open sat without an ounce of glow left in it.

The soft sound of a click at my back startled me, and I turned to see Ellis locking the door behind me. He smiled brightly, bright enough to warm the cool night air, and waved a final goodbye to me before slipping back into the darkness of the empty diner.

When I returned home, Rae was already tucked into her bed.

"What happened, Brooke?" Jill asked me, perched on the edge of my sofa as she adjusted a pair of reading glasses, a book splayed across her knee.

Shame and annoyance peppered my mind with everything I should have done differently. Why was it so hard to say the right things in the moment?

"I just really messed up, I guess. Said one thing wrong, then instantly self-sabotaged," I explained, sinking into my favourite La-Z-Boy with a disgruntled huff.

Jill smiled, "I don't think it was too much of a loss," She said sweetly, pushing herself from the sofa and stretching her arms above her head. "She told me you had too much baggage."

The words brought a soft snort to my nose, and I pinched the bridge between my eyes, "She isn't wrong, I guess."

My friend laughed lightly, stooping to collect her purse from beside the couch, "You need to get some sleep," She ordered, "There's always next time."

She was right.

I knew she was right.

I stood to walk her to the door, waving goodbye to her as she drove away, but as the door closed before me... I couldn't help but feel the annoyance in myself for not having the right amount of money for Ellis tonight. He was just a waiter at an urban diner that was trying far too hard to be reminiscent of the American Dream...

Guilt bit down into my chest, and I walked to a small safe located in the cabinet door of my TV stand. Inside was a gun that I'd owned since my rebellious teenage years, and enough money to get me the hell out of here... but not yet. Not now.

For now, it was enough for me to spare $10. I pulled the crisp bill from the pile and closed the door, spinning the lock closed and then placing the bill in my wallet for tomorrow.

Content, I made my way up the stairs to the hallway, where

my eyes fell onto a door which stood slightly ajar. Pink paint that needed another coat or two, and butterfly stickers embossed the surface of the entrance.

I crept into Rae's bedroom, peering over the edge of her crib to see her precious sleeping face, then dipped to gently pull her from the mattress. I clutched her to my chest.

That night, she slept in my bed... she was the most genuine comfort a man could ask for. Her love was everything to me, and as I lay in my bed with a mind full of racing thoughts, all that it took to silence them was the feeling of her tiny hand as it gripped tightly onto my shirt.

Fuck... I would burn the world down for her.

You're Late

I counted out the tills for the last time tonight, staring anxiously at the clock as I felt the ticking of the second hand burning through my ears. I was already ten minutes late, and it would take me half an hour to get there... *Zophia was going to be pissed.*

After one final check of all the lights and facilities, I stepped out through the back door of *Broadway Diner* with a bag of rubbish in one hand and my phone in the other. Endless missed calls. The annoyance grew strong on my face, and I tossed the bin bag into the large green bin at the back of the alleyway before starting my walk towards the *Midnight Raven.*

The back door to the club was wedged open by a tattered old heel with torn rhinestones. I smiled lightly, pushing the heavy metal panel open to reveal the welcoming scent of latex and perfume. The halls were full of laughter and music. You could feel the vibrations of heavy bass from the front performance area as you stepped.

I pushed open the door to the dressing area and all heads within instantly turned to me. About twenty people of all shapes and sizes, wigs and diamonds, and enough makeup to paint all of Atlanta one shade brighter.

The attention triggered an ache of embarrassment in my chest, and I turned my nose to the sky, "Come now," I waved my hand dismissively, "We all know that a Queen arrives precisely when they intend to!" I boomed, swaying my hips as I approached my dressing table. It was untidy and cluttered. The chatter and laughter returned, and I sank into my seat to begin working on my makeup.

I was nearly finished with my mask when the door to the dressing room slammed open and Zophia's screech silenced the room.

"Flare Femme!" She squawked, stamping over towards my dressing table with a vengeance. All four-foot-nothing of this woman approached me, her beehive black hair waggled atop her wrinkled scalp.

I groaned and closed my eyes, then glanced down at the woman with my lip liner clutched tight in my hands, "Hello to you as well Zophia," I said sardonically.

"You're late! I've sent on six girls in your place now! How do you think Lorenzo is going to feel about this when he-"

I cut her off abruptly, "I am here now!" I said in a nonchalant tone, "Give me five minutes and I'll be ready to go. No need to throw your toys out your pram." I grabbed the long red wig from its resting place atop a beauty school head and pulled the seam to cover the black of my hair.

Zophia fumed, stamping her feet, "You best be glad you're even welcome here anymore, Flare! One more stunt like this and you'll-"

"I get it," I pushed myself to stand, moving away from the vanity towards the rack of clothing beside it. I pulled a pair of denim shorts that were wider in the front to protect the jewels and sceptre from the rack and then a tattered white t-shirt with an American flag on it.

The woman at my heels continued to bark, but I ignored her senseless prowling and folded my uniform from work up as I changed.

A few wolf whistles from behind me as I shamelessly stripped in front of the other Queens. Once I was dressed, I pulled on a pair of knee-high gold boots with an eight-inch heel. I stepped back to check myself in the mirror. I won't lie... I was stunning. Perfect plump lips and a tight arse... this is why people come to see me.

I twirled the strands of my red wig around my finger as I glanced down at Zophia, "Right, Darling. Take me out!"

The performance was jaw-dropping as usual. Nothing in this world could ever tell me that I wasn't damn good at my job. I made a decent killing from Drag Nights at the Midnight Raven, and I enjoyed it. The dancing, the lights. The other Queens were nicer to me than pretty much any other human on this earth... and I even enjoyed being screamed at by the human embodiment of a chihuahua for being late so often.

As I stepped down from the stage, sweat beading on my forehead, I noticed a familiar face in the crowd. A disgusting man with beady black eyes and a black cane. He lifted one of his meaty hands to me, then hooked his finger aggressively towards himself, summoning me forth as he disappeared into one of the private dance rooms.

A pit grew in the base of my stomach as I followed him wordlessly into the room. The door shut behind us, sealing us within the dark room with a chaise lounger and a single pole in the centre of the room.

"You were late again today, Flare," Lorenzo said in a stern tone as he sat on the centre of the chaise lounge. It creaked lightly under his weight.

A shiver ran down my spine, and I crossed my arms in front of myself, "Give me a break, Lorenzo, I had shit come up at work!" I spat, turning my head away to avoid his eyes.

Lorenzo grumbled again, "Do you know how much money we missed out on because you were late? I had to send Kiki Vajay out twice… TWICE!" He shook his head, placing a hand on his forehead in annoyance, "Do you forget that the only reason your ass is still standing free right now is because of me?"

My eyes narrowed and a cold blade of fear punctured my gut. "It was a simple mistake, Lorenzo," I muttered, pulling my eyes to the dingy carpet beneath my heels as I drew my arms closer… now more for self-preservation than to project my attitude.

"Simple mistake?" Lorenzo launched himself to stand, and his meaty palm wrapped around my bicep, pulling me down to his level. "You fuck around with my money one more time, and I'll make sure to hand your ass in to the fuzz myself," he spat. I could feel the percussion of his words as droplets of his spit collided with the makeup on my face.

I winced from the pain, but my ego got the better of me, "Fuck off, Zo!" I shouted.

In an instant, the heel of his palm collided with the socket of my left eye and a searing pain struck me to my core. Lorenzo's grip tightened on my arm and he swooped a leg against the back of my knees, launching me to the floor. He delivered a solid kick square to my ribs, and I let out a yelp of pain and I curled into the fetal position, clutching my ribs and reeling from the sudden... immense pain.

"You fucking ungrateful piece of shit. I own your ass!" He snarled, reeling back to finish me off with one more kick to my spine.

I gnashed my teeth together as I bit back a howl, throwing my hand over my mouth. My body writhed uncontrollably from the pain.

"You'll learn better than to speak to me like that. You know what I'm capable of. Stupid bitch!" He spat, then dipped to grab the red hair on my head into his tight fist. I could feel it separate from my scalp, breathing a soft sigh of relief that the hair wasn't actually connected to my head. He knelt down beside me with a feral expression across his greasy face. "You're booked for a special dance tonight, Flare. You'd better get yourself fixed up. Can't have our clients seeing you whipped like this."

My heart ached as the rate of its beats rose, and I closed my eyes tight, allowing the softest whimper to leave my lips. It wasn't until I heard the door sound, and I realized that Lorenzo was gone, that I was able to fully collect myself. I pushed myself to sit, then crawled to the chaise to brace myself to stand.

The ache in my torso was strong, but I didn't quite understand the damage he had done until I made it back to the dressing room. As I opened the door, one of the other performers' eyes widened. The others stared at me, watching as I trudged myself back to my vanity and sank onto the stool.

My eye had already begun to swell, and I felt a sigh fall from my lips as I folded my arms before myself and sank into their brace. The exhaustion from a full day of work and mental overload pulled at my faculties as I wished for nothing more than to go to sleep.

Unfortunately, that isn't always possible when you're a fugitive under the control of a megalomaniac. He had me on a tight leash... and I did as he pleased... even when that meant I'd be sore and sleepless for yet another full day's shift tomorrow.

"I'll never understand your tenacity," a voice said to my side.

I glanced to the side to see a tall, slender Queen with a giant curly red wig atop her head. One of my best and only friends, Ginger. Ginger was also English, but she hailed from London. I was born in the Shires.

Ginger pulled her right arm horizontally across her stomach, resting that hand in the crease that formed in her other arm as her left hand perched lightly in the edge of her painted face. She had a classic beauty to her, one that I mimicked to the best of my ability as often as I could. I considered her my Drag Mother...

My eyes fell again to rest on my vanity as Ginger placed her long, slender fingers on my back. I instantly tensed, recoiling in pain.

"Bless," she said softly, retrieving her touch from my skin and sighing "You should really save the back chat for Zophia.

She seems to handle it significantly better than Zo." She adjusted the fabric of my intentionally tattered shirt and brushed her fingers through the wig that was pinned to my head.

"I fucking hate him," I grumbled, "why is it okay for him to beat me like a fucking…" I stopped myself from falling into the habit of comparing myself to animals who probably deserved far better treatment than I did.

My friend shook her head behind me, "Sit up, Flare." She ordered. A task that I resisted for merely a few seconds before I slowly pushed myself into an upright position.

I stared at myself in the mirror of my vanity, Ginger at my side with her hands placed softly on my shoulders.

"This, what you're doing right now, that is called 'being a little twat,'" she chuckled. "Queens aren't twatty, they're fucking sassy."

A chuckle lifted a nearly imperceptible smile to my lips, and I nodded slowly.

She smirked, pressing a finger under my chin and guiding my face to look at her. "Fix your fucking crown, babes. The only way to win against that asshole is to take it in stride. With style."

Her words instilled a confidence in me that pulled me from the ledge to rock bottom. Though, I couldn't help but feel like she would never fully understand how different my situation was from hers. From everyone else here tonight.

Lorenzo had stakes in the Raven. He came in most days to make sure the dancers danced and the Drag Queens were on time… but there is a deeper, more sinister tie between myself and Lorenzo.

Six years ago, I made a stupid fucking decision. My mum

called me in floods of tears saying that she had found the drawer where I stored everything I used for drag. A drawer that I had tried my best to conceal from her... and the result was just as volatile as I thought it would be. She disowned me, kicked me out of my house... so I did what any reckless little shit with no direction in life would do, and I fled to the US.

I convinced this rich old man to sponsor me on a K-1 visa and skived to the safety of his massive mansion in the hills of Georgia. I trusted him, but I was a naive twenty-one-year-old gay man who didn't understand himself, much less the world around him... or the dangers of the situation he'd created for himself. He started pimping me out two months after I arrived.

One night, I went to bed with him and he asked me to tie a belt around his throat while I sucked him off. All I remember is that the belt secured too tight when he pulled against it and I didn't understand his pleas for help.

He died. I killed him.

When I called the police to explain, they came to the house and discovered that I was part of a massive drug and sex trade that this man had organized... and because I was designated as his spouse, they didn't stop to think that I might have been a victim.

Fifteen counts of accessory, possession of marijuana and cocaine, and an involuntary homicide case. I was tipped off that the police would be by to collect me in the morning by one of the other men this man had kept in his captivity.

The dead man's lawyer called the house and as I explained what was going on, he told me to contact Lorenzo. Lorenzo would make it all disappear.

And I did …

And… he did make it all disappear.

Within days of signing his contract, my face disappeared from the Most Wanted registry. The cops stopped looking my way when I walked anywhere in the city.

I was able to start my life over and reinvent myself. I started working at the diner, and I still got to participate in the drag nights that I adored… but Lorenzo had a clause in my contract that meant my body was his to sell until I had worked off the debt he'd garnered through clearing my name. A debt I would probably never see an end to in my lifetime.

I was on call with him 24/7. At the ring of my phone, the ping of an email, I'd present myself to him for his sick and twisted desires… or the desires of his friends.

In that respect, Ginger would never understand. She believed that the dances I gave in the private… soundproofed… locked room … were simply private dances and nothing more.

I focused in on Ginger's soft blue eyes as they rested on my face like a protective parent would gaze at their child. Pressure built in my lungs, and I became keenly aware that I had not taken a breath for a moment.

As my lungs expanded, I felt the tension in my shoulders ease, but the ache in my ribs and spine burned. I closed my eyes, pulling in deep, regular breaths.

Ginger reached forward to grab a makeup brush, proceeding to fix the mess of cosmetics on my face. "There, now you look like you were just a bit heavy-handed with your concealer," she said brightly as she returned the brush to my table. "All the best queens are."

I pulled my eyelids open and glanced at myself in the mirror. She definitely fixed me up for now. I returned my eyes to

Ginge and my lips pulled into a half smile "Thanks Ginge," I muttered softly.

She smirked "You're a badass bitch, Flare Femme. Don't let them break you."

My face pulled into a confident smile, and I tightened my fists, "I am a badass bitch, aren't I?" I said, the confidence burning on my face as Ginger signalled me a final wink, then waved and slipped back away to join her group by the stage entrance.

Flare Femme

BROOKE

"Fulton County 911, what is your emergency?" I asked, pulling the bulb of my microphone close to my lips. The woman on the other end of the phone was in great distress, worried that her husband was having a heart attack.

This type of call was probably the most common, and some education on the use of defibrillators and chest compressions would go a long way in helping to reduce the casualties on this fact alone. I spoke to the woman through the whole ordeal, ensuring she stayed calm until the ambulance arrived, then told her she did well as I signed off the call.

I glanced up at the clock above my cubicle, it was lunchtime for our section. There was a crisp $10 bill burning a hole in my pocket, and it was destined for the man at the diner. I searched the office for any sight of Brian and Jill, but it seemed they were still quite busy with their own calls.

Brian spotted me as I stood near the entrance of his cubicle, then waved to me with a smile, telling me to go on ahead. I'm sure he would join me later.

With that, I found myself pushing through the doors of the Broadway Diner once again. It felt like I had been here more in the past two days than I had been home. It was busier today, and the only seats available were at the bar itself.

As I climbed onto one of the chrome-plated bar stools, I noticed a pretty young woman in the seat next to me. She offered me a kind smile, then returned her attention to her book.

This was about a good a time as any to strike up a conversation as I awaited service, so I took a glance down at the book she was reading. It was a book by Viktor Frankl, I knew the name… but only the name.

"Is that any good?" I asked her.

Her blonde curls bounced lightly as she turned her gaze to meet mine. A soft sparkle of her blue eyes. "It is," she said softly, "Do you know much about Frankl?" She asked.

I shook my head, "No ma'am," I admitted. "But if you're keen to share, I'd be happy to learn."

The woman's eyes twinkled and she placed a napkin inside of the book before placing the closed tome upon the bartop. "Viktor Frankl was an Austrian psychologist," she hummed sweetly, folding her hands into her lap. "This book talks about his experience in the concentration camps and how that experience encouraged him to create logotherapy!"

The intense joy she seemed to find from sharing this

knowledge summoned a smile forth to my face, and I nodded slowly. "What is logotherapy?"

She spun from side to side on her barstool, "Frankl believed it was a tool to help people find a sense of purpose," she explained, "And a lack of purpose is the reason behind our neuroses... or... what brings us down the most in life." She reached forward to grab the mug of black coffee before her and bring it to her lips. As she pulled it away, the soft outline of her pink lipstick stained the edge of the white rim.

I watched as she placed this mug back down on the table, thinking about the things she had said to me. "I think my daughter is my purpose," I said honestly, my eyes falling upon the book.

She brightened once more, "My husband is mine!" She said sweetly.

The excitement in my head faded, and I smiled softly, nodding respectfully to her. "It is good to know that true love exists," I said softly, a thought that dug a hole beneath my barstool, where I wanted to bury myself alive.

The woman giggled sweetly and nodded, moving to dismount from her seat. "It was lovely speaking to you, Mister!" She said with a gentle wave, then slipped out the front door.

I watched as she left, feeling the sullen reminder of my own loneliness whap me in the face.

"That was brutal," A voice chirped from in front of me.

My head reeled around to see Ellis standing before me. His elbow rested on the bar top and his chin secured atop the brace. There was a grin on his cheeks. "I was really rooting for you till she said she was married," He teased.

Around his eyes, his makeup was thicker than it had been yesterday. Obviously so. I rolled my eyes and plunged my hand into my pocket before retrieving the $10 bill from it, smacking it onto the counter.

Ellis laughed, "What is this?" He glanced down at the bill with a curious lift of his glittery eyebrow.

"For last night," I said softly, aware of the other patrons.

The maroon-clad man chuckled, placing his slender, well-manicured fingers over the bill and sliding it towards himself. "I don't remember the exact change to give you, but-"

"Keep the change," I said abruptly, turning my head over my shoulder to see that Jill and Brian had entered the diner. I pulled from the counter before Ellis could say anything else and stepped towards my friends. "I realized I left my wallet at home, so I'll just head back to the office," I explained softly.

"What?" Jill said, "No, absolutely not." She boomed.

Brian nodded, "We will cover it for today, okay?"

I felt a burning sensation in my chest, "No, no… I don't want to owe anyone," I admitted.

Brian chuckled and put his hand on my shoulder, guiding me to the booth where I had grown accustomed to sitting. Apparently, my protests were not enough to dissuade them. Once Jill and I were seated, Brian turned on his heels to find the jukebox.

"Here we go," Jill teased, fluttering her eyelashes as the song began to play overhead.

My friend returned to his place beside Jill and grinned, "Brooke, I was wondering… would you be interested in coming out with me tonight?" Brian asked.

The question struck me quite abruptly, and I tilted my head. "Tonight?" I asked.

In for another award for saving the day, Ellis swooped by with his pad at the ready. "Hey, Hey!" He called to us, "Are we doing our usuals again today?"

Brian nodded, then pointed to me, "Put Brooke on our tab today, please. I'm trying to butter him up to come out with me tonight."

"Oooh? Going out?" Ellis grinned, "Anywhere fun?" He inquired as he scrawled our orders across the pad in his hand.

Jill smirked, "He is trying to take him to Drag Night at the Midnight Raven."

My attention pinged to Jill, who maintained that devious smirk as Brian bashfully tried to shush her.

Ellis hummed and something in his expression changed, his eyelashes fluttered closed as he tilted his head to the side. "That sounds lovely!" His tone was off. Even for the superficial act that he had put on for most parts of conversation, that tone in particular felt wrong.

I turned my eyes to meet his gaze, and the softer lighting on this side of the dining room lent itself to reveal swelling beneath his eye where the makeup was thickest.

I then turned to Brian, "I don't know... with everything that happened with Kelly yesterday, I just don't know how comfortable I am with leaving her alone."

"I'll take her to my house. You can pick her up in the morning." Jill said sweetly.

"Did you want your BLT?" Ellis interjected; the smile still plastered on his face had fallen half an inch. I glanced over at him and nodded, and he quickly disappeared back into the kitchen without another word.

"That was odd..." I muttered.

Jill tilted her head, "What do you mean?" She asked.

"Did he not seem off to you?" I asked, turning my head back to glance at the silver swinging door.

Brian smiled, "I think you're just avoiding the invitation," He said in a light tease.

I returned my gaze to my friends, then shrugged, "I like drag racing, I guess."

The looks on their faces were priceless...

I knew exactly what Drag Night was.

By the time Ellis brought our food out to us, he was bright and peppy again, dancing from table to table like there wasn't a care in the world. I watched him curiously as he placed a glass of Coke down in front of me.

"Oh, Ellis... I think he has orange juice," Jill said softly.

Ellis glanced down at the glass in front of me, his hand moving to reach for the glass, but I quickly shook my head and blocked his grasp, "Coke is fine!" I said abruptly.

The pair in front of me seemed to tilt their heads, and Ellis laughed.

"Well, you're having it now whether you want it or not." He teased, placing Jill and Brian's drinks down as well, then folding the circular tray the drinks had balanced on under his armpit. "Food will be out soon, if you need anything-"

"Ask for Ellis!" a voice shouted from another table.

Ellis' eyes darted to the other end of the dining room and grinned, "You've got the spirit!" He said with a waggle of his manicured fingers, then winked back at us before disappearing into the busy dining room.

I pulled the glass of Coke closer to me and breathed in a soft sigh, I guess I would be going to a Drag Show...

* * *

I pulled my rusty old shit-box into the parking lot beside the

Midnight Raven. Bright pillars of light shot from beacons bolted into the concrete outside, waving from side to side as crowds of people pushed through the front doors. Near the entrance, I spotted Brian leaning against a railing, a lit cigarette poised between two fingers.

As I grew near, the intoxicating smell of tobacco pulled an ancient addiction from inside of my chest, and I chuckled. "Didn't realise you smoked," I commented.

Brian spotted me, throwing the bud down and stamping it, "I don't! And if Jilly ever asks, you saw nothing!" he laughed, then reached to pull me into a soft hug. "Glad you could come tonight. I was afraid I'd end up going alone… not a good look for an engaged man."

"Why not?" I asked, "Is it any better of a look for two men in precarious romantic situations?"

He tilted his head, then glanced at the building, "Man… what are we doing?" He laughed, "I'm surprised Jill was even happy for me to go, to be honest."

I shrugged, "We are men. Confident and secure in our sexuality. What is the big deal about watching other men who are also secure in their sexuality dressing up and dancing?"

Brian laughed, "I think you need to listen to the words you've just said."

A laugh rolled off my chest and I shook my head, "Let's go before we get shitty seats," I said, pulling myself from the gravel earth towards the club.

Inside, the world was alight with bright crimson colours. Neons that painted everywhere we walked with a soft radiating glow. Brian grabbed the scruff of my collar and pulled me to sit at a small table near the main stage, where a pole that must have been at least twenty feet high was centred.

I took a moment to glance around at our surroundings. People were dressed in everything from bathing suits to business suits, and I felt simultaneously under and overdressed.

The lights began to flicker and music shook the floor, silencing everyone in the room as a spotlight drifted to the top of the pole.

A performer in denim shorts and a tattered top began to descend the pole in mystifying circles while lip-syncing along with the song that played overhead. She had stunning long red hair... and for a moment I began to question everything I thought I knew about myself as a thirty-three-year-old man with an estranged wife and child.

As her knee-high, golden boots delicately graced the floor, she plucked a microphone from the stand on which it rested and pulled it to her lips.

"Welcome ladies, gentlemen, and gentle-thems... to a night of mystic wonder!" She called in a voice that felt eerily familiar. I was transfixed by her face. The way her bright red lipstick seemed to boast a classic sort of elegance that extended into sparkling shadows above her eyes. I recognized her face... the tone in her voice... that smile... everything about this person was setting off alarm bells and yet I couldn't think of why.

"It is so lovely to have you here tonight at our soiree. This is our last Drag Night for the fortnight," She sang in a sickeningly sweet British accent. "I'm Flare Femme, and I cannot wait to start off your festivities for the night with my own little *flare!*"

She threw her head back, dismounting the pole into a deep squat that pulled the fabric of her jeans tight against her ass, and I'm not ashamed to say that my eyes hovered there for a few beats longer than they probably should have... but then again... I do have a thing for redheads.

Flare dipped into a light bow as she explained the rules of the evening. "No touching unless consent is expressly given, no pinching, plucking, pruning, or otherwise vulgar p words to the Queens under any circumstances." Flare pulled her hand to dramatically adjust her shirt, "And the biggest rule of all is to have a fucking ball, Darlings!"

She placed the microphone in its mount, then spun around to grab the pole. The lights shut off entirely and a hush fell over the crowd and the room grew eerily quiet until the harsh shutter of a stage light clapped, pointing directly at Flare's position in the stage. She had somehow managed to change into a golden shimmering dress that reached her ankles. It had a slit that ran all the way up to her hip. There was a white faux fur draped across her shoulders and the bright sound of a saxophone started to play *Champagne: Electro Swing Spin.*

I was absolutely dazzled by the production value. Cannons released golden confetti throughout the room, and as Flare stepped down from the stage, an entire production of other Drag Queens joined the stage with procedural introductions from Flare herself.

As the song wound to an end, the dancers funnelled back to their backstage hideaways and left Flare to finish the song in the most eccentric way possible. She took a few steps towards the pole, swung a leg around it, and spun at high speed until the song finally came to a conclusion and the stage darkened once more.

Brian and I clapped, and when I glanced back at him, he didn't seem half as impressed as I was.

It was strange to me, the way I felt... my whole life I lived under the idea that everything I thought was *normal* was the only qualified beauty in life. And yet, here I was, sitting by the stage with a man I hardly knew intimately, watching this show that I never would have come to without his urging.

This… this was beautiful.

My joy seemed about as short-lived as ever, though, because as the next song began, the screen of my phone lit up in an annoying blue glow as yet another incoming call flickered onto the screen. My eyes flicked down to meet the glow, and I sighed as I realized it was Kelly.

With a roll of my eyes, I tapped Brian on the shoulder, "I'll be back. I need to grab this." I said, then slipped out the back door to find myself in the alley behind the club.

The first call ended before I could answer it, and just as she had done the night before, Kelly's call came through again. I answered it on the first ring this time.

"Hello?" I asked.

"Why do you keep ignoring my calls, Brooke?" She asked immediately.

Annoyance stitched itself between my eyebrows, and I stared down at the gravel beneath my feet, "I was busy, Kell." I kicked a larger rock a few inches.

"Too busy for your wife?" She asked.

I winced, "That isn't fair. You know it isn't fair," I said.

"Oh?" She questioned, "Why not?"

"As if," I spat, "You literally abandoned me with a newborn, now your little fling isn't working out so you think you can just crawl back into my life and expect me to be open to you?"

"I want to see my daughter!" Kelly bulldozed through the statement I'd made.

Frustration burned behind my eyes as her blatant disregard

for my words only confirmed my suspicions, and I lifted my hand to my forehead to rub the skin, "She is my daughter too, Kelly... in fact, she is more my daughter than she is yours! The only thing you've ever done for her is give birth to her!"

"I carried her for nine-fucking-months, you dick!" She shouted back.

I tried to compose myself, but the anger that boiled in my veins made the brick wall beside me look like a compelling punching bag. "You need to stop this. Get some fucking therapy, yeah?" I snarled, "I can't deal with these psychotic interactions anymore. You need to get fucking help!"

"You think I'm crazy?" Kelly asked, "I'll show you fucking crazy!"

The phone call ended, and I sucked a breath of air in through my teeth. My eyes stared at the brick wall before me, then I balled my hand into a tight fist.

"I wouldn't do that if I were you," a strikingly familiar voice called, though it was distorted... different.

I glanced up, snapped from my rage as though a bucket of ice water had been doused over my shoulders. Flare Femme was sat on a metal staircase, her elbow propping her up as she leaned back against the chequered metal. A lit cigarette in her hand.

My eyes narrowed, and I turned to face her, my arms crossed before myself. "I'm not too sure you have the qualifications to tell me what I should do," I said flatly.

"Ha!" Flare laughed, throwing her hand over her chest. "You think I need qualifications to boss you around?" She pushed herself to stand, stepping closer until our chests nearly touched, staring down at me from that high place where she towered six inches above me, "Darling, most men

56

would pay me for that honour."

Flare Femme smelled phenomenal. A sweet mixture of hairspray and a floral perfume that overwhelmed me the more I breathed near her. I stepped back and sighed, "Sorry, that was rude," I apologised.

She shook her head with a smirk as she returned to sit on the staircase, "I sure hope you are," She teased as she retrieved a carton of pre-rolled cigarettes from the breast of her sparkling dress, pulling one out to place it between her lips. She struck her lighter to ignite the end.

I glanced over, feeling a pang of anxiety wash over me. Was I really arguing with a Drag Queen? One that… I kinda had the hots for?

"You're really good at this, by the way," I said softly.

A laugh rolled off of the smoke that she exhaled and she nodded, "I do get that quite a lot," she said, then pat the stair beside herself to beckon me to have a seat.

For a moment, I hesitated. Then, I gathered my hands, shoving them into my pockets as I walked to sit beside the Drag Queen. She held out the cigarette that she'd lit to me, a soft expression on her face. After another brief bout of hesitation, I accepted it.

I pulled the smoking roll to my lips and breathed the smoke into my lungs. A practice I had grown habitual of years ago before I decided to quit. The relief was almost instantaneous, and I passed it back to Flare.

"That phone call sounded rough… need someone to talk to?" Flare asked softly, her brown eyes stared at me with a gentle glitter catching on her eyelashes.

A weight lifted slightly from my shoulders, and I shook my head. "Nah… No use, really."

"Why do you think that?" She asked with a chuckle. I swear... I swear I recognized that chuckle.

I turned to glance at her, my heart stopping dead in my chest as I realized that her eyes were already soldered onto me. I searched the heavily painted face of this person for a moment before my focus was drawn to a patch beneath her eye that had swollen.

"Ellis?" I asked softly.

Flare's face fell in an instant, and she turned away from me quickly. "It isn't polite to use a Drag Queen's real name when she is in character," She muttered, avoiding my gaze.

"This is why you were acting weird in the diner earlier," I vocalized my own realization, pushing myself to stand.

The expression on her face mixed with a hint of fear and hurt as I now stood taller than her. That simple fact broke my heart, and I crouched before her.

"I'm sorry, I didn't realize."

She turned away from me, her eyelashes batting in the moonlight and catching the softest glints of its rays. "The magic goes away when you know," She muttered, pulling the cigarette to her lips again.

"Well, I mean you look fucking stunning." I pushed a hand through my brown hair to smooth it, and Flare glanced at me. She was right, though... now that I realized who she was... Ellis is all I could see.

Flare sighed, checking her phone to gleam the time. "I have to go back inside now, Brooke." She said softly, "I'm due back on stage."

I would be lying if I said that the idea of Flare leaving at that moment didn't upset me, but I nodded.

"Do you think..." I stopped myself, shaking my head quickly.

"Nevermind… it's nothing."

The Drag Queen pushed herself to stand, crossing her arms. "It doesn't seem like nothing," She said with a grin. That same artificial, half smile that Ellis had given us earlier.

I frowned and pulled my phone out. "Could I possibly get your number? I need advice from someone with style." I said. "I've been swiping on Tinder… might lock something down, ya know?"

Flare smirked and snatched my phone from my hand. She typed her number into my contacts and saved it under *Flare Femme* with a winking face. She then winked and slipped back in through the back door, leaving me completely alone.

Until Brian came stumbling out through the entrance. "Brooke!" He called, "Brooke! You missed the best act!" He hiccuped, then spontaneously vomited all over himself.

I chuckled as I turned to face him, "Dear God, Brian… What have you done to yourself?" I asked, gathering the man into my arms and guiding him towards my shitty old car. "You're coming to mine, I'll sort your shit out in the morning." I chuckled, helping him throw himself into my backseat.

I took Brian back to my house that night. Made him comfortable on the sofa in the lounge with a puke bowl and some water beside the couch. He knocked out pretty much the second he touched the cushions. So with him sufficiently sedated for the night, I made my way upstairs to my bedroom.

The urge to call Jill and ask about Rae weighed heavily on my mind, but I knew she was safe where she was… I messaged Jill anyway to tell her that I brought Brian home early because he got himself smashed off his face. Then, as I lay there in bed, I pulled open the contact for Flare and stared at an empty draft message.

Why did it feel so daunting to speak to someone new? Was I not worthy of friendship? The blinking line flashed lightly in the bottom of my screen, and I just shrugged it away, placing my phone on the charger on my bedside table and falling asleep as quickly as I could manage.

Stood Up?

BROOKE

Two months have passed since I first saw Flare Femme at a drag show with my only real friend, Brian. Ever since then, I hadn't made it a habit of going into Broadway Diner for regular meals. Back to saving money and brooding on my lonesome.

As I dressed myself, I heard a ping from my phone as a Tinder notification rolled along the top of my notifications bar.

This girl I'd been speaking to, Renee.

She was a beautiful redhead with bright green eyes and every time her name came across my screen, I melted.

Renee: Hey Handsome

My cheeks warmed.

Me: Morning beautiful!

I sent the message, then lay across my bed as I saw the bubbles bouncing along the bottom of the messenger. Teeth perched on my lower lip as I nibbled at the soft flesh; her new message arrived on the screen.

Renee: Are you still excited to meet tonight?

My heart fluttered, and I smiled brightly as I tapped out a response.

Me: Absolutely! I just need to make sure my babysitter can watch my little girl.

An instant later, a response came.

Renee: Bring her!

That flutter in my heart turned to a throb, and I glanced at the baby monitor in the corner of my bed. Rae was awake, but sitting up and playing with the stars on the sheet of her cot.

I really felt like this girl may be the one. She said all the right things, we agreed on everything. It felt far too good to be true… but I didn't want to subject Rae to anything too soon.

I pulled up Jill's contact and sent her a message.

Me: Hey Jilly! Are you still okay to watch Rae for an hour or so tonight?

Jill took longer to respond, but it gave me time to finish getting dressed and to get Rae ready for daycare as well.

By the time I'd finished dressing her and packing her things, a notification from Jill pulled across my screen.

Jill: Yes!!!!

Relief washed over me, and I opened Tinder once more.

Me: Everything is set up! Where would you like to meet?

Renee: Have you got any suggestions?

I thought for a moment, then shrugged.

Me: I'll meet you at Broadway Diner at 6?

I arrived at the diner half an hour early, like I usually did, and sank into that booth that I'd chosen as my preferred place to sit. Within seconds, I heard the kitchen door swing open and the light footsteps of Ellis approach.

"Ah, Welcome back!" He cheered. "It has been ages,"

A warmth grew on my cheeks as I noticed the sparkling, pink highlight that dusted Ellis's cheeks. My words caught in my throat and I ended up just staring at him like a deer caught in headlights.

Ellis tilted his head, the pencil that was secured in his ear didn't budge. "You alright, mate?" He asked with a confused lift of his eyebrow.

I pulled my eyes from the maroon-clad waiter.

"S-sorry," I said, "Just...nervous."

"On another date, are we?" He asked brightly, a grin pulling his white teeth into view.

All I could do in that moment was nod, but that seemed to please him for the most part.

"That's lovely, then! Shall I bring out the gallon of Coke?" He teased lightly.

"Yes, please," I nodded affirmatively, "She should be here soon!"

A chipper laugh rolled off of Ellis' tongue, and he nodded slowly, "I can see you're already fumbling this one, mate." He turned on his heels and waved to me with a cheerful tut as he disappeared.

Why was I so fucking nervous around him? What is going

on?

My heart pounded in my chest as I watched the clock on my phone tick by. Ellis brought me my drinks, leaving me to my misery for the vast majority of the evening.

Six o'clock came… then six fifteen… six thirty… and Renee never showed.

I held onto some sort of hope that she would turn up… late and anxious, maybe clutching an umbrella from some invisible storm beyond the confines of the diner, but she never did. I emptied my fourth glass of Coke and laid my head on the table, blocking out the heartbreak and annoyance that burned in my chest, when I felt the soft collision of glass against the table.

Peeking out, I saw Ellis standing there with a solemn look on his face. "You just can't catch a break, eh mate?"

I scrunched my nose, shaking my head softly, "I think I need to commit myself to a life of celibacy at this point if I'm being totally honest."

Ellis let out a burst of laughter, and I saw a flash of Flare in his face. He looked around at the empty dining room, then back at me, "Well, maybe you should have reached out for that advice," He hummed, slipping into the other side of the booth.

A chuckle tumbled from my misery, and I pushed myself to sit upright, albeit slouched quite a bit. I looked up at this person who I think I could call my friend at this point.

"Are you hungry?" Ellis asked. This time, his tone was soft. It sounded real. I liked that tone.

My stomach wouldn't allow me to lie, as it lurched at the thought of consuming food. I nodded softly.

The man in the other half of the booth chuckled, "Me too.

Mind if I join you?"

I thought for a moment, then nodded softly.

Ellis' eyes brightened and he leapt from the booth, running back into the kitchen where he remained for about ten minutes. When he returned, he brought forth a tray full of food.

"This is my favourite meal that we offer here," He explained as he passed me an oval-shaped plate with scrambled eggs, bacon, pancakes, and a piece of buttered toast. He then placed a freshly filled Coke beside me and retrieved his own plate from the tray.

I stared down at the food for a moment, and once Ellis had dug into his bacon, I think it felt safe for me to do the same. The pancakes were fluffy and warm, exactly what my stomach wanted at that moment in time.

"I never get to do this," Ellis chuckled, washing down a mouthful of food with a glass of iced water. His actions pulled a smile to the edges of my lips, and I found myself fixated on his face once again. He seemed to notice this, and he turned his gaze away.

"You know, you don't have to stare."

The statement snapped me back into reality, and I quickly turned my eyes back to the food.

Ellis sighed, "You haven't come in since that night..." he said softly, his fork shifting around to poke at his eggs. "Part of me hoped that you were just really busy, but I saw your friends come in on their breaks."

I rubbed my neck, "I've been trying to save money, so I stopped eating out as much."

This brought a bit of a smile back to his face, and he shook his head. "I thought you were weirded out when you saw..."

"What? Saw you dressed in drag?" I asked.

Ellis' face lit up bright red as he looked around the empty diner to ensure it was well and truly empty, "Jesus Christ, mate," he sighed, sinking back into his seat. "This is why you scare women off!"

I grinned, "Why are you embarrassed?" I asked softly, scooping a mouthful of eggs into my mouth.

The shimmer of his eyebrows twinkled in the fluorescent lighting as he furrowed his brows, "What do you mean? That is the kind of shit that'll get me chased out of most southern towns," He pulled his hand to rest on his forehead.

"It isn't like I'll tell anyone it was you," I said quickly, "And anyways... I don't think you should be ashamed of it at all. You're really good at it."

Ellis moved his eyes to glance at me, his cheeks glowing lightly with a blush. He crossed his legs before himself.

"Do you... want to be a woman?" I asked softly.

His eyes widened, and he chuckled. "I guess I should have expected this question," He hummed softly.

Ellis pushed himself to lean against the table, his long arms resting at the elbow against the sticky surface of the table.

"No, mate. I don't want to be a woman. I am fully secure in my gender... I just..." he lifts a hand to his neck, "I like feeling pretty. Drag is the only thing that keeps me grounded. I get to sing my sorrows away and paint myself in pretty colours."

I nodded slowly, keeping my eyes on him. "What are your... um... pronouns?" I asked, the query felt alien... this was the first time I'd actually considered this question, but... it seemed important.

"I like he or him... when I'm Flare... I'm no longer Ellis, so I prefer to use the character's pronouns. Flare is a woman."

Ellis said, fidgeting with one of his almond shaped nails as he avoided my eyes.

"What made you start?"

"Start Drag?" He asked.

My head bobbed in a soft nod.

He ran a hand through his black hair, "My mum used to watch RuPaul… I really liked the show, but when I showed interest in it, she flipped. Kicked me out… I was on the streets for a while and the only money I could get was from doing occasional drag shows. They'd fund me a little ways until I… made a few more bad choices and ended up here."

He shifted, leaning back against the seat once more as he locked his eyes onto mine. There was a shield that glittered around his iris, sealing me off from getting any closer to chipping away at his lore.

"Tell me about her…" he changed the subject.

I tilted my head, "Who?" I asked, polishing off the last of my bacon.

"Your wife," he said, dipping his hand to retrieve the abandoned fork.

"Why would you want to know about her?" I asked.

He lifted an eyebrow again as he stared up at me, and I think I got this hint. I pulled a napkin to wipe my chin and sighed.

"We were childhood best friends. It took me nine years to finally marry her. Part of me wonders if that is why she left me," I chuckled, glancing out the window. "She started to become really mentally unwell about two years ago. She'd hit me, throw things, she would scream in my face until I was on the ground shaking… and then when she saw how scared and broken I was, she would sob uncontrollably." The ache in my chest returned, droning a low and steady beat into my lungs. "When she got pregnant… things got better. Lots better."

Ellis was still, listening closely without interruption. Every time I managed a glance in his direction, his brown eyes hovered on my face. It didn't feel menacing, but kind.

"The last month of her pregnancy, the symptoms of her illness started showing up again. She was violent with me, and I called the hospital… They came and picked her up and I didn't see her again until Rae was born. I didn't even get to be there for her birth." I looked down, tracing the dotted pattern of the table. "Then she left me for her co-worker. Moved all of her stuff out… took the car I bought… she begged me not to take her to court, so I didn't. Anything to keep Rae safe." That is what I told myself at least.

"That's rough," Ellis said in a genuine voice. Chills rolled down my skin as I met his gentle gaze. "I'm sorry you went through that." He glanced down at his untouched pancakes with a look that detailed a slight disinterest.

I noted his expression, smiling and nudging his foot under the table, "Cold pancakes are shit," I said softly.

He chuckled, and I swear I saw his cheeks dust a light pink as he nodded slowly. "They are shit, aren't they?" He leaned in to finally take a bite of the cakes. After a moment, he placed his fork down and pulled in a deep breath. "I hate this shithole, mate," He looked out the window, "I wish I could leave."

"Why don't you?" I asked, pulling a sip of my drink through the straw.

He chuckled, shaking his head, "It isn't really anything I could explain on a first date," he said.

I choked on the drink as it nearly missed my oesophagus,

coughing up a lung as Ellis burst into a soft laugh.

"I only tease," he said, leaning his head back against the wall behind his seat. His eyes wandered around the diner that he'd circled thousands of times at this point in his life.

As I regained myself, I noted the heavy silence in the air, the way he seemed to disappear into another universe in his mind. When he sank into that place of comfort, the mask he wore fell away. He unclenched his jaw. He rested... and god damn, did he look like he needed rest.

My eyes softened as I glanced over his shoulder to see a picture on the wall. A classic car driving on a long empty road.

"If you could go anywhere in the world... where would you go?" I asked.

The question perked the man's lips into a soft smile and he changed his position to sit completely upright. He leaned over the table slightly. "I'd go to Iceland!" he chuckled, "Nice and cold, lots of fish! You can see whales swimming in the water during the day... and volcanoes!" He hummed, "So... I would go to Iceland," he said confidently.

I nodded slowly, taking in the sparkle that had grown in his eyes as he spoke. It was different than the superficial joy he typically spoke with. My heart raced, and I felt the smile on my face growing less and less forced.

"I have always wanted to drive around America. Go to all of the places we see advertised on TV, but never actually get to see."

"I'd love to see the Grand Canyon," Ellis chirped, a smile now present on his face as well.

"Me too!" I laughed softly.

Ding!

Ellis' eyes darted to the front entrance of the Diner, "Welcome! You find a seat and I'll be right with you!" He said, pushing himself from the booth.

"Wait," I muttered, grabbing Ellis' fork and stabbing the last bite of pancake onto it. Ellis turned and I presented the fork to his lips. I watched as the colour drained from his face, and his eyes locked onto mine.

In an instant, I threw the fork back down onto his plate, throwing my hand over my mouth as I realised what I'd done.

"S-sorry," I muttered.

His brown eyes fixed on me for a moment, but he glanced back to look at the customer. They hadn't moved from the door.

"Come on in," he assured, "We are still open for half an-"

"Shut up!" A deadly familiar voice shouted.

Ellis froze dead in his tracks as he tilted his head, "Whoa, miss..." he tried to say, but before I could come to grips with what was happening, a steel chair was hoisted from beneath a table and launched at the wall beside my head.

I leapt from my place, reeling around to see Kelly standing there, her blue eyes burning with righteous fury as she seethed. "I knew you were a bottom-feeding fucker, but to stoop so low as to arrange a meet-up with some slut you met online!" She snarled at me.

Defence was my first plan of action, and I threw my hands up in front of myself, "W-wait a minute! Why are you here?"

"Where is my daughter, Brooke?" Kelly screamed.

Ellis' eyes narrowed and he crossed his arms, knowing better than to get involved in this sort of dispute.

Meanwhile, my head was reeling from the sudden presence of an incredibly mentally unwell woman. I felt the undeniable urge to sink into my own skin and perish at the top of my mind.

Kelly stepped forward, closing the distance between us at lightning speed as she continued to scream at me. Suddenly, Ellis stepped between us.

"Madam, you need to leave before I call the police." He said in a stern voice. This only seemed to agitate her more and she reeled back to shove Ellis.

In a split-second decision, I grabbed him by the arm and pulled him behind me, then I let go, my face burning with the heat of rage as I grabbed Kelly by her wrists.

"You need to fucking go, Kelly!" I shouted, louder than I ever shouted at my wife in our entire lives… louder than I ever wanted to shout at anybody. This virile anger poured out of me at rapid speed. "You're fucking with my life and you need to go!"

She froze, instantly recoiling, and I knew the tears were en route. It took everything in me to stop myself from dropping to my knees and wallowing to apologise. I knew that she was unwell… but she was pushing that onto me, and that wasn't fucking fair.

I couldn't take it anymore, so I pulled her by the wrist and guided her out through the front door so that we could exit the building. Once outside, I released her wrist.

"Go the fuck home and don't ever come near me again. If I ever see you again I'll have you put in prison." I shouted, jabbing a finger in her direction.

Kelly trembled before me, a face of utter terror drawled across her pink cheeks. People were beginning to peek out of the businesses nearby, staring and watching in concern, and I turned on my heels to re-enter the diner. I quickly walked to where I had sat moments before with Ellis, removing my wallet from my jacket and thrusting a wad of money in Ellis's direction.

He scrambled to grab it, watching as I stormed out through the front door and back to my car. I sank into my seat, locking the doors the second that I could. Panic coursed through my veins as I felt the tremble of utter adrenaline. I'd yelled at my wife… I'd made her cry… Fuck.

I pulled out my phone to see hundreds of missed phone calls and unread messages. My mind flooded with terrible thoughts, and the air within the car became suffocating and stagnant.

Each breath I drew in through my mouth felt like razor blades along my windpipe, slowly cutting into the tissue until I would eventually drown in my own blood. The vision in the corners of my eyes was drawing nearer, blacker. I breathed in quick, uncontrollable succession, my whole body locking up. I was burning with the bites of thousands of fire ants that I fucking knew didn't exist.

I balled my hands into fists, striking them hard against the wheel before me until the skin on my knuckles tore and my muscles throbbed. Every single atom in my body begged to shut down. Begged to be permitted to cease function, and yet my heart beat so fast within my chest that it seemed I could run on pure unfettered adrenaline for ages.

Just when I felt like I had reached the climax of the attack, I saw her again. She was standing at the entrance to the parking garage, staring at my car with bloody murder written in her eyes. I panicked, searching the seat for my phone. When I finally grabbed it, I dialled 911 as fast as I possibly could.

"Fulton County 911, what is your emergency?"

"He-Hello? I- I need police," I begged into the receiver, the panic drowning out my own words, as well as those of the dispatcher in my ear.

"Sir, what is going on?"

"My-my wife.. she… she is going to kill me," I whimpered, watching Kelly with wide eyes. I was terrified that she would appear right in front of me if I blinked.

"Where are you?" The dispatcher asked impatiently.

I whimpered, "F…fuck," I muttered, "Um… I'm downstairs… in the p-parking garage for th-the dispatch."

"Why are you in our parking garage, sir?"

Annoyance bubbled in my brain and I groaned in frustration, "I w-work here! I went to d…dinner after work!" I explained, though I shouldn't have had to. There was silence on the other end, and then finally…

"Officers are en route, sir. Please stay on the line until you see blue lights." The woman on the other end of the phone call said.

I blinked, finally, rubbing my eyes… and when I opened my eyes again, Kelly was gone. "W…what the fuck?" I said aloud.

"Sir, what is happening?"

"S-she is gone! Vanished into thin f-fucking air!"

Then, I heard the single most terrifying sound in my life as the passenger side window was delivered a steady thump three times. My soul left my body as I turned to see Kelly standing right outside the right-hand window, her eyes glassed over and her face stone cold. I could feel my life fading from my body as I dissolved into screams and whimpers.

Her tapping remained consistent. Long slow taps… then she tightened her fist, striking the glass harder, then harder. I reached for my keys to turn on the ignition, but they weren't there. She was going to break through this window any moment now.

Out of the corner of my eyes, the flashing of red and blue lights emerged. Just as I heard the squeal of their tires, Kelly's hand crashed straight through the glass, spraying me in her blood as well as shards of glass. Within seconds, the officers had incapacitated her. Then and only then, could I relax... and by relax, I mean absolutely fucking black out.

Mr. Unlucky

ELLIS

What the fuck is my life, right?

I asked myself this question most nights as I locked up the diner... but this night in particular was one for the books. The cash that Brooke had thrown at me burned a hole in the pocket of my apron as I pulled the shutters down on the front windows.

Blue and red lights flashed beyond these shutters, and my heart ached as I turned to collect the chair that had once resided on the other side of the room. Brooke's half-empty glass of Coke sat on the table where we had just been sat together.

I'd be lying if I said I didn't feel a pull towards him... He was a kind man with a really unlucky life. I guess you could say that I was projecting my own feelings onto him, though.

I pulled the cash from my pocket and counted out the change, placing the excess into a small envelope that I would keep until the next time I saw him. Then, I told the cooks I closed up shop early, and began my walk toward the Midnight Raven.

There was no Drag Night tonight, but Lorenzo had sent me an email with details on one of his more high-profile clients who wanted a man with womanly features. I intended to be early. This was a streak I had maintained for a fair number of weeks now.

The twenty minutes it took for me to walk from downtown Atlanta towards the club always seemed to breeze by. I can't remember the last time I actually took a moment to observe my surroundings, but today was definitely not one of those days.

I pushed through the back door of the club to see a group of girls huddled around the dressing room entrance. Some of them sneered as I entered, but one of the girls smiled in my direction and waved.

This girl was known as Scarlett, but I knew her as Valentine. She was nice to me because she was also wrapped up in a trap set by Lorenzo with no escape in sight.

I smiled lightly at her and wiggled the tips of my fingers in her direction, then slipped past the group of scantily clad women towards the dressing room. My vanity was still just as cluttered as before, and I would probably never tidy it at this rate.

"Ellis," A soft voice came from behind me. I turned to see Valentine stood nearby. Her long blonde hair was tied into a high ponytail.

Closing my eyes, my head fell to the side as I smiled at her, "Hey, Val!" I said softly, beckoning her closer.

Valentine stepped closer, glancing down at my worktop, "I will never understand how you got so good at makeup," She said softly, "I have been doing mine since I was twelve, and I could never turn myself into a completely different person like you do every night."

I chuckled, shaking my head as I turned my attention to the piles of makeup at my station, "To be honest, Val… it is the reason I keep this up. Every night I can come in here and become someone other than who I actually am." I reached to pick up a lip liner, scooping my hand beneath Valentine's chin. "You have a stunning cupid's bow… if you overline it like this…" I painted an arch over each side over her lips, then pulled back and smiled, "It gives you a more *darling* look, Darling!"

She turned her head to catch a glimpse of herself in the mirror, and her brown eyes shimmered for a moment. "You're a miracle worker," She giggled, then glanced over her shoulder. "Zo has you working with a guy who likes whips… are you gonna be okay?"

"Babes," I laughed, pulling a drawer of my vanity open to retrieve a black choker from within. "I have taken far worse than a whip, and I'll deal it back tenfold if they cross me."

Valentine giggled, then winked. "Be safe, Ellis." She said softly before scurrying out for her stage call.

Her absence filled me with dread. On nights that didn't host Drag, it was extremely rare to have any men in the club who were performers. It was usually just the normal dancers… and I always felt so out of place.

I pulled on a skimpy outfit with plenty of mesh, then painted my face a pale shade of cream, tracing my lips in a vampiric bloody red. My eyelashes had begun to lose their shimmer, so I added some falsies in for volume. Finally, I picked a simple pair of leather boots with a six inch platform. The boot came up to a few inches above my ankles and zipped on the inside, but there was a zig-zag cross of laces that tightened them and made the pair snug on my feet.

My alarm dinged on my phone, and as if by the grace of God, Zophia pulled the door open at the exact same time. "Flare!" She screeched.

I whipped my head around, securing a black bobbed wig to my scalp, "I'm just here, Zophie! Stop your shouting!" I said in a boisterous voice.

"Your client is in room six!" She called, then slammed the door shut abruptly.

The urge to roll my eyes was strong, but I contained myself, choosing instead to push myself from my seat and saunter through the hallway towards the private rooms.

The second I entered the room, I recognized the man. I had been his pet many times before, and though he had a tendency to be rough, he was almost always respectful.

"Good evening, Alfred," I said sweetly, pressing my weight back into the door to close it, then flipping the lock to seal us within.

Alfred's face brightened. His bright silver eyes flickered with lust as he smoothed a hand through his red hair, "You've changed your look up, Flare," he commented with a slight growl in his voice.

I could feel my cock twitch beneath the restrictive shorts I had tucked myself into. I always enjoyed Alfred's nights.

He was a gentleman who knew exactly what he wanted. He wanted to cum... to cum hard... all over my back.

"Shall we dim the lights?" I asked, pressing my finger along the dimming light switch until the only light that remained was the haunting red glow of the floor lamps.

Alfred approached me, extending his hand to lift one of mine to his lips. "You know the rules, Flare... get up on that stage and dance for me," He demanded, his hand wrapping around my wrist as he thrust me forward toward the pole and tiny intersecting stage.

A rush of mischief flooded my mind and I stepped up onto the platform. "Yes, sir." I began to strip tease for him, and Alfred watched me, sinking into the chaise lounge before me.

Sexy, sultry music flowed from the speakers above as I danced for Alfred, and when I was finally nude, he beckoned me towards him, grabbing me by the elastic of my choker and forcing me to my knees before him. "Milk my cock, Flare. I want you to get me right there on the edge so I can fill your asshole with my cum." He demanded.

Chills dotted over my exposed skin and I reached into his trousers to remove his smaller-than-average penis... you can see why he needs to pay for this kind of entertainment.

I made fast work of getting him nice and hard, spitting on his manhood and tugging at it just the way I knew he liked it. Alfred's head rolled back and he groaned with pleasure, his hips occasionally bucking into my hand as I pumped his cock.

Before too long, he reeled his hand back, delivering a decent slap across my face. It stung... but I liked it. I liked it a whole fucking lot.

"What do you want to do to me, Alfie?" I groaned out,

thickening the gravel in my voice. He melted beneath me, his hips bucking up into my grasp.

"G-get the whip," He demanded.

My heart raced in my chest as I pushed myself from between his legs and strolled with a sultry roll of my hips towards a toy chest on the wall. I selected one of the whips and turned back to him, placing the hilt in his hand.

Alfred smirked, "kneel," he ordered me, and I did as told. I knelt before him. He stood up, grabbing me by the back of my neck and dragging me to the chaise, "Hands on the couch. Don't you dare fucking move." He ordered.

Obediently, I pressed my hands to the chaise, feeling the soft velvet of the fabric beneath my skin as I pulled in a deep breath.

Thwack!

Alfred struck me with the whip. I whimpered, allowing the high-pitched noise to roll from my chest like a plea for more. Again and again, he struck me until the skin of my back was marked with the imprint of the soft leather throughout. Then, he tossed the instrument to the side.

I heard shuffling from behind me, and then the sound of a tube being squeezed. Another reason I liked Alfred, he fucking knew not to go into an ass raw.

The cold lubricant splashed onto my exposed asshole, and Alfred knelt to rub his fingers delicately around my entrance, occasionally slipping his fingers inside until I was lubed up. Then, he straddled my hips, pressing his manhood into my hole.

A gentle moan left my lips, and I played up the pleasure of his size to please him. He began to thrust, not that I could feel too much, but it was pleasant nonetheless. Faster, harder,

I moaned like he was the biggest cock I'd ever taken until suddenly, he pulled from within me and emptied his load all over the seething skin of my back.

He groaned, slowly pushing himself to stand before he collapsed on the chaise in front of me. A dim smile crossed his lusty face and he smirked, "When are you going to marry me, ay?" He said.

I straightened myself with a smirk, "You'll have to fight Lorenzo for me," I teased with a light expression on my face.

Alfred reached to cup his hand under my chin, and though I felt the apprehension in my chest grow, I sank into his touch like a lovesick puppy. I craved this sensation... this level of care and adoration. I flicked my eyes up to look at him, and for a split second, I swear I saw Brooke staring back at me.

I blinked quickly, and Alfred's gentle face stared down at me.

"I could save you, you know. You'd never have to do this for anyone else but me," He said, and my heart gripped at the thought of being his fuck buddy until he died... but I simply giggled.

"I appreciate your offer, but I am happy where I am," I lied through my teeth. I lied as though I didn't cry myself to sleep most nights, dreading the next day. My chest ached as Alfred's warm touch faded from my skin and he nodded respectfully.

"Okay, Flare. I will see you next time," He said softly, adjusting his belt and placing the money he owed on the chaise beside me before slipping out of the room.

Alone on the ground, I felt the world spinning. The smile that I'd forced for Alfred faded and I crumbled into myself, feeling wholly and truly empty.

As I straightened, I felt the sting of his strikes ache with every movement I made, and the sticky sensation of his fluids pulled at my skin. I shuddered and pulled a black silk dressing gown down from the box of toys, then escorted myself to the onsite showers. Lorenzo would be in to collect the money from that room soon, so I simply tidied myself and slipped on back to my miserably tiny apartment nearby, where I could take a full shower and decompress.

Once home, I threw my uniform in the laundry and curled up on my futon, a rerun episode of Supernatural queued up as I sipped at a can of cider.

Just before I progressed from my state of calm to sleep, my phone dinged beside me with a message from an unknown number.

Unknown: Hey, is this Ellis?

I tilted my head as I stared at the screen. Exhaustion threatened to pull me into its grasp, but I grabbed the device and typed out a response

Me: Who is this?

There was nothing for a moment. I stared at the open conversation and rubbed my eyes to keep myself from drifting off, The soft hum of the washing machine behind me pulsed with a soft siren song.

Unknown: Brooke

The pupils of my eyes expanded slightly as I processed the response. A brief wave of confusion as I wondered how he had gotten my number, but then I remembered the night outside the Midnight Raven.

I nibbled the skin at the back of one of my lips, and rolled onto my side, pulling the thin fleece blanket over my shoulder.

Me: Hey! Did you manage to get home okay? xx

There was a brief period of silence, then Brooke sent through an image of a car that I assume was his own. The passenger side window was smashed and the seat was full of glass. A terrifying streak of blood was painted on the edges of whatever shattered glass remained on the edge of the window.

A chill pulled through my spine, and I felt the edges of my lips pull to a tight purse.

   Me: Oh my god, Brooke! Are you okay? xx

The beat of my heart began to pulse violently in my chest as I stared anxiously at the bouncing bubbles from an incoming message.

Brooke: I'm fine. Physically at least. They've taken her into custody for the night... not sure for how long

The breath that I didn't even realize I was holding suddenly released, and I felt myself relax significantly.

Brooke: She has really fucked my head up after tonight.

   Me: Oh? xx

His response was taking a decent amount of time, and in that space the hum of my washing machine stopped almost entirely, resounding a jarring buzz that pulled my exhausted, aching body from the mattress of the futon. As I stood, the healing skin of my back pulled, and I winced in pain.

"Fucking piece of shit whips..." I grumbled as I trudged towards the washing machine and removed the load of clothing, draping the pieces across a clothes horse that I splayed out in front of the machine. The soft vibration of a notification pulled me back to the futon, where I perched myself on the edge of the tatty cushion. Its metal frame creaked beneath me.

Brooke: I checked Tinder after I got back to see if the date

I had tonight had messaged me and I just hadn't received it. The account was closed. Pretty sure that it was a long con by her to get me to bring my daughter out so she could see her.

I stared over the message and I felt a pang of annoyance in my chest. This guy just couldn't seem to catch a break and I felt bad for his circumstances. I saw how that woman was when she came into the diner. How she seemed to just see red the second her eyes fell over him. I've felt the helplessness that he felt. I understood the rage that pushed him to scream at her.

My legs that hung over the edge of the bed pushed back against the shoddy wooden flooring to press myself back into the bed, and I sighed softly.

Me: Damn…

Brooke: Yeah.

The words that could soothe him didn't seem to find me, and I sighed again in deliberation.

Me: Tonight was pretty heavy, mate. I think you really need to get some rest. Come into the diner tomorrow and I'll treat you to some cheesecake. xx

I didn't know if that was the right thing to suggest or not, but it was all I could really offer him. The money I made at the diner funnelled straight into bills and the maintenance of my unproductive lifestyle. I never saw a cent of money from Lorenzo, and what little money I could scavenge from Zophia on Drag Nights hardly filled my cabinets with food.

Brooke: I will come in. I need to get out of the house.

I'm not sure why, but my heart leapt at this. The idea of seeing him again. But it did. I felt a smile grow on my face and I let out a final sigh of relief.

Me: Fantastic. I look forward to seeing you again Mr.

Unlucky. xx

The bubbles rolled once more, and I anxiously stared at them as they rolled. Suddenly, they stopped. I think I stared at the screen for ten minutes, hoping to see them reappear. They never did, and the green dot that highlighted his activity turned grey.

I leaned across my futon and placed my phone on charge after setting my alarm for 6:00 a.m., then laid on my stomach to help ease the pain I felt against my burning spine. Slowly, I managed to fall into a gentle, slightly buzzed sleep.

Chocolate Cheesecake

BROOKE

I pulled open the door to Broadway Diner, Rae's car seat draped over my arm as I stepped through the threshold that would funnel from the busy streets of Atlanta into the buzzing diner.

The events of the previous night vanished like a distant memory into thin air, and I found myself searching the busy dining room for a table where I could set Rae's carrier next to myself.

In a far corner of the restaurant, there was a small table with a seat just big enough for me to place Rae in a safe little corner. I placed the carrier in that nook and then sat down, pulling the menu that I had already read hundreds of times now across the table to mindlessly fidget with.

Rae babbled sweetly at my side, something that she had been doing much more of in recent days.

Sometimes it felt like she was arguing with me, and I would fall into a cyclical argument with a four-month-old... she was usually the winner of these disputes.

In the distance, the silver door of the kitchen swung open and Ellis emerged with a bright smile. His eyes scanned the diner for new patrons until they settled upon my face. There was a split second of electricity that coursed through my veins, and I grinned at him as his lanky legs tugged his sassy torso along with them towards my table.

Ellis stopped dead in his tracks as he noticed the carrier stuffed into the seat beside me. His brown eyes twinkled as they fell upon Rae and he pulled his hands over his face.

"Oh. My. God." He squealed, placing a hand on the back of my seat as he dipped himself across to see her better. "Is this your little girl?" Ellis asked. The scent of his cologne hit me hard as the warmth of his presence spread.

The pride that burned in my chest when someone first met my daughter is one that I enjoyed thoroughly every time that I got to experience it. I turned to Rae and unstrapped the buckles that held her in place, pulling her from the seat and turning her so that Ellis could see her better.

He squealed, placing his pen and notepad on the table in front of me, "Can I hold her?" He asked.

I grinned, shifting to hold her out to him, and Ellis' gentle arms pulled her close to him. Rae stared at him with her sickeningly sweet green eyes, cooing and reaching to grab onto his badge.

90

Ellis spun her around, which triggered a squeal of joy from Rae.

My heart leapt with joy and I stifled a laugh as Ellis tickled her belly. Soon enough, he returned her to me with a bright smile on his face.

"She is officially my favourite customer," Ellis said happily, "You've got to bring her in more often, I need at LEAST an every-other-day fix of her brilliance."

"Noted," I chuckled, pulling out a premade bottle from the diaper bag and removing the cap. I clutched Rae close to me as I fed her and Ellis watched with a shimmer in his eyes.

"What kind of cheesecake would you like?" Ellis asked, retrieving his notepad from the table.

I chuckled and shook my head, "I appreciate the offer, but I am gonna get myself something nice before I head to the gym. Could I have a BLT?"

Ellis fluttered his golden eyelashes with a laugh, "Only if you're buying *me* cheesecake," He teased.

"Deal," I said with a grin across my face.

His eyes flickered up to meet mine and he shook his head, "It was only a joke."

"What kind of cheesecake do you like?" I asked.

Ellis narrowed his eyes and smirked, crossing his arms before himself as he flicked one of his hips to the side with a sassy sway. "I like the Hershey's Chocolate one we've got the most," He said with a chuckle.

I nodded, "I'll have one of those as well then," I said, pushing the menu away from me with a smile.

The server chuckled, jotting the order down and then turning on his heels to skip away. Rae eventually finished her bottle, and I held her against my shoulder, patting her back gently until she burped. I then cooed and kissed her forehead, snuggling her close to my chest.

I had decided to return to my roots today. Something I hadn't really done for a few years.

When I was about ten years old, my father enrolled me in mixed martial arts lessons. I had been quite good at it, and I'd made it through to a few championships. The rush that I felt in the ring was unmatched, and it was exactly the kind of release that I craved at the moment.

The only reason I stopped is because Kelly had demanded it of me. She told me I'd wind up dead... or at least brain dead. But now she is gone, so it doesn't really matter.

I found a gym nearby that offered childcare while parents trained and I figured with everything going on, I may as well join.

What is the worst that can happen?

A few moments later, Ellis returned to the table. His apron was no longer around his waist, and his shoulders were covered in the soft knit fabric of a jacket.

"Cold, are we?" I asked as he placed my food in front of me.

Ellis grinned brightly and shook his head, "Just about to head on home for the afternoon, my relief has come in." He sang, "Don't rush though, Shelley is more than willing to close off your check for today."

I won't lie, my heart sank in my chest at the thought of Ellis leaving, and it obviously displayed on my face.

My eyes drifted to the slice of dessert in front of me. "You haven't eaten your cheesecake," I protested softly, turning to place Rae back in the comfort of her carrier.

The black-haired man before me let out a belting laugh as he shook his head, "You ordered that for yourself," He said plainly, crossing his arms before himself and hooking his hip.

"No, I asked what your favourite cheesecake was and that is what you asked for," I said, pushing the plate towards the seat on the opposite side of the table. "Go on, you'll make Rae sad if you don't eat it."

Ellis chuckled again, glancing around, "I can't," He said softly. A dusting of pink rose to his pale cheeks.

I glanced down at Rae with a sigh, "Your God-Father seems to be in quite the hurry to leave you, Princess. What ever will we do with this cake?" I said, my eyes shooting back to stab Ellis lightly in the sass.

A glint of mischief lifted to Ellis' eyes and he shook his head, throwing his hands up in defeat as he sank into the seat opposite to me. "I apologize, Your Darlingness, I will sit and eat cake." He said, though I could sense the uncertainty in his voice. It burned through the flamboyant act that he put on... but it made me smile.

Rae squealed as Ellis sat down, her babbles increasing as I tickled her feet.

"See?" I asked, a smug expression painted across my face, "It would have made her cry if you left her so soon," I grinned.

Ellis lifted an eyebrow and his lips lifted to form the ends of a smirk. "You're an evil man, using a precious little girl to entrap me here," he declared dramatically, sinking his fork into the cheesecake in front of him. He stared down at the punctured cream on the tip of his fork for a few seconds before lifting it to his lips and placing the bite in his mouth.

His eyes closed tight and a buzz of joy radiated from him. He likes chocolate, noted.

As his eyes fell open again, I couldn't help but notice the flecks of gold that floated towards the edges of his irises.

The way the threads of amber mixed with deep mocha tones. Golden sparkles intertwined in the trees that rooted themselves in the obsidian centre of his pupils. Black discs which seemed to widen the most as they fixed themselves on the things he loved most, like chocolate or cute things.

Right now, they fixed on me.

My heart pounded heavily in my chest as I found myself transfixed by these orbs. It must have been an uncomfortably long time before I realized that Ellis was trying to speak to me… in fact, I wouldn't have noticed unless he hadn't broken the contact of our eyes, reeling me back into life.

"Are you taking the mick, mate?" Ellis sighed, stabbing another piece of cheesecake onto his fork. "Why do you do that?"

"Do what?" I asked softly, pulling my hand to rub my cheek lightly. I tried my best to keep my embarrassment to a minimum.

Ellis frowned, and I felt myself falling through thin air at light speed. The expression stripped the air from my lungs, and I tilted my head in confusion.

"You keep staring at me," He said in a hushed tone.

My chest instantly began to ache and my eyes shot to the sandwich that had yet to be touched in front of me. "Oh," I said softly, pulling my hands together in my lap to fidget anxiously. "Sorry… I just," a blush pulled across my face. I didn't really know what I wanted to say here… I hadn't even fully grasped what I felt.

Ellis sighed softly and looked around, "Listen, Brooke," he said, placing his fork down on the edge of his plate. "You're sound and all, but you have no idea what my situation is. You have no idea who I am. You can't just keep staring at me

94

and then not fucking tell me what is going on." His accent thickened as he spoke.

The skin on my face tightened as I raised my own eyebrow to the man before me.

"Well," I said softly, then looked down at Rae. The words I wanted to say found themselves caught in my throat, so instead I asked, "Are you busy after work?"

He leaned himself to sit back in the seat, pulling his lanky arms across his slender chest as he lulled his head to one side. His bouncy black curls rolled the slightest bit with gravity. There was a wordless question here. A beckoning for me to continue my statement before he made a judgement.

Anxiety prickled my skin and I found myself looking at my daughter for support. She had fallen asleep in her carrier, her tiny hands balled into sweet fists. I pulled a breath in through my nose. "I haven't been to the gym for ages... My membership comes with a buddy pass. Would you like to come with me?"

My nerves trembled beneath my skin. Truth be told, I was terrified of going back into something that I hadn't done in a while. Maybe being there with a friend may help?

Ellis chuckled, the darkness which had fallen over his face zipped away as a veil of brightness cloaked him. "Why would you want me to join you?" he asked in an almost accusatory tone.

I blinked once. I could never really understand why people read into my words as if I were some asshole. My shoulders lifted in a helpless shrug, "It would be nice to do something with a friend that isn't Brian or Jill?" I explained.

Something in his expression shifted. There was a no-ticeable change from cautionary uncertainty to a mystified innocence.

Ellis glanced across the table to where Rae slept peacefully. He gripped the fabric of his jacket tight in his hands and then looked back at me, "I'm sorry, Brooke. I can't today…" he said in a hushed, but genuine tone. It was almost as though he didn't want anyone else to hear that he had this tone. Where his English accent grew thicker and sweeter.

His true voice was hauntingly beautiful to me. It had to be my favourite part about him. "My other boss has me booked in for an afternoon business meeting," Ellis explained, but he leaned forwards, placing his elbows on the table before himself.

"Oh, okay," I replied.

I didn't realize that drag queens had business meetings… but I didn't want to make him uncomfortable. I glanced down again to the sandwich that I had lost the appetite for. I don't know why I felt like this. Nausea and anxiety.

He reached across the table to place a hand on mine. The warmth was immense, and for an instant, I felt like the world came rushing into my hand, sucking me into Ellis' touch. My eyes flicked up to meet his and I found a gentle, friendly smile awaiting me.

"If you're around later on tonight… I'm performing at a smaller venue," He offered, slipping his slender digits from my touch to grasp the fork on his plate. "Maybe you can bring Jill and Brian… Rae can come as well. She might like the music and the lights."

Ellis pulled the final bite of cheesecake to his mouth, finishing off the dessert , and I felt my heart thud in my chest. I think I wanted to go. To see him perform again. Ellis then reached into his coat pocket and placed a business card on the table.

"It is a nice open venue. Lots of space. If you can make it, I'd like to see you there!" Ellis was back to normal now. That over-the-top excitedness in his voice that I couldn't entirely discern the realness of anymore.

I picked up the business card and placed it in my pocket, nodding softly.

He smiled, pushing himself to stand, "Right then," he hummed brightly, "It seems my debt to my *god-daughter* has been repaid. She can now sleep in peace knowing that I'll be bloated for the next three hours!" He grinned, then spun on his heels with an animated wave, "Goodbye, Mr. Unlucky!" He called as he high-tailed it out of the diner.

I felt a void within me that continued to haunt my aching body as I asked for the new waitress, Shelley, to help me box my untouched sandwich and settle the tab. It hung over my shoulders as I stepped through the doors of the gym and handed Rae over to the childminders.

The class was torture, I felt this aching feeling resonating through my body, pulling me further and further from reality. The coach seemed to notice the distance between us, and he ordered me to go home and return on a day when my head would be better sorted for something of this nature.

I paced the floor of my lounge. Rae watched me with her beautiful, curious eyes as I burned a rut into the carpet. Something in this world was gnawing at my mind and I think that I knew what it was.

Fuck.

How have I lived my whole life without understanding I had the capacity for these feelings? Was I really falling for Ellis?

I pulled my phone out of my pocket and dialled Jill's number. My heart throbbed in my chest as it rang. Every second that passed between rings felt like an eternity where my lungs would cease pumping at any moment.

"Hey, Brooke. You alright?" Jill's voice pulled through the other end of the line with a gentleness that I expected from a mother.

My heart pounded in my throat, "Um… Hey! Would you and Brian like to come with me to a show in town tonight? I'm bringing Rae," I asked, fidgeting with a strand of my long brown hair.

There was hardly any hesitation from Jill as she let out a laugh, "You are inviting us out?" She asked.

"Well… yes?" I responded.

She hummed sweetly, "Where are we going? What should we wear?" Jill asked.

The pounding in my chest switched quickly to a soothing racing. "Um, one of the drag queens that Brian and I met the other day has recommended a show. She said it would be a more child friendly venue so I thought maybe we could have a nice night out? the venue is called…" I dipped my hand into my pocket and retrieved the business card for the location, "The Blue Lagoon,"

"Oh! I've been there. It is beautiful. Very classy." Jill said, then turned to Brian who must have been nearby, "Brooke has invited us out for the night. Shall we say yes?" She asked.

I couldn't quite catch Brian's response, but Jill soon returned to the speaker, "We are gonna say yes. I recommend you dress quite nice as it is quite a lot nicer of a place than somewhere like the Midnight Raven. There is a separate area we can sit in from the performance space if it gets too much for Rae."

Excitement built in my chest as I looked down at my little one who had rolled onto her belly and was playing with a tiny plastic piano that chimed when the keys were struck.

The card listed the start time at 6:00 p.m., and it was currently 4:00. "Shall we meet in town at about five?" I suggested.

"Cutting it a bit close for me, but I'll make it work," Jill said, the grin audible in her voice as we ended the call.

The silence that followed jettisoned me back into my own racing thoughts.

I sat down beside Rae's playmat, crossing my legs beneath myself as I hunched over to play with her. She was usually the only thing in this world that kept me sober in mind, but now even in her presence, my mind raced with a million thoughts. I kept picturing Ellis, sometimes my mind would flash to images of Flare Femme. The way his smile lingered in my mind like an imprint.

My face warmed and I pulled my hands to cover the flesh of my cheeks. What was I doing? What was I thinking? Why does my hand still feel the buzz of Ellis's touch?

I had spent my entire life being one way, this is all I have ever known… so why the hell is my head craving his presence more than I think I ever craved Kelly's?

Rae rolled onto her belly, lifting her head to stare up at me. She giggled sweetly and grasped a strand of my long brown hair that had fallen over my shoulders.

She pulled me from the crisis in my mind and I found my eyes falling on the beautiful smile that she so often held on her beautiful cheeks. I softened and the stress began to fade, if only slightly. I hooked my thumbs beneath her armpits and scooped her up, snuggling her close to my chest and running a thumb down her cheek.

"You know you're the most important thing in the world to me, my Rae?" I asked softly, pressing my lips to her forehead. She didn't respond, not that she could have... but she cooed sweetly as she touched my cheek with her tiny palm.

My heart ached and I nuzzled into her cheek. "Do you want to come with me to see Ellis perform?" I asked in a sweet tone, one that she mimicked with a giggle.

I pushed myself to stand, holding the little girl who wasn't as tiny as she used to be against my shoulder as I searched for a pair of ear defenders that I'd bought for noisy outings like this.

Once the headphones were packed securely in her bag, I carried her through to her bedroom where I dressed her in a sweet pink dress and brushed out the fluff of brown hair that was growing on her head. She was patient and calm the entire time, and I appreciated how docile of a baby she was.

Then, we moved through to my bedroom and I laid her in the centre of a c-shaped pillow where I could see her so I could dress myself.

I decided on a pair of black skinny jeans that pulled slightly tighter than I wanted, but enough to still be functional. The shirt I chose was a simple red button up with a braided pattern throughout in a deeper wine colour.

My curls were a menace to style, so I stuck with the horrible task of dragging a comb through them to at least make myself more presentable. I sprayed a few squirts of my favourite cologne onto my neck and wrists, then turned to Rae with a smile as I rubbed my wrists together.

"You ready to go, baby?" I asked sweetly, polling the long

sleeves of my dress shirt up to cuff at my elbows.

Rae squealed, reaching her tiny hands towards me as I climbed onto my bed and crawled towards her, hovering over her so that I could pretend to eat her belly. A roar of the cutest laughter known to man spilt from her, and her tiny hands swatted at my face.

I couldn't help but laugh as well, backing off of the bed and scooping her into my arms. I sang loudly to her as I lifted her above my head, tossing her just slightly into the air and catching her.

She didn't like this, and as I caught her, her face scrunched into a tearful whimper. My heart dropped and I pulled her into me, pressing kisses all over her tiny face.

"I'm sorry my beautiful," I muttered apologetically, placing kisses all over her cheeks.

Eventually, she calmed down, and I was able to finish getting everything ready. I loaded her into the car and made sure her stroller was stowed in the trunk, then climbed into the front seat.

My passenger-side window was nonexistent. A haphazardly taped trash bag blocked the opening so that nothing could get in. I had vacuumed the floorboards multiple times, but you could still see the occasional sparkle of glass remnants in the beige flooring.

I glanced back at Rae in my rearview mirror, a flutter in my chest as I gripped the steering wheel. "Okay, Rae... You can't tell anyone, but we are gonna go see someone who Daddy really likes. You've gotta turn on all of your cute charms for me, okay sweetness?" I said softly.

A resounding squeal sounded from her seat, and the mirror that I'd positioned in front of her seat captured a cute smile on her face. It brought a smile to my own face, and I shrugged my shoulders a few times to encourage myself before setting off towards the venue.

Not So Starry Night

ELLIS

Today has been shit.

I don't remember the last time I got more than three hours of sleep in a single night, but the weight of that deprivation is weighing heavily on me now. I sat before a vanity in the green room of the Blue Lagoon with a throbbing migraine that pulsed in the front of my brain.

On the tabletop before myself, an array of my makeup sat in organized rows, untouched. My face was plain, unpainted and exhausted. I hardly ever went anywhere without having makeup on now, it was weird to see myself beneath everything. The sight made my skin crawl. Every time I saw my bare face, I flashed back to the image of my mugshot. A version of myself which seared itself into my memory like a branding iron. That burned in my mind as a vivid, gutting reality check that reminded me of the addiction to depression.

My hips ached from the session I had gone through earlier in the afternoon. A dull throb of muscle that climbed from the depths of my sacrum all the way up to the middle of my spine.

I came straight here after I'd showered and calmed myself down. There was no point in waiting, and even less of a point being late. Though within me, I felt an ache that was much deeper than the physical pain that I had mostly learned to embrace.

A gnawing anger that raptured my bones.

Overwhelmed by the reality of my life, I grasped a glass of caramel-coloured liquor from the tabletop and pulled it to my lips, downing the entire glass without taking a breath.

The weight of my arm increased rapidly as I slammed the empty glass onto the table with a wince. I sealed my eyes shut for a moment, waiting for the warmth of this drink to burn at my core enough to distract me from the throb of my chest.

Soon enough, I opened my eyes and finally felt the courage to face that image of who I used to be. That past self whom I tried to hide from at any turn.

It was his fault I was here.

I plunged my hand into a makeup bag, retrieving a beauty sponge. Concealer first, to hide the deep bags beneath my eyes. Foundation to deepen the pallid tone of my cheeks. Contour to sharpen my cheekbones and jawline, then highlight to bring forth some sort of shimmer to my face.

The more I worked, the better I felt. The more I concealed, the more I locked who Ellis truly was away, and the more I felt who Ellis should be coming to the surface.

My confidence built, growing within me as I dusted my cheeks in a deep blush. Crimson bases to a black smoky eyeshadow that starchly underlined my lids with deep black liner and dotted the tear ducts with a shimmering white.

Finally, I pulled on my favourite long red wig and began to style it. I curled the strands until my shoulders were encircled by the ringlets of red. Fuck. I looked good!

I pushed myself to stand, removing the outfit I had brought for the night from its garment bag and placing it on the hanger beside my vanity. The door behind me pushed open and I heard the roaring laughter of a familiar Queen.

Ginger entered the room with a glass of wine in her hands. She was already dressed to the nines in a slinky purple dress that was absolutely covered in sequins, and her elegance escaped me. I paused where I was to greet her with a bright smile.

"Hello!" I called to her, turning to face her entirely.

She brightened, and the silver shimmer on her cheeks glistened beneath the fluorescent lights above. "Flare!" she beckoned, setting her wine down on the nearest empty vanity and approaching me with her arms outstretched for a hug.

I practically dove into her arms, doing my best to avoid smudging either of our makeup.

"You look like shit," Ginger said with a smirk, "Got a new fella?"

My shoulders tightened as I remembered Lorenzo's goon from earlier in the day, "You can say that, I guess," I laughed, peeling back to return to my garment bag.

Ginger's hair was black today, but styled up in her classic poof style at the top of her head. "Should I grab you a drink?" She teased, "or are we trying to keep ourselves as sober as possible so we don't accidentally snog another audience member."

An instant heat shot to my face, and I laughed anxiously to hide the embarrassment, "Ginger! It was one time, and-"

"And they liked it," She completed the train of thought with a sassy twirl of her fingers in the air.

I tossed a handful of hair over my shoulder, "Bet your bollocks they did."

Ginger laughed and spun around to grab her drink, pulling the rim to her plump lips, "You know, Flare... I think this opening act you've got is sickening."

My heart rushed as I removed a pair of leather trousers and a jacket from their hangers, turning to glance back at her over my shoulder. "Really?"

She smiled, swallowing a gulp of her wine, "When I was running shows in London, this kind of entrance would have blown the socks off of most venues. You should be proud of yourself."

The world seemed to stand still in that moment, and I steadied myself. "I really love Drag. It is one of the only things that keeps me going," I admitted, pulling a flyaway strand of red hair behind my ear.

Ginger's eyes focused on me, staring at me for a long time. People tended to do that... stare. It unnerved me, but also sent a rush of emotions through me.

All I wanted was to be seen, but people never really saw me for who I was... just what they expected me to be.

"I have been thinking about starting my own Drag Company," she said softly.

My heart instantly shattered in my chest, and my brown eyes saddened. "What? You're leaving the Midnight Raven?"

A wry laugh fell from her lips, "I have been debating it for a while, and I have finally saved enough for it to become reality." She placed the wine glass down again, stepping close to me and placing her hand at the centre of my chest. Her palm was warm, calming. It soothed the aching thud of my heart as it pounded against my ribcage.

"I want you to come with me, Flare," she declared.

That earth-shattering heartbreak began to consume me once more, and my eyes fell to the carpeted blue floor beneath my feet. "Ginge... you know I can't leave," I muttered sadly.

She frowned, pulling back from me, "Why not?" Her hand fell back to her side.

I groaned, glancing around the room to ensure we were alone. "Lorenzo has me on a leash," I muttered.

"Could you not do both?" Her eyes glittered with hope... hope that I didn't have.

"I am hardly surviving right now, Ginger. Life is really, really shit right now." I finally lifted my eyes to see her face again and her expression knocked the wind out of my chest.

Sadness. Disappointment. An expression I hoped I'd never see on her face.

"Well..." She grabbed the wine glass again, tossing back the remaining wine before setting it back down, "If anything changes, you know how to find me... this is my last show with you."

Fucksake.

Fuck... fucksake...

Every ounce of joy and confidence that I had built up

for myself came crashing down around me like raindrops, careening towards my psyche.

"Okay," I muttered in a dejected whimper, then turned abruptly to my vanity. I scrounged through my bag to search for a cigarette, but there were none... I guess I'd smoked the last one during the walk here.

Great.

I stripped down so that I could continue getting dressed for the show, and before I knew it, Ginger had vanished from the green room, leaving me alone with all of these toxic thoughts.

I sighed, pulling the leather trousers up to my hips. The boots that I brought were next, just plain black leather with a six-inch platform and heel.

A click sounded from the door behind me again.

"Why're you so pissy?" Lorenzo's voice shot through me like a bullet, and I practically lost my shit, stepping back and falling into the chair before my vanity.

"W-what?" I asked, sweat beading across my bare chest.

The evil man before me smirked, "So caught up in your own head that you didn't hear the bell. It is nearly call time."

I glanced at the clock on the wall of the room and groaned. Ten minutes until the show began. My shoulders fell and I shook my head, "I'm literally just finishing getting dressed, Lorenzo. Can't you fucking see?"

His beady black eyes fixed on me with a gaze that made me feel incredibly uneasy. "You're lucky that I need you to go on soon, you'd think I taught ya a lesson about that mouth of yours," he snarled.

"My mouth?" I snapped, "What? You expect it to function as nothing more than a pocket pussy for your filthy cock?"

He stepped towards me, his amber-coloured cane hooking

109

itself behind my neck and drawing me closer. "Listen here, you little shit. I am supremely fed up with your bullshit. You know your role here. You are nothing more than a filthy little whore that serves me! Me and only me!" He tugged the cane to one side, spinning me out of stead and toppling my balance so that I crashed against one of the empty tables. "You're wholly and truly testing my patience,"

The rush of fear pooled adrenaline through my veins and I smirked. This is exactly what I needed.

"What are you gonna fucking do? You can't break a contract because I pissed you off!" I snapped, moving from the table where I had fallen.

Lorenzo frowned. He knew he couldn't do anything to me right now, he needed me to look my best... that didn't mean that I was safe, though. I was far from safe.

"We will continue this conversation once you have finished the opening act," he declared with a hiss of his tone.

My heart raced, but I pushed it to the back of my mind and shoved past him to grab my leather jacket, pulling it over my shoulders and zipping it midway up my torso. Outside the room, the final bell rang and I stepped out through the doors without another word.

I knew I had royally fucked up. My mouth was getting me into far more trouble than I could cope with, but I couldn't help it. It felt so wrong to be pushed around like that, so when I could get away with it... even for a few minutes, I would.

The hallway leading through to the stage was dim, and I could hear the soft chatter of a crowd beyond the threshold. I stopped here, pulling a deep breath in through my nose as the stage manager approached me with a microphone. She smiled.

"You look lovely, Flare! Are you ready?" She asked.

I galloped lightly where I stood, feeling the energy pulse through my veins. I shook my whole body violently, allowing the nerves to flow through and disappear through my fingertips. With a final deep breath, I gently took the microphone with a nod and lifted it to my lips.

"Hit it, Darling," my voice ripped a silence through the crowd and the lights shut off. Deep red lights flashed on as the intro to Scarlet Opera's 'Riot' began to play.

Pulling a deep breath in, I strode out onto the stage, beginning to sing.

"Say what you want, there's a great big world and a billion of us so say what you love! If it's money you need and your pockets are shot then run to the club! I'm buying a round, oh, the Queens are in town tonight, so dress to the nines!" I sang, continuing the lyrics with an all too confident smirk, a hand reaching out to captivate the audience. "And if luck is on your side, just take the shot and sign on the dotted line!"

I stepped down from the stage, dancing around the tables of adoring viewers as I sang.

This song filled me with unrelenting dopamine. Joy that crashed through me like waves of pure light. When I performed, the world melted away... until I spotted a group of familiar faces.

Brooke and his friends, his little girl sitting sweetly in her stroller with a pair of chunky pink headphones over her ears.

My heart swelled to a fever pitch of excitement and I locked eyes with Brooke as the next verse started up.

"Light of my life... you know who you are, you're drunk at the bar and looking to fight," I sauntered towards him, feeling my inner slut taking over as I twirled in front of him, sinking back to sit in his lap and pressing my back against his chest with an arm outstretched to reach behind us.

He smelled amazing, and though he seemed to tense at my actions, he didn't push me away. In fact, I swear I felt his hands brace the flesh of my hips, his eyes fixed themselves on my face as I sang.

"But you're better than that and your mother is here, and she's giving the eye!" I motioned to some random woman in the distance before pushing myself away from Brooke's lap.

"And I'm not gonna lie, it's turning me on! Oh my! Oh my!" I dipped to gently poke Rae's nose. She watched the glittering, abhorrently painted version of the man who'd cuddled her earlier strike a pose. "And if luck is on my side," I snatched a shot glass from the table where Brooke sat and raised it high, "I'll take a shot and sign on the dotted line!" I sang before knocking back the shot and clapping the glass back down on the table.

As the song continued, I drifted from Brooke's table, though I felt his eyes soldered to my body. A familiar rush that seemed to buzz through me any time he stared.

Lust?

The more I sang, the more the music ramped up, and as the chorus droned, the other Queens of the night emerged from backstage. I soon returned to the stage with the line of other drop-dead gorgeous Queens, standing in the middle as Ginger looped her arms around my waist and we all sang in harmony.

"Oh I kinda like it! Gets me excited! Let's start a riot, we could start a riot!"

Our heads fell to the ground as the stage lights flashed off and the room filled with darkness.

Adrenaline coursed through my veins as I stumbled my way back to the corridor at the stage exit. Brooke's cologne still clung to my jacket, intoxicating and strong. My heart fluttered at the thought of him coming just for me… even after I hadn't joined him at the gym.

I definitely would have… if I hadn't been booked.

I distinctly remembered the feeling of his hands as he touched my hips, the way he looked at me over my shoulder with a soft silence. He didn't push me away or flinch.

The daze I was in came to an abrupt stop as Lorenzo's meaty palm wrapped around my throat, pinning me to the wall of the corridor.

"I told you we would continue our conversation," He growled, his fingers tightening around my neck.

Fear burned through me, but I wouldn't let him see it. I tightened my face into a distinctive glare and stared into his beady black eyes. It was a miracle he could even reach me from the height I stood in my boots.

"Jokes on you, ya daft cunt! Whores like me enjoy being CHOKED!" I spat.

His palm crashed hard across my cheek and I instantly silenced myself.

"I've booked you in for another session tonight. Free of charge!" Lorenzo smirked, dragging my back down the wall so that we were eye level, "Your customer is supremely happy with the discount I have given him. You'll be pleased to know he is one of the gentlest men I know," A horribly crass laugh left his chest.

I struggled against his grasp, feeling the consciousness fading from the edges of my vision. I pulled a hand up to pry at his hand, but he was far stronger. My body began to tremble.

"You… fucking… cunt," I managed out.

This only triggered another whooping laugh and Lorenzo tossed me to the floor of the empty hallway.

Air returned to my lungs and though I could breathe, the gasps it took for me to be able to inhale were numerous. I coughed, grasping my throat that now bore the imprint of Lorenzo's bones and fingerprints. He dipped to grab me by my jacket.

"This is your last chance, Flare. You either kick your ass into gear, or I'll be kicking your corpse into a ditch on the side of I-85." He snapped aggressively.

I bit back the urge to say something sarcastic that would get my teeth kicked in, fearing that the results would be instantaneous. Instead, I pushed myself to stand slowly and crossed my arms. Still requiring deep, shaky breaths.

Lorenzo stalked away from me with a grumble in his step and Ginger stepped past him to try to console me.

The rage that boiled in my stomach was too much, and I bulldozed past her. I needed a smoke... I needed a fucking drink. I needed to fucking end myself before Lorenzo did it himself.

"Flare!" Ginger called to me, reaching to grab my shoulder. I ripped it from her grasp.

"Leave me the fuck alone, Ginger... please!" I snapped, reeling around to face her. My hands balled into fists as my arched shoulders lifted and fell slowly.

Her face hardened and she shook her head, "You're absolutely batshit if you think you're gonna speak to me like that," she said flatly.

My heart pounded in my chest and I pulled my hands to my face, whimpering.

"Ginger, please..." I muttered, "I can't think, I need to find nicotine before I find a bridge to throw myself off of!"

She sighed softly, approaching me and placing her hands on my shoulders, "Flare… you can't keep this up. You need to leave him."

My face twisted into a distraught grimace as I noticed another Queen passing by us with a concerned look painted across her face.

Ginger waved her away and pulled me through the back exit. She removed a vape pen from her cleavage and pushed it against my chest.

"Take this, you need it more than I do." She said with a sigh. "Listen, Ellis," she dropped her voice to a natural level as she addressed me by my real name, stepping away from me, "I get that whatever the fuck you have going on with Lorenzo is feeding your crazy fucking mental state that you're in, but there are better things for you. Better places."

I groaned in frustration and pushed my back against the brick of the building, "You don't understand. You'll never understand."

"I understand that he is your pimp. I understand that you must have done some shady ass shit to become a puppet for a piece of shit like that," Ginger stared at me with all the affection of a mother. "You have to make the decision to leave. Whatever consequences that follow are-"

"No," I said flatly.

Her head tilted to the side, "No?"

"I won't leave." I reaffirmed.

Ginger sighed heavily, looking away from me in defeat. After a few uncomfortable seconds of silence, she returned her gaze to me. "Right, when you come to your senses and stop being a dickhead… my arms will always be open for you. You're a gifted performer. I'll give you the spotlight you deserve. A salary that pays you well."

The hope in her words filled me with an equal amount of dread as I sank down the red bricks of the club in defeat.

"I'm going back inside. Your next song is in twenty minutes… so pull yourself together or else I'll find someone else to put on the stage." She turned, grabbing the back door and pulling it open.

Before she returned, she offered me one final glance. "For what it is worth, you were the only reason I stayed at the Raven as long as I did…" she sighed heavily, "You're so much better than this. Figure your shit out."

The door slammed closed behind her.

There I sat, on the floor behind some high-class restaurant that I couldn't even afford to eat at. A diva in clown makeup, sulking.

I pulled the vape pen to my lips and pulled in a breath that filled my lungs with the harsh vapour of her menthol-flavoured pen. I held it in my chest for as long as I could, then coughed as the smoke choked me.

Part of me didn't want to perform again. I didn't want to go out there and parade around like I was happy when all I wanted was to fucking sleep. I didn't want to dance for Lorenzo, I wanted to dance for me.

With Ginger.

The nicotine clung to my senses and I crossed my arms, resting my forehead against the brace of my arms as I allowed myself to finally breathe out the frustration that had built in my chest.

"I figured I may find you out here."

Brooke.

I lifted my head to find the source of his voice. He was standing not far from where I was sitting. His green eyes fell over me in a respectful gaze.

The softness of his stare sent shivers through my spine, and I looked across the car park to try and find something else to concentrate on.

"I'm sorry for dancing on you, I should have asked permission first," I said softly, feeling a wave of guilt crash over me.

The adrenaline and excitement was beginning to fizzle out of me, and I had begun to think and feel like a normal person again.

Brooke chuckled, "It didn't bother me. Brian and Jilly teased me a bit, but it was fun to be part of the show for a moment," He said softly, rolling a stone beneath the toe of his boot.

My eyes wavered from my new focal point and fell to the tarmac beneath me. They inched along the ground until I could see Brooke's shoes. Then I slowly followed his frame until our eyes met. That gentle gaze held firm.

"How is Rae doing with the music? Is it too loud?" I asked.

The edges of his lips pulled into a soft smile, "She has some ear defenders on, and it hasn't seemed to bother her. She loved it when you were singing to her. You have a lovely voice."

The superficial blush on my cheeks grew deeper and I reached a hand up to tangle in the strands of red hair.

"Thank you," I said softly.

"You're upset," Brooke said, crouching down so that we were at eye level with one another, "What's wrong?"

I shook my head, "I'm not upset, Brooke." I said, trying to

force a smile. It didn't work, it only looked as unnatural as it felt right now. Once again, I averted my gaze.

Brooke watched me in silence.

I noticed that he did this when he was thinking really hard about something. At first, I thought he was being a creep, but the more I interacted with him… the more I understood that he was just a very contemplative person. He thought about what he was going to say before he said it… it just didn't always work out for him. Mr. Unlucky.

His eyes felt warm. Warmer than any other gaze I had felt for a while. I think it is the fatherly part of him. He cares about broken, fucked up people… because he was also broken and fucked up.

After another moment, Brooke moved to sit down at my side, his head leaning back against the brick to stare up towards the sky.

"I don't think I've ever really seen the stars," he muttered.

When I glanced over at him, his eyes had sealed themselves the the black, light-polluted sky with no visible stars. I turned my gaze to that very sky and sighed. "I have. I was born in a really small village on the Welsh border. The street lights shut off at eleven… you could see endlessly."

"Sounds nice," Brooke hummed, his eyes falling to stare into the distance. Not that there was much available to view in the close-knit carpark full of strangers' cars.

I allowed my own gaze to wander to the left, away from Brooke's eyes. I rested the side of my head against my arms and closed my eyes.

"Is it the show itself that has upset you?" Brooke asked.

Anxiety simmered lowly in my stomach, and I shook my head. "No, I love performing," I said softly, twirling a strand of hair around my finger.

He shifted, placing a knuckle on the toe of my leather boots. "Then why do you seem so broken down?"

I rolled my head along the support of my arm until I had returned my gaze to him. For a moment, I didn't quite know how to explain it to him. I got that he was worried and all, but it isn't exactly like he would even understand.

"My boss is just shit," I muttered in a whispered response.

A hum rolled through through the air from his side, "Why do you stay? You can leave things that don't serve you." He asked.

"I signed a contract with him. I've got to stay until he relinquishes control," I explained, finally allowing myself to look to where his eyes should have been.

"Like an abusive marriage," Brooke chuckled, "I know the feeling." He lifted his hand from my boot, hooking a finger to gently push a strand of hair behind my ear. The contact sent a buzz of electricity through my veins and as much as I wanted to pull away, I couldn't.

Did he even know what he was doing?

That smile that had pulled across his lips a moment before returned and he looked away with a somewhat bashful chuckle. The absence of his gaze coated my skin in chills.

"What is it?" I asked.

He glanced back in my direction, his teeth positioned on his lower lip as he pushed a soft sigh from his chest. "I am going to be honest," he began, pulling his arms in front of himself to cross in front of his chest.

His eyes moved back to the starless sky. "I have been feeling some things that I'm not really used to feeling."

A light chuckle, one that felt nearly genuine. "Oh yeah?" I

asked, "Not so used to being so statistically unlucky with the ladies?" I teased lightly, hoping that this brightening of the mood would last in both of our spaces.

Brooke turned to me, his whole body turning ninety degrees until he faced me head-on, his legs crossed before him. "I think I have a crush," he said softly.

"Ohh?" I grinned, poking his chest lightly, "You don't have the hots for your friend Jill, do you? Isn't she engaged?"

"No," His voice deepened and he shaded his eyes away from me. Had I gone too far with that joke?

"S-sorry, Brooke," I said softly, "I didn't mean to upset you."

He chuckled again, shaking his head, "No, Ellis." He reached across to place a hand on my boot again. His warmth lingered, a welcome pressure against my aching feet. "I think I have a crush on you," He said finally.

My heart stopped in my chest. Suddenly the sound of distant cicada chirping ripped from existence and there was a rift in the world where Brooke at I sat. I felt my face fall, a frown that I wasn't in complete control of, so I turned my head away and buried my eyes into my arm.

The pressure of his hand on my foot lifted, leaving behind a chill in its wake. I instantly straightened my posture, "Please don't leave," I pleaded, my voice hardly above a whisper. I noted that his face had fallen and he was staring at the ground. I lifted a hand from its position on my bony knees and extended it towards him, brushing his curls from his face.

I took in a deep breath, my manicured fingers trembling. "Brooke... I like you too," I admitted in a hushed tone, "But I am not worthy of your care. There are so many things you don't know about me... do you even like men?"

Brooke's hand took hold of my trembling fingers, pulling

121

them down into his lap. Both of his hands gently encased mine, a thumb running soothingly against the skin.

"I don't know... I have never liked a man before," he admitted.

"I think you have a crush on Flare," I said softly, "Ellis and Flare are two separate people, Brooke."

"I don't think I do," he muttered, his grasp tightening ever-so-slightly, "I mean, don't get me wrong... Flare is beautiful," He chuckled. "But yesterday, when you sank into the seat across from me. You spoke to me like I was your friend. No expectations or offence. Even when I said stupid things, you laughed... and..." He released the hold of my hand.

My eyes settled on him once again, "And?"

"And..." He pulled his hands to cover his face, "Your laugh, the way that you speak when you're genuinely excited about something... the way you listen to me... like... really listen to me. I don't know." He pulled his hands through his long curly hair. "I think of you all the time, when you came to me during your intro... when you leaned against me... I wanted to hold onto you, to keep you there."

My cheeks burned with a blush and I frowned, feeling a burning pressure behind my eyes. I blinked quickly, "F-fuck... I can't cry. I have to perform again in a minute," I muttered, pressing my fingers along the tearline of my eyes.

Brooke chuckled, "Sorry," he muttered, looking away.

"I think that you really need to think about this, Brooke." I cleared my throat, drawing in another puff of smoke from the vape pen.

"I have done nothing but think for the past few days. When I think of you, my heart races." He said softly, warranting a flutter in my own chest.

I dipped my head down again, "I don't know," I muttered.

Brooke placed a hand on his cheek, "Is it me?" He asked.

My head shook immediately, "No, Brooke.. it isn't you at all."

"Then what is it, Ellis?"

I bit down on my lip, "You'd grow to resent me for the things I can't really share with you..."

"Like what?" He asked.

Frustration built in my chest and I leaned my head back, "I just said I couldn't tell you," I grumbled, "That is the point..."

He sank back, resting his palms against the concrete behind himself and leaning into their brace, "But if I don't know then how will it affect me?"

"Brooke," I snapped, straightening the bend in my knees so that my legs stuck straight ahead. I looked around, then dipped my voice into a low whisper. "My boss... he makes me do things that no human should ever have to put up with."

His eyebrow raised in confusion, a silent request to expand on the issue. I sighed and wrapped my arms around myself in a defensive hug, "I got into trouble years ago... he got me out, but on the condition that I'd..." I paused as the pain of admitting my debauchery gathered in my throat like nails. "I have to... repay him for his services."

Brooke nodded slowly, his eyes drifting from me, "He makes you perform sex work, doesn't he?" He asked.

That ache in my chest grew, and shame drenched my shoulders. I nodded.

He pulled in a shaky breath, then nodded in return.

Silence fell between us, and so too did a blade of distance, disapproval. I felt my heartbeat slow.

"Do you like the other men when they touch you?" Brooke

123

asked.

My face fell deadpan, and I nearly laughed at the question. I pulled my hands over my face to hide the smile, trying my best to avoid my makeup that I had probably already sufficiently fucked over.

"I don't enjoy the sessions. It is just a job at the end of the day." I said simply, "They almost always have a saviour complex. Want to rescue me... but I always turn them down. No way I'd fall for the trick and become someone else's full-time sex slave when I just need to pay off a simple debt with Lorenzo," I muttered, though I felt myself cringe as I realized that I had said his name.

Brooke rubbed his shoulder, "I don't... I don't think I would mind that," he said softly. "This is all really new to me... it could not even work out."

"Have you ever even kissed a man?" I asked.

He shook his head, though his eyes flickered to my lips. My heart rushed in my chest, and I'm not sure what came over me, but I reached over to cup his cheek, gently running my thumb along the skin.

His cheek was warm, a soft layer of nervous sweat. I pulled his face so that he was looking directly at me, then I leaned in and placed a gentle, respectfully sweet kiss against his lips.

Fuck...

Brooke's lips were soft and gentle. That intoxicating smell from before filled my nose and I allowed my eyes to flutter closed as I relished that moment where I felt free.

When I pulled back, the soft sound of our kiss punctuated the moment, and my lips buzzed with the sensation and taste of his. Salty from whatever he'd eaten inside, but the familiar undertone of Coke as well.

I opened my eyes slowly, expecting to see him peeled away with a face of pure disgust. To recoil and realize that he was wrong about his feelings.

I was wrong.

His emerald eyes glittered with some sort of affection, a soft lull in his eyelids as he stared at me… curly wig, feminine makeup, and all… and drank in my appearance with the most refreshingly kind adoration.

My heart leapt.

Fuck. Fucksake…

"Was… was that okay?" I asked anxiously.

Brooke blinked, reeling himself back to reality from whatever place he had been in the moments prior to my query. At first there were no words, just a simple smile that pulled across his face. Then, he spoke.

"If… if that was your attempt at dissuading my feelings… I'm not sure it achieved what you wanted." He muttered.

Chills ran down my spine, and I nibbled the back of my lip, "I- I have to go back on soon…" I whispered breathlessly, my hands trembling.

He nodded slowly, pushing himself to stand. I watched the way he moved without hesitation when I expressed myself.

His hand extended to me, a silent offer for gentle assistance.

I accepted, taking his hand and pulling myself to stand. It took a moment to steady myself on the heels which put me quite a few inches taller than Brooke. He smiled at me, and I felt my heart steady for the first time all day.

His eyes held my figure with that same adoration he'd shown me a moment before.

"We should talk later," he said softly, "I don't want to pressure you… so just reach out whenever you feel like you're willing to talk. Okay?"

That blush softened, and I nodded softly, "Okay," I replied, placing a hand on his forearm to deliver a soft squeeze. "Will you stay for my song? I know Rae probably needs to go home soon," I asked.

He nodded definitively, "I'll stay."

A smile returned to my face. One that was genuine. I felt butterflies in my stomach as I looked at the back door, "I should go…"

"Message me when you get home, yeah? So I know you made it safe." Brooke said kindly, then pulled away from my soft grasp. "Go out there and rock that stage, Flare." He grinned.

I nodded quickly and fluttered a gentle wave to him, watching as he disappeared back into the front of the building.

My heart raced again, and I pulled open the backstage door, to step through to the green room and quickly fixed my makeup.

Ginger smiled at me, her gentle eyes fluttering as if she could sense the shift in my mood. I approached her, placing the vape pen on the tabletop before her.

"Thank you, Ginge… I'm sorry for being a twat," I said softly.

She brightened and reached to fluff her hand through my hair, "Fix your crown, gorgeous. You've got a show to put on!"

Do You Want Me To?

BROOKE

Ellis didn't message me that night.

I felt a bit dejected, I won't lie. After laying my heart out for him, hearing his reasons... I can't help but worry if I've fucked this up like I have fucked every other possible relationship up.

Mondays are hard, I hate how much I have to do in the mornings and I wish that I could just wake up and cuddle Rae like I did over the weekends. Today, I decided that I'd drop her off an hour and a half before my shift so that I could go to the gym and see if I could manage through a boxing class.

The other people in the class seemed like they knew each other so well. Conditioning was rough at first, but the longer

I persisted, the more the muscle memory kicked in and I started to do quite well.

Coach split us into lines. The person at the front of the line would practice a technique and then fall to the back of the row. This was nice because even though we had to keep ourselves low and in a good fighting stance, it gave us a break from constant moving.

I was the first in the line. Coach demonstrated a jab and dodge, one of the more basic techniques that I didn't have any problems completing. One of the instructors readied in front of me, bracing the pads for the attack and impact. He swung, and I dodged, reeling in for a quick jab immediately after. My fist collided heavily against the pad and I felt a tingle of pride in the front of my mind.

Towards the end of my class, as the instructors and Coach were leading a cool-down stretch, I turned over my shoulder to stretch my back and I spotted a familiar face standing by reception. A tall and slender man with curly black hair and brown eyes.

It was Ellis.

He was dressed in a simple white t-shirt and a pair of basketball shorts that just about reached his knees. How he could cope with shorts when the chill of autumn raged on outside, I'll never know.

My heart fluttered in my chest, if only for the relief that he was okay.

After Ellis finished signing in, our eyes met for milliseconds and his face softened into a brief smile. He lifted his hand slightly to offer me a gentle wave, then disappeared towards the men's fitting rooms.

My session wrapped up, and I thanked the coach before

heading off towards that very same fitting room. Chest tightening as I pushed through the doors. Part of me hoped that he would already be dressed for his workout.

In front of the lockers, Ellis stood in a pair of even shorter black biker shorts. He was rooting through his bag for his top when he spotted me in his peripherals and turned his head to offer me a smile.

Everything in me wanted to stare at him, but I knew it made him uncomfortable, so I returned a closed-eye smile and sat down in front of my own locker to remove my tennis shoes.

We were alone in that moment.

He removed a thin black tank top from his bag and pulled it over his shoulders. There was a deep set slit along the spine of this tank top, and I swear I could see some sort of scarring that patterned his pale skin with thin white tiger stripes.

"You're staring again, Brooke." Ellis chuckled, turning around to face me, his arms crossing over his chest as he sank onto the bench on the opposite side of the locker quarters.

I pulled my eyes back to focus on removing my socks which were now absolutely drenched with sweat, and opened my locker to remove a towel and toiletries for my quick shower before work. I didn't know what to say… or rather, if I should say anything at all.

Ellis pulled a pair of slip-on shoes over his feet and then glanced in my direction.

"Sorry that I didn't message you when I got home… it was so late and I think I just crashed on the sofa. Wasn't the greatest end to the night." He explained in a hushed voice.

My eyes lifted to him and I smiled softly, "It's okay, you know? I understand."

His face brightened and he pushed himself to stand, walking towards the shower portion of the locker room and leaning over a mirror to inspect his makeup. I couldn't help but watch.

"What are you working on today?" I asked softly as I made my way towards the showers, still fully dressed at this point.... save for my bare feet.

His eyes found my reflection in the mirror and he smiled. "I attend a pole dancing workshop every morning," he explained. "It is one of my favourite workouts."

"That's cool," I muttered, anxiously gripping the towel in my hands as my eyes drifted towards the showers.

He spun around and leaned back to perch himself against the sink. His soft brown eyes held my gaze for a moment, and then he faltered, pulling a hand through the coiled black hair on his head.

"Do you have time to talk?"

I didn't... the class had been an hour long, and I realistically had to be at work in twenty minutes. Every second I wasted standing outside of the shower was one that I could count on losing of my lunch break.

"I don't have much time," I admitted, "But if you want to talk then I can stay for you."

His eyes flickered with understanding and he lowered his gaze to the floor. "I'm sorry," he said softly, "For kissing you... it feels like I forced something you might not have been ready for,"

The words almost felt wrong coming from him. My brain had a hard time connecting Flare to Ellis now that I had confessed my feelings. A soft warmth rose to my cheeks, and I chuckled.

"You don't need to apologize… if anything," I lifted a hand to rest on my neck, "Maybe I should… for putting you in a position where you felt like you had to?"

Ellis smiled and his eyes slowly raised to meet mine again, "Was it okay?" He asked.

My heart raced in my chest as I remembered the feeling of his lips against mine. The instant shockwave of certainty that doused my shoulders. I blushed, full-on blushed… and then I stepped closer to him.

As the distance between us shortened, I felt the hairs along my body stand on end. I stopped just in front of him, a respectful distance.

"I think it only solidified my feelings, to be honest," I said softly, reaching across with my free hand to request his hand.

Ellis relaxed, allowing that touch.

His slender fingers rested lightly in the cradle that my own palm formed.

I brushed my thumb along the smooth skin on the back of his manicured hand, and I pulled in a soft breath.

"I don't want you to feel forced… but I do like you. I'm certain of that fact," I admitted, averting my gaze now that we were so close. His own eyes settled on my face and for a few seconds we stood in silence until I broke through it once more. "May I kiss you?"

He tensed.

My heart raced in my chest, bounding thuds against my lungs hard enough for me to feel physically ill in the silence.

Ellis met my eyes once more, and locked onto me, beckoning me into his space. "If you want to," He muttered, a breathless acceptance… but it didn't sit right with me.

"Do *you* want me to?" I asked.

His eyes widened and a shine of respect glimmered through them. He was quiet for what seemed to be forever, and then his face softened significantly. The tension in his jaw lessened and his fingers twitched lightly in my grip as he moved to intertwine our fingers. "I-"

The door to the locker room pushed open, and he instantly dropped my hand, his eyes averting away. There was no confirmation, and I stepped back to allow that tension to lessen.

Men filed in through the locker room and Ellis trembled lightly, pulling that flamboyant persona from within him and blocking out the real him with that bright smile.

"Will I see you at the diner later?" He asked, his vibrant tone returning.

My chest ached, and I stepped towards the showers, "Maybe," I said softly.

He nodded softly, "It would be nice to see you again," he said, then moved towards the threshold of the shower area, "Have a nice day!"

I sent a wave his way before hopping into one of the fastest showers I've ever taken in my life.

As I was leaving, I could see one of the classrooms with a glass wall. The room was lined with six chrome poles that reached the ceiling, equally spaced. Ellis was there, currently running through the conditioning which would make any proficient person look like an Olympian.

I was already late enough for work, so I couldn't stay to watch as much as I would have liked to. I slipped out the front door and made my way to the building two blocks away.

Jill was sitting at her desk when I arrived. A grin on her face, "You're not usually one for being late," She said as she noted my hair that was still quite damp. "Sleep in?"

"Actually, no," I laughed, "I just lost track of time at the gym. Trying to get back into boxing," I explained. "I used to be an MMA fighter, but I think I'm too old for all the grappling now."

She smiled, and nodded sweetly. "Brian is sick today. Think he had a bit too much to drink last night."

I placed my bag on my desk, logging into my computer as I listened to her. "Oh, damn. Is he alright?"

A gentle laugh rolled from her chest and she nodded, "He'll be fine. I'm gonna go see him on my break. You know, bring him some hangover cures." Jill typed away on her keyboard.

My phone was the first to ring, so I turned my attention to my workstation and pulled the phone to my ear. "Fulton County 911, what is your emergency?"

"Um, hi... I just came back to my apartment and it looks like the place has been ransacked." A male voice called across the line. My alarm bells started ringing instantly, and I started to pull up the software I needed.

"Okay, sir. Could you tell me your location?" I asked.

He gave me the address, and as I typed it into the search, he continued explaining. "I live with my ex... she isn't here, but there is a broken chair and lamp in the hallway and I think there is blood on the floor."

"Have you been in contact with her?" I asked, pinpointing the address and sending the details to dispatch.

"No. She won't answer her phone." He said flatly.

This guy seemed far too calm about this situation, almost like he had something that he wasn't telling me. "Sir, where were you when your house was broken into?"

"Um... I don't know, man."

I lifted an eyebrow, "Okay, I have police on the way to see you. Can I get your name please?"

"Finn."

"Finn?" I asked, "What is your surname, sir?"

"Anderson."

"How old are you, Mr. Anderson?" I asked. Getting answers out of him was like prying teeth out of a crocodile.

"Twenty-nine."

"Okay, and what is your ex-partner's name?" I asked with a hint of frustration hanging in my voice.

"I hear the sirens," He said dismissively.

"That is brilliant, Mr. Anderson, I just need your ex-partner's name for the record so we can chase up her possible location." I rested my forehead against my hand as I awaited a response.

Finn was silent for a moment, but he sighed. "Rebecca."

"Great, Rebecca. I just need her last name and her age." I coaxed.

"Cassidy. She is twenty-six." He said, then immediately snarled, "She's a fucking whore though, so she is probably deepthroating some freaky motherfucker right now."

I rolled my eyes, "I understand sir. Do you see any officers coming your way?"

"Yeah."

I breathed a sigh of relief and closed my eyes, "Brilliant, I will leave you in their more than capable hands, then." I said.

Before I could even register the call dropping, the man had ended the call.

"What a freakazoid," I muttered, then dialled one of my colleagues to pass the details on about the missing woman who was quite possibly injured.

Today was busier than most. With Halloween coming up next week, there were plenty of calls regarding harmless or mundane things… but that first call of the day stuck with me in my head.

When it came time for my lunch break, I was on a longer call than we usually tend to take. I decided to forgo lunch, as I wasn't exactly sure how I would approach Ellis in his workplace as of right now. I didn't want to risk making him uncomfortable… but I did message him.

Me: Hey, are you busy this evening?

My phone propped against my monitor. Ellis was marked as inactive on his end. He must not have his phone on right now. I decided to scroll through Rae's daycare app and check in on her.

They were doing spooky-themed arts and crafts, and there was a picture of Rae playing in a sensory pit full of ghost-shaped pasta. She seemed to be having fun.

I liked to read her notes throughout the day, it lessened some of the guilt that I had about leaving her somewhere else while I worked.

She was absolutely thriving under Nora's care. It gave me hope that she would have a positive female influence in her upbringing.

My phone buzzed, pulling me back to reality as Ellis' name popped up on the notification. I selected the message immediately.

Ellis: I finish at the diner around 10:30… and as of right now I'm not booked this evening.

Ellis: What have you got in mind? xx

I don't think I really had anything in mind, to be honest. I just wanted to see him. I stared at his messages, reading them over in my head. I watched as the green dot beside his name faded to grey once again and I felt a bit of relief as it would give me time to think. I really didn't want to leave Rae with someone else again.

Me: Would you like to come to my place for a late dinner?

We can sit down and really talk things through.

The bubble remained grey, though I stared at it for an achingly long amount of time.

Soon enough, the office filled with my co-workers returning from their breaks and Jill returned to her desk behind mine. She approached me with a bag in her hand.

"Did you go to the diner?" she asked, leaning against the frame of my cubicle's entrance.

I turned to her with a chuckle and shook my head, "No, I just stayed here. I was late enough this morning and I'm not super hungry."

"Aw," she hummed, "I passed a bakery on my way back and grabbed you an eclair. Would you like it?"

My heart leapt at the offer and I spun the spinny office chair around to face her, "You didn't have to do that, Jilly."

She grinned, "So you *are* hungry?" She teased, outstretching the small bag to me. The plastic crinkled with her movements. I reached out to accept the gift, pulling it back in front of me.

My eyes fell to the bag in my hands and I stared at it for an unusually long time.

Jill hummed, "What is on your mind?" she asked.

I glanced up at her, contemplating whether I should talk about this with her… but there was probably nobody in my life that would be better to discuss it with. I turned slightly to place the bag on the desktop, then rested back in my chair.

"I think I am falling for someone," I admitted in a soft tone.

Her eyes widened and she clapped a hand over her mouth, "Oh my god, really?" She asked in an excited tone, then stepped inside the cubicle to lean back against my desk. "You have to tell me more!"

My face warmed and I averted my gaze as the blush crept over my cheeks, "There is this person I've been talking to quite a bit recently… I don't know, I just get really excited about seeing them and then when we talk I just lose myself in their voice."

"Have you met them face to face?" She asked.

I nodded, "Yeah… we exclusively see each other in person," I explained, rubbing my neck.

Jill clapped excitedly, "Oh my god, have I met her?"

My body tensed, and I didn't quite know what to say to this question. She absolutely had met Ellis… I pulled my hands into my lap, anxiously fidgeting with the digits. "Um…"

Her eyes softened, "What's wrong?"

"Nothing is wrong… it is just…" I glanced up at her, "This person is a man." The words left my lips and I winced in preparation for some sort of backlash, but my friend only softened further.

"You have feelings for a man?" She asked, and then her eyes widened. "That Drag Queen from last night… is that why you disappeared?"

The blush burned a raging crimson across my cheeks, and I pulled my hands to my face. Jill quickly placed her hand on my shoulder.

"There is nothing wrong with that! I just didn't expect it coming from you," She laughed sweetly, squeezing my shoulder as the phone in her cubicle began to ring. Jill quickly stood, rushing to her own cube to get back to work.

I turned myself back to face my desk and saw that my phone had brightened with a response from Ellis.

Ellis: That sounds nice... I don't drive, though. xxx

The words lit a fire in my chest and I quickly responded.

Me: I'll pick you up from the diner and bring you back here.

The bubbles from his end began to roll instantly.

Ellis: Are you sure about this? xx

I nibbled my lip as I stared at this message, thinking long and hard. Was I being impulsive? Should I just back off? I began to question everything I'd felt over the past few days and the reality of this decision was sinking in hard and fast. Was I just seeking out Ellis' approval because he was the only person who seemed to care about me?

The apprehension grew loud within my mind, screaming confusing things over and over. It was overwhelming. Terrifying. Falling for someone new when your life was so hard already was no easy matter... especially when you've never tasted this experience before in your entire life.

Have you ever even kissed a man?

His voice rang loudly in my ears. I sank against my desk as the rush of a panic attack began to pull me into its waves again, but I knew I couldn't slack... not here. This was the only place that was keeping me afloat right now.

I picked up my phone as the panic burned deep inside of me, silencing all thoughts that had previously screamed. Now I was left with little more than an anxious electricity that surged through me just enough to dull my logical thought.

Me: I don't really know too much right now, I'll be honest... but I'd like to talk this through with you.

Me: If that is okay.

He responded quickly

Ellis: Okay, I'll see you at 10:00, Mr. Unlucky xx

Dolled Up Lunatic

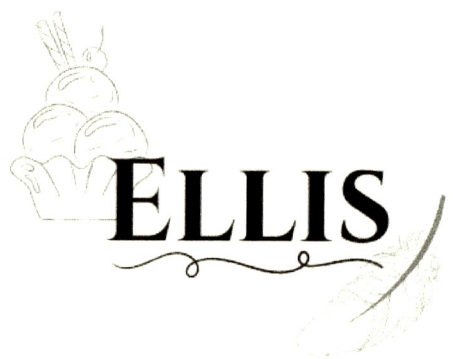

ELLIS

I had swept the floor of the diner about three times now. Monday nights were usually dead on this side of town, but tonight was taking the piss. I hadn't served a single customer since six, and the streets outside were empty.

One of the cooks has already left, so it is just me and one other person here. Aaron has locked himself in his little cosy kitchen corner to watch YouTube videos and I have subscribed to trying to get as much rest as I can against the bartop in the main dining room.

Silence was something that I couldn't quite cope with at this point in my life. It was odd to me, uncomfortable… and the more it persisted, the more my mind raced. The more my mind raced... the worse the voices in my mind raced.

A creeping, aching anxiety crawled up the centre of my chest, and I knew now that I absolutely needed to find a way to drown it out.

I pulled out my phone and started scrolling through Spotify, searching for my favourite band: The Scarlet Opera. I'd performed one of my favourite songs by them the previous night, but the sound of Luka's voice never dulled in my heart. I scrolled until I found my all-time favourite song by them and selected the one at the very end of the list: *God Damned Beautiful.*

The piano scrolled along vibrantly through the speaker of my phone, and I maxed the volume before strolling around the dining room and lowering all of the window shades.

I sang word for word with Luka, feeling every single syllable of his lyrics beating the tone into my heart. This song was about so much more than it let off... and to me... it was my everything.

He sang about the way he felt as a queer man in a world that didn't understand. A man with an identity he couldn't comprehend himself. A battle with who he was versus who he was expected to be. The disappointment and shame he felt... and how he learned to embrace every single flaw of himself, because it made him who he was.

"All the bridges I've burned, and the taste that I lack, don't mean nothing at all... cuz the facts are the facts: I am Goddamn beautiful... Yes I'm goddamn beautiful. I'm a dolled-up lunatic who's shouting at the wall." I sang with conviction in my heart, and the acoustics of the dining room lent me the charm.

I danced, finding my footing around the white tile beneath

me as I spun and dipped. A performance that would never reach the stage. My heart swelled as the music grew more intense. I threw my head back and belted the song with all of my might, paling in comparison to Luka's brilliant voice, but giving it my all nonetheless.

So intensely consumed by the music that I almost absolutely lost my shit when the door opened and the bell above it let out a gentle ding.

I scrambled to grab my phone from the bar top, pausing the song.

"Hi, Welcome!" I said quickly, shoving my phone into my apron as I spun around.

Brooke stood at the entrance with a soft smirk painted across his face. Rae's carrier hung over his arm and the beautiful little girl sat inside with a curious expression.

"Don't you dare stop on my behalf," He said, moving to place her seat on a table, sitting on the edge of the booth.

My heart thudded against my lungs and a bright blush painted my cheeks, but he just smiled and nodded, lifting his hand as if to wave a continuation. I shook my head quickly and lifted myself onto a barstool in minor embarrassment.

Brooke's smirk faded and he tilted his head to the side. His brown curly hair was tied into a bun at the back of his head and he glanced at his daughter.

"I think we should wait in the car, Rae Rae. It seems like he doesn't want to sing to us," He said sweetly.

Rae babbled cutely, her tiny hands grasped the air before her, and she stretched her little arms out as if to ask for me to hold her. I glanced between her and Brooke, and he grinned.

"It seems the princess has demanded your affections," he said softly.

I slipped down from the stool and approached the table where her carrier sat, "Hello, Lovely," I muttered, reaching to stroke her cheek. She giggled and grunted as she tried to lean towards me.

Brooke moved to unstrap her from the restraints that held her in place and pulled her free from the seat. He then turned her around in his lap so that she was facing me.

"She isn't big on being left in the carrier for very long. She's a snuggle bug," He chuckled.

"I don't blame her," I said with a bright smile on my face. The little girl's arms outstretched to me again.

"She wants you to hold her," Brooke said softly.

I dipped to a more accessible height and pulled her into my arms. Her hands instantly latched to the fabric of my maroon uniform, and she snuggled into my chest.

Damnit, this was so fucking cute.

My heart ached as I ran my fingers over the soft hair on her head, my pink almond-shaped acrylics carefully avoiding her soft skin. She smelled of baby powder and remnants of Brooke's cologne.

His eyes softened as he looked up, but for a moment the softness wavered and his eyes fell to the floor as he twirled his thumbs around one another. I watched him with a sincere curiosity as I cuddled the little girl in my arms.

"Had a busy day?" Brooke asked softly, finally meeting my gaze again.

I pouted and shook my head, "No, it's been painfully dead. Haven't served anyone in four hours." I said in a subtle whine, "I'm so ready to finish for the night."

Brooke chuckled and pulled his phone out, "Only ten minutes left. Anything I can help you with that'll get you out of here faster?"

A grin lifted the corners of my lips, and I shook my head, "Sit there and look pretty," I said, twirling on my toes as I rubbed Rae's back. "I've cleaned everything… Might as well count down the tills and clock out," I pressed a kiss to the little girl's forehead and then peeled her away to return her to her father's arms.

There was slight protest from the little one, but she soon settled and I was able to slip into the kitchen where I could finish up my tasks for the day.

I was quite nervous about going home with Brooke… there were so many things I was uncertain of, and he didn't seem to know anything either. I didn't really know what would come of tonight, but I really did like Brooke… and if anything, it is a good bit of fun isn't it?

Soon enough, everything was finished and Aaron slipped out the back door with the final bin bag of the night. I returned to the front where Brooke was swaying with Rae in his arms, humming softly to her. My chest ached lightly at the sight. The absolute love and adoration in his eyes.

I stepped closer to him and placed a hand on his shoulder, "Shall we be off?" I asked in a hushed tone, trying not to disturb the little one who was beginning to fall asleep.

Brooke glanced back at me with a smile and nodded, gently transferring Rae to her carrier. The exhausted little one whimpered, wanting to be held. Her father leaned in and kissed all over her face, "I know my beautiful girl. I will give you so many cuddles once we are home, okay?"

Rae started to cry, and my heart ached at the sound, I nibbled m lip, "I can hold her until we get to the car," I offered softly.

He glanced at me again, "Are you sure?"

I nodded, stepping between him and the carrier to retrieve the fussy little girl and pull her into my arms. She whimpered, clinging to me. I pulled my jumper from the coat hook behind the bar and pulled it around her, smiling at Brooke once she had settled and was comfy.

His eyes displayed something that I wasn't entirely familiar with, a caring expression that recognized me as something far more than friendly. He nodded and grabbed the car seat by the handle, pulling it from the table and moving towards the front door.

I pulled the door closed behind us, slipping the key into the lock and securing the building for the night. There was a chill in the air, one characteristic to October.

Brooke led me though the city streets towards his car, where I had to bear the heartbreaking burden of returning Rae to her car seat. Once he secured the seat in the base, I leaned over it and placed her inside, then strapped her in. She began to fuss again, but I curled my index finger, gently running the knuckle along her nose until she settled once more.

"You're so good with her," Brooke muttered from behind me. His presence was warm and comforting. I stepped away from the car to let him shut the door and smiled bashfully.

"Children are a sweet spot of mine," I said softly, "They remind me of the beauty I can't see in the world anymore."

He chuckled, "Any world with you in it is beautiful, Ellis," he said.

He said that shit with a straight fucking face.

WHAT THE FUCK IS MY LIFE!?

I blushed deeply and tugged at my ear, "You say some

charming things," I whined, "Why don't you say this kind of shit to girls?"

Brooke chuckled and reached to cup my cheek, his eyes locked onto mine and he nibbled the back of his lip.

I wanted him to do it… to kiss me. I wanted him to make me forget whoever the fuck I really was and fucking kiss me.

"I have to really like someone for the right words to come," He explained in a husky voice.

I practically melted into his touch, blinking wordlessly as I took in his face.

He was truly a handsome man, and the dim lighting of the parking garage gave him just that little bit more credit.

My aching chest returned and I stepped back, "Alright, Tiger," I smirked, "Lets get going."

The drive back to his home was faster than I thought it would be. He was lucky enough to live outside of the metro area, if only just, in a small duplex. I followed him through the front door as he carried Rae's car seat. The aroma of bolognese hit me the second I entered the house. Basil and thyme, savoury tomato.

Brooke motioned for me to have a seat on the couch in his lounge, then he slipped upstairs to put Rae to bed. The whole ordeal took about fifteen minutes, and I happily waited for his return.

As he descended the stairs, I felt a rush of excitement ebb through me. I put my phone away and crossed my legs, leaning back against the soft couch. "Did she fall asleep okay?" I asked in a whisper.

His green eyes closed slowly as he nodded, "She is a pretty good baby. I'm very lucky that she didn't inherit her mother's temperament." He chuckled and entered the kitchen, which I could see through a half wall that peered into it. "Do you like cheese?"

"I don't trust people who don't like cheese, Brooke," I smirked, pushing myself to stand and anxiously stepping towards the half wall.

Brooke was dishing out the food he had prepared earlier in the day, spooning the meaty sauce from the crockpot.

He grinned, pulling out a fancy-looking cheese grater with a spinning handle. The cheese grated perfectly over the pasta and my stomach grumbled.

"Wow, I haven't had a genuine home-cooked meal in years," I admitted.

"Really?" Brooke asked, grabbing the bowls and extending one hand to me, "That is something I'll have to change," he said as I accepted the bowl of warm food into my hands. He then led me through to the lounge again where I sat in the same spot I had chosen earlier.

We ate in relative silence, and as the food settled in our bellies, I found myself growing more comfortable in this cosy little home.

"Your house is cute," I said.

Brooke laughed lightly, "Thanks, it isn't much but it is more than most people have. I'm fortunate that Kelly decided to leave without too much of a fight." He placed his empty bowl on the coffee table.

I stood, dipping to grab the other bowl and carrying them to the kitchen where I washed them and set them to dry on the rack.

"You definitely didn't have to do that," Brooke said as I returned to the couch.

"I felt like it, so deal," I said with a nervous grin, now aware that the barrier of eating was no longer between us.

I worried that Brooke would try to leap directly into the hard conversation, but he seemed to relax now that he was comfortable in his own home. He sat back in his seat and stared at the swirling pattern of his ceiling.

"How did you find out that you enjoyed Drag?" He asked softly.

One of my eyebrows lifted and I smiled, "I like to perform, and I love everything makeup," I said simply. "It is fun, you can choose a different personality to become every day and nobody can question it. Drag is an escape from everything for me."

He nodded slowly, "You keep saying that there is a lot about yourself that I wouldn't be comfortable with… would you be open to talking about it?"

Apprehension began to tingle in my fingertips as I felt the joy of discussing things I loved slowly drain from my expression. I tilted my head and sighed. "You know how it feels to be totally and completely alone in the world?" I asked.

A nod.

"I've been there… far too many times to really count." I sighed, pulling in a shaky breath as I ran a hand over my forearm. "I was really young, and I wanted to get away from the loneliness so badly that I ran into the arms of a man who used me." I felt a familiar pressure building behind my eyes. "Unfortunately, it has been a theme that runs quite consistently throughout my life. Trusting people that are evil monsters and becoming more and more fucked up."

Brooke moved closer to me, sitting on the other end of the couch with his body angled in my direction. "You've been hurt a lot," He said softly.

I shook my head, biting back the emotions that gripped my throat. "No, Brooke… I've been fucking destroyed. Over and over again."

His knee brushed against mine, and I felt the chill of his touch ache against the skin and I recoiled. Panic flooded my chest and I couldn't find a focal point to draw me back in. "I've been broken down to the point of crawling. I've been fucked… beaten… used… and I-" the words I sought to spill choked me and I felt Brooke's warm touch encroach on my knee.

"You don't have to hold it in, Ellis." He said softly.

The kindness in his tone sent waves of confusion through me and I shook my head again.

"I don't think I could give you what you need," I said softly. "I'm so… so fucking broken that I don't know how to trust. I don't know how to love."

"It doesn't have to start with love," he whispered, his hand moving from my knee to gently take one of mine.

The desire to pull away was just as bitingly strong as the desire to sink into him, and I bit down hard on my tongue.

"Listen, Ellis," he muttered. "I will admit, this is all brand new for me. I've spent twelve years in love with someone who used my insecurities as target practice in daily mental gymnastics." Brooke pulled his hand away from mine and the feeling sent an instant bolt of worry through my body. "You may not think you are enough for me, but I can assure you that I will never feel like I am enough for you."

The words fell over me like poetry and I was able to look at him once more. He wasn't finished.

"I don't know how long this will last, and I don't know if

you'll ever feel the way I do… but I can honestly say that I've never waited on bated breath for a message from anyone as I do with you. I've never felt the hairs on my arms stand up when someone sings, or felt electricity in my bones when I locked eyes with someone." He met my gaze. His green eyes locking onto mine, and the very electricity he spoke of shot through to my core as well.

"I don't know if this is love… or if I am just confused and lonely… but I think you're one hell of a person."

I held his gaze for a moment, "I am worried that you will realize that you aren't okay with the things I need to do to survive."

"Well, if it comes to heartbreak then that is just another mountain that we have both travelled before, isn't it?" He asked.

My heart pounded and my eyes followed over his face. The freckles that dotted the edges of his cheeks, the curls of his hair that had fallen from the bun at the back of his head.

The energy in his eyes felt compelling, drawing me into him. And I faltered, falling back against the back of the couch.

"What if you hate me?" I asked, feeling the sting of tears as they pulled to my eyelids.

Brooke leaned forward to cup my cheek once more, "What if you love me?" his thumb pulled soothingly along my lash line to gather a fallen tear and swipe it away before it could smudge the black of my eyeliner.

He was close. So close that I could feel the heat of his breath on my skin. I reached up to cup his cheek as well. Our eyes burned into each other's souls and Brooke inched closer.

"May I kiss you?" he asked softly, his voice hardly above a whisper.

My heart hitched in my throat, and I felt my cock harden against the restraint of my skinny jeans. I nibbled the skin at the back of my lip as my eyes fell to his. I remembered how they tasted last night and I wanted to taste them again... I needed to taste them again.

I reached my other hand to rest on his shoulder and pulled him closer, nodding in response.

In that instant, our lips met and the throb in my chest erupted into racing. The hand on his shoulder slipped along the back of his neck before my fingers tangled into the mass of curls restrained by a simple hairband.

He deepened the kiss, pressing his weight into me as he did, a hand moving to run along my chest.

I removed my hand from his face and guided the wandering hand to rest on my throat, where his grasp tightened just enough to send me into a full-on frenzy.

I gripped his hair and pulled him away from my lips, gasping for air as my cheeks dusted deep red. His emerald eyes glittered as he stared at me.

"I definitely... definitely want this, Ellis," Brooke muttered anxiously, reaching to clutch my hand that had tangled in his hair.

He pulled my hand free of his hair and drew my wrist to his lips, placing a soft kiss to the skin.

Chills ran down my skin and I pushed myself to sit forward, leaning closer to him. I pressed my hand to his chest and then pecked his lips with a quick kiss.

"Have you ever... had your dick sucked?" I whispered the question as though the world could hear my words.

Brooke blushed and nodded softly, "A few times," he muttered, "But I never enjoyed it." He admitted, his hands

153

instinctively moving to rest over his groin.

A signal which told me he had already grown stiff beneath the cloth of his trousers.

"Would you mind if I tried to change that?" I whispered, my own hands moving to rest over his.

He shuddered at my touch, but his eyes glazed over with lust. He nodded softly, "I-if you want to," He said.

"Do *you* want me to?" I asked, stealing the question he had asked me earlier that very same day from thin air.

Brooke's eyes deepened and he nodded, "I do…"

I pressed a hand to his chest, pushing him to lay back against the couch. As his head connected with the cushion, I straddled his waist and leaned in to press our lips together.

The kiss deepened, and I rolled my hips against his. I could feel the tent in his trousers as it twitched against the bulge in the front of my own.

Pulling from his lips, I expertly placed kisses along his jaw, watching as his whole body reacted to each and every touch. I sank down between his legs and undid the fastener of his belt, placing it lightly to the side of the couch as I unbuttoned his trousers and slowly pulled the zipper down.

"If you feel uncomfortable at all, I'll stop…" I assured him softly, "Got it? No fancy words, no conditions. You say stop, and I stop."

I locked eyes with him and he nodded in understanding. Only then did I continue. My hands slipped around his hips to loosen the fabric of his jeans, and then dipped into his boxers to extract his already engorged cock… he was massive. I practically moaned at the idea of having him inside of me, and my cock twitched again in anticipation.

For now though, I worked on making Brooke comfortable.

"I want to learn your body, yeah?" I said softly, "I'll teach you everything you need to know." I wrapped my hand around his girth and began to pump him gently.

His length twitched in my hands, and I noted that Brooke pulled a hand to his mouth as if he were trying to hold himself back from making any noise. I tightened my grip just enough to apply a good pressure and as I pumped, I dipped my mouth to take his tip in. My tongue lapped lightly against the sensitive nerves at the base of his hood.

Brooke pressed his head back lightly and a soft grunt escaped his chest. The slut that existed within me sank his lips down the shaft of Brooke's cock, taking his whole length in until he reached the back of my throat. I bobbed my head slowly, cupping his balls lightly as I worked my magic on his shaft.

I could taste the salty secretion of precum as it began to leak from his tip, and I pulled away. My hand returned to the length, pumping him faster now as I flicked my eyes up to make eye contact with him.

He was watching me intently, that sparkle of lust in his eyes glimmering as he watched my hand stroking his length.

"Better than you expected?" I asked in a taunting tone.

His head bobbed in a soft nod, but his eyes remained fixed on my hand as it pumped him.

That was so... fucking... hot.

I soon replaced my hand with my lips again, allowing my tongue to trace the ridge of his cock as I sank to the base of it.

I felt the urge to gag as his tip twitched against the back of my throat, and that only made me want him more. I increased the speed of my sucking, my own cock throbbing as I did.

This wasn't the time for me to seek pleasure, it was time for me to deliver.

As I sucked, Brooke reached to grip at my curly black hair, tugging at the strands as his hips bucked into my throat.

"F-fuck…" He muttered, biting his knuckle to keep himself quiet.

I pulled my lips from his cock, a string of fluid peeling away as I stared up at him, "Don't hold back now, Mr. Unlucky, if it feels good, you need to show me." I then took him in again, deep throating him.

Brooke moaned out, his legs trembling beneath us as I struck that nerve in the back of my throat over and over, choking down every inch of his long manhood. The thrill of it all made me tremble as well and the fabric of my jeans began to absorb the liquid that was dripping from my own member.

The twitch of his cock signalled to me that he was about to cum. That paired with the bucking of his hips and the sudden helpless moaning, I took his cock deep into my throat and he filled me with his cum, dissolving into a moaning mess of a man beneath me as I swallowed his load.

I pulled back, wiping the back of my hand across my lips as I stared at Brooke's trembling body on the sofa. His eyes closed as he shuddered with pleasure. A feeling of pride overcame me, and I sat back where I had been, adjusting the throbbing muscle in my pants as Brooke returned back to earth.

"I- I don't think I have e…ever felt like that," He muttered, his voice had risen in pitch to a soft whimper.

A chuckle built in my chest, and I relaxed back, "Never been sucked off by a prostitute then," I teased lightly.

Brooke pushed himself to sit up slowly, glancing down at

his cock as it twitched against his trousers.

His eyes then drifted to my own groin. "That must hurt," he muttered anxiously.

I glanced down at my bulge, then at him, "I can take care of myself," I muttered softly.

He shook his head, "Let me try?" he asked softly.

"Brooke," I whispered, "you really don't-"

He silenced me, pinning me to the back of the couch and crashing his lips against mine.

His hand sank between my legs to grope at the twitching, leaking mess that I had become. I ached beneath his touch, pulling away from his kiss to press myself further against the couch.

His eyes lingered on me, "Forgive me," he said softly, "I've never done this... so you'll have to live with the fact that it will probably be the worst you've ever experienced."

I laughed, a real... genuine laugh. "You don't have to," I muttered.

"I want to," he said assuredly, slipping down from the couch and positioning himself between my legs. This was a position that I didn't often experience. I was so used to having my body used with no hope of having the favour returned. This was new to me as well...

Brooke undid my tight jeans and lifted my hips to slip the fabric down to my knees, he then did the same to my briefs, watching as my cock stood erect without any prompting.

I was just as big as he was, and I worried that he would shy away from this now when all I wanted was for him to take me further than any man had taken me for the longest time.

He encircled his hand around my shaft and glanced nervously up at me as he began to pump. He had lived his whole life with a dick, so he knew exactly how to treat one.

It showed.

I pressed my head back into the sofa and allowed him to work.

It truly didn't matter if he was good at this or not, the point is that he was trying.

He cared enough to try.

Brooke placed his lips around my tip and slowly lowered his head. He didn't quite take all of me in, but his technique was strong nonetheless and now I was the one trembling beneath him. He pulled himself back up, then started a steady rhythm that was a good enough speed to simultaneously keep me grounded and push me towards the edge.

My eyelids fluttered as I rolled my hips into his touch, "Mmm... Brooke.." I whispered sharply, reaching back to grip the fabric of the cushion behind my head.

His eyes darkened as he glanced up at me, and I placed a hand on the back of his head to guide his speed.

Brooke followed my guidance, slowly growing comfortable with deeper strokes. I had a lot of stamina... so much that it usually took me forever to cum at this point. But I don't know if it was the way he looked at me or the sentiment behind him trying so hard to get me off, because in this very moment I was so close to orgasm that I could feel it in my toes.

"B-Brooke," I muttered, "I... I'm close... you can pull away if you don't want me to c-cum in your mouth,"

He accepted this offer, pulling his lips from my shaft and replacing them with his hand. He pulled my hand from his head to place it on the hand that pumped me.

"Guide me. Show me how to make you cum, Ellis," He whispered in a husky tone.

I bucked my hips at his order, feeling more in control than I ever had. I did as he demanded of me, and together, we pulled through into a searing ecstasy that ripped me from my body as I came, a mess of moans and soft whimpers.

The second that I came, Brooke pushed himself to close the distance between us, kissing me deeply. There was a passion in his kiss that I'd never felt before. A true, rampant desire for me and only me. I tasted his lust as he pinned me back to the couch.

Soon, we pulled from each other, and Brooke pressed himself to the back of the couch beside me, breathless.

I glanced over at him, the passion and buzzing fading and soon being replaced by genuine calm. I reached over to gently grasp his hand and squeezed his fingers. As I did so, Brooke squeezed in return. A silent gesture that spoke a thousand words between us.

The whole situation was still quite uncomfortable, uncertain… but he said the right things to me. He tried. Maybe it was worth trying for him as well?

Brooke placed his other hand on my knee and chuckled, "Was I terrible?" He asked softly.

A grin rose to my face, "Bloody dreadful," I teased, then pressed closer to him, placing my hand against his chest, "No, Brooke. You did fine considering you've never done it before," I placed a peck on his nose, and saw his face brighten with something akin to pride.

I stared into his sleepy green eyes for a moment, trying to figure out how the hell I got to this point, sitting in his lounge with a full stomach and a banging come down with this amazing man who seemed to see me for everything that I was… and somehow wasn't.

"What is this, then?" I muttered softly, tracing the pattern of his shirt with one of my acrylics.

Brooke smiled, then pushed himself to stand. He adjusted his trousers and tucked his goods away before sitting back down beside me.

"I… I haven't dated anyone in over twelve years," He chuckled.

A soft laugh left my lips, "Is that what you want, Brooke? To date?" I asked with gentle scrutiny.

He pulled his hands into his lap, eyes flicking down to intensely stare at his own nails.

"Is… is that okay?"

The rush that question sent through my body was unreal. Thoughts raced in my mind and I couldn't tell if I was actually as terrified as I felt or if it was simply the possibility of it all going wrong that frightened me the most.

Brooke seemed to gauge my worry, "If you'd rather take things slow, I understand," He said.

"I don't want you to call me your boyfriend," I said softly, "I think *boyfriend* is such a childish word. Maybe partner is better?"

His eyes widened, a smile burning bright across his face, "Is that a yes?"

I narrowed my eyes playfully at him, "You think I'm going to let you cook me dinner, confess your undying affections for me, suck me off, and I wouldn't at least humour your feelings?" I asked in a playful tone.

Brooke fist-pumped the air and laid back across the couch, covering his face as he tried to conceal the joy in his expression.

This made me feel so unbelievably happy. To think that he

was so overjoyed about me was the highest of compliments.

My heart buzzed lightly in my chest, and I grabbed a tissue from the coffee table to clean myself, then smiled and stood. I pulled my own trousers back up around my waist, securing the button and sinking back into the seat.

Reality struck me a bit too hard as the familiar sound of a bell strummed on my phone. It was a unique notification that I had set for one person: Lorenzo.

I glanced at Brooke with a sadness that overtook my face far faster than I thought it should have.

"That's him," I muttered sadly.

Brooke pushed himself to sit up, "Do you need to leave?" He asked softly.

My hand shook very lightly as I grabbed the phone and opened the notification. A name and location. My face communicated everything I wanted to say to Brooke and he nodded slowly.

"I can call you an Uber, I'd drop you off myself but Rae-"

"I can call the taxi, Brooke, you don't need to worry about that," I assured with a soft smile.

It was forced, and by now Brooke knew it was forced.

He placed a hand on my shoulder, "Will you be okay?"

I laughed, nodding, "I'm always okay. It sucks, but... I try to tell myself that it is only temporary."

Brooke moved closer, pinching my chin to guide my face to his. His lips pressed against mine with such gentleness that it actually made my heart throb.

In this moment, I wanted nothing more than to stay in the safety of his gaze.

When he pulled away, he smiled at me, "Please make sure you message me when you get home tonight. I won't be able to sleep until I know you're safe."

I chuckled, "Possessive," I teased, poking his chest.

"Not possessive, territorial." He smirked, and I felt the shock of his forwardness strike a flame in my stomach. I laughed, shoving him lightly.

My Uber pulled outside just five minutes later, and as I sank into the back seat, Brooke stood, leaning against the frame of his door with his arms crossed in front of himself as he watched.

Protective and steady.

Something changed within him, something lit. I don't quite know what it is.

That night, as I trudged through the front door of my studio, I threw my keys down on the counter and tossed my aching body onto my futon. Exhaustion pulled me in, but I kept my word.

Just before I slipped off to sleep, I sent Brooke a message.

Me: Home xx

A Match Made in the Ring

BROOKE

"Alright, guys! Split into sparring partners. We are running ring drills today." Coach Murphy called out through the small space of the gym that was dedicated to boxing.

I glanced around the room until I found a guy who was about the same height as me, with a similar enough build. He seemed like the perfect person to go against.

It had been about four years since I had last entered the ring. Back then, Kelly had begged me to quit just when my coach offered to take me to a national tournament, and because her mental health had been declining so rapidly, I agreed.

There was definitely a rush that came from boxing matches, the adrenaline was immense and I knew I was good at it… I just didn't know how well my skills would show with the test of time.

I approached the other man and extended my gloved hand to him, "Brooke," I said.

"Alex," he reciprocated the gesture, and we tapped our gloves together. A pairing. The two of us sat down on the mat and waited to be called upon.

Most of the other people here today were men, but we had three women as well, which meant that one of them would have to spar exhibition style or twice with a different opponent each time.

Sparring was the best part of boxing. They don't usually have you in the ring for a good amount of time, but because I had experience, Murphy felt more comfortable with me sparring with the more advanced students.

The ladies went first. Both of the girls in the first pairing were on the smaller size, but it was incredible how powerful their punches were. They were both clearly more advanced than a lot of the people here, and their spar was professionally done.

As they exited the ring, the third young lady stepped inside. Her arms were long and lanky, she was slightly awkward but it was definitely a facade. Coach Murphy looked around the room for a younger man who was a similar weight class when one of the burlier men piped up.

"Why not grab one of the pole dancers?" He smirked. This man's hair was buzzed to his scalp, and his jaw was as thick as his brains. Probably more useful to him, though. Seeing as eating took priority over thinking.

He jabbed his finger in the direction of a group of girls who were waiting by the glass wall of the pole room.

Murphy chuckled, "Rodney, I can guarantee that you do not want to fuck with a pole dancer," He said with a shake of his head.

Coach Murphy was jacked, absolutely jacked. He had salt and pepper hair and a neatly trimmed beard. He stood with his arms crossed, hands resting on his protruding biceps.

Rodney chuckled, then turned around to jab his disgusting finger in the direction of someone who had just entered the building. "Why not ask him to do it? Ain't much of a man anyways."

That person was Ellis.

My blood instantly ran cold as I watched this man sneer at the clueless man with curly black hair who was checking in brightly at the reception desk.

Coach Murphy shook his head again, "You should really keep some things to yourself, Rod. Opinions are like assholes," He turned his attention to Ellis and held his gaze there for a moment.

Having only just finished checking in, Ellis skipped towards the group of women with a bright smile on his face.

Rodney tutted, and I felt anger bubble in my stomach.

"Do you have a fucking problem?" I snapped, turning myself to face Rodney. His wrinkly head which resembled that of a Shar Pei jutted in my direction.

"I'm only trying to help Coach find a suitable opponent for Lorraine," He said, shrugging his shoulders as though he hadn't done anything wrong.

My fingers twitched, and I remembered why it wasn't always the best idea to put me in a contact sport... my tendency to think with my fists.

I turned my eyes to Ellis briefly before I silenced myself and watched the girl in the ring.

"I'll spar you, Lori!" One of the previous girls offered, pulling herself back into the ring. It was clearly an exhibition match. They were nowhere near the same weight class or height.

I settled, thinking the brunt of the annoyance must be over.

I was wrong.

As the match started, I could hear sniggering coming from Rodney's side. Usually in response to something one of the girls in the other class had done. He was becoming more and more annoying, and it was becoming increasingly difficult to focus on the girls in the ring.

"All I'm saying is," Rodney attempted to whisper, though it carried through to my ears, "there is no way in hell I'd ever let my son do something like that. Pole dancing?" He chortles to the man beside him, who seemed to ignore his senseless prattle. "I mean, there isn't much of a man there. It has pink fingernails."

It.

I turned to the man whom I had paired with, "I want to knock his brains out," I grumbled under my breath.

Alex smirked, glancing past me to see Rodney continuing on his tangent. He then nodded.

"Seems he needs someone to teach him a lesson," He chuckled.

Ellis innocently turned his gaze to fall upon the boxers, chatting with the girls around him.

"Oh look, he's staring at us. Watch yourselves," Rodney smirked, "Maybe we *should* have put him up there with the girls."

I pushed myself to stand, "Want to fucking say that to his face?" I snapped.

All eyes fell on me, including those of the people waiting for the pole workshop.

Rodney turned to me with a glare and pushed himself to stand as well, stepping towards me with arms like carpet rolls. He stopped inches from my chest, flexing his biceps as if to make himself look bigger, like a fucking ape.

"I'll say whatever the fuck I want to say," He snapped.

I clenched my hand into a tight fist. I'd had my fair share of experience with bare-knuckle boxing, and I was prepared to lay his ass out.

"You even look at him cross again and I'll knock your fucking teeth out," I growled, standing my ground.

"Hey!" Murphy halted the match and climbed down from the ring, "Both of you, knock it off."

I glared at Murphy, but Rodney's filthy smirk only grew on his face.

"He's stuck defending the fairies," He said, the filth leaking from his tongue.

My glare on Murphy deepened, and he shook his head.

"In the ring, both of you." He demanded.

I stepped towards where I had been sitting with Alex moments before, sinking to grab my gear and moving towards the ring where the girls were just exiting. I couldn't fucking wait to lay this man out.

Rodney was bigger than me. He looked like he had been a construction worker all his life, and his mouth reaffirmed this idea. The thing with big, muscly men, is that they gas out a hell of a lot faster than leaner men like me. I wasn't in my prime by a long shot, but neither was he. I had something else going for me, though… a territorial defence mechanism that had been activated.

The coach pulled us in close, "If you can't sort your differences out in the ring, one of you will have to leave. There is no team without showmanship," Murphy said.

My eyes narrowed as I traced the path of Rodney's gaze to fall upon Ellis, who had approached the half wall that divided the boxing gym from the rest. A few of the girls from his class had joined him there to watch the match unfolding.

He was none-the-wiser to the things said about him, and if I had any power… it would stay that way.

The man in front of me scoffed and turned to look at me, "fucking filth," He grumbled, then shoved his mouth guard in, stepping back to prepare.

I looked at Murphy one last time, and his face displayed an annoyance that seemed to resonate with all of the people who surrounded our ring as well. I shoved in my mouth guard and stepped toward Rodney in a fighting stance.

Low and agile. That was my speciality.

Murphy gave the signal, and Rodney launched at me with one of his carpet rolls for arms. He was precise, but I could just about miss the brunt of his attack by stepping away. He immediately followed up with an uppercut that graced the side of my jaw. It definitely fucking hurt, but my pride was bigger than that.

I retaliated by jabbing him in the shoulder, just enough to throw off his balance, then slipped behind him. Inherent training to grapple burned in my mind, but I knew that the rules of MMA were different from boxing, and that would instantly disqualify me. I wasn't going to let anything take away the satisfaction of rocking this man's world.

The match continued on with quite a few evenly distributed punches from each of us, but just as I expected, Rodney began to gas out. His heavy feet collided with the floor of the ring with a much more percussive sound, and that is when I knew it was my time.

I launched forward, delivering an uppercut that would send his head back at just the right angle for me to follow it up with a jab straight to his throat. Rodney reeled back, stepping away as he threw off his glove to clutch his throat.

"That's illegal!" He shouted through the suppression of his rubber mouth guard, coughing as he held onto his throat.

Murphy narrowed his eyes at me, crossing his arms… but there was something else hidden there. He turned to Rodney. "Not illegal, just not very nice." Coach approached the other man and placed his hand on his throat, "No damage done. He's just winded you. You should really protect your neck in a match, hands up next time."

I won't lie… I still wanted to hit him. I wanted to absolutely smash his face in. This rage burned inside of me that I concealed behind a placid expression. I stared at Rodney with eyes of steel and he glared back in anger. This wasn't over.

Coach dismissed Rodney from the ring, and I went to exit but he halted me, placing a hand flat against my chest. I turned to meet his gaze, and he lowered his voice.

"That was illegal," He said in a soft whisper. "You may be able to get away with it in MMA, but not here. Not on any other occasion."

My eyes fell, and I nodded, "Yes, Coach... sorry."

"Don't apologize. He was being a dick. I see how angry you are. Don't go causing trouble outside of here because that is exactly what he wants." Murphy sighed, then straightened. "Alex," He called.

My original partner stood and approached the ring. Murphy beckoned him in and crossed his arms.

"I want to see you spar with someone who is more your level," Murphy said, then signalled for us to fight.

Throughout this match, I could feel his eyes on me at all times. He was reading me.

Alex was a good opponent, I'd had a good eye when picking him before. He was advanced, far more so than Rodney had been. He got quite a few good shorts on me, and even winded me at one point, I lost count of the points in the end.

As the bell sounded, we backed away from one another and tapped our gloves respectfully. Murphy dismissed Alex, but once again held me in the ring. He couldn't possibly ask me to fight anyone else. He could see that my energy had been depleted. I was panting, sweat dripping from my brow.

"What time do you finish work, Brooke?" Murphy asked. The question halted me, and I tilted my head.

"Four," I said, dragging my forearm across my forehead to clear away the sheen of sweat.

Murphy nodded once, "Come back at five tonight. I have an advanced MMA class then. We are working on the techniques you've been using, and I think it is a better fit for you."

Excitement buzzed in my chest, and I felt relief fall on my shoulders. I nodded quickly. I'd been worried that I had pissed him off, but he was actually just scouting me for the evening class.

"Go on and stretch, you've done enough for now. Tonight's conditioning will wreck you, so head off early." Murphy said as I slipped down through the ropes.

I stepped towards the stretching area, placing all of my equipment beside me as I pressed my back to the wall, catching my breath. Rodney had disappeared, and I realized that I actually hadn't seen him since our match finished.

"That was pretty cool," a familiar voice said in a hushed tone over my shoulder.

I glanced up to see Ellis perched against the wall, leaning over slightly. My heart fluttered in my chest, and I couldn't suppress the grin that lifted my lips as I rested my head back against the wall to look up at him.

His arms crossed along the top of the border wall and he nodded towards the ring, "I heard you shout at him," He hummed lightly.

I closed my eyes, sighing lightly, "He was just being a dick," I explained.

"Seems you've taught him a thing or two," Ellis chuckled, watching the next group of fighters as I started stretching. A light groan left my lips and Ellis smirked. "Your back is arched. Straighten it if you want a deeper stretch," he explained, reaching one of his long, slender arms from the wall to rest on the small of my back.

His face twisted into a light grimace, "Fucksake, mate. Absolutely drenched, you are!"

His laugh filled my ears and I straightened my back as he suggested.

"Do you blame me? Did you see what I just went through?" I asked with a soft grin that he couldn't exactly see.

"I did, it was hot. Make sure you stretch your hamstrings,"

172

He said with his usual chirpy demeanour.

"Yes, dear," I muttered in a soft tease.

He grew silent, and when I glanced up to where he was stood I could see a blush burning at the height of his cheeks. This summoned a smirk to my lips and I turned my head away with a smugness that could be sensed in the air between us.

Ellis looked around, then leaned over the wall so he was closer to me, "I have to go change. Will I see you later?" He whispered the question with a hopeful tone.

"I'll be finished here in a few minutes," I said softly.

His face fell in contentment and he nodded. "See you in a few minutes, then," He said sweetly, then peeled away from the wall and disappeared towards the men's changing rooms.

When I lifted my eyes again, I could see Rodney sitting at the edge of the mat, glaring at me with annoyed daggers. I simply waved at him, then pushed myself to stand. I needed to pass him to leave this section of the gym.

As I did, I turned to him one final time, "Watch your mouth. Next time you open it like that, I'll make sure not to hold back," I promised, then pulled the gate open before he could get a word in and slipped towards the changing rooms.

I rolled my neck side to side as I entered the locker room, pushing the door closed. Ellis was already dressed in a black tank top with a matching pair of black short-shorts, sitting in front of his locker with a distant, unsettled expression on his face... like he was sad. Really sad.

As his eyes fell over me, though, the expression zipped away. His eyes brightened significantly, and he closed them to tilt his head to the side. "Early finish?"

"Coach told me to head off early... he wants me to come

173

back after work for a different class," I explained.

"Exciting," He grinned, clapping his hands in front of his face lightly.

I smiled and sat down beside him, leaning back to rest my head against the cool metal of the lockers behind me. "I don't know if I'm going to do it," I said softly.

Ellis tilted his head and matched my posture, his black curls pressed against the lockers as well, "Do what?" He asked.

My eyes moved to capture his face in my gaze, "The intensive training," I said softly, resting a hand on his thigh and delivering a soft squeeze. "Rae's daycare closes at six... I wouldn't be done until nearly seven. The childminders here at the gym close at five. I wouldn't have anywhere for Rae to go." I said softly.

"But wouldn't you enjoy it?" Ellis asked, placing one of his hands over mine as it rested on his knee.

A soft chuckle rolled off of my chest, and I nodded, "I would. There isn't much of a point in enjoying something if I don't have anyone to watch Rae."

He pushed himself to sit forward, angling his knees in my direction, "Drop her off at the diner. I'll set up a seat for her in the kitchen and we can all keep an eye on her."

He spoke with conviction.

The thought brought a smile to my face, and I glanced at him for a moment, trying to read the determination on his face.

His lips were painted with a soft gloss and his eyes were dusted with his signature golden shimmer.

I chuckled and shook my head, "You know the diner can get busy. What happens if she cries or needs a bottle? I can't expect you to risk your job for me, Ellis."

He scrunched his nose up, "I will literally carry her around in a kangaroo pouch if I need to," He crossed his legs, then mimicked the fold with his arms. A stubborn upturn of his nose followed.

"I don't know," I muttered, pressing my palm to my cheek.

"I do," he said matter-of-factly. "I've already made the decision, bring her in on your way back for the late class, then you have an excuse to come see me afterwards." The left side of his lips lifted in a sweet smirk as he fluttered his eyelashes.

My breath hitched in my throat, and I blushed softly. "You'd do that?"

Ellis' eyes narrowed and he scrunched his nose again, "I don't think we can really count babysitting as a moral high ground for me," He chuckled.

"It isn't a moral high ground… it is just pretty awesome that you're willing to do something like this for me," I explained, fidgeting with my hands.

His eyes shifted from teasing to sweet, and he glanced down at my hands as they wrung one another.

"Why wouldn't I? Rae is your world, but you need to be happy outside of her as well."

I softened my gaze on him, pulling a hand to his cheek and gently pressing my lips to his.

Cherries.

His lip gloss tasted of cherries.

As I pulled away, he grinned at me, pressing his palm to my chest.

"Darling," He muttered in a soft chuckle, the title spread hives of bashfulness across my cheeks. "As much as I adore your ravenous masculine energy… you're absolutely soaked through with sweat." He peeled away from me with a grin.

My lips lifted in a smirk, "You don't like a sweaty man?" I teased.

"Not unless I am the reason you're sweating. Get your arse in that shower this instant!" He demanded playfully, rolling a towel into a whip and firing the tip at me.

I leapt off the bench to avoid the strike, laughing with my hands up in defence.

"Ah!" I laughed, "I'm going, I'm going!"

Ellis grinned and tossed the towel at me, "I'm going now, class starts soon," He said softly.

A pout fell over my face, "Oh," I said sadly, staring at him with an exaggerated longing in my eyes.

His face brightened with mischief as he waved sweetly to me.

I watched him turn to leave, knowing that I was going to be late again just because I sat around talking for too long.

Just as Ellis reached the door, it swung open and Rodney entered the locker room with at least four of his buddies alongside him. I froze as I watched his interaction with the man he'd insulted.

"Well well well," Rodney smirked, "If it isn't the pussy and his princess."

My blood began to boil again in an instant, but Ellis took me by surprise. He switched, completely and totally.

His arms pulled behind his back and he leaned forward.

"Rodney Corbin!" He hummed sweetly, "It is so good to see you again."

He knew Rodney?

The brute of a man who had said such nasty things about him earlier froze in his stead and shook his head, "How do you know my name?"

Ellis laughed, his eyes darkening as he fluttered his gold-tipped eyelashes at the man, "Don't be daft. Remember me? You blew your brother's entire stag-do fund on an all-night private dance with me!"

"I-I don't know what you're talking about!" Rodney looked between his friendly quickly, clearly flustered and caught out.

"Oh, of course you don't recognize me!" Ellis boomed with laughter and pulled a hang through his bouncy black curls, "It was Drag Night, after all. You requested that I stay fully in character while I stripped for you. Don't worry though, Darling... I'm off shift now, so I won't tell your friends the gory details. That would be a violation of client-escort confidentiality."

He pressed his manicured fingertips to Rodney's chest, pinning him against the wall as he glared down his glittery nose at him.

"I seriously recommend picking better battles, especially when the person you slander has had their fist deep enough inside of you to class you as their puppet." His tone was malevolent and biting. Spiteful even... it was hot.

As Ellis pulled away, he pinched his fingers together, holding his hand like a pincer. He opened the tips of his fingers to mimic the mouth of a puppet, then grinned slyly.

"I like teasing hot gay men because I'm too insecure about my sexuality to admit that I like twinks," He mocked in a bastardized variation of a Southern accent. Then, he laughed brightly, slipping out the door towards his class.

When Ellis disappeared, the room fell eerily silent, and Rodney didn't say another word. I simply took my shower and went off to work.

* * *

Ellis did exactly as he promised that evening.

I arrived at the diner at 4:45 on the dot with Rae's carrier in tow, and he was there waiting with open arms.

"Hello, my darling!" He called to Rae, extending his arms to steal my daughter away from me.

Rae lifted into his arms without an ounce of hesitation, instantly sinking into the maroon-clad waiter's chest. This instantly melted the man before me, and… me as well.

I loved watching him hold her, the kindness he exuded. When Rae was in his arms, the world was set to rights.

As he snuggled her, he motioned for me to follow him through the silver doors of the kitchen, a mysterious place that I'd never visited.

Through the doors, he pointed to a high chair he'd set up near a staff table where the other waitress, Shelley, was currently sitting with a fork full of peach cobbler.

"Shell! This is my little love!" Ellis said brightly, bouncing Rae against his hip sweetly.

Shelley glanced up from her phone to acknowledge them, then her blue eyes lit up in sparkles.

"Oh! Isn't she an absolute dear!" Shelley returned the bright energy, pushing herself to stand and approach Ellis.

He nodded cutely and glanced at me, he extended his hand and I reached out to accept it.

This triggered a soft laugh from him, and he squeezed my hand kindly, "I was asking for her bag, but this works for now," He said sweetly as he intertwined our fingers.

My heart raced lightly in my chest, and I felt a blush creep over my cheeks. I looked away bashfully. He ran the end of his thumbnail over the skin of my wrist, then released my hand from his grip.

I passed the diaper bag over to him, anxiously going through the procedure for bottle-making and diaper changing.

"I've changed a fair few nappies in my lifetime, Brooke," Ellis snickered, pulling the bag over his shoulder confidently. "Try not to worry, I won't let anything happen to her, kay?" He reassured, running his hand soothingly across Rae's back as he held her.

Anxiety buzzed in my chest nonetheless, and I stepped closer, cupping my hand along the back of her head as I leaned in to kiss the top of her hair.

Ellis placed a hand on my chest as I did this, and I unconsciously positioned my hand on his waist. His cheeks warmed; a shift that I could feel in our proximity.

I took a deep breath, unsure about everything at the moment... and I think he sensed this uncertainty as his fingers moved together to smooth the fabric of my chest.

"Hey," he dropped his boisterous tone, "I've got her. You trust me, right?"

A slow nod, but with hesitation nonetheless.

Ellis lifted his hand from my chest to gently rest on the side of my face, "You're going to be late. I'm only just around the corner," He assured kindly, leaning in to press a kiss to my lips.

He was so tender and kind. Moments like this made me question how he ever fell into such a shitty life. I savoured our kiss for the few seconds that it lasted, then pulled away.

"I love you, Rae," I said softly, "Be a good girl for Ellis." I pulled away, feeling Ellis' touch fade as I did so. There was a dull ache in the absence. I looked around to see that Shelley had returned to scrolling on her phone, and then waved at Ellis one more time before slipping out through the kitchen door.

No Merciful Gods

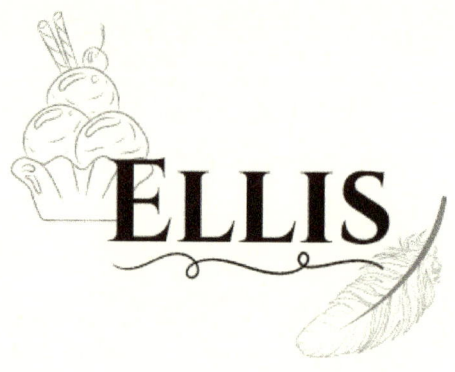

ELLIS

The diner was surprisingly empty for a Wednesday evening. I was so used to getting the church crews coming in, but there must be something going on elsewhere in the city to make this week so dead.

Luckily, this meant that I had a fair amount of time to hang out with my new best friend.

I had a lot of apprehension when Brooke first came to drop Rae off. There was a self-sabotaging moment when I remembered that I was the one who initiated this arrangement, but I think being left alone with anyone's baby for the first time is daunting enough.

Brooke was right, though, she was an absolute dream. I

moved her high chair out into the main dining area so I could keep an eye on her as well as the two tables that had most of their needs fulfilled. She was easily entertained and communicated when she wanted something, but overall a very low-maintenance little girl.

As I sat behind the bar chatting to Rae in baby babble, the front door of the diner swung open and a face that I recognized instantly entered. Searing blue eyes twinkled beneath a neatly styled head of brown hair. The woman smiled at me as if she knew me intimately.

"Hello!" The woman said, "Is my husband here?"

I felt the eaves of panic begin to surge in my chest as I realized the woman before me was the mother of the baby sat in the high chair beside me. After a momentary scramble trying to think of what to do.

"Hello, Darling!" I sang, pushing myself to stand. "I am so sorry, I don't quite know who you're looking for. Could you expand on that?"

Her eyes closed slowly, and when they re-opened I watched as her eyes found themselves situated on Rae. I stepped forward with my arms crossed, moving to place myself in the line of sight, leaning back against the bar top.

As soon as I blocked her view, the woman's eyes lifted to mine. She seemed oddly quiet, "Why is my daughter behind the counter?" She asked.

I tilted my head, "Madam, I can assure you that I have no idea what you're talking about."

This seemed to frustrate her, but she shrugged. "My husband's car is parked nearby. I saw him here last time," she said in a deadly cool tone. She shifted something in her hand. Slim and metallic. My heart rate instantly spiked as I recognized the shape to be a pocket knife.

"Listen, I don't know who you are talking about," I said plainly. Frustration burned in my mind as I realized that the other guests were now watching. I was also keenly aware that Rae was unsupervised behind me.

The woman sighed, "Brooke. Brooke Morris." She said in a tone that explicitly laid out how fed up of me she was.

"Oh, right." I turned from her to situate myself behind the bar beside Rae's chair once more.

She raised an eyebrow, "You know him?"

I flicked my eyes up to glance at the clock. Ten minutes past seven. Brooke would be back any minute now. "I've met him a few times," I said plainly, pulling out my phone to send him a quick message.

Me: Psycho stalker wife is here. ETA? xx

"Why is his car parked outside?" She asked, "Why are you in possession of my daughter?"

My eyes fell to Rae. She was staring at the woman with a confused, silent stare. It was almost as if she understood what was going on.

I pulled in a sigh, returning my attention to the woman. "Your name is Kelly, right?" I asked.

She stiffened her shoulders, pulling her arms across her chest. "How do you know my name?"

"Lucky guess," I sighed, glancing down at the screen of my phone as Brooke's response flashed up.

Brooke: 2 minutes

Relief began to wash over me, and I narrowed my eyes at Kelly. "I would like to request that you leave, please," I said sternly, "I will call the cops if you don't."

The idea of being anywhere near police officers was actually the worst possible thing that could happen to me, realistically, but I know better than to tempt fate, especially when that fate involves the life of an infant.

I think that the level of relief that washed over me when I saw Brooke push through the front entrance was actually indescribable.

He was dishevelled, obviously having just thrown on clothing and run straight here. I could smell the sweat on his clothes from where I stood, and he looked far less pleased to see her standing in front of me. His eyes immediately darkened.

"Kelly," He snapped.

She whizzed around on her toes to face him. Her face displayed a terrifying combination of annoyance and anger as she continued to fidget with the currently closed blade in her hand. My own eyes locked onto the metallic item, wondering if there was a way to disarm her before something terrible happened.

"Brooke!" She beamed, "I missed you!" She threw her arms around his neck, puckering her lips to kiss him.

He grabbed her hips and pushed her back to her feet. "You can't be here. We discussed this," He said in a gentle tone. "You need to go home."

Her face fell, and the expression that appeared on Brooke's face demonstrated how much that affected him. He still cared for her, even though she had done everything in the world to warrant his annoyance.

"Why Brooke?" She asked softly, "Why are you doing this to me? I just want to come home."

His eyes glassed over and he pulled in a shallow breath, "We already made this decision. You can't come back," he said, though his voice trembled.

Kelly balled her hands into tight fists, the one containing the blade still prominent in my peripherals. "Let me see Rae. Let me hold her!" She pleaded.

Brooke glanced up at me, his green orbs searching for support. They then moved to settle on Rae.

He was torn.

He knew he couldn't deny Kelly the right to see her daughter, but the whole ordeal made him understandably unsettled.

He pulled in a shaky breath and stepped past her, leaning across the table to pull Rae from the high chair. I placed a hand on his forearm briefly to comfort him, and he nodded once in appreciation of the gesture.

Rae whimpered as she was pulled from her seat, and he tried to soothe her by rubbing gentle circles in her back with his thumb. Kelly's eyes brightened and she slipped the blade into her pocket, extending her arms to Brooke.

"Sit," he demanded, motioning to a booth.

She narrowed her eyes but obeyed the command, slipping into the booth. Brooke then sat on the end of the seat, sealing her inside. Only then did he pass their daughter over to her.

Kelly pulled Rae close to her chest, cooing and stroking her face. The little girl began to whine, but Brooke allowed the woman before him to handle everything.

I watched, perched on the edge of my seat. Brooke turned to glance at me, a haggard expression rested on his face.

"Ellis!" One of the customers called, pulling me from the incredibly tense interaction at present.

I turned my attention to them and pulled on my signature smile as I approached them.

"We'd like the bill. Is everything okay over there?" One of my regulars asked.

I tilted my head to the side with a soft smile, "Everything is fine," I assured, "Did you enjoy everything this evening?"

The woman nodded, then pointed towards Brooke and Kelly, "I've seen that woman before. She has some serious issues," she said softly. "Is that her baby?"

"I am so sorry, I'm not really able to discuss this," I muttered, "I'll just grab your bill-"

Shit hit the fan faster than my brain could process.

"You can't take her away from me!" Kelly's scream sent a silence through the dining room that halted my heart. I turned to look at them and Kelly was holding Rae away from Brooke. The little girl began to cry, and I abandoned the table to present myself at Brooke's side.

Kelly was thrashing in the seat, trying to climb over with Rae in her arms. My kneejerk reaction was to rush to where she was struggling. The expression on Brooke's face was distraught as he tried to remove Rae from her mother's grasp.

Within seconds, she had managed to worm her way free of the booth, moving towards the door at lightning speed.

I slipped between her and the doors, grabbing each of the bars that ran along the inside and holding them in place to keep her from shoving past me. Brooke scrambled from the booth, but Kelly was quicker. In an instant, she had retrieved the pocket knife from her pocket and flicked it open.

We froze, eye to eye with one another as Rae's sobs could

be heard.

She placed the blade at my throat, "You better fucking move," she demanded. The cold tip of the knife grazed the skin of my neck.

I clenched my teeth, my eyes drifting to Brooke who now stood completely and totally frozen as his wife held me at knifepoint. His daughter cried.

"Kelly!" He said in the calmest voice he could muster. "Kelly, put the knife down." He urged, his arms trembled. Frozen in indecision.

She growled, pressing the blade against my taught skin, "Move!" She ordered.

Every alarm bell that could go off in my brain was screaming, I could feel the sting as her blade pierced my skin. I stood my ground, teeth clenched together so hard that I could feel them grinding.

"E-Ellis," Brooke muttered helplessly, "L-let her go," his voice trembled.

My eyes widened, and I frowned, "Let her go?" I growled, but Kelly stepped closer to me. She was at least a foot shorter than me, but her reach to my neck was deadly accurate.

"I'd do what he said if I were you," she snarls, "I'll slit your fucking throat!"

The pounding in my chest continued, and I gulped down the fear that was building in my chest.

Would it be wrong to say that a part of me wanted her to do it?

I held onto hope that one of the other customers had called the police, though I couldn't hear anything outside of the constantly racing thoughts in my mind, paired with the blinding pain that was beginning to build with the pressure against my throat.

Something inside of me surged with a rage like no other, and I glared down at her with a fire in my eyes.

"Do it, you freaky bitch!" I growled through my teeth, "You'll never see your fucking daughter again if you do it."

"Ellis, stop it!" Brooke begged, his eyes searching for any possible way for him to break through without harming me or Rae… it seemed hopeless, though. One of us was bound to get hurt.

I drew in a deep breath and closed my eyes, selling them shut as I channelled every ounce of strength I had left inside of me. Tears brimmed my eyes and I bit into the hard-ass information to swallow; I'd be the one to go.

Brooke whimpered, "Kelly…Kelly please come back… we-we can go home." He bargained, holding his hands out, "You know this is wrong. You can't just kidnap her," His voice was calm and gentle, but I could see the genuine terror in his face. "Just put the knife down and we can go back to normal."

The blade moved. Not completely, but enough to signal Kelly's body was trembling. I turned my attention to her, and the fire that burned in her eyes persisted. But her teeth clenched. She stared into my soul with angry, trembling features.

Brooke stepped forward, placing a hand on her shoulder, the other reached to gently encircle the wrist that held me pinned to the door. His eyes locked on mine as he slowly pulled her hand from my neck.

As the blade released from my skin, I pulled in a deep breath. Every one of my muscles ached as I felt the whole facade of who I had built myself to become melt away.

My arms shook anxiously as I watched Brooke pull Kelly

into his chest, the hand which held her wrist slipping further to grab the knife and quickly close it with a snap.

Kelly crumbled into his arms, sobbing against his chest. He pulled her into a tight embrace, trying to soothe Rae in the process.

My chest ached, eyes falling as I pulled myself from the door. I brushed past him before entering the kitchen and moving into autopilot.

I comped the bills for both of the tables who had sat through the chaos and re-emerged to explain what I'd done to them, asking them to leave at their earliest convenience. I then sank into the chair I had been in before this all went down, my head fell into my hands as I allowed myself to disassociate for the next few minutes.

Before too long, the white tile beneath me began to flicker with blue and red lights. My heart raced as I heard the doors to the diner open and Kelly once again kicked off. The police retrieved Rae from her, placing her back in Brooke's arms, then escorted her to a patrol car.

I could hear the distant, muffled voices of officers talking to Brooke about what happened, but the world felt unreal. It was like I had been placed here against my will, thrust into a dimension I couldn't comprehend.

A hand rested on my shoulder, "Sir," an officer spoke. I couldn't move. I was paralysed with abject terror. What if they recognized me? What if they took me away?

"Sir, are you alright?" The officer asked again. A woman.

I bit down on my tongue, still fighting back the rush of anger and panic... terror. Lorenzo was going to have my head on a silver platter if I was late tonight, so I genuinely couldn't see the harm in just finding Kelly's knife and ending it all myself.

"Ellis," Brooke's voice pulled through everything. His presence grew stronger as he sank to his knees in front of my raised stool. He cupped my face in his hands and pressed his forehead against mine. "It's me, Ellis. Take a breath please," He muttered.

My eyes fluttered, and I could see his eyes pressed close to mine. His touch was so gentle... I wanted to crumble into his arms, but something kept me cemented to this seat.

Was it anxiety?

Jealousy?

Brooke gently stroked his thumb over my cheek, "I'm so... so sorry that you were ever put into this situation," he muttered. One of his hands fell to rest on one of my knees as my legs bounced underneath me.

"Does he need medical attention?" The female officer asked, and I felt the comforting touch peel away from me as he turned to speak with her.

Only once she had stepped away was I able to bring myself to speak. I lifted my eyes to search for Brooke and found that he hadn't moved from in front of me. Exhaustion fell over my shoulders. "Where is Rae?" I asked softly, feeling the tremors in my voice as I spoke.

Brooke turned his gaze back to me and softened his expression, "She is safe, don't worry. She is being checked over by the paramedics just in case," he said reassuringly, pushing himself to stand now that I was back from my catatonia.

I followed his position with my eyes, "Where is Kelly?"

"They've arrested her... again," he mumbled, then his eyes locked with my own. "Are you hurting? She nicked you with

191

the knife."

My hand lifted to touch my neck and though I felt the soft sting of pain, it didn't hurt nearly enough to warrant more than a bandage. "I'll be okay. I've had worse."

His eyes fell and he sighed, "will you come home with me tonight?" He asked softly.

I glanced down at my phone, countless unread messages from Lorenzo and the diner didn't close for another half hour. "I have a job tonight," I muttered flatly.

"A job? You're going to make yourself work after all of that?" He asked.

My lips pulled to a tight smile as I chuckled, "It doesn't matter. He'd lose money if I didn't show up. Lorenzo losing money is the same thing as killing his dog. He's already pissed enough at me so I can't exactly just not show up."

Brooke turned to me, narrowing his eyes, "What happens if you don't show up?"

"Then the next time I do turn up, he beats me within an inch of death and throws me off a bridge to make it look like an accident." I said flatly, a low whisper to my voice.

He frowned and crossed his arms. "I want to meet this Lorenzo guy," he said in a tone that matched my own.

I scoffed, shaking my head, "No chance in hell," I declared.

Brooke turned, walking away from me abruptly. His absence struck me to my core, and I immediately began to regret the projection of my insecurity onto him.

Next thing I knew, he returned, Rae clutched in his arms. He had only gone to collect her from the medics...

My head fell and I messaged my temples as I tried to steady myself. My phone started to ring and I could see Lorenzo's fucking name peel across it. I growled and stared at it on my knee, feeling a seething anger pull through me as his name pulsed with the vibrations of my phone.

In a split second, the device disappeared.

I blinked, looking around... then I heard it.

"Hello?" Brooke asked, and when I finally brought myself to look up, I could see the pink rhinestone case clutched in his hand, the speaker pressed to his ear.

Fuck.

"I'm so sorry, who the fuck do you think you're speaking to right now?" Brooke asked.

Fuck.

The brunet scrunched his nose, nuzzling into Rae's hair as he listened. His shoulders were tense and his beautiful fucking green eyes narrowed in annoyance.

"Well I mean, I can pass on a message to him, but if you're going to continue to speak like this then I'll have to conveniently go through a tunnel."

My body was frozen in terror as I stared at Brooke in blatant terror.

Dizzy... sick...

"I don't think he will be in tonight,"

My jaw dropped, I wanted to scream.

Fuck.

Fuck.

Fuck.

Brooke's eyes finally fell into me and concern painted across his face, "Mmm, no. I don't think you'll be doing that," he said in a warning tone.

My heart was beating so fucking fast that I genuinely thought it might explode out of my chest at this point.

"B...Brooke," I stuttered out.

He lowered the phone from his ear and I noticed the call had ended. My blood ran cold and that familiar pressure returned behind my eyes.

"W....what the fuck did you just do?" I asked, the abject... blatant fear dripping off of every word.

Brooke extended the phone back to me, "he seemed to be fine," he said.

"No." I snatched the device away from him, staring down at the blackened screen. If I thought I'd felt fear earlier with a knife to my throat, reality was staring me in the face right now. "No. Lorenzo doesn't do fine!" I snarled.

He lifted his eyebrow and pulled Rae closer to himself, "what are you talking about, Ellis?"

I stood abruptly, turning on my heels to slink into the kitchen behind me. My whole body vibrated in pure adrenaline as the screen of my phone lit up once more.

Fuck...

I clenched my teeth together as I slammed my shoulder into the back exit door, answering the call.

"H...hello?"

"Where the fuck are you?"

I could feel the icy grip of his hand on my throat, and I pinned my spine to the brick wall behind me. I drew the heel of my palm to my eyes as I swallowed.

"I- I am finishing up at the diner," I said, voice breaking from fear.

"You have twenty minutes. If you aren't here before then, your ass is grass." Lorenzo snapped.

I pulled in a shaky breath "I c-can't leave yet... m...my boss will kill me if I don't lock up."

"Well if you aren't standing in front of me in nineteen

194

minutes, I'll make sure he doesn't have to." His voice was a thick, deadly warning.

"It's not possible… it takes me half an hour to walk there, Lorenzo! This isn't fair!" I whimpered. Even though I stood outside, it felt like walls were closing in around me.

"Figure it the fuck out then, Flare." He ended the call abruptly.

The silence was fucking deafening. I stood for a few seconds in stark paralysis as darkness encroached the edges of my vision. My phone vibrated with a taunting message.

Withheld: 18 minutes.

Fuck. My. Life.

Like… actually fuck it.

I stuffed my phone into my pocket and turned to storm back into the kitchen, but the back door had locked behind me.

Fuck it.

I turned away and ripped my apron and badge off, throwing them to the ground and storming from behind the restaurant. All I could think to do was run. Run fast.

A distinct numbness buzzed in my fingers as I followed my path.

My phone rang, I glanced at it to see Brooke's name… which I had affectionately punctuated with a heart emoji…

I silenced the call and kept running.

When I burst through the back door of the Midnight Raven, I saw the concerned face of the House Mother of the night. Zophia wasn't here… where the fuck was she?

I raced through the back stage area, shoving past girls in hardly any clothes as I spotted Lorenzo standing at the end of the hall. His eyes locked onto me, and I felt the wind zip from my lungs as I froze, folding in half so that my hands propped on my knees.

Sweat dripped down my face and my lungs burned. My makeup ran. The crusted blood on my neck itched. My entire body surged with equal levels of numbness and pure, unadulterated panic.

Lorenzo jabbed his meaty fucking finger at the door of one of the private dance rooms to his left.

I panted, forcing my spine to straighten enough to be considered standing, and I took a step towards the room. My knees felt as though they were going to buckle beneath me, but I persisted until I had entered the room.

The door behind me slammed shut, and the sound of the deadbolt lock rotating and clicking shut rang like the slamming of a cell door. I was locked inside this fucking prison with Lorenzo.

"Who was he, Flare?" Lorenzo asked in a sickeningly sweet query.

Bile built in my throat, and I was still trying to catch my breath.

"Flare." His saccharine tone dropped away.

"He... he is a f-friend," I muttered, my own pitch increasing. I couldn't bring myself to look at him.

The floorboards behind me creaked and chills ran up my spine as the sensation of his steaming hand burned against the small of my back. When it connected, its heat surged up my spine and my head fell forwards. My black curls fell to shade my eyes.

"Why does he think he has any right to intervene with our work?" Lorenzo hissed in a low whisper into my ear and my shoulders convulsed in anticipation of his disgusting fucking lips as they graced the flesh of my neck. His wirey moustache sent an itch of irritation over my skin.

"I.." I tried to speak, but Brooke's expression flashed into my mind. Fucksake... I couldn't help how much I cared for him. I remembered how he'd held my face and pulled me from the panic earlier. I choked on the phlegm in my throat.

Lorenzo kissed my neck again, his large hands gripping tight to my hips. I wanted to cry...

"P...please..." I muttered helplessly, "please just kill me."

"Oh, Ellis..." Lorenzo smirked as he dragged the sharp edged of his canines up my neck, finally settling on my ear. "That would be far too merciful for a disobedient slut like you." He whispered sharply into my ear and presented a flat substance at my lips.

I closed my eyes and parted my lips as Lorenzo placed the tab onto the tip of my tongue.

It dissolved instantly, the taste of a harsh chemical forced me to gag... but the effects were almost immediate. My skin bubbled with goosebumps as my hair stood on end and a warmth enveloped me. The fear slipped away, dissolving into the air through the heavy exhale that I released.

I clenched my teeth together and... I submit... to all of it... every single fucking second of that six hour period.

Masquerade

BROOKE

I have well and truly fucked up this time.

Why did I have to answer that phone call?

Why couldn't I have just shut the fuck up and kept my head out of Ellis's business for five fucking minutes?

I had been staring at my phone for the past hour, sat in the empty darkness of the diner with my daughter clutched to my chest.

He hadn't locked up... he just vanished.

There wasn't any point in blowing up his phone, if he wanted to speak to me ... he would have answered me already.

Rae's tiny fingers clung to the sweat soaked fabric of my

grey gym-shirt, her tiny chest rising and falling in a soothing rhythm. She was absolutely the only thing keeping me sane at this moment in time.

Every single atom that buzzed within my skin wanted to run away. Fast. I was so fucking tired. So fed up of fucking everything up. So fucking done.

Why is it that I do stupid things that push people away?

I pulled Rae closer, bouncing her lightly as I glanced to the coat rack. Ellis's knit jacket still hung there, the silver and red threads casting dark shade through the dim lighting of the diner. My chest ached from the uncertainty of everything, and I really, really wanted to see him. I needed to know he was okay… that I didn't just fuck everything up… again.

My hands trembled as I tapped the screen of my phone, and as the lock screen brightened I could see the picture I had set of Rae playing with an elephant toy.

A shaky breath pulled through my lungs and I stared through the silent diner… should I go home?

What was I even doing here still? Hours had passed since the commotion had died down and it was way past closing time.

Midnight would be approaching soon.

I pushed myself from the booth, slowly feeling my feet brace against the ground as I pushed my phone into my pocket and approached the front door. There was a simple turnkey style latch on the door, so I twisted it to lock the front door, then turned around. Through the kitchen door, and then finally through the very back exit which emptied into an alleyway. The cool night air of October pulled through my hair, and I felt a sobering wave of annoyance pulse through me.

The door pulled to a soft close behind me, and just as I

turned to find my exit… I noticed a bundle of fabric on the ground. Black, with ties torn asunder. I stopped down to collect it, realizing that it was an apron… something golden glinted beneath it.

Rectangular and shiny, with a pin sticking out the back.

As I turned it over, my heart sank. It was Ellis's badge.

My head fucking hurt.

I picked up the badge, running my finger along the letters of his name as Rae shifted in my arms. The exhaustion was beginning to hurt me now… that on top of the ache from my classes today. It was becoming too much to handle at this point, and all I wanted was to sink into sleep.

With a heavy grunt, I pushed myself to stand upright, Ellis's badge and apron clutched in my hand as I made my way out to my car… which I was only just realizing had also become a victim of my mentally ill ex-wife.

The entire piss-yellow driver's side paint was scratched up with the most terrible keying I had ever seen. In big, bold letters, she had drug her keys out to the words 'Wife beater'.

Fucking Jesus…

I glanced down at Rae, she was fast asleep at the moment… but I knew the second I put her in the car seat she would rouse and probably cry, so as I opened the door to her seat, I braced myself for her squirming and crying.

Surprisingly, she didn't.

The entire ride home, she stayed calm. Not once crying, even when I removed her from the car to take her inside and out her to bed. Not even as I tucked her in… not even when I slipped out of her bedroom and stepped quietly through the hall to my own. She went down easy, and stayed asleep.

Four a.m. rolled around, and I still hadn't managed to

fall asleep. Staring up at the ceiling with every possible thought racing through my mind. Chaos reigned supreme, and though I knew I should sleep, I just couldn't bring myself close enough to relaxation to allow myself to slip into rest.

Against my chest, the soft vibration of my phone roused me from my wandering thoughts, and as I lifted it to check the notification... The name that flashed across my screen sent chills down my spine.

Ellis: home x

He messaged me?

I stared at the notification, reading into every single detail. The fact that he hadn't capitalized his words, the single x when he normally sent two or three. It almost didn't hit me that the strangest part of it all was that he had messaged me in the first place.

Before I knew it, ten minutes had passed, with me just staring at the message on my lock screen. When I eventually opened it, the active bubble beside Ellis's name was red.

Do not disturb.

My eyes fell, and I nibbled my lip... maybe I should leave him alone?

Ellis: you're staring

My eyes widened. I hadn't even noticed the bubbles popping up. How did he know I was staring at his messages?

Ellis: will you please reply?

Me: I don't really know what to say, to be honest.

I nibbled the back of my lip anxiously as I awaited his response. The bubbles never appeared at the bottom of the chat… he must have disabled the visibility.

After an excruciatingly long few minutes, my whole screen brightened as his name pulled across the centre. I answered within a nanosecond.

"Hello?"

"Hey," Ellis muttered. The drawl of his accent was thick. He sounded inebriated… loopy.

There was a moment of hesitation as I reached my hand into my hair, tangling my fingers within the mass of curls. "Ellis… I am so… so sorry," I muttered softly.

He didn't respond, and every second of silence felt like a death grip on my heart, choking me.

"I-it was wrong of me to try and intervene with something I didn't understand…" I offered into the silence. The sound of my own voice seemed to echo from the other end, as though I was on speaker.

Finally, he pulled in a breath. His face was right next to the microphone, and the sound of his breathing was sharp against my ear.

"I understand," He said plainly.

A frown spread across my face, and I allowed my eyes to lull closed. Attempting to picture him standing in front of me, my imagination ran wild. Bruises on his face … cuts. Things I had allowed to happen to him… caused.

"Can you speak to me?" He asked. His voice dipped to some tone just beneath a whisper with his question.

That tone was new… he had never spoken in such a soft

and helpless way before.

My heart ached more. "W...what do you want me to say?"

"Anything ... I just..." he paused, the line crinkled as he adjusted himself. "I need something to keep myself from slipping over the edge."

My eyes fell open, but I could see his face clear as day. As though he was right in front of me. I search the recesses of my mind for some sort of conversation.

"Um... why do you put x's at the end of your messages?" I asked, rubbing my neck anxiously.

A soft, nasally exhale sounded from his end.

"It isn't common here," he muttered, shifting again and placing the phone where the microphone was a bit further from his face.

"They're kisses..." he said softly. I imagined that he was lying on his back, phone resting on his chest as he stared at the ceiling of some classy apartment.

"Oh, that makes sense... like x's and o's?"

He didn't respond immediately, like he was searching for the words to say.

"It is common in England. You put kisses at the end of your messages."

The explanation pulled a soft smile to my lips. "So you put them at the end of everyone's messages? Not just mine?"

Ellis chuckled softly... almost entirely silent. "Would it make you jealous if I did?" This time was brighter. Sassy. This sounded like the Ellis that I knew... albeit, still obviously under the influence of some mind-altering substance.

A warmth built in my chest and I felt relief wash through me. "Do you want me to be jealous?"

"Hmm," he hummed softly, and for a moment... I worried

that I'd lost any progress with pulling him out of the funk. "Brooke…"

"Yes, Ellis?"

"Have you ever just wanted to disappear?"

My heart fluttered in my chest, and I nodded softly… why the hell would I nod? I know he can't see me. "I think about it frequently, actually…"

My mind flashed to my safe downstairs. The money I was saving for the perfect time… to get me and Rae the hell away from all of this bullshit. It felt cruel, though… leaving him behind. I think that is why I have stayed.

"Hmm," he hummed again.

There was an inexplicable distance between us. I wanted to see his face, to be able to reach out to comfort him.

"Brooke,"

"Yes?"

"Would you miss me … if I disappeared?"

The flutter of my heart shifted into this throbbing pang of worry.

"Absolutely…" I managed, choking softly on the word.

He fell silent again, but this time the silence set off the racing of my heart once more.

"Ellis," I muttered into the air.

"Hmm?"

My face softened, and I turned my head to stare at the rectangular digital clock at my side. The red LEDs flashing up 5:00 a.m. in the darkness of my bedroom. The sun would be rising soon.

"Did he hurt you?"

In an instant, the line dropped. The cavernous silence of his presence suddenly erased from the world. I felt an instant cessation of my pulse, baring my teeth down on the back of my lip. I held my phone to my ear in disbelief that he had hung up. After a minute, I felt my resolve fade, and I allowed the phone to slip from my grasp, sliding down my pillow.

Exhaustion is a state of being that I have found myself living in frequently this year. Every time I thought I was coming out of the clearing, something would prove me wrong.

I didn't manage to sleep during the night. It felt selfish… considering the issues I had caused for Ellis.

As the sun rose through the blinds of my window, a weight pressed into my chest. I wanted to sink into the darkness that remained. Sunlight felt like acid against the pale sheen of my skin.

The clock at my side began to screech with its grating alarm tone, and I delivered a solid hand to the silence button along the top. With a full, exhausted sigh, I pushed myself from my bed and forced myself into the shower.

Even though Ellis hadn't said anything, his response was everything I needed to know. This Lorenzo guy… he had absolutely hurt Ellis.

As the steam gathered in the bathroom, I pushed my long brown curls beneath the stream of water, feeling the weight on my scalp increase with the hot water.

The more I thought, the more fed up I was with everything… in fact…

Fuck everything.

I shut off the water and pulled myself out of the cubicle to angrily rake a brush through the mess of curls that now dripped into puddles around my feet, collecting on the bath mat. I threw my hair into a haphazard bun and quickly dressed myself.

When I pushed into Rae's bedroom, I froze for a moment as I realized that she was sitting up, fully awake and clutching a teething ring in her hands. My entire disposition shifted greatly within an instant and I softened my gaze.

"Hey beautiful, how long have you been up?" I asked sweetly, dipping to hook my hands beneath her armpits and pull her into my arms. Of course, she snuggled into my chest, her tiny hand gripping at the neckline of my black dress shirt. She soothed my heart... she had no clue how much I needed her right now.

I dressed her in a sweet pink dress with a frilly white bow head wrap, then carted her off to school. The gym was calling to me. I needed to punch something... hard.

During my workout, I kept an eye on the front door... hoping to see Ellis step through with his bright smile and swaying gait that I couldn't keep my eyes off of.

He never did.

I walked by the diner on my way to work, glancing into the window.

Shelley was standing, chatting happily to customers. The joy pulled a string of guilt through my chest, and I quickly stepped towards the Dispatch building.

"You look like shit, Brooke," Brian grinned, adjusting his glasses as he peeled around the entrance of my cubicle.

A pang of annoyance sprung to my chest, and I turned to glance over at him. I nodded succinctly, then turned my eyes back to my screen.

"Okay..." he offered again, and I could feel his energy encroach upon me as he stepped closer to me.

His hand clamped down on my shoulder and he dipped to

pull my attention to him. I darted my eyes in his direction, a soft glare in my expression. Brian chuckled.

"Rough night?"

"Brian, in the nicest way I can possibly say this… fuck off," I grumbled.

He lifted an eyebrow and crossed his arms, "Okay, dude." He turned to walk away, but stopped just before he reached the entrance of my cubicle. "What happened last night?"

"Kelly happened." I snapped, "She held Ellis at knifepoint in the diner while trying to kidnap Rae." My annoyance was clearly audible… though it may have been eclipsed by my fatigue.

"Shit," Brian muttered, and I finally glanced back at him. He stood, facing me directly. A soft expression on his face. "Should you be here right now?"

I allowed my shoulders to fall, then shook my head softly. "I don't know, man. I don't know what to do with myself," I admitted sadly.

My friend nodded slowly, "Do you think you'd like a night alone? Jilly and I can take Rae for tonight."

"I've asked Jill to watch her so much recently, and I feel like I'm grifting off her kindness," I said with a soft sigh, allowing my head to fall into my arms.

A laugh lifted from his chest, and he shook his head. "Jilly told me about your crush," he changed the subject. "I know it may feel selfish, but there is a Masquerade Drag Show at the Midnight Raven tonight. Maybe you should go? Ask for a private dance? Get your mind off of things. We can watch Rae for the evening."

Drag Night…

I glanced up at him, feeling a flutter in my chest. Did Ellis even want to see me? His messenger said Do Not Disturb still … would he even be there tonight?

"Well, you seem keen. It's sorted then." Brian grinned, "Now come to lunch with us. You need to eat something before you pass out."

The reality of his statement hit me hard as the mention of food summoned a great gargle from my stomach. I lowered my eyes to the betraying organ in my abdomen, then nodded softly. Part of me… most of me hoped that Ellis would have shown up for work in the time since I had walked by this morning.

"Nah, sorry honey! Ellis called in sick," Shelley sang, pulling a hand through her blonde hair.

I sank back into the booth, feeling my chest ache.

"Well that is just terrible," Jill says softly, "He is the best part of our lunch breaks."

Shelley grinned "I'm sure I can do him justice," she teased lightly, "He sounded drunker than Cooter Brown when he called me this morning!"

I allowed my eyes to fall onto the menu. Any appetite that I had previously was now vanquished. When I finally lifted my eyes once more, everyone was looking at me… expectant.

"Um…" I tapped the table anxiously, "Hello?"

"What do you want to eat, Sugar?" Shelley asked as though she had asked it multiple times before.

Embarrassment struck and I nodded "oh, um…" I scanned the menu. "P-pancakes. Just a three stack please," I said softly.

The waitress smiled softly and closed her notepad, "Cute," she said softly "that's what he would've gotten too," she winked and I felt my skin flush dark.

As Shelley walked away, Jill perked up, "He? How does Shelley know?" She asked breathlessly in a hushed tone.

My eyes snapped to Jill, "um..." I blinked slowly.

"Come on, Jilly. Let the man breathe," Brian said, then tried to engage me in casual conversation about some sort of football game going on tonight. A conversation that I was neither interested in, nor listening to.

When the food came, I tried to gather myself. Looking down at the stack of pancakes, I pulled in a slow breath and sank my fork into the soft dough.

Cold pancakes are shit... at least, that is what Ellis would have said.

I wanted to see him... I needed to see him.

"Are you sure about watching Rae tonight?" I asked softly, poking the fluffy cakes with my fork. My eyes never lifted from the food.

Brian placed a hand over Jill's hand that perched on the table before us. "Without a question, Brooke," he inserted into the tense air around us.

Later that night, in a sticky corner booth at The Midnight Raven, I pulled the hair tie from my messy bun, allowing my unkempt curls to fall around my face. A shoddy, twenty-dollar pirate outfit from Party City clung tight to my skin, but it was the best I could do.

My face was partially obscured by the simple black plastic of a bejewelled mask which tied along the back of my head with a cheap bit of elastic.

This was about the most effort I had invested into my outfit for quite some time. Here I was, sitting in a dark booth at the back of the Midnight Raven. A glass of untouched Jameson on the sticky black table in front of me.

Scantily clad girls with dollar store masks walked around the main dining area, enticing the patrons around me. Luckily, I was hidden right enough in a shaded corner to avoid the majority of these batting eyelashes.

Three drag queens had already been on. It felt weird for Flare to not be the opening act, but I guess if he wasn't at work … he would definitely be here, right?

I opened my phone to scroll through notifications that I had been ignoring. Just needed to do something with my hands. In front of me, a girl with large breasts and bright blonde hair dipped down to press her palms against the table.

"You've been awful quiet, Mister," she sang in a saccharine voice. "Think you'd be keen to sample any of the girls?"

My thumb pressed to the power button, casting my screen in darkness as I glanced up at her. There were stunning brown eyes behind her red mask, black feathers outlining the perimeter. I nibbled my lip, then looked at the stage. "Um… do you know if Flare Femme is performing tonight?" I asked, anxiously shifting in my seat.

She smirked, shifting her weight as she sank into the booth beside me. "She isn't performing," she said softly, pressing herself against my arm. The warmth of her skin against the shitty polyester of my sleeves sent chills up my skin, and she leaned to rest her head against my shoulder, a hand walking her pointer and middle fingers across my thigh.

"I can get you a room with her, though, she may have a few minutes to spare for deeper pockets."

That throbbing organ in my chest started up again and I looked down at the woman. She was much smaller than me, delicate and sexy features that sent a thrill through my mind.

I reached into my pocket to pull out my ratty wallet, then opened it to retrieve the only bill inside… a wrinkled twenty. This woman snatched it in an instant.

Her hands braced at the edge of the table, pulling her from the seat as she beamed dramatically. Then, she twirled as she dipped to grab my wrist. The long golden locks of hair swayed in against her movements as she pulled me through the side of the main hall which soon dissolved into a hallway with golden wallpaper and deep red carpets.

"This will get you five minutes," She said, pressing her hand to a door to ensure the lock was not engaged. She then pressed inside, revealing a simple couch with a pole and a wall length mirror. "You go on in… I'll send Flare down," she coaxed.

I stepped past her to enter the room, and without another word, she had sealed me within the room.

It was dark in here, and though there were light switches on the wall, I had no clue what they did… so I stepped closer to the mirror to take in my appearance in the mirror.

To an untrained eye, I looked mysterious. Shoulder-length brown curls and striking green eyes that peered from behind the black mask which covered the top half of my face. Even though the party store pirate outfit gave me an edge of camp, I think it fit me to an extent.

Shitty, but useful for a bit of fun once in a while.

The door behind me clicked, and the room filled with the soft light of the hallway as a figure stepped inside. Tall and slender with long black curls that encircled lace-covered shoulders and a faux leather corset. Her long legs were wrapped in black fishnet leggings. Knee-high platforms in shiny black leather and a mini skirt of the same material.

212

I stared at her in the mirror, hands planted firmly in my pockets as my eyes held the face of my guest.

Her skin was painted in a pale white coating with crimson lips that dripped at the edges in a slightly darker shade of red, like blood. Those deep brown orbs that I recognized in an instant, even despite the change of face and the shading of her velvet and lace mask which she had clearly spent more time and effort on than I could even imagine.

For a moment, I didn't know what to do. My shoulders softened as I realized that this person whom I had grown to care for was okay. Flare stood at the entrance to the room, pushing the door to close behind herself as she sank back into the black lacquered wood. A solid click sounded as she twisted the lock with a hand behind her back.

"Ooh, a pirate?" She sang, placing her hands on the curves of her hips. "Probably my favourite kind of masked man." Flare stepped closer to me, but suddenly… froze.

"Brooke?"

I allowed my head to fall, staring down at my boots as I shuddered lightly.

Flare crossed her arms, "Why are you here?"

My chest started to ache, and my throat filled with saliva. I forced a swallow and a tingling sensation climbed from my fingers. For the first time in a long time… I felt the real things that I had pushed away.

What is life?

Why bother?

Ellis was the only person whose presence I craved… and that question… I think it would be my final straw. That numbness climbed through my limbs until it reached my chest and transformed into a dull, heavy throb. My face eclipsed in warmth and I truly felt like I might collapse.

I thought back to the glass of Jameson on my table and craved the sensation of its burn in my throat.

Behind me, the soft thud of Flare's platforms grew in volume as she stepped closer to me. A soothing warmth burned on the small of my back as she pressed a hand to the fabric of my shirt. The soft wisp of her breath brushed my neck between the strands of hair that cloaked that skin.

"Where did you get this piece of shit costume?" Ellis's thick English accent pulled from the higher feminine tone of Flare, and two slender arms wrapped around my hips.

Crimson lips, soft and full, pressed to the exposed flesh of my shoulder and Flare rested her head on that platform of bone and muscle.

She was so warm... and she smelled like that beautiful concoction of hairspray and makeup that I had grown to crave.

I pulled in a shaky breath, feeling myself instinctively sink into her touch. "Party City."

I could feel the shrug of her shoulders as she exhaled a soft snort of a laugh. She lifted her head and rested her chin against where her hair had been, a hand moving to lift my chin so that I was looking into the mirror.

There was the softest of smiles on Flare's face. A kindness that made my whole body ache. This was a gift, this connection. Nobody else would ever see the softness of Flare like I would.

She turned her face to place a gentle kiss on my jaw, and I watched every minuscule movement that she made. How her eyes would flutter in the most alluring ways. The soft lift of her shoulders as she breathed.

214

"Next time, you're not allowed to dress yourself," She whispered into my ear, the hairs on my neck stood on end. Her brown eyes fluttered open again, and settled up on mine in the mirror.

My thoughts raced aimlessly in my mind, but nothing came out. Every second I stared into her eyes was a second I had wasted.

Flare pulled away from me, and I felt panic ebb through my whole body as the contact lessened, but she stepped around me to stand in front of me. Of course, she was taller than me. Towering at least six inches above me with the help of those black platform boots. She pressed her manicured fingers to my chest and pulled my eyes up to hers.

I wavered, stepping back so that I could sit at the centre of the sofa on the wall beside me. My head fell into my hands.

"I'm so sorry," I whispered.

She stepped closer to me, a hand on my shoulder. I could feel the sharp ends of her nails resting against the polyester of my tunic. "Brooke," Ellis's voice pulled through again, as though he couldn't maintain the energy of his facade.

It took every ounce of resolve in my body to lift my eyes to look up, and when I did, she slipped a leg over my waist, sitting in a deep straddle of my hips. Her hands pressed to my chest to push me back against the cushion of the sofa. My own hands instinctively situated themselves on the platform that her waist provided and she lifted a hand to my hair to rake her fingers through the messy locks.

Those soft brown irises pulled me into her hypnotic gaze, her free arm hooked around the back of my neck to brace herself.

"Thank you for coming to see me," Flare whispered softly...

though I knew for certain that it was definitely Ellis speaking. "I needed to see you… but…" She cast her eyes away, "I'm… coming down from a pretty shitty high."

I nibbled the back of my lip, "Shelley mentioned that you sounded drunk on the phone this morning."

She winced, "You saw Shell?"

A soft, slow nod. "I went to see if you had gone to work on my break," I explained softly.

Flare's eyes softened for a moment and she reached to remove her mask. I could see the remnants of Ellis in her features, and my heart fluttered as her hands moved to pull my own mask away. Her eyes deepened and she placed coverings to the side.

"This is what I meant when I told you that I didn't think you'd approve of the life I live …" she muttered, and her gaze fell away from my own. "It means you have to let me suffer, because if I don't suffer…" Her words halt for a few seconds as she bit down on her tongue, "he only becomes more of a demon… and he will stop at nothing to destroy me."

Understanding pulsed in the front of my mind, and I tightened my grasp on her hips. "I don't know what you went through… but I am genuinely, so beyond sorry for making it worse," I said softly, feeling the tremble of my vocal cords.

Her face brightened softly and she shook her head, a hand pressing to my chest. "You couldn't have known" She muttered anxiously, "but…"

"But?"

I waited on bated breath for her to speak again, my body aching in need.

"I think I am ready to die…" This time, I was certain that Ellis was the one speaking. His thick vowels dragged lightly through the air as he sank back against my thighs.

The racing of my heart stopped, and my eyes widened. "What?" I muttered.

All I could see now when I looked at Flare was the genuine pain painted across her beautifully sculpted features. Features which Ellis had crafted with his infinite talents.

Her brown eyes welled with the lightest sheen of tears, and she turned her face back to the mirror at our side. "I think that is the only way to escape all of this … you know?" She muttered.

Every single ounce of my own turmoil ripped away from me in that instant, and all I cared about in this world was Ellis. That warmth, that friend who knew me completely and wholly. My eyes fixed themselves on his face and though he wasn't looking at me, I felt him calling to me.

"I-I don't have much time left, Brooke," Flare's tone lilted his voice, "And I can't have the girls see me crying… but I am glad you came to see me tonight. I needed to see you one last time."

"Ellis…" I muttered desperately, feeling the weight in my lap shift as Flare moved to pull away. My hands grasped tight to her hips to hold her in place, "No… look at me, El," I begged.

Flare glanced my way, but her eyes focused on the couch beside me.

"How much is an hour?"

"W-what?"

"How much does it cost to keep you here for an hour?"

Flare froze, shaking her head, "No, Darling… it doesn't work like that," she sighed. "I have an appointment in ten minutes and another an hour after that."

"How much does he want for me to have the night?" I asked, clutching at the leather mini-skirt that currently hid the plump rear-end of the drag queen on my lap.

She softened and leaned in to press a kiss to my forehead, "Brooke, you need a window for your car... nappies for your daughter," her hands smoothed the rough polyester of my tunic, "You don't need me, Mr. Unlucky. I am nothing more than a placeholder for whoever is lucky enough to take my place."

"Don't you dare," I snapped, a hand reaching up to guide her eyes to meet mine. "Don't you dare pretend like I wouldn't burn this place to the ground for you."

She held my gaze with a glassy, numb expression. "Darling..." she choked, but I shook my head.

"No, stop it... you're coming home with me tonight. I will wait for you outside," I said plainly, "you're coming home with me and I'm going to cook you a hot meal. I'll run you a shower and we will turn our phones off."

"I can't turn my phone off, Brooke," Flare whispered, shaking her head, "you don't understand, I can't escape him no matter what I do."

I reached up to cup her cheek in my hand, "Then I will be your transport. I'll take you wherever you need to go, whenever you need to go. I'll make sure you're safe and okay-"

Flare dipped to press a kiss to my lips, the words caught starkly against her crimson flesh as her intention of silencing me punctuated the air.

As she pulled away, I met her brown eyes again. Flare... or rather... Ellis stared into my soul.

"Darling, you have to understand that every man I have

ever invested any time in has ended up dead," he whispered. "I am a curse. A living… breathing curse."

Frustration creased between my brows and I shook my head, looking away from the man in drag before me. "Jesus Christ, Ellis," I muttered.

"Don't you get it, Brooke?" He snapped, pushing himself away from me to stand. He dipped to retrieve the mask from beside me, pulling it over his face, "I am not worth loving. I'm not worth saving… I should have been sent to prison for what I did, but now…" He looked away, his shoulders heaving. "I-I have to go… I can't be late."

Ellis turned to the door, but I pushed myself from the sofa, grabbing his wrist and pulling him back to face me.

"Ellis, please," I muttered, my voice trembling, "Please, you have no idea how much I need you."

He sighed, the curly black hair of his wig swaying with the movement. "You don't need me, you need attention," The words stung, mostly because they were true. Only to an extent though, I absolutely needed Ellis in this moment in time.

I pressed his slender frame against the wall behind him, feeling adrenaline course through my veins as I stared up into his eyes. "I will wait for you, I promise. I will be here when you leave tonight."

"P-please," Ellis whimpered, "I-I can't do this right now, Brooke… I need to go."

The headstrong, stubborn, sassy, witty man before me trembled with something I had never recognized in him before. Even yesterday, when I saw him confront death head-on, he had faced the prospect of death as though it was a challenge. Now, he seemed to have been broken.

This was my fault.

I released my hold against Flare Femme, allowing the trembling figure to move with ease. The room began to spin, the metallic taste of anxiety brimming in my chest as I stepped away and once more allowed my eyes to fall to the floor.

Without another word, Flare slipped from the room, disappearing into the hallway. All that was left behind was the echo of her receding footsteps down the corridor and the ache of this tragic premonition in my chest.

On the Count of Ten

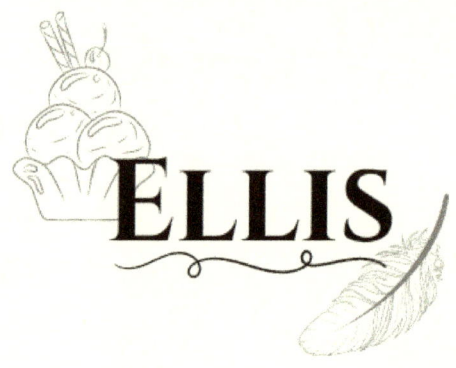

Hi friends, this is the author speaking. I wanted to
check in and let you know that this chapter contains
scenes depicting an attempt of suicide, and details of a
declining mental health. Please read on with your own
discretion and please, please be gentle with yourself.
Thank you for being here with me today. You are so
worthy of having your story written.

Sam

Sometimes it feels like life knows when you're down on your
luck.

Luck doesn't even sound like the right word to describe

what I have been down on. Makes it sound like I was ever lucky to begin with.

With a deep sigh, I pulled the lip of an open bottle of Alize Bleu to my own lips, drawing forth the fruity liquor and dousing the anxiety that burned at the base of my stomach before it could erupt and consume me whole again for the fourth time today.

"Jeeze, Flare," A sunshine, sugar-coated song of a voice pulled from my friend Valentine (Even though everyone here called her Scarlett). She crossed her arms over her full chest, looking me up and down as I swallowed a fourth of the massive glass bottle.

I glanced over to her, the gorgeous girl who every man dreamed of getting their hands on. My only remaining friend here at the Midnight Raven now that Ginger had left.

"What? Never had a shit day?" I asked.

Valentine smirked, slinking down from her chair to snatch the bottle from my hand and pour a gulp of the bright blue tequila into her mouth. A smile gracing her lips as she placed it down on my vanity with a resounding thud, "Far too many to count."

Our shared misery bonded us closer together for a reason. A sad, pitiful reason. The blonde woman before me looked around, her deep brown eyes surveying the room. "Wasn't that your last appointment of the night?"

A stitch of annoyance pulled a grimace to my face, and I turned my attention back to my vanity, where numerous makeup wipes lay coated in the white face paint and colourful accents from my recently removed face.

"I'm killing time," I muttered beneath my breath, a soft cry for help beneath these words.

She threw her arms around my neck, large breasts pressing against the top of my shoulder as she pulled her arms in a drunken hug around my face.

"Killing time for what? You're usually far too eager to leave this shithole," She grumbled with a tipsy hum. She smelled like the softest hints of coconut and vanilla, a lotion which soothed her aching knees after a few too many drops from the top of the pole.

I didn't want to answer her question, despite her being right. Maybe I was hoping that Lorenzo would come along and apologise for the shit I had gone through last night... as if. That dickhead wouldn't apologize for anything.

"Did you enjoy your five minutes of freedom earlier?" Valentine hummed, pulling back to finally allow me to move freely, "That pirate dude seemed like a real piece of ass."

That pirate dude WAS a real piece of ass.

I nibbled the back of my lip, thinking back to how Brooke had held me against the wall, begging me to stay. He had gotten dressed up, even if the costume was from a cheap party store. I doubt he even knew that Halloween was my favourite holiday, and yet he came to see me because he wanted to apologise.

"He was nice," I responded softly, sinking my face into a brace of crossed arms that rested against my vanity. "I think I will go," I muttered, pressing back against the tabletop until I stood, then changing from my outfit into a large hoodie and sweatpants.

When I looked back at Valentine, she was finishing off the last few drops of my bottle of alcohol, a glassy look in her eyes. She gave me a thumbs up, a soft hiccup rocking her small frame as she stepped down to give me a hug.

The warmth in her touch was soothing, but not enough to fight my demons. If only she knew that her hug was the last one I'd feel...

As I finally pulled from her, I felt certain about my next steps. I reached into her hand and placed the stack of dollar notes from my collection today in her palm, then turned to leave without giving her time to catch on to what was happening.

I exited through the backstage, pulling my hood over my curly black hair. My eyes remained heavy on the road beneath my feet as the gravel underneath my tennis shoes crunched with every step.

My vision was just beginning to blur a bit as the alcohol soothed whatever remaining sensations I had left, and the subtle buzz from the first moment of drunkenness settled over my ears.

The world around me simultaneously raced with life while droning to a grinding, screeching trudge of muffled noise. I didn't really know where I was going, but I put one foot in front of the other nonetheless.

Halloween was my favourite holiday. A day where I could truly be myself without people questioning me or criticizing how I dressed.

Even though it wasn't a big deal in England, my mother never batted an eye at my costumes and face paint. And yet, here I was, on my favourite day of the year. Alone and absolutely finished with life.

The emotional blunting that you feel when you have resigned yourself to death is addicting. I understand why people fall into these cycles of intense depression, hovering the line between life and death. In this moment, I felt nothing but the sting of tears that brimmed my eyes for a reason that my mind couldn't possibly comprehend. And though no thoughts pulled through to my consciousness, my feet moved without question.

Truth be told, I knew exactly where I was going... even though my mind had shut itself off from the world around it. I had planned this before, over and over again in my head. Usually when I was alone in my flat, feeling the intense call of the void from somewhere outside of my corporeal understanding.

This route I had walked many times before with intent, but no action. I was a coward then... too afraid to do what Lorenzo would do without a second thought.

Maybe that is what made me so angry, to feel like I had to prove to him that I was worth more than he claimed. To prove that his shows were nothing without me... and maybe that just demonstrated how dependent I was on Lorenzo as well?

I could have fought back.

I could have read my contract in depth before I signed my name.

But I didn't.

This is my fault.

The ground beneath me changed from gravel to solid concrete, and I lifted my eyes warily to the path before me. I stood at the base of an interstate bridge. Cars passed by, their lights casting a sharp light across the dark overpass. I pulled in a deep breath, trying to gather myself enough to move my feet forward.

My body weighed millions of tons, and as much as I wanted to move, I also wanted to collapse right there, maybe fall into the road and have some sorry sod in a car that was far too big for them take care of the deed so I didn't have to do it myself.

Another deep breath, and my feet began to move. Again and again, I stepped until I had reached the centre of the bridge.

Vertigo rushed through me as the wind on the overpass knocked my hood from my head, sending my black curls into a mess of wind. I winced, placing my hands on the concrete barriers as I looked over the side.

As above, so below. The interstate beneath this overpass carried all of the traffic coming and going from downtown Atlanta.

As I stared, this sensation of a tether latched onto my chest. Taut and soothing. It welcomed me, beckoning me over the edge. In its grasp, I felt warmth. I felt freedom.

Those tears from before traced their warmth down the pale, dry skin of my cheeks as I felt the colour draining from the world. I wanted nothing more than a sign, a reason to fucking stay. Something that would save me from all of this.

I grit my teeth, reaching my long, slender leg over to the other side of the barrier.

A platform.

Solid ground.

Then I stepped over, pressing my back to the barrier which I had just crossed. Suddenly, that beautiful warmth, that numbness, the emotional blunting...

Suddenly it was fucking gone.

Something about the sudden, imminent risk of death while standing on the ledge of an overpass was very fucking sobering.

In an instant, I could feel every cell in my body screaming

at me. Intense, mind-shattering pain that I had managed to keep at bay throughout the day came rushing forward, and my knees weakened. Those tears shifted to heartfelt, whole-body sobs and I was gasping for air.

Below, horns from approaching cars began to sound, cars pulled over to the sides of the road and I groaned, clinging to the barrier behind me like my life depended on it.

Because it did.

"F-fuck," I choked out between gasping breaths of air. The comfort of that call had silenced, but now my head raced with all of those terrible, toxic thoughts that demanded my exit, stage left.

A burden.

A freak.

A waste of space.

Nothing more than a plethora of holes.

A sob left my chest, and I closed my eyes tight.

Just take a fucking breath, Ellis... just count to ten and jump...

One...

Two...

Three...

Four...

I struggled, biting hard on my lip as I whimpered anxiously.

Five...

Six...

Seven...

Eight...

My left foot lifted from the concrete beneath me and I leaned forward to finally end everything. All of the pain… the suffering… the isolation. It was all so close to being over, and-

"Ellis!"

His voice.

"Fuck, Ellis!"

My strength wavered, and just as I felt my grip on the wall behind me lessen, two solid arms encircled my shoulders, sealing my spine back against the concrete.

The intoxicating scent of Brooke's cologne filled my senses, and I lifted my hands to cling to his arms. Pure, genuine anguish bubbled from within me in hauntingly deep bellows as I gripped tight to his strong arms.

"C-come back over, Ellis, please!" Brooke struggled, his words trembling as he spoke. "L-let's talk about this."

I sank back against the barrier, my chest burning with the pain of my heart as it thrashed within its cage of bone and muscle. Even in his hold, I wanted to die. I wanted him to let me go, to push me.

How the fuck did he even find me? How did he know where to go? I thought I had done a good enough job of disguising myself… even if he had been at the club, how did he know to follow me? And why didn't he stop me sooner?

Helpless, heartbroken sobs escaped from my chest.

"Just let me go, Brooke!" I begged, feeling the disorienting comfort of standing on this ledge to be far too much.

He doubled down, a hand dipping into his pocket to retrieve

his phone. There were a few seconds where his other arm's grip had lessened enough that I could have bolted... but I didn't. I began to worry that he would be phoning the police, and ambulance... the very last thing I would ever want. But after a few more seconds, he placed his phone on the top of the concrete barrier, turning the volume up all the way.

Familiar notes from a piano that I had heard hundreds of times before. Brooke pulled that free arm back around me, pressing his face into the crook of my neck as he acted as my anchor. Holding me strong and steadfast, gentle and yet so firm that I could understand his desperation in his silence. The song continued... the sound of Luka's voice singing the lyrics which I had danced around the diner to just a few days ago. The day I had given in to my feelings for Brooke.

More tears fell down my cheeks as the music swelled and the man behind me held tighter to me. I could feel his trembling arms as they held tight to my torso, soft sniffles emitting from where his face rested on my shoulder.

Beneath me, the cars beeped and sirens began to sound, but Brooke held me through every single second. His strength never once wavered.

I grit my teeth, allowing my head to fall forward as I finally gave into the reality that I was absolutely fucking terrified of throwing myself off of this bridge.

My hand tightened on the rough polyester of Brooke's costume sleeve, the other moving to grab the lip of the barrier between us. With a deep breath, I hooked a long leg over and Brooke stepped back, though his hands grasped firmly onto my biceps.

When I made full contact with both feet on solid ground, I crumpled.

My knees gave out beneath me, colliding hard with the tarmac.

Brooke sank to his knees in front of me, once again pulling me into the tightest hug he could manage.

One of his hands tangled into the hair at the back of my head, and he sank his face into my shoulder again. The music behind me continued; another song that I recognized. Another Scarlet Opera.

"F-fuck, El," Brooke whimpered, pulling his head back so that he could look at me, "I-I didn't recognize you… I heard the cars and I…" he bit down on his lip, "Jesus fucking Christ, don't you ever do this to me again!" He sniffled.

I stared at him, his panic was clear in the deep green of his eyes. A forest of concern. He was still wearing his mask, framed in those stunning brown curls of his.

My heart fluttered as he stared back at me with the worry of an adoring, doting partner.

Why did he fucking care about me so much?

He pulled the hand from my hair, pressing the palm to my cheek as he cleared away the sticky residue of my own tears. His teeth perched on the base of his bottom lip, but I cast my eyes away.

"Why didn't you let me jump?" I whispered softly.

Brooke frowned, his hand gripping at the base of my jaw to coax my eyes back to his face. "If you ever ask me a stupid question like that again, Ellis, I'll handcuff us together so you can't escape me even if you tried."

I lifted an eyebrow, my eyes locking onto his. Kindness. Care.

Fucksake… why was he so fucking fit?

My breathing calmed slowly, and I lifted my hands to my

231

face to steady myself. Brooke sat down, crossing his legs in front of himself as he kept one hand touching my body at all times.

After a few deep, resounding breaths, I felt the warmth from my buzz return to my stomach. My face tingled with soft euphoria, and I allowed a deep, heavy breath to fall from my lips.

"Where would you get them?" I muttered, my eyes cemented onto the tarmac. I became keenly aware that Brooke's car sat idling not far from where we currently sat, the amber hazard lights flashing brightly.

"What?" He asked.

"The handcuffs," I whispered, finally pulling my eyes back to meet his. "Where would you get them? The ones from Party City make me break out in hives."

His face shifted. A softness reached his eyes and the edges of his lips lifted as if he wanted to smile, but still felt the moment wasn't right.

Brooke chuckled, though the laugh was breathless. "Fucking hell, Ellis," He shook his head playfully, then leaned in to pull me into a gentle hug.

The song ended and another one began. This was another one of my performance songs as well. I tilted my head, bracing my hand against the small of his back. "Do you just have a playlist of all of my numbers?"

Brooke pulled away, but this time he allowed the smile to come. "And what if I did?"

"I'd say that it is cringe," I chuckled dryly.

He lifted an eyebrow, "You're telling me that you, Ellis, Flare Femme, don't want to be worshipped?"

"Do you worship me?" I asked softly, finally able to utilize my humour for the coping mechanism it had always been. I wanted him to laugh, to roll his eyes, but Brooke simply smiled and pushed himself to stand.

He collected his phone from the concrete railing where he had left it, then turned to me.

"Come on, you," He urged softy, extending a hand to me "Back to mine?"

Well… this was the only option with a somewhat positive outcome.

I took hold of his hand and pulled myself to stand. My knees were shaky and my vision blurred with the residual touch of alcohol. As I stood beside him, he turned the music off on his phone, and I could see the title of the playlist: *My Dolled Up Lunatic.*

His…

God, how I wanted to be his.

My heart fluttered, and a new kind of warmth spread through my cheeks. I don't know what the hell I have done in this world to deserve such a gentle guardian angel… but I hope that he stays this way.

He glanced over at me, smiling softly, "We will talk more at home… you just take the next little bit to breathe, okay?" Brooke reached across to cup my cheek. Without my heels, we were eye level with one another.

His touch was cool against the burning flesh of my cheek, and I allowed myself the vulnerability it took to press into that sensation, nodding softly in response to his command.

Brooke pulled away, guiding me back towards his car. As I sank into the tattered seat of the passenger side, my mind fell silent for the first time in nearly 48 hours.

The man in the shitty pirate costume beside me started

the car and began the drive to his house. It was short, sweet, and when Brooke got to a comfortable coasting speed, he reached his hand over to gently intertwine his fingers with my own acrylic-tipped digits. This offered a pleasant sense of normalcy that I wasn't really used to.

He maintained that gentle grasp of my hand, even as we pushed through the door to his duplex. As it shut behind us, Brooke kicked his boots off and released my hand, then turned to face me completely.

His eyes were soft, exhausted.

I anxiously rubbed the pit of my right elbow as I held his gaze, half expecting him to scold me... he didn't.

Instead, Brooke lifted his arms to hover around my hips. He placed his hands on the bony sides of my waist and pulled me against him, our foreheads pressed together. Those tired emerald eyes fluttered closed, and he breathed in slowly.

My own arms lifted to circle his neck. This was peaceful... far too peaceful.

This horrible voice inside of me began to list off all the ways this could go wrong. All the reasons Brooke was silent. All the things I have fucked up.

"You looked beautiful tonight," Brooke whispered, shattering the racing thoughts in my head.

I tilted my head, a motion which caused him to pull back his own. He opened his eyes, smiling softly.

"You looked beautiful, I like mini skirts," He grinned, reaching a hand to gently cup my cheek. His touch summoned goosebumps over my skin. "I've never seen you without makeup."

My cheeks dusted with a bright pink blush, eyes searching for elsewhere in the entryway to focus their attention on, but his gaze felt magnetic. I released my hold from his shoulders and allowed my hands to pull down the front of his blouse.

"I hate how I look without it," I whispered.

Brooke hummed, his thumb brushing across my skin lightly as he inspected my features. "Ellis," He said softly.

I turned my gaze back to him, the dip in his smile.

"May I kiss you?"

Fuck off.

Every time he asked me that fucking question, I could feel my heart melt. He knew I wanted him to kiss me. He knew I needed that touch… and yet he asked me. He made sure he wasn't overstepping his boundaries.

I softened in his arms and nodded.

"Please," I whispered, hardly perceptible.

In an instant, he had sealed our lips together.

I needed him. I needed Brooke so badly that his absence made the ache so much worse. I needed the way he looked at me, the tenderness of his touch. The relentless respect and assurance. I needed the worship without overbearingness, the lust within the love. I needed his arms holding me down, keeping me from stepping over the edge.

Fucksake, I needed Brooke.

I was falling for him. So fast and so hard… and that realization was the most terrifying thing I think I have ever experienced.

He pulled back, the sound of our kiss echoing lightly in the hallway.

"I am going to make dinner… go upstairs and have a shower. Use my things, you can wear my clothes if you want to," Brooke pressed a gentle kiss to my jawline, and I ached for his touch. "When you're finished, come back down here and we can watch a movie. Any movie."

Why did this make me want to cry?

I stiffened, anxiously fidgeting with my hands as I glanced up the stairs. My eyes drifted back to him… to be honest, I didn't want to be alone right now.

"Um…" I let my eyes fall to the ground, "Could you… sit in the bathroom with me?"

Brooke's eyes shifted, and he chuckled. "There aren't any monsters in the closet… I checked this morning," He smiled.

My eyes rolled and I pouted, this seemed to get the point across.

"I will, let me just throw some pizza in the oven?" He leaned in to press a kiss to my lips, then turned to walk to the kitchen.

A few minutes later, he returned to me, a hand extended in my direction which I took without hesitation. Brooke led me up the stairs and into his bedroom. It was mostly empty aside from the bed, definitely the space of a bachelor.

He looked me over. "Do you want anything to wear, or are you comfortable with what you've got?"

I glanced down at my hoodie and sweats, "I am fine in this, I think," I muttered.

Brooke nodded and stepped into his en suite, turning on the shower for me to allow it to warm up.

He then turned back to me, a soft blush on his face. "I'll let you get sorted," he said softly, stepping aside to allow me to enter the bathroom.

My heart fluttered in my chest as I removed my hoodie, laying it across his bed. My bare chest was exposed, revealing the scars and bruises from lashings and beatings I had earned over the past few years. They didn't really hurt anymore… except for the bruises.

"Do you want me to wait outside?" Brooke asked. A question which summoned a soft snort from me.

"You've literally had my dick in your mouth, Darling... I'm not sure prudishness is a thing we should be concerned with." I slipped my joggers and pants down around my ankles, stepping out of them without a shred of insecurity. My life is sex-work... so undressing in front of another man doesn't exactly faze me.

My eyes met with Brooke's, and I could see that blush had grown much deeper on his cheeks. He glanced away bashfully and I felt a smirk pull the edges of my lips.

"I won't blame you for staring. I do have one of the highest requested bodies in all of the Peach State," I teased, stepping closer with a shameless wave of my hips.

He chuckled, hands settling quickly on the bare skin of my waist to hold me in place. "You always scold me for staring at you," He hummed, leaning in to press a gentle kiss to my cheek.

I pouted, "I scold you, but that doesn't mean you should stop. You're the only person whose stare doesn't creep me out," I said succinctly, moving past him to enter the bathroom.

His absence was immediately obvious, and I tried not to show how much the dwindling of his gaze affected me... though it was great.

Brooke lingered by the door, back pressed to the door frame as he hummed softly.

"Brooke," I muttered, peering back at him from just outside of the shower cubicle.

He glanced my way, a wordless response.

"Will you... join me?"

Brooke paused for a moment, then turned his head to meet

my gaze. His eyes softened, falling swiftly over my naked body to take in my appearance, and he chuckled.

"Fine, but we have to be quick or else we will burn the pizza," He said softly, pulling himself free from the binds of his shitty party store costume.

His body was nice. Clear muscles that ran throughout his body. I could tell he had been a fighter for the majority of his life.

Brooke stepped closer to me, his curly hair falling around his face in ringlets that set my heart aflame. I pressed a hand to his chest, taking a moment to shamelessly stare at his body.

"Perv," He teased, pinching my chin lightly as he stepped into the water, thus pulling me beneath the stream alongside him.

The warmth sent a rush of comfort over my body, soothing aches that I had gone numb to. I shuddered and closed my eyes, releasing the clench of my jaw and the tightness in my shoulders.

Steam filled my lungs with an intoxicatingly sweet sensation of comfort, drawing me further and further from the waves of depression I had been feeling just an hour before.

When I finally opened my eyes, Brooke stood in the corner of the shower cubicle, his twinkling emerald eyes cut sweetly with his upper lashes as he took in my appearance. The rush that his gaze sent through me was unreal.

To a sex worker whose entire life was putting their body on display, the expression on his face pulsed a shy blush to my cheeks.

You would think that being stared at like I was the subject of someone's affections would be lost on me by now, but when it came to Brooke... I was experiencing sensations that felt new… dangerous.

Brooke made me want to change my entire life. If only I had met him six years ago… maybe I could have been the man he deserved.

The bashful dusting of pink on my cheeks faded as a throb of insignificance once more overtook my thoughts, pulling my eyelids to close. My head grew heavy under the weight of my own anxiety and lulled back, dousing my face in the overhead downpour.

"Damn," Brooke whispered softly, the wet percussion of his footstep echoing in the cubicle as he moved closer to me.

"You were doing well for so long," He says, gently pressing a hand to the skin of my chest.

I shuddered beneath his touch, adjusting my head slightly so that the water would cascade down the side of my neck rather than head-on.

His other hand braced against my shoulder and suddenly, he pulled me from under the water to press into his chest.

He smelled nice.

Brooke placed a gentle kiss to my temple, then pulled away, reaching behind himself to grab a bottle of soap and a folded cloth from a shelf. He doused the fabric with a dollop of soap and held it beneath the water until it began to foam. Then, he pressed the cloth to my skin, gently lathering the soapy cloth along my collarbones.

My heart fluttered in my chest, and I nibbled the back of my lip. Brooke pulled the cloth along the curves of my body, gentle and respectful… but so fucking arousing at the same time.

His actions were bizarre to me, truthfully. Who in their right mind would wordlessly scrub down a suicidal maniac?

He did these things that made no sense… and yet… I adored every odd action this man did.

As he finished with scrubbing my upper body, he crouched down, giving each of my legs a thorough pass of his cloth. He was diligent. Silent. Once he had finished, he returned to a standing position and placed the cloth in my hands.

"I figured you may want to do the more intimate areas yourself," He muttered, a soft smile on his face as he turned to grab a second cloth to wash himself.

I glanced down at the item in my hands, a flannel which Brooke had used to clean almost every inch of me, and yet he maintained my dignity by leaving my private areas alone. A blush encroached upon my cheeks, and I finished what he had started.

He poured soap onto his cloth and turned to steal the stream of his shower to wet the fabric. Finished with my job, I threw my flannel over my shoulder and reached forward to take his cloth from his hand. His eyes snapped to mine in a momentary confusion, but they softened as I held his gaze with a stubborn silence of my own.

With the wet cloth grasped in one hand, I stepped closer to Brooke. My free hand reached to situate the palm against the side of his neck, fingers wrapping in a gentle clasp along the back of his spine so that my acrylic nails nested gently against his skin.

Without a word, I completed the same routine that Brooke had done for me, down to the very last motion where I handed back over the cloth when I finished with his legs.

Brooke hooked a finger underneath my chin, pulling me to look at him. For a moment, we stood in silence. Every second passed through me like a rapture, my heart sounded loudly in my chest.

He leaned in closer until our foreheads touched.

"I think I fall for you more every time I see you," he whispered. I could taste his breath, the scent of a distant drink of Jameson burning in my senses. My knees weakened beneath me, but I stood still.

The hand which I had situated on his neck pulled him closer, and in an instant, I had sealed us together for a kiss.

My toes curled beneath me as I pressed back against Brooke, pushing him into the cold tile wall. The contact briefly pulled his lips from my own, but I swiftly returned the passion to him. My hand crawled slowly up the back of his neck to tangle into the mess of wet curls, gripping the strands as I kissed him hungrily.

His hands moved to hold tight to my hips, pulling my dripping, soapy body against his own as he returned the fervour in my present attack.

This only made me crave him even more.

Unfortunately, the distant sound of Brooke's timer sounding from the pocket of his abandoned trousers sliced the throes of our passion, and the man whom I had sealed against the wall pressed back against me with a strength that far outweighed my own.

He gently pushed me to the side, sending me a smug wink as he stepped from the shower and grabbed a towel from a holder on the wall. I watched, a pout present on my lips as he pulled the towel around his waist and sank to retrieve his phone.

In the blink of an eye, he had disappeared.

His absence sent a pang of grief through my body, and I sank back against the wall of the shower, moving a hand to shut off the water. Now, only the occasional sound of dripping water accompanied my racing heartbeat in the stark white, tiled room.

I dried my body with another towel, dressed myself, then slipped down the stairs with all of my anxiety returned to my system.

But the house smelled like pizza… and as I rounded the corner to the lounge, Brooke met me at the coffee table with a plate of hot food, a smile on his face. "You sit, I'll go sort myself out," He grinned, passing me a plate of pizza. He was still naked, dripping from our shower.

The plate felt warm in my hands, and I nodded as I sank into the soft embrace of his couch. Brooke disappeared up the stairs.

When he returned, he was dressed in a plain black t-shirt and a pair of matching black joggers. His hair was tied up into a bun. He sat down on the couch beside me, retrieving his own plate of food from the coffee table.

We shared the silence of this home as we ate our pizza, comfortable in the presence of one another. And when we had finished, Brooke didn't demand my words, he simply stacked the plates, took them to wash, then returned to the couch beside me where he lifted an arm to beckon me close.

I obliged, laying my head against his chest as his extended arm fell around my shoulders. He held me close to him, and for this moment, all of my worries seemed to fade.

The fatigue from the events of the past few days pulled at my eyelids, and I nuzzled into the crook of this fucking crazy man.

"Are you feeling any better?" Brooke's soft, soothing voice asked.

The answer to this question escaped me in this present moment. Was I feeling any better? I turned my head slightly to glance up at him, allowing a hand to press into the warmth of his chest as my sullen brown eyes met his green orbs. "I am going to be honest, Darling…" I muttered, my fingers grasping gently at the fabric of his shirt. "I feel okay right now… but I still have to face the world outside of this safety."

His eyes softened considerably, and he shifted so that his legs moved onto the couch. With a simple tug, he pulled me onto his lap. My legs fell over each side of his hips and I pressed both hands flat to his chest. The slow rise and fall of his chest was soothing.

"Ellis," Brooke muttered, a hand rubbing gentle circles into the small of my back. I lifted my eyes to meet his. God, I fucking loved his eyes… "Could you tell me more about why you have signed a contract with this demon of a human?"

My stomach lurched, sloshing the digesting pizza in an uneasy squeeze. I looked away and sighed.

"I killed someone."

The Plan

BROOKE

"You killed someone?" I asked.

A breathless question that didn't even feel real when I asked.

Ellis had sunk back on my thighs, and every second, I felt him drifting further from me. He turned his gaze away from my own, but I reached to gently grab hold of his hand.

He seemed to hesitate, but he allowed this touch.

"He was a massive dick... which... I know isn't an excuse for my behaviour," Ellis muttered, "He wanted to have sex one night... most nights really, but this night was significant." He pulled completely away this time, moving to sit at the end of the couch. "This guy had a thing with auto-erotic asphyxiation... the belt tightened too much, so he suffocated."

245

There was an energy that surrounded him that I had never felt before. A darkness which consumed him.

Ellis was like a black hole, pulling in the energy of everything around him in order to sustain his own existence. I think he feared that being too close to me may pull me into his negativity as well.

I hooked my legs to my side, rubbing my shin lightly. "That isn't your fault, El," I offered, but he shook his head.

"I think I wanted him to die, really..." The slender man said softly. His brown orbs sealed upon the coffee table in front of him. He pulled his hands into his lap to anxiously fidget. "I noticed that he was struggling, but I pushed it to the back of my mind, hoping that he would just figure it out himself... The most fucked up thing is that... he actually fucking came..." Ellis began to tremble, and his eyes flashed with painful, haunting memories that I couldn't even begin to imagine. "I ha-had a dead man's cum on my fucking face," He trembled, tears gathering in his eyes.

Fuck.

This handsome, charismatic, talented man before me was completely and totally traumatized. Here I was, lamenting about things that were well within my control to change. He was trapped in his mind with all of these terrible fucking memories, and all he could do was grin and bear it.

"I-I was on the Most Wanted scene... because that bastard trapped me into a marriage I couldn't escape. I was going to be put in prison," His breath hitched, hands reaching to grip onto his black hair as he began to breathe faster. "Drugs... so many drugs. They blamed me for it all, I was going down for murder and..." Tears cascaded down his face as his eyes widened in a manic stare into the distance, "Lorenzo... made it all go away. He saved me…"

My heart shattered.

That is why he served this fucking psychopath blindly, no contest.

I moved to sit closer to him, a hand resting on the fabric of his sweatpants as I pressed into the flesh of his leg. He seemed to tremble beneath my touch, but I looped my other arm around his neck, pulling him against my chest.

"Seems like we are both pretty shit about picking who we marry, hm?" I muttered, pressing a kiss into his damp hair.

He broke down into helpless sobs in my chest, clutching at my shirt as he did. My chest ached from sympathy as I held him. This man who had taught me more about myself than I ever knew… I had never cared for someone as much as I cared for Ellis, and all I fucking wanted was to have the power to bring this pain to a stop.

My eyes flickered to the door of my TV stand's cabinet, and all I wanted to do was save him…

"How much do you think it would take for him to relinquish your contract?" I asked softly, eyes seared into the soft wood of the unit.

Ellis sniffled, shaking his head. "I-I don't know," He said helplessly, his fingers gripped tight to the fabric of my top, "I th-think he wants to work me until the day that I die."

That wasn't a fucking option.

No way in hell was I going to let that be a fucking option.

I pulled in a soft breath through my nose and allowed my eyes to flutter shut. This frustration and annoyance burned within me, and I was ready for everything to be over.

The sound of a subtle buzzing triggered a genuine leap of fear from Ellis as he helplessly glared at his phone where it sat.

It took all of my self-control to keep myself from silencing the device, but Ellis steadied himself and grabbed his phone with a shaky hand.

He stared down at the screen for a moment, as if he wasn't quite expecting the name that he read, then swiped to answer it.

"Hello?" He asked, his voice full of the rasp he had achieved from his tears. Ellis pressed himself into my chest, reaching up to mindlessly fidget with my curls as he listened.

Something in his posture relaxed, and a feminine tone pulled through the line. I couldn't quite make out the words they said but it soothed Ellis tremendously.

"No, no… I'm okay Ginge," Ellis muttered, "I-it is really nice to hear your voice."

I ran my hand along his thigh, gently smoothing the fabric of his sweatpants.

He stiffened. Something she had said tightened the bones in his spine and hitched his breath.

"I know you are just trying to do what you can for me… but…" He pulled away from me, placing his head in his hands, "I just can't keep doing this."

That calm from before was washing away from him quickly, and I could feel his light draining rapidly again.

Ellis sank into his hands, nodding slowly along with the person on the phone.

"I know, I understand…" he muttered, "Thank you, Ginge. I'll keep that in mind… love you too, ya minge muncher," He said softly, then hung up the phone.

His shoulders eased as he allowed the phone to fall from his face, resting it on the coffee table before pulling both hands to cover his face, hunched over.

I rested a hand on the small of his back, feeling the arch in his spine.

"Everything okay?" I asked softly.

For a moment, he didn't speak. He stayed hunched, face in his hands, wordless. I permitted the silence, my hand maintaining that ever present contact with his spine.

"That was my friend Ginger," He said in the softest tone, reminiscent of Flare. "She is a Drag Queen that worked with me at the Raven… but she left recently. Keeps trying to get me to come with her as a leading act." The promise in his words was bright, but his tone and my knowledge of his circumstances sliced the hope in that prospect in half. "She is going back to England… wants me to try and run away, disappear back to London."

I nibbled my bottom lip, "Is that what you want to do?" I asked softly.

Ellis sighed, hands falling as he turned to face me. His beautiful face was haggard with exhaustion and pain. Those hypnotic brown irises gazed at me with a longing that told me everything I needed to know.

He did… he wanted that more than anything.

To disappear… to be free of this megalomaniac.

My own gaze shot to the TV unit, holding them there for a moment before I returned to him.

"Do you trust me?" I asked softly.

He lifted one of his manicured eyebrows, tilting his head to the side. "Why?"

My own eyes narrowed, and I reached to cup his cheek, "I have a plan… but I need you to trust me," I explained.

The confusion on his face deepened and he pressed into my touch. "I… I guess?" He muttered softly, blinking slowly.

249

I smiled, pushing myself forward so that I was on the edge of the couch with him, pulling both of his hands into my lap and pressing my forehead against his.

"I'm going to make this happen for you," I muttered softly.

"Huh?" Ellis pulled away from me, tilting his head to the side, "What do you mean you're going to *make this happen*?" He asked in warranted confusion.

A chuckle rolled off my chest as I shook my head, "You said it yourself that the only way to escape Lorenzo is to die," I said softly… which didn't exactly seem to calm his anxieties.

"Listen, Brooke… If you're planning on killing me, maybe you should have just let me do it myself…" He interjected, great offence on his face.

I leaned forward, pulling him closer so that I could silence him with a kiss. When I pulled away, I rubbed my nose against his. "I need you to listen to me before you start going sassy, okay?" I teased.

He straightened, the lull of his eyes demonstrating a stray from the constant barrage of his low mood.

"What if Lorenzo… *thought* that you were dead?" I asked.

Ellis nibbled his bottom lip, his eyes flickering down to his hands in my lap as he slowly nodded, "I… I don't think I ever really thought about that," He muttered softly.

I hooked a finger under his chin, "So… what if we were to fake your death… then disappear to London?"

The soul seemed to return to his eyes, and he continued to anxiously nibble at his cheek. "Brooke… you need a visa… it takes time, and neither of us has the money to move an entire household across an ocean," He muttered.

"Well, I can take care of everything for Rae and me… all you need to do is give me time to sort everything," I said softly, resting my palms against his thighs. "You'll have to hold on for me... for a few months... I know it is hard and it will suck, but-"

"Yes," He said.

"Yes?"

"Yes... I want to do this, Brooke," Ellis muttered, his eyes sparkling, "I... I can cope... for a few months," he murmured softly, but his entire demeanour shifted. Excitement buzzed in his eyes, and he threw his arms around my neck, locking me into a deep, passionate kiss.

My heart raced, nothing set me off more than when Ellis initiated intimacy. I looped an arm around his waist, sinking forward into his embrace.

He was far more proficient in these acts than I was. It was obvious by my sloppy attempts to keep up with his kiss. This didn't seem to bother him, though, as he pulled his arms from around my neck to press those manicured fingers to my chest.

I reached my free hand up to gently cup his cheek, pressing back to separate our lips.

Ellis opened his eyes, an instant blush coating his pale cheeks as he searched my face for reasoning.

Why had I stopped him?

"Ellis," I whispered, pulling my thumb over the skin where a soft shimmer usually lived.

He stared at me, clear anxiety displaying with a soft chew of his lip, sloping eyes which begged me to speak.

I lifted my hand from its gentle hold on his face to brush through his hair. My own eyes fluttered with an unspoken buzz of nerves.

"Will you stay the night?" I asked softly.

His eyes flickered briefly with a million silent thoughts.

He sank back to sit on the couch, resting back into the soft cushion. The black fluff of hair atop his head smoothed as it pressed against the seat and his eyes fluttered closed.

This silence filled me with worry, and I looked away. Was this too forward?

"I haven't slept in another person's bed without expectation in years, Brooke," he muttered, finally.

I shook my head softly, "No, El. No expectations. No obligations," I pressed a hand to his knee. "I will sleep down here if you'd prefer... I just...don't want to send you home in a taxi tonight."

When I managed to return my gaze to his, his eyes were open. The pull of their magnetism drew me in. Ellis absolutely was a black hole... and he was pulling me into him at light speed. Every fucking cell in my body burned with the desire to be completely and totally consumed by him.

It was crazy to me, I had never even looked at another man before, but I couldn't stop myself from staring at Ellis and wanting to understand him, pure and whole.

He lifted a hand from where they had retreated to in his lap, placing it on his neck in a bashful pull.

"I don't want you to sleep downstairs," he admitted softly, his eyes soldering onto mine with an intensity that halted the beating of my heart.

Fuck...

If this is what it feels like to be seen... to be wanted... I never want him to break this stare.

Every brick in the walls that Ellis had built up to shield himself from me crumbled to dust before me, and I had never felt a stronger connection to anyone.

I adjusted myself, sinking closer to him on the sofa. My hand reached to retrieve the hand which had rested on his neck, intertwining our fingers and leaning in to gently press a kiss to the skin which had been concealed by that hand.

His eyes fluttered closed, and his teeth pinched his bottom lip. A soft squeeze resounded from his hand, and I smiled.

"You know, Brooke…" Ellis whispered, opening his eyes to search for me. They narrowed in a mischievous glare, "if you'd said half of this shit to a woman, you wouldn't be so unlucky." His lips parted to send me a sneaky grin.

A chuckle left my lips, and I lifted an eyebrow, "Well, Ellis… I don't consider myself the least bit unlucky that I get to say these things to you," I sank to that soft skin on his neck again, placing a gentle nibble on his skin.

He silenced, but his eyes sparkled with something that I recognized. He was flustered.

I smirked and gently pulled my hand across his thigh.

"Are you going to work tomorrow?" I asked softly.

Ellis softened, but his eyes saddened, "I lost my apron… and my badge," he muttered.

I chuckled, pulling away from him. The panic was etched into his expression, but I winked and slipped into the kitchen, where I had placed his belongings the night before.

His eyes widened as I returned. "What? How did you find them?" He asked, standing up to approach with his hands outstretched to take the items from me.

"When you left… I waited," I said softly, "I hoped you'd come back, but when you didn't… I locked up the front door and left through the back. Found these on the ground…"

He bit down on his lip, "you've washed the apron," he muttered.

I nodded softly, a blush spreading across my cheeks, "That night was stressful enough... I figured-"

"Thank you," he interrupted me. "Nobody has ever done something so thoughtful for me before."

A laugh lifted from my lungs, and I shook my head, "it is just an apron, El," I said softly.

He shook his head, "That diner is the only thing that keeps me afloat, Brooke... I don't get paid for my work with Lorenzo, so if I had fucked up with the diner, I would have been homeless within a week."

I softened my gaze, shaking my head, "I'd never let you sleep without a roof over your head, dude."

His eyebrow lifted, and he tilted his head. "That's an interesting term of endearment," he teased, immediately slicing the romance of the moment with his comic relief ... he did that when he felt vulnerable.

My lips pulled into a smirk and, and I shook my head softly, "I mean, you call me mate," I offered.

"Well... I also call you Darling!" He pouted.

"You call EVERYONE *Darling*," I chuckled.

Ellis frowned, pulling his uniform against his chest as he stiffened his shoulders. His eyes narrowed as he thought for a moment about what he was going to say.

"I like when you call me El," he said softly, his voice dipping back into that range of insecurity.

I smiled softly, reaching to grab the hood of his hoodie and pulling it over his hair. Then, I grabbed the drawstrings for the hood.

"I'll call you something different anytime I see you, you tell me when you like the name," I grinned, then pulled the strings, cinching his hood so that his face was concealed.

thumb along his lip, where the pink ceased in a sudden line. The aching in my chest subsided, replaced by hunger.

Ellis fluttered his eyelashes, but something in the glittering brown orbs, which I found myself transfixed upon, seemed uncertain.

A soft dust of pink coated his cheeks, and his gaze wavered. It seemed that his reaction was due to discomfort…

My hand fell from his face to rest as my side, and I stepped back warily.

"N-no," he muttered, taking his own steps to bring me closer. "Sorry… it's just…" Ellis looked away, clutching the apron in his hand against his chest. "You make me want to…"

My head fell to the side in a silent confusion, and I studied him like I had found myself doing for months now.

Ellis's free hand reached forward to clutch mine, and his eyes found their place resting on the hands which bound us. "I used to hate being stared at my anyone," he muttered softly, "but when you stare at me… it feels like my skin is on fire."

Guilt washed over me, and I allowed my own eyes to fall.

"I'm sorry," I whispered.

He squeezed my hand, "no, Darling…" when he called me this, I felt my own skin surge with a wash of goosebumps. He did call everyone Darling… and yet, when he said it to me, the whole word felt different. It felt personal.

"I… don't know how to be a good partner," Ellis admitted, a genuine sadness painting his tone, "I have… never felt like this before, Brooke… and it would be an absolute lie to sit here and say that I will always do the right things."

"Ellis,-" I tried to speak, but he sent a silencing squeeze to my hand.

"Please, let me speak," he said through a trembling tone as

he closed his eyes tight and steadied himself. His shoulders rolled back to tighten, and he leaned his head back so that he faced the ceiling above.

I held my gaze on him, watching as he bit down on his bottom lip. His brown curls, still damp from our shower, clung to his scalp.

"I am not a good person… or a truthful person. I am vain and I am nasty… sometimes I'm an absolute cunt," his eyelids pulled open and he lowered his chin so that he could lock eyes with me. "I'm an alcoholic… a drug addict… and a fucking diva that can't control his mouth." He released his grip on my hand, but only so he could move to place his apron on the coffee table.

Once he stood straight once more, he lifted both hands to rest on either side of his neck.

"I want to be better, Brooke. I want to try to be what you need… but… if you ever feel like you're falling out of love with me… please tell me," He asked softly.

I nibbled the back of my lip as his words sank into my mind. Ellis was every single bit of the man that he was when I first met him… and to see him so raw and emotional… that was fucking beautiful.

My lips pulled into the softest, most understanding of smiles. "Is that what this is?" I asked in a whisper.

His eyes twinkled in confusion, head tilting to the side. "Is… is it what?"

"Love?" I muttered, closing the distance between us to wrap my arms around his waist. "You said… if I ever fall out of love with you…"

A blush darkened on his face, and though he seemed uncertain, he sank into my arms.

"I…" he struggled, "I don't know, Brooke… I've never been in love."

My arms tightened around him, sealing him securely in place against my hips as I placed a line of gentle kisses along his jaw.

"I think I might love you, Ellis," I whispered to him as my kisses reached his ear.

This boisterous, headstrong man fell completely silent as he became the one who stared… and I understood what he meant now. Because as I looked into his eyes, my skin set alight with the flame of his attention.

I allowed my hands to slip from his waist, gently caressing the fabric which concealed his ass from my touch. Every inch of my body craved him… and yet, I could still sense this intense push from him.

He was still holding me at bay, his energy serving as a barrier between us.

Exhaustion had darkened the bags beneath his eyes, and I felt my own sleepiness pulling me in. I leaned in to press my forehead to his.

"We've both had long days, El," I said softly. "Should we go to bed?"

He blinked a few times as a relived expression washed over his face. He pulled away with a slow nod. "That would be nice," he said softly.

"Would you like me to sleep down here?" I asked.

Ellis scrunched his nose, "Um… no?"

I lifted an eyebrow, "Ellis, you have to tell me what you want… not what you think I want," I said softly.

He frowns, "I want you to sleep with me," he said. That nasally tone hinting within his thickening accent… I loved how he sounded when he was annoyed. Almost made me want to piss him off even more.

A smirk lifted my lips, and I nodded, "lead the way, then," I hummed. "You know where to go."

Ellis lifted an eyebrow and crossed his arms, a cement of stubbornness welding him to the floor. "You first."

I laughed, shaking my head lightly. "You confuse me, babe," I said softly.

His face instantly snapped to one of shock, and he blushed, a dark red colour which spread to his ears.

He liked that.

This ammunition that he has supplied me with fuelled my own mischief, and I simply turned away from him.

Ellis reached forward to grab the cuff of my sleeve, pulling me back to a slow stop. He blushed, allowing that hand to slip down my arm until it reached my hand. He intertwined our fingers and bashfully stepped behind me.

Pleased, I sent a gentle squeeze to his hand and led him up the stairs to my bedroom, where my party store costume still lay across the floor. I plugged my phone into its charger and climbed into the bed, turning to beckon him in as well.

For a moment, he blushed, then turned to the door, closing it softly behind himself as he flipped off the light. The mattress dipped as Ellis climbed onto it, searching the darkness for me as he crawled under the blanket.

The darkness brought a new sensation. I couldn't see him, so as he rested his head on the pillow at my side, I didn't even register how far from me he was at first.

My hand crawled across the mattress to search for his, eventually intertwining our fingers. His breathing was all I could hear.

"Babe," I muttered softly into the darkness.

There was a moment of silence, then I heard him shuffle. "Yes Darling?" He asked in a whisper.

I ran my thumb over his knuckles, closing my eyes, "will you come closer?"

Ellis didn't respond for a moment, but then he slowly inched towards me. I lifted an arm to hook under his neck, and his face nestled into my shoulder. His free hand pressed to my chest.

Comfort is the only way I can describe the sensation of holding him like this... and as I slipped into a deep sleep, comfort was the only thing that mattered.

Ask For Callum?

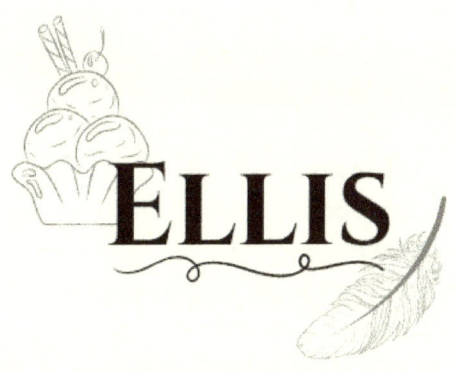

ELLIS

Five Months Later

A gust of warm air descended upon my head as I sat back in the salon chair. My friend and stylist, Magnolia, danced sweetly around my chair in her neon pink pumps and matching jumpsuit.

"I think this suits you, Flare!" She sang as she switched off the blow drier, storing it in a nest along the side of her table.

I glanced at her in the large mirror before us. Mags stood at the back of my chair, her ebony skin showing a stark contrast to my obvious Irish heritage. A new feature now bleaching my skin even further. I had decided to dye my hair bright blonde.

Mags grinned, wrapping her long arms around my neck as she placed her chin in my hair.

"Thank you, Mags," I said softly, looking myself over in the mirror.

Blonde was my natural hair colour. A fact that I tried my absolute best to run from… but things were changing. I'm not sure whether they were changing for the better, or not… but they were changing.

Mags's lips lifted in a teasing smile. "You're never usually so quiet, babes. What's on your mind?" She pulled her slender fingers over my shoulders to remove the black cape from around my neck to reveal my maroon-coloured uniform.

Deliberation tingled in my fingertips, and I nibbled at my bottom lip. She held my eye contact in the mirror, her brown eyes outlined in a pretty, sparkly pink liner.

Finally, I relented, exhaling in a long and excited breath. "My partner's visa has cleared… and he got the job he wanted!" I sang sweetly, clasping my hands together in front of myself.

Her smile brightened, and she squealed. "Oh my god! That is amazing!" She cheered, plucking her long acrylics through my hair to fluff up the blonde ends.

My phone buzzed in my pocket, an alarm that I had set to ensure that I would leave the salon in time to get back to the diner for the second half of my shift. Something that I didn't exactly want to miss, especially because Brooke would be stopping by for his lunch break.

I removed my phone, glancing down at the lock screen; an image of me laying on the couch with Brooke. Rae was asleep on my chest between us. My face lifted into a content smile, and I pushed myself to stand.

"Thanks for fitting me in today, Mags. I really appreciate

it… the black was giving Greaser," I grinned, skipping towards the front computer so that I could pay her for her service.

She rang me up, and I added quite a generous tip… her eyes brightened as she saw the extra zero at the end of my usual ten-dollar tip.

"Flare, what the hell are you doing?" She said in a sharp, hushed tone, "You know as well as I do that you can't be giving out money like this…"

I lifted a hand with a smile and rolled my eyes, "Magnolia, Darling, I have to go, but we will definitely continue this chopsing the next time I see you!" I sang happily as I slipped out the salon's front door and skipped towards Broadway Diner.

The diner had served me quite well over the past few months. I had been promoted to the Assistant Manager, just beneath Shelley on the totem pole. We had a few new staff members, which meant that I had a bit more free time… which meant that I got to see Brooke more between my shifts at the Midnight Raven.

The busy streets of Atlanta felt a lot brighter recently… and my fleeting thoughts of ending my life were dissolving.

As I approached the diner, I felt a buzz in my pocket. A phone call. Assuming this would be Brooke, I swiped without looking and pulled the phone to my ear.

"Hey!" I called into the speaker, nearing the door. The sun shone bright and the energy of the day was so warm.

"You sound bright," Lorenzo's voice pulled over the speaker.

I had extended my arm to grab the door, but upon hearing his voice, I froze dead in my tracks. "L-Lorenzo," I muttered under my breath, turning on my heels to face away from the diner.

A soft, menacing chuckle pulled through the line. "You're about to go in to work, aren't you?" he asked in a knowing tone. He already knew the answer to this question.

"Um, Yes," I said, rubbing my neck anxiously as I looked around. The brightness that had surrounded me suddenly felt quite dull.

A hum pulled through the line, and he chuckles. "You finish at six?"

My eyes narrowed, and I pressed my back to the glass of the diner behind me. "Yes."

"Perfect," He hummed, "I need you to come in. If you can get here for seven, that would be lovely."

I frowned and stared into the concrete beneath my feet. Annoyance stitched a thread between my eyebrows, and I sighed. "Okay, I have to go now," I said, then hung the phone up without warning.

My heart fluttered in temporary annoyance as I rolled my eyes and spun around on my heels to enter the diner.

The dining room was full, quite busy, so I slipped through to the kitchen and pulled my apron and badge on, clocked in, and got straight to work.

The new guy, a younger man named Callum, was working his magic on customers. He was really good... at least at the actual customer part.

In the window of the kitchen, a plate of fries was sat under the heat lamp going dry. I scrunched my nose as I glanced through the window to Aaron at the stove.

"What table is this for?" I asked.

"Don't know, Ellis. Callum rang it in twenty minutes ago and never took it." Aaron called back, wiping his brow with

266

a black and white chequered flannel before turning back to the stove.

I grumbled, turning to see Callum coming in through the swinging doors of the kitchen. He grinned at me.

"I like the blonde!" He said in a sickeningly sweet voice.

A chuckle left my chest as I adjusted the metallic gold badge on my chest. "Thank you, Cal," I said softly, then motioned to the plate. "Which table is going to complain that their fries have gone rank?"

His blue eyes flickered to the plate, and he chuckled, "Actually, those are mine," He said with a grin, "Been starving!"

I glanced out to the dining room through a porthole window in the door. "Okay, mate. Just make sure you aren't letting the actual guests' food die in the window. I can't comp tables every shift." I said as I slipped out the door to greet a few tables.

Throughout the afternoon, I kept an eye on the clock. Brooke usually went on his lunch break around one in the afternoon. He would come in and sit for half an hour at the bar with a BLT and a glass of coke.

It was currently 1:15, and Brooke hadn't come in yet.

I won't lie, I was a bit bummed. Seeing Brooke was the highlight of my day. One of the only things that would get me through these busy rush shifts.

"Thank you for dining with us, next time you're in… Ask for Callum!" That saccharine voice of this new server cut through the busy diner like a knife.

The guests at the table in front of me stopped mid-statement to turn their attention to the other man a few tables down. My own attention snapped to him as well.

I tilted my head as he grinned in my direction, then skipped towards the kitchen.

"That was kinda weird," One of the guests said. Most of the diners here were regulars, and all of my regulars knew my line.

The pad in my hands crinkled beneath my grip as I shrugged, "He's learning," I chuckled as I scribbled down their orders from memory. "I'll have your drinks out in a second!" I sang sweetly. "If you need anything-"

"Ask for Ellis!" The dining room recited in chorus.

Some semblance of peace rolled over my shoulders, and I made my way towards the kitchen.

"Ellis!" One of the other patrons called from a corner seat.

I smiled and sauntered over, "Hello! What can I do for you?" I asked brightly.

The woman blushed softly, "Actually... I have already ordered. Callum hasn't brought my food out yet, and I really have to go soon or else I'll be late coming back from my lunch break."

"Oh!" I stood straight, "Don't you worry your little cotton socks," I sang as I placed the notepad into the front of my apron. "Is it the french toast and egg scramble? I'll have Aaron make it now and we will box it up for you."

She nodded with a soft smile, "That's it! That would be lovely, thank you!"

I nodded happily, "Legend, I'll be back in a minute!" I turned on my heels to enter the kitchen.

As I did so, I saw Callum sat on the silver prep surface of the kitchen window, stuffing his face with the dried-out french-fries from before. I sighed.

"Cal, you're missing tables again. You can't seriously be back here eating. I'll take care of your corner table. Can you at least go out front and do something productive?"

The young man scrunched his nose, rolling his eyes as he placed the fries back on the plate. He wiped his greasy fingers on his apron and shoved by me to return to the dining room.

An annoyed sigh fell off my shoulders, "Sorry, Aaron. Could you throw together a french toast scramble to-go for me?" I shouted over the noise of the kitchen as I started to fill up the soft drinks for my newest table.

"Damnit, Ellis," Aaron shouted back, tossing a spatula into the dish-washing sink, "Get that kid together. I'm tired of him messing up orders."

I rolled my eyes, "You and me both, bud."

Tray of drinks now fully prepped, I pulled the tray onto the flat surface of my palm and pushed the door open. The instant I stepped through the doors, Callum spun around, knocking straight into me.

The red plastic cups spilled, some leaping from the tray to clatter messily onto the tile beneath me. I was absolutely soaked through with water and Coca-Cola... the citrusy smell of lemon slices adding a surprisingly sweet scent to what I was going to be wearing for the foreseeable future.

Every single ounce of annoyance that bubbled in me wiped the superficial smile from my face, and I narrowed my eyes into an angry glare.

"Callum," I growled in the deepest voice that I had been able to muster for most of my adult gay life.

He looked at me with an anxious expression, "I'm so sorry Ellis!" He said... but it sounded so fake. I knew what fake sounded like... and this was fucking fake.

I pulled a deep breath in through my nose, steadying myself as I didn't want to kick off in the cafe. After a few seconds, I placed the tray with the surviving glass of ice water on the bartop, stooping to clean up the carnage of our collision.

Callum stepped over me to return once more to the kitchen and I stared down at the floor in annoyance.

The bell from the front door sounded, and my eyes snapped up, "Welcome in! Please be careful as we've just had a spill!" I said, then registered that the man who had entered was none other than Brooke.

Some semblance of relief washed over me, and I smiled.

"Hey, stranger!" I chirped, standing with the fallen glasses. "Sit in your usual spot, I'll get your stuff sorted." I hummed.

Callum exited the kitchen with a new tray of drinks, and my annoyance faltered slightly as he took the drinks to my table.

Maybe he wasn't so bad.

I returned to the kitchen and grabbed a glass of coke and the to-go box for Callum's other table before once again coming out of the back. I took the boxed food to the woman from before and apologized for her wait.

When I turned to greet Brooke, I noticed that Callum was already speaking to him. I lifted an eyebrow and looked at him with a confused expression.

"I've got him, Cal. You sort your tables out, please," I said softly, Brooke's drink clutched in my hand. My uniform was still soaked from our collision, but I was pushing it to the back of my mind.

Callum ignored me, continuing to speak with Brooke... he reached a hand up to fidget flirtingly with his brown hair.

My eyes narrowed in a lack of amusement as Callum rolled onto his tip-toes and leaned on the edge of Brooke's table.

"Callum." I snapped. My voice dropped to a less-than-enthused tone as Cal whipped his head around to look at me.

Well and truly done with his bullshit today, I placed a hand on my hip. "I told you I've got him. Please do something productive."

"I am being productive, Ellis. I'm literally serving a guest!" Callum fired back, crossing his arms in front of himself.

Brooke glanced between us, clearly recognizing the tension.

"I told you I've got him, Cal," I reasserted.

"Fuck off, Ellis!"

The cafe went silent.

Rage bubbled in my blood as I felt purely sick to my stomach. The sensation of my saturated shirt as it stuck to my skin added to the ticking time bomb that was my very short fuse. I stepped closer to the table, setting Brooke's drink on the table and slipping it towards him.

I dipped down, pressing a hand between Callum's on the table as I hooked my index finger under Brooke's chin and angled his face upwards. I sank closer to him, shoulder brushing against Callum's chest as I leaned in to press a kiss to Brooke's lips.

My ego flooded as Brooke sank into my kiss, and I pulled back to release him from my grasp.

"Sorry, Darling," I said in a hushed tone, my eyes narrowed from frustration. "I guess I'll see you after work." I pulled back, then walked back towards the kitchen. My shoulder knocked against Callum's as I shoved the doors open and disappeared behind their swing.

I grabbed my bag from the staff locker area and rummaged through it to find my pack of cigarettes, then threw my apron on the prep table. Turned to walk out the back door, pressing my back to the bricks as I lit the end of the cig.

A few minutes passed where I stood there, trying to regulate myself.

If we were in England, I would have knocked Callum clean out when he spoke to me like that... but here, things are different... and I couldn't risk our plan going tits up because I couldn't control my temper.

"Thought you were trying to quit," Brooke hummed as he rounded the corner with a grin on his face.

I glanced over at him, taking in the look of him.

His long hair was tied up into a loose and messy bun, and he had grown a bit of a beard. He stalked towards me with his hands in the pockets of his dark-wash denim jeans.

A sigh rolled off my chest with a fresh exhale of smoke, and I shook my head. "I haven't had one all day," I said softly.

"Ah, deserved, then." He hummed, stopping right in front of me.

I chuckled and dropped the remaining bud onto the floor, crushing it with the toe of my non-slip kitchen shoes.

Brooke smiled and looped an arm around my shoulder, pulling me against him for a soft hug. I obliged this embrace, but the second I pressed into him, he recoiled.

"You're soaked," He chuckled, looking me over.

I grumbled, nodding softly. "Fucking dickhead knocked a tray full of drinks over me."

Brooke chuckled, hooking a finger under my chin to summon me forth for a kiss.

Once more, I obliged.

As he pulled away, he smiled softly. "Sorry I was late," he said, "I can't stay too long today. Brian and Jilly are throwing me a surprise party that I'm not supposed to know about."

I laughed softly, leaning back against the brickwork of the building. "Oh? You told them about your visa?" I asked.

He lifted an eyebrow, "I can't tell if you're serious or not," He said softly.

Confusion wrecked my brain as I tilted my head, "What are you on about?"

Brooke chuckled, stepping back a pace as he rubbed his neck, "Um... it's my birthday," He said softly.

My eyes widened and I felt the colour drain from my face. "It isn't..."

"It is," He said with another wry chuckle. "Do you not remember? We have reservations for tonight..."

The thrum of my heart stopped suddenly and I pressed back against the bricks. "W-what time?" I asked softly.

Brooke's face fell further, "Seven thirty,"

Fucksake.

My eyes saddened instantly, and Brooke seemed to understand without a word being exchanged. He lifted his hand to rub his neck.

"Ah... I can see if I can push them back to later?" He offered, but the annoyance of the day had already drained me so much.

My attention wavered, falling to my feet as everything positive that had started this day seemed to disappear into the ether. A weight of guilt pressed heavily on my shoulders.

"I'm so sorry, Brooke," I muttered sadly. That insecurity bubbled in the front of my mind.

He reached to gently cup my cheek, pulling my face to meet his eyes. "Hey... it's okay. We knew this might happen, anyways," he said softly, pressing a quick kiss to my lips. "I'll come back with Rae after work to see you before you go off, yeah? That way she can see you before she goes to bed."

I lifted my eyes to meet his and nodded softly, "I'd really like that," I muttered.

A smile returned to his face, and he nodded, "I love the blonde, by the way," he said as he pressed a kiss to my cheek. "Suits you."

My heart fluttered, and my eyes fell once more. "Today was going to be a really good day," I muttered sadly. "Now I'm soaked… I forgot your birthday… I've got a cracking headache… and the trainee is doing my fucking nut in."

Brooke chuckled, pressing a hand to my chest to seal my back against the wall. He leaned in to kiss me with a bit more vigour this time, pulling back after a few seconds.

"I said, I love the blonde. It suits you," he repeated softly.

A blush graced my cheeks, and I felt the corners of my lips lift, "Thank you, Darling," I said softly.

He smiled, then pulled off his sweater to reveal a plan black T-shirt underneath. Brooke passed me his sweater, "put this on or you'll freeze out here. I'm amazed you've lasted this long in that shirt."

I smiled softly and took the article of clothing into my hands, peeling off the wet maroon shirt and replacing it with Brooke's grey, knit jumper. It was warm… and it smelled like his cologne. Probably the one good thing that had happened since I left Mags earlier in the day.

"No more smoking," he scolded sweetly, then wrapped his arms around me for a final hug. "I've got to go, babe," he whispered into the embrace.

My arms wrapped around him to send a final squeeze his way as I nodded softly, "okay Darling," I muttered softly, "come see me later. Bring my princess as well," I whispered.

As Brooke pulled away, I felt my heart quicken in my chest. He always managed to make me feel better.

"Can you take care of my tab? I'll pay you back tonight," he asked sweetly.

I scowled "it's on me. I am the one who threw a tantrum and walked out the back," I said softly.

He laughed, and my heart skipped a beat.

Fucksake I loved his laugh.

Brooke turned away to make his way to the corner, but just before he turned it, I called after him

"Brooke!" I shouted, summoning his attention. My eyes softened as I rubbed the sleeve of his jumper over my arms, "Happy birthday, Darling."

He grinned, "Thank you, baby." He waved lightly and left.

After another moment, I returned inside of the diner and got back to work. Significantly less on edge, satisfied with existing for now.

"Where is your uniform top?" Callum asked as I pulled my apron back around my waist.

I glanced over at him with a lift of my eyebrow, "I felt like fancy dress today," I said curtly, walking out to check on my tables. They had all coped quite well in my absence.

Brooke's table contained the empty glass of coke, a plate that had once been host to a sandwich... and an untouched slice of the Hershey's Chocolate Cheesecake that he knew I loved. My face brightened slightly, though I wish I had been able to enjoy it with him.

"He ordered the cake and then left," Callum said at my heels, "I didn't know you were sleeping with him. I would have-"

"Listen Cal," I cut him off, "I need you to leave me be for a bit, okay? Just do your own thing, please."

I personally believe that I was being exceedingly nice under the circumstances. Callum, I guess, did not.

He grumbled, crossing his arms and stalking off to speak to one of his tables. A drama king.

I rolled my eyes and gathered the dishes from Brooke's table, then took the slice of cake into my free hand and stepped through to the dish area to hand the dishes over to Colby, the dishwasher. I then sank into a chair near the staff table to sink a fork into the slice.

Chocolate was one of my favourite things, though I didn't often partake in it. I tried to keep my sugar intake to a minimum because it made me bloat quite badly... but I think I deserved something a bit cheeky today.

As I pulled the fork to my lips, Shelley pushed through the kitchen doors with a bright smile on her face. The tension in my shoulders immediately eased, and I brightened.

"Hi Shell!" I sang, then proceeded to demolish the bite of cheesecake on my fork.

The woman with bleach blonde hair and pretty blue eyes turned to face me. She was an older woman, about fifty. I considered her a motherly figure... especially since my own mother was quite a negative feature in my mind.

"Hey there, honey!" She said brightly, her thick southern accent pulling through. Shelley was from Tennessee, and she'd tell you that any chance she got.

"How's the shift been today?"

An annoyed chuckle left my lips, but Aaron was the first to pipe up from behind the silver structure of the kitchen window.

"Been a shitty day, Shelley. That Callum kid keeps fucking orders up and he's driving me and Ellis both to criminal levels

276

of annoyance," Aaron peeked through the window to stare at Shelley, his eyes flickering over to me at the staff table as I stuffed yet another bite of chocolate into my gob.

Shelley frowned, "Naw," she shook her head with a tsk. "I was hoping he would start improving soon," She grumbled, then glanced over at me. "Why aren't you in uniform?"

I placed the fork down, then pointed to my maroon shirt that was currently hung on a coat rack, "Callum ran into me as I was leaving the kitchen with a full tray."

Her eyes widened, "Jesus in heaven… I hope you weren't carrying any coffee!"

"No, no," I shook my head, "just iced drinks, thankfully."

She sighed, "well, Callum is finishing off with his last table and then he is going home for the day, so we can all take a breath."

I nodded softly, my eyes lifting to the swinging doors to the dining room as I heard Callum reciting the same thing he had earlier.

"Next time you're in, Ask for Callum!" He sang to his departing patrons as he entered the kitchen with a flamboyant smile.

His eyes fell on me, "Wait a minute… why do YOU get to sit and eat when you have tables but I don't?"

This kid has a fucking problem with me, I just know it.

"Listen, Mate," I snapped, placing my fork down on the table beside me, "What is your fucking problem?"

He rolled his eyes, "You go off on your break to get your hair done and leave me alone with a busy cafe!"

I narrowed my eyes, "I'm entitled to an hour break because of the shift I work today. I was back before it ended."

"That isn't how it works here, you dick. If we are busy,

you're supposed to help!" Callum snapped back. "Not go around all prissy, getting your hair done and blowjobs out back."

Shelley stepped between us, "Callum, you're way outta line here, honey…"

"Shut up, Shelley," he said crassly.

In an instant, Aaron emerged from behind the steel frame which divided the kitchen and grabbed Callum by his collar.

"Listen here, don't you DARE speak to a woman like that," he snarled, pinning Callum to the wall. Aaron's skinny arms with far too many kitchen burns held strong against the young man. "You're being a fucking brat, and brats get punished for misbehaving. I suggest you apologize to the people who have been kind enough to deal with your bullshit today and fuck off."

The younger, but not smaller man shoved Aaron back and adjusted his collar. He glared angrily at me, then grabbed his bag and keys from the coat rack and stormed out of the front.

Once he had gone, I felt my shoulders ease, and I sighed softly.

Shelley shook her head in annoyance, "If he bothers coming back, I might just send him home," she muttered beneath her breath as she aggressively tied the strings at the back of her apron.

I glanced down at the rest of the cheesecake and sighed softly, shaking my head. Appetite was gone again, but I was okay with that.

Shelley and I got to work getting the diner back into tip-top condition, and by the time five o'clock rolled around, I was in a significantly brighter mood. I was practically dancing around again. My name badge was now affixed to the breast of the jumper I wore, leaning against the bar top to natter a bit with Shelley.

She grins at the sound of the front door's chime, nodding for me to turn my attention to the front.

Brooke stepped inside, holding Rae on his hip. She was so much bigger now, her hair fell in sweet loose curls around her adorable cheeks.

I smiled brightly, skipping over to snatch the little one from Brooke's hip. She fell into my arms without a second to waste, squealing in sweet laughter as I peppered her face in kisses.

"My little love," I said in a soft voice, running a hand through her curls as I lifted my eyes to meet Brooke's.

He was smiling, bright. He usually had this expression when I held Rae. It was one of the sweetest expressions in his arsenal.

"Hey," I said in a hushed tone, allowing Rae to nestle her legs around my hip. A hand placed securely on her lower back to hold her in place.

"Hey," he repeated, adjusting the strap of Rae's bag on his shoulder. He glanced around the dining room at the few occupied tables. "Busy night?"

I grinned, "nah, it's been nice actually," my free hand lifted to gently rub Rae's cheek.

The little girl in my arms nuzzled into my touch, "Nana?" She asked in her soft little voice.

My heart swelled, and I turned back to look at Shelley.

"Mind if I sit with them for a minute?" I asked, spinning around to remove my apron and place it on the bar top.

She grinned and nodded, "just keep an eye on your table," Shelley looked past me to Brooke, "Happy birthday, Doll!"

I glanced back at Brooke to see him smile thankfully and

nod as he sank into his usual booth.

"Thank you Shell!"

A warmth lifted my face, and I glanced down at Rae. "Shall we get your nana?" I asked her.

Her bright emerald eyes lifted significantly and she clapped her hands, "Nana!"

I grinned, carrying her into the kitchen with me and snatching a banana from the fruit counter. I handed it to her.

"Hold this, Darling," I pressed a kiss to her forehead as her tiny hands clasped her fruit. She stared at it with bright curiosity as I collected a plate and a knife, then made my way to Brooke's table.

He had already set up Rae's highchair, and was speaking to Shelley when I moved to place the plate and knife across from Brooke on the table, then sat Rae down in her chair. I placed a final kiss on her forehead before gently retrieving the fruit from her and sitting down.

I pulled the peel open, slicing the soft yellowy flesh of the banana and handing Rae a piece. She grasped it in her tiny hand and shoved it into her mouth.

She loved bananas, it was probably one of her favourite things to eat. Which came in handy when trying to decide on her meals.

Beneath the table, I felt the warmth of Brooke's leg as he brushed it against my own. The warmth summoned contentment to my face, and I flickered my glance to him as I continued to slice the banana up into manageable pieces for Rae.

"How was work?" I asked softly.

"Fine. I missed you," he replied with a smile. "Are you

performing tonight?"

A hum rose in my chest, and I passed another slide to the little girl at the end of the table. "I'm not sure what he wants me for. There is a show tonight, but I can sneak out if you want to go to that restaurant instead," I explained in a hushed tone.

Brooke had this way of bringing me down to earth that isn't often (or easily) achieved. When I was with him, I wanted to make myself compress. To keep these perfect, happy moments as personal as I could.

"No, you love performing. It is the only good thing you get from that place," he said softly.

There was something in his eyes that told me he had more to say. An energy that ebbed through the space between us.

"Is everything okay?" I asked, "You were looking forward to that dinner."

A smile pulled to his face, and his eyes fell over Rae. He reached forward to smooth her hair out, then relaxed back in his seat. I felt his knees press on either side of my left knee.

"Everything is fine, babe," he reassured in a soft tone.

"Ellie!" Rae shouts, jabbing her tiny finger towards the pile of banana slices in front of me.

I turned to her with a soft smile, "Sorry, gorgeous girl," I muttered, handing her another slice. Apprehension still rang in my mind, though.

"Are you still dropping Rae off with Jill?" I asked softly.

"If I do, would you mind if I come watch you dance?" He asked in return.

Something was off in his energy. It wasn't negative... but noticeable.

I handed Rae another small slice of banana and glanced

up to meet Brooke's eyes. "Are you sure everything is okay? You're being weird," I muttered.

A chuckle left his lips, and he pierced an elbow on the table, "I'm fine, Ellis. Everything is fine."

My gold dusted eyebrow lifted in inquiry, and I tilted my head. In my quest to search his features for the unspoken answer to my questions, Brooke grinned.

"You're staring," he said in a teasing tone, then glanced at his daughter.

I broke my stare and crossed my arms, leaning back in the booth as I tried even harder to read his mind.

"Is this some sort of Gay Jedi mind control shit?" Brooke inquired as his hands fell into his lap, then he moved, reaching under the table to touch my knee. His hand scooped under my calves, pulling my legs into his lap.

My feet rested on his thighs, and Brooke gently ran his hands along the trouser covered skin. His touch soothed the subtle ache that had grown in my legs from a day of being on my feet.

I rested back in the seat, allowing my head to lull backwards as I closed my eyes.

"Ellie!" Rae called to me again. Her voice pulled a soft smile to my face, and I sat straight to smile at her.

1. "Yes, babs?" I asked softly with a feminine lilt in my voice.

She pinched her fingers together, then touched the pinched tips of her hands. American sign language for 'more'.

I smiled and handed her yet another slice of her favourite food, which she gobbled up happily.

"You're tired," Brooke said softly. "Did you sleep at all last night?"

My attention turned to Brooke, and I shrugged. "Not much less than usual," I said in a hushed response.

"Ellis!" A guest from one of my tables called.

I instantly removed my legs from Brooke's lap and turned to the customer. They smiled at me, beckoning me over, so I glanced at Brooke apologetically, then kissed Rae's head before running off to see to my actual responsibilities.

Brooke stayed with me until my shift ended, then as I clocked out and met him out in the dining room, he pulled Rae into his arms and walked out with me.

I turned, placing a hand on his forearm, "I'm so sorry about dinner, Brooke," I said softly, a sad expression donning on my face.

He smiled, stepping closer so that our chests touched, though at an angle so he didn't crush Rae. Brooke pressed his lips to my forehead.

"Don't apologize, El." He pulled away with a soft expression.

Anxiety buzzed in my chest... this wasn't normal. Something was off. I rubbed my neck, "will I see you tonight?"

"Most definitely," he grinned, "Please be safe..."

I offered him a soft smile, leaning in to press a kiss to Rae's hair. My arm slipped around Brooke's waist as I turned my head to kiss his neck. "Get home safe," I whispered.

Brooke slid a hand down my back, resting to squeeze firmly on the flesh of my ass. "I love you, Ellis," He muttered softly.

My heart raced at the statement, and a blush darkened my cheeks. I felt so guilty for not saying it back to him... despite all we had been through, I couldn't even manage to humour him. That guilt weighed my eyes down, casting them from his view.

"Thank you," I managed instead.

Just as he did every other time I said this, Brooke smiled and pulled away. He waved to me one last time before watching as I turned to walk away.

A Masked Man

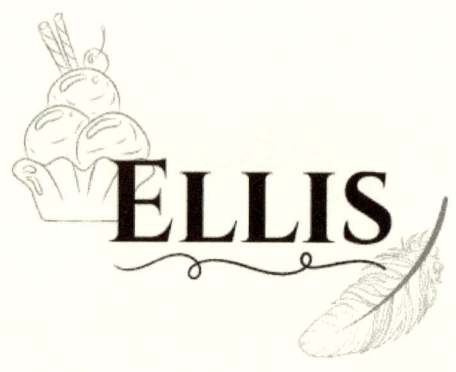

ELLIS

"You're early… for once," Lorenzo snorted, a smirk pulling across his round face as he stared into my soul. He was perched on the velvet lined sofa of his creepy, dark office. Zophia sat silently beside him with her beehive hair sprayed so stiff that it could probably be considered a deadly weapon.

I stretched my arms over my head, feeling the tension in my shoulders subside with the relaxation. "You told me to be here by seven thirty," I said simply.

"So I did," He grinned. His eyes flickered to his wife for a few seconds. "We have had an interesting day, Flare," His tone dropped into a frustrated grumble as he rolled his head on his shoulders. "Two of my operatives have been murdered.

Executed in the home of one. I think we know who is behind it all… a marksman," Lorenzo cracked his knuckles.

My eyes fell wide, and I tilted my head. "Are you seriously insinuating that I killed these people?" I asked, gobsmacked at the thought of it being a consideration.

Lorenzo laughed, "No, no." He shook his head dismissively. "Do you remember a man by the name of Ernest Sawyer?" He asked.

The name rang a bell, and the image of this man's face flashed in my eyes… a man scarcely old enough to be under his reign. Red hair and massive blue eyes. Ernest was the silent, moody type. Another one of those stupid, vulnerable souls to fall into Lorenzo's trap… not that I was one to talk.

"The tailor? He is the one that refitted all of the seat covers… and designed my first few performance outfits."

"Indeed," The greasy man hummed.

"Isn't he dead?" I asked, "I swear Huxley said he was at the bottom of Lake Lanier."

A cold, ominous chuckle pulled through Lorenzo's chest, "Huxley is one of the men who was murdered."

A chill ran down my spine as Lorenzo pushed himself to stand, stalking towards me with heavy footsteps. Strings affixed themselves to my muscles, pulling at them until the tightness burned a deep throb. This monster of a man grabbed me by the scruff of my shirt and pulled me closer to him. I could smell the stench of alcohol in his breath.

"Do you know where Ernest is?" He asked, spit pattering onto my face.

"W-what?" I asked, "No! Of course I don't know where Ernest is… I only barely knew him when he was still alive… we all thought he was dead!"

"Ghosts don't kill people, Ellis."

My name... Lorenzo never called contractees by their names.

I felt my heart racing in my chest as he growled and shoved me back.

"Fuck!" He snarled, grabbing hold of a table full of empty glasses and tossing it. Glass shattered upon the floor, shortly followed by the resounding sound of the table crashing hard against the carpet. A vein bulged from the top of his forehead and his neck, and his face grew a deep red. "First Cain... then Valentine..." He stomped around the room, but my eyes widened in panic when he mentioned my friend's name.

"What happened to Valentine?" I asked, eyes flickering to the last time I had seen her just a few days before.

Lorenzo spun around with a snarl, "Shut the fuck up, Flare!"

I bit down hard on my tongue, my breath slowed to a near halt as I trembled in my stead.

He growled, stepping towards me again. Aggression radiated from his skin as his boots crashed into the floor beneath him. When he finally stopped, he had managed to make himself big enough to shove his face into mine, pulling in slow and irritated breaths from a jaw that hung open to reveal scraggly white teeth.

"I'm losing money faster than I can send out product, and that makes me incredibly fucking angry," Lorenzo grabbed me by the scruff of my shirt and tossed me to the ground, "You're going to dance all night, Flare. Every fucking second that you breathe... you better be making me money!"

I yelped, staring up at the devil who stood above me, darkness casting a shade of evil over his eyes as he sank to wrap his meaty palms around my throat.

"Go fucking get dressed… and if I see you talking to anyone, I'll make sure you're fucking sorry!"

For once, I felt completely and totally lost. I hadn't done anything to warrant Lorenzo's anger this time… and yet it felt so much more real. He plunged his hand into his pocket and retrieved one of those drug-laced tabs, forcing my mouth open and placing one on my tongue.

I gagged as the taste of bleach coated my tongue, feeling my faculties leave me as he ripped me back to my feet yet again… my head was already spinning.

These drugs were nothing to fuck with… I don't know how he expected me to be able to perform under their influence. They usually made me go completely limp.

"Get out!" He snarled, reaching to clasp the handle of his door and throwing me out.

My shoulder collided with the wall on the opposite side of the hallway, a wave of pain striking through me as I felt my bones rattle. Fear pulled through me, but I simply stared in silence at Lorenzo.

He growled, "You're on in twenty minutes. Get fucking dressed!" The door slammed shut.

Panic ebbed through my limbs, and I looked around the hallway to see other dancers staring in confusion.

"Are you okay, Flare?" One of them asked, stepping forward to place a hand on my trembling shoulder.

I bit down on my tongue and nodded, already feeling the warmth from the drugs in my stomach. My nose and lips began to tingle and I shook my head to recant my nod.

"I don't think so… but I don't think we should stand here," I urged, motioning for the girls to follow me towards the dressing room.

This apprehension grew over my shoulders, paranoia beginning to spiral out of control as I began to feel presences that weren't usually there.

As the time ticked by towards my stage-call, I felt myself moving in slow motion. The world around me seemed to warp, and panic flushed through my whole body at warp speeds. I absolutely did not want to risk being late to this stage call.

I fumbled around my station, my hands shaking uncontrollably as I tried my best to apply my makeup as quickly as I could.

The tingling of my nose and lips spread to reach my entire face, my tongue… breathing became so much harder. It took more and more effort to exist normally… if I had been managing it at all in the first place.

I pulled in a deep breath, trying my best to maintain my composure, but I couldn't feel my face. The deep breath choked me, halting in my throat.

Desperate for something that could calm me down, or at least distract me, I plunged my hand into my pocket to retrieve my phone.

My hands were shaking violently now, and I dropped the device on the tabletop of my vanity. Teeth clenching together, I grabbed onto it again and clumsily unlocked it.

I selected an icon on my home screen with Brooke's name beneath it. Speed dial. The screen filled with a picture of him holding Rae as she took her first steps.

Forcing myself to remain somewhat calm was almost impossible. I was feeling increasingly numb… increasingly nauseous.

In front of me, my phone rang quietly and my eyes locked

onto Brooke's face in the background, trying desperately to focus on something.

The screen shifted as the line connected, and I snatched the phone to my ear.

"Hey, you!" Brooke called through the speaker.

"B-Brooke," I muttered, a tight whisper hissing into the microphone.

He was silent for a few seconds, then asked: "What's going on babe?"

I whimpered, the room was beginning to spin faster now, but I tried to compose myself. "H-he dr-drugged me," I whispered again.

My eyes shot about, looking around the dressing room. I could hear whispers, people's eyes sealed onto me like watchful serpents. I wanted to crawl into a hole and die.

"He drugged you?" Brooke asked in a sharp, accusatory tone that almost felt like a blade to my own heart.

I nodded, not that he could see me. "I'm... so scared, Darling..." I whimpered in the softest voice I could. My words slurred drunkenly, "H-He was acting s...so weird... I need to get dressed for t-this dance... but I c-can't stop shaking," I balled my hand into a fist, pressing my knuckles into my eye socket.

A soft, steadying ring pulled through my ears, and Brooke hummed. "Ellis, you've got to perform... if he is willing to drug you to make a mockery of you then he is willing to do so much worse."

He was right... not that I could comprehend that.

"I-," I couldn't speak, I just pressed the phone closer to my face, trembling. "I wish you were here," I whimpered, a single tear slipping down my cheek. My head began to ache... a biting, crippling sensation of a migraine which pulled from the base of my skull in an intense warmth. "Th-the thoughts are back, Brooke."

"I will come up now, okay?" Brooke said reassuringly, "I'll be there soon... just need to drop Rae off, okay?"

I threw my phone against the vanity, pressing my fingers into my eyes as I desperately tried to perceive something other than pins and needles.

"Ellis," his voice was loud enough to reach my ears from the speaker of my phone on the vanity.

"Darling, I can't breathe," I muttered hopelessly, a hand slipping down from my face to grasp at my burning chest. My whole body was aflame.

"You need to breathe, El. Take slow breaths," he advised.

My hands lifted to the blonde curls at the top of my head, gripping tight as I trembled.

There was a biting fear in the forefront of my psyche... Lorenzo may kill me tonight...

"I love you, Brooke," I whispered, needing to get those words off of my chest, just in case I never got the chance to do it again.

A hand rested on my back, and I turned slowly... the world moved around me at a snail's pace. When I managed to turn completely, I saw one of the other drag queens standing beside me. Her hair and makeup were done, and she had my wig clutched in her hands.

"You're really struggling right now, Flare," she said kindly... her words echoed in my head like screams on a cave walk, and I grimaced in displeasure.

I clumsily moved my hand to end the call with Brooke before he could say anything else.

This new person stepped forward and gently pulled the wig over my hair, ensuring everything was tucked inside.

"I don't know why Lorenzo goes after you, Flare… but I think he's gone too far this time. You really need to get out of here," she said softly, turning to the rack beside my vanity and grabbing a decent outfit.

I pushed myself to stand, though my knees shook.

"You can't even stand independently, how are you supposed to dance?" She asked sternly.

My eyes flickered to her, finally focusing in enough to try to place who she was. This was Gold Dust, a friend of Ginger's… I wasn't super close with any of the other Queens here, but Ginger was.

I removed Brooke's jumper, placing it haphazardly on my vanity as I took the sparkling golden bralette from Gold Dust and clumsily pulled it over my head.

It wasn't that I didn't want to speak… it is just that speaking felt absolutely nauseating at the moment. Standing, alone, was more than I could really cope with right now.

Goldie braced me, her arms acting as scaffolding which held me upright. Something I definitely needed as I reached into my trousers and adjusted myself so that I was sufficiently tucked, then allowed my trousers to puddle around my ankles.

I struggled to kick these away, then climb into a pair of knickers.

The numbness was creeping down my neck now, it made my mouth water hopelessly, but I couldn't quite tell if I was swallowing.

Goldie stepped back, sighing as she looked me over. "I really don't think you should go out, Flare," She said softly.

My eyes lifted to... attempt to look at her, but she was skewed by double vision. The migraine shot through my head, radiating at the back of my eyes intensely as an involuntary twitch rolled over my shoulders.

"I... would much rather go home," I admitted honestly, conjuring my best fake smile... a talent I had honed after years in customer service. "But... the show has to go on, right?" I staggered towards the doorway as Zophia pulled it open.

The mousey woman stared up at me with her arms crossed in front of her chest.

"Pathetic," she snarled. "I told Zo to wait until after to dose you," Her stubby arms crossed in front of her. "If you fall off the stage, you're done for. We are tired of entertaining your trash, Flare."

What the fuck was going on?

I wasn't responsible for killing those men, and I sure as hell hadn't done anything wrong... I was early today, I wasn't even backchatting Lorenzo. Just when I thought I'd reached the depths of his malevolence, the ground opened beneath me to reveal an even darker, even more disgusting place.

My feet felt heavy as I peeled them from the floor. Every step echoed loudly in response to my heels clacking across the ground. To the naked eye, I'd come across as drunk... but I knew better.

"You have to dance, Flare," Zophia said with a grumble at my side, "You better not fuck this up."

The warning was loud and clear in her voice, and I gulped down a pit that had formed in my throat as I emerged through the backstage curtain into the main stage area.

The lights shut off, sending an eerie silence through the

crowd… then a spotlight sliced through the darkness, pairing well with the ringing in my ears as I reached my hand to block the rays from my eyes.

One of my songs began to play, and as the music droned on I could feel my body moving more fluidly… at least that was a plus. Muscle memory might just save my life.

I danced, feeling the jittering of my skin slow as I entered a world of my own, dancing mindlessly. I shut off my perception of everything else in the room until …

A table collided hard with the floor.

Glass shattered.

A scream.

The music continued like nothing was happening, but my eyes fell in the direction of the scream. There, in front of the stage, a shadowy figure in black stood with a menacing stare burning through my intoxication.

His face was obscured by a black mask with a white skull imprinted on the face, and as I pulled myself up from the reclined position of a dip, I noticed the shiny muzzle of a gun pointed straight at my head.

My heart stopped beating… it seemed like everything in that room stopped.

The most gut wrenching part? Nobody even tried to stop him. Those who didn't run just seemed to stare silently.

Was I really worth so little?

The figure leapt onto the stage, a long black trench coat dragging over the neon lights embedded in the black floor as he stepped towards me.

The room was a chaos of screams, people running… but

the security guards didn't flinch. They watched carelessly as this fucking freak approached me with a weapon.

My life began to flash before my eyes in quick succession, and I stood straight. The effects of the drugs snapped away in a sudden, extreme sobriety that rattled my bones as I stared death in the face once again.

The marksman...

He was here for me now...

Tears began to seep from the corners of my eyes, slipping down the crease of my nose as I grit my teeth.

Brooke... he was on his way.

Panic surged in my chest as I thought about him trying to burst through the door and save me.

What if he got shot?

What if Rae lost her father?

What if I never got to see him again?

What if he was the one to find my body crumpled up behind a dumpster in a back alley?

What if I never got to tell him that I loved him to his face?

I allowed my head to roll forward, feeling that familiar call of the void beckon to me as I trembled once more before this harbinger of doom.

"P-please," I whimpered.

The figure stepped forward, pressing the muzzle of the gun firmly against the soft palate of my jaw, forcing my chin to raise as I coughed out a soft sob.

His arm grabbed me, looping the pit of his elbow around my throat as he turned to face the only remaining people in the room, body tucked securely behind my own. He moved his gun from my neck and pointed it at the spotlight which shown on both of us.

He squeezed the trigger.

The sound of his shot rang out loud and clear, and the room was plunged into darkness.

Two more shots rang out, loud in my ears. I flinched with each shot as the chaos in the room continued to develop.

My ears began to ring.

He pulled me from the stage, slipping through the darkness like a man in a mission. One of his hands squeezed tight to my bicep as he pulled me along.

My wig slipped from my hair, falling somewhere behind me.

I stumbled through the darkness, my heart racing with every step. The effects of the drugs remained poignant in my stumbling clumsiness in this darkness.

After walking for what felt like ages in the pitch black, a door opened and the cool night air rushed through my body. Streetlights illuminated the world around me.

The figure released me from his grip, then pressed a hand to my chest, sealing me against the brick wall of the Midnight Raven. My head, now absent of the protective cushion of my wig, collided with the wall. The ache of my migraine returned to my consciousness as I let out the softest groan of pain.

I stared at the man in the mask with confusion spelled across my face, a throb in my chest as I reached the eye-slits of his mask... to see green orbs peering through to me.

My eyes widened as the electricity from his stare washed through me. One of familiarity and safety.

"Brooke?" I whispered sharply.

The masked man held that stare over me, his hand resting firmly against my chest. He lifted the hand which held his gun, and my heart stuttered as I felt my eyes had deceived me.

He turned his hand, pressing a single finger to the lips of his mask as we listened in silence.

The sound within the Raven was audible... angry, lecherous howls from a man that I recognized. Terror flooded my system... we had to leave... if Lorenzo found me now, I'd be dead faster than you can think.

The masked man released his pressure on my chest, that hand then moved to grab hold of my hand as he tugged me in the direction of an alleyway.

We slipped through the streets, hardly making a noise aside from the clock of my heels... then as we emerged into a back street a few blocks away, Brooke's beaten up station wagon sat running.

My face washed over with relief as the figure pulled his own door open, ushering for me to get in on the other side.

As I collapsed into the passenger side of the car, the rush of adrenaline and fear slipped away, replaced by the existential warmth of relief. Tears fell down the roughly painted skin of my cheeks and I pressed my hands to the panel of the door to steady myself.

The figure turned the key in the ignition, and the engine sputtered a few times before kicking into gear. He reached to grasp the base of the mask, peeling it off to reveal the one fucking face that I would have killed to see in this moment.

Brooke tossed the mask into the back seat, pulling a hand through the sweat-slicked hair on his head as he pressed his foot to the accelerator and peeled out of the alleyway.

Once we emerged onto the main road, I could see the Midnight Raven in the rearview mirror... it was eerily still.

No police presence… no panic. It was silent.

I closed my eyes tight, pressing back into my seat as I felt the buzz of the drugs pulling at my faculties once more. This was far too fucking much.

"Sorry,"

My eyes snapped open, and I glanced over at Brooke.

His green eyes were sealed on the road before us, one hand clenching the steering wheel tight enough to bleach his knuckles while the other perched against the driver's side window. His temple pressed into the knuckles of this fist.

"W-what?" I asked.

Brooke flashed his eyes over to me, but only for a millisecond.

"I didn't tell you the plan… the fear in your eyes back there was enough to kill me ten times over," he muttered softly.

My heart fluttered, and I bit down on my lip. "I…is this why you were acting so weird earlier?"

He chuckled… the sound warmed my chest, calming the race of thoughts in my mind. I closed my eyes again to bite back the throbbing of my head.

"Open the dash, baby," He said softly, turning onto the road which would take us to my apartment.

I grimaced with the annoyance of having just closed my eyes again, but did as told, reaching into the dash.

Inside, there was a large manilla envelope and one much smaller envelope with my name scrawled on it in Brooke's handwriting.

My eyes darted to him for a split second, then I collected the smaller envelope.

"Open it," he whispered.

I obeyed, peeling the lip of the envelope open.

Inside, there was a single plane ticket.

Ellis Evans, Atlanta Hartsfield-Jackson International Airport to London , England. It had today's date on it March 26th, 2025.

My heart fluttered in my chest as I gripped the ticket tight in my hand, tears gathered at the corners of my eyes again.

There was only one ticket.

I sniffled, pulling the back of a hand to press against my pink lipstick.

"I need you to get just enough to last you for a few weeks," Brooke said softly, pulling up to the curb outside of my apartment.

A sharp pain struck through my chest, and I glanced over at him... his eyes were already on me, a sadness twinkling behind the stunning emerald irises.

My eyes flickered to the building to our right... then back to Brooke.

"Will you... come inside with me?" I asked softly, my tone hardly above a whisper.

He held his gaze over me, and for a moment I thought he'd refuse... but his hands released from the steering wheel and fell to the buckle of his seatbelt. It clicked, and Brooke stepped out of the car.

He stepped around the bonnet of the car, then pulled my door open. My eyes held his shape as he held a hand outstretched to me.

I accepted his hand, shakily moving from my seat. I led him towards my building.

Brooke had dropped me off here quite a few times in the

past few months... but I never allowed him inside because I didn't want him to see how I was living.

As I pushed the door open, the tiny squalor came into view. A room scarcely bigger than a standard living room. There was a futon with my laptop plugged into the wall resting on top of a single sweat stained pillow. A chrome pole in the open space between this futon and an empty wall. A kitchenette with a single hob and a microwave sat next to a sink, mini fridge beneath the hob, and a washing machine that hardly held a single load tucked into the corner.

Admittedly, the evidence of my addictions was everywhere. Empty wine bottles and cans of lager strewn about the floor. I cringed in embarrassment and kicked off my heels, feeling some of the difficulty with walking fade as my bare feet graced the unswept concrete floor.

I walked to my futon, sinking to my knees in front of it and pulling a storage capsule and duffel bag from beneath it. Slowly, I stuffed a few pairs of normal clothes (of which I possessed very little of... mostly oversized hoodies and sweatpants). Then, I unplugged the chargers for my phone and laptop from the wall and stuffed them into the duffel, followed by the laptop itself.

Finally, I collected a small reddish-purple booklet from the base of the storage capsule. A shaky breath pulled in through my nose, and I pulled it open to glance down at the pages.

There I was... that fucking terrified 20 year old gay man running from disappointment and confusion, straight into the exact traps that are meant to detain vulnerable people.

I flipped through the booklet, finding the vignette for my initial visa pasted to a page. My name was different... Ellis Worthington... that fucking bastard's last name.

My face twisted into a soft grimace, and I turned my head to look at Brooke. He was stood in the doorway, his eyes sealed onto me as his hands stuffed into his pockets.

"You okay?" He asked in a hushed tone.

I glanced back down at my passport, sniffling softly and nodding as I folded it and pushed it into the side pocket of the duffel.

Standing on my shaky legs once more, I removed the outfit I had worn for my dance, pulling on one of the remaining pairs of trousers. My mind flashed back to Brooke's jumper which was still laying on my dressing table at the Midnight Raven. An ache burned behind my eyes as I sighed and slipped on a jumper of my own. It fit me snug... and it smelled like me.

The duffel bag's strap slung over my shoulder with ease as I returned to Brooke's side and slipped into a pair of ratty tennis shoes, bracing my hand against the wall to steady myself.

"Ready?" Brooke asked.

I turned around to take in the room one last time, then met his eyes with a resounding nod.

He extended a hand to me, slipping his fingers between mine as he intertwined our grasps. His warmth was soothing.

I stepped closer to him and pressed myself into his chest.

Brooke looped his other arm around me, pressing his lips against my temples as he breathed in slowly. This was an embrace that I craved, I needed... especially right now.

I truly believe that if Brooke hadn't come to kidnap me... Lorenzo might have actually killed me today.

His hand ran down the centre of my spine, and I pulled back slowly to meet his eyes. He simply smiled and pressed a soft kiss to my lips.

Then, he turned to lead me down to where his car sat... still idling.

We sank into the seats and he pulled off towards Hartsfield-Jackson.

The nearer we grew to the airport, the more terrified I felt... but Brooke's free hand rested on my knee, and I wanted to revel in this peace for as long as I could.

Brooke pulled into a parking garage, and finally... stopped. My heart fluttered in my chest. His gaze fell onto me, and his hand squeezed at my thigh.

None of this felt real... I was still fucking reeling from the fact that not an hour ago, there was a gun pressed to my throat.

The car silenced as Brook turned the key to shut off the ignition, his hands fell into his lap and his beautiful brown curls shaded his face as his head fell forwards.

Heartbeats swelled in my ears as I felt reality encroaching.

"How long?" I whispered the question in a soft, pleading tone.

Brooke's head turned slowly to face me, the green of his eyes locking onto the brown of my own. He blinked, a slow... exhausted blink.

"Two months."

My heart broke, and my eyes fell. "T-two months?"

He nodded slowly, reaching across the front seat to pull the dash open. He retrieved the large manilla envelope and tapped it with his fingers.

"I have to serve Kelly with divorce papers," he muttered, "and... I can't leave until she signs them."

I stared at the yellowish parcel in his hands, teeth perched against my bottom lip as I sank into my seat.

Steaming tears flooded my vision, and I wrapped my arms around myself. Brooke was sending me away... what if he never came for me?

Brooke placed the folder back inside of the dash and pressed it closed, then turned to face me completely. His eyes softened, and I felt him take in every last inch of me... the smudged makeup and the gaunt eyes. I wanted to sink away from him, to hide from what he thought of me.

He is going to leave me...

I'm never going to see him again.

The stinging tears slipped down my cheeks and coated my face in the salty sensation of despair.

"Hey," Brooke reached across the seat to stroke my cheek, swiping away a tear or two as his strong hands braced against my skin. "You've got this, Ellis... you know what to do. You know how to get by... I just need you to be safe, okay?" He leaned in to press his forehead to mine.

In the darkness of the can of his car, I felt fear like never before... not the fear of death... nor of pain... nor of malice... I feared that emptiness that I had felt before returning to eat me alive.

I was terrified of living one day in this world without feeling the warmth of Brooke's gaze... the roll of his eyes in response to my sass or the sound of his laugh when I needed it most. The thought of missing out on Rae's life... on never seeing her grow up into the beautiful little girl she would definitely be.

I feared grieving this... this was love, and I was fucking terrified of losing it all now.

"Ellis," Brooke muttered. His calm voice sliced through my racing thoughts, and I glanced up at him.

There was an equal sadness expressed on his face. Sadness. It only made me ache more.

"Promise me," I whispered.

He tilted his head.

"Promise me... you're going to come for me... please..." I reached forward to press a hand to his chest. The steady thrum of his heartbeat rocked against my palm. I hooked my fingers lightly into the fabric of his shirt.

Brooke sank closer, his lips connected with the sweat-slicked skin of my forehead and he breathed in deeply.

When he pulled away from me, he nodded.

"I promise you, everything is going to be okay, baby..." he whispered softly, pushing his fingertips through my hair. "I promise I will be there, I will come for you."

I sniffled lightly, nodding slowly.

"Did you mean it?" He asked softly.

It was my turn to tilt my head in confusion. His eyes conveyed mysticism to me... intrigue... excitement.

"What you said... on the phone..."

My cheeks flushed dark with a pastel rouge colour. I held his eyes for a moment, but nodded slowly.

"Will you say it?"

I grit my teeth as the anxiety rushed through me... but I sank into his touch.

"I-," I wavered, the sensation of being totally starstruck overwhelming me. "I love you."

He kissed me.

Not just any kiss... Brooke pinned me to the pillar beside my seat, blocked from external view by the still present bin bag duct taped to the windowless... window. His hands reached to tangle in my hair as he leaned across the centre console to press into me.

His tongue pressed to my lips, pushing them apart so that he could explore the inside of my mouth... and the more voracious and hungry he grew... the more I craved from him.

My hands slipped along his chest, moving up until my slender fingers could wrap around his throat. I tightened my grip around the flesh, able to feel each of his breaths against my palm.

Brooke let out a moan, soft and poignant in the cab of his beaten up wagon. The sound sent a flutter of warmth to my groin, and I disconnected from his hungry kiss. My teeth pulled at his bottom lip as I sank back into the seat, eyes sealed onto the panting man before me.

The darkness of the car park lent him this stunning ambiance, a shadow which cloaked him in a thrilling air of mystery.

My cock throbbed in my trousers, begging for Brooke's lips to take it in. He had gotten significantly better at giving head in recent months... not that I was taking notes.

His eyes flickered down to my bulge, a sinister smirk pulling across his face.

"I can't let you go in there with that, now... can I?" He asked, reaching his hand across to a lever on the far side of my seat. The back of my chair sank back beneath my weight.

A gasp left my lips, my eyes fluttering open wide as I watched Brooke sink his hand beneath the seat. A metallic trill sounded as my seat rolled as far back as it could... and he crawled across the front so that he was straddling my waist.

I stared up at him with a bright, confused look in my eyes... he was never the one to be forward about intimacy. My whole body vibrated in excitement as I felt his hips sink against mine.

"B-Brooke," I muttered breathlessly as my fingers rested against his lower stomach.

He sank down, sealing our lips together for another deep kiss. His hands gripped at my hips in ways that made me want to call out for him. I couldn't believe how intense he was, it is like he wanted to fuck me right here in the middle of this parking garage.

Brooke peeled his lips from mine, sinking to the soft flesh of my neck where he began to place soft nibbles. A hand slipped beneath my hoodie to inch along my skin.

"I want to fuck you, Ellis," he whispered sharply into my ear as he nipped the lobe.

My heart exploded, beating hard against my ribcage as I whimpered... I wasn't keen on being submissive, but I won't lie... Brooke could dominate me any fucking day of the week and I would let him.

"I-I can suck your dick," I whispered, trying my best to add a sultry tone to my words.

He shook his head, a hand tangling into the short blonde curls on my head as he left sloppy kisses along my jaw. "No. I want to *fuck* you," He clarified.

Fuck...

We had never crossed the line into anal before... I think I was worried he may realize that I was actually a man and lose interest in me if we did, so I never pushed.

"A-are you sure?" I asked, my tone sharpening.

He kissed my neck, his free hand intertwining into mine as he pinned that arm above my head.

"I've never been more sure about anything in my life," Brooke muttered, "I won't see you for two months... I need

307

to make sure I give you something worth waiting for."

My eyes flickered in seduction, and I grit my teeth. "We don't have any lube," I said with a forlorn expression pulling at the desired ecstasy in my eyes.

Brooke chuckled, turning around and pressing the button to open his dash. He removed a tube of Aquaphor, then winked at me with a knowing smirk.

"Always prepared," he hummed, placing the tube on the centre console.

My cock twitched in my trousers, and I practically drooled. This man was going to be the death of me... and by god... I wanted to suffer every second of it.

"You want to fuck me right now?" I asked, slipping a hand beneath my own hoodie to pull the fabric upward, revealing the crest of my muscular abdomen. My face twisted into the seductive stare that my time as a sex worker had prepared me for.

I wanted this so bad.

I wanted Brooke to fuck me... to make my last moments with him so fucking mind-blowing that he'd crave me every second that we were apart.

Brooke wavered, my words obviously hitting him deep in his core. His right hand pressed to the now exposed flesh of my stomach as he sank to kiss that skin.

Goosebumps raised along my torso, following the placement of his kisses as he knelt in the floorboard between my legs. He guided my hips up, then pulled my joggers down until they had puddled around my knees.

My throbbing dick stood on its own, and I watched as Brooke's eyes fell to meet it. The green of his irises glittered with need, and he poised his lips around my dick. He sank all the way down until he had taken my whole length to his throat. Just as he took it as deep as he could, his eyes flickered up to meet mine.

Jesus.

Fucking.

Christ.

I trembled, feeling warmth encroach on my whole body as a blush crawled it's way across my skin.

By this point, it was clear that Lorenzo's drugs still had their hold of me.

Brooke pulled back, allowing my tip to grace against his tongue for a few seconds before he sank back down.

"Nng... Darling ..." I reached to tangle my fingers in his hair, guiding his speed very slightly. He respected every demand I made of him, no matter how silent, and proceeded to rock my world exponentially.

Soon, he pulled his lips away, rolling his jaw to adjust from the lockjaw he had obtained, then pressed kisses along my shaved inner thighs, pumping me slowly.

I rolled my head back as Brooke pulled my joggers off the rest of the way and perched my ankles on his shoulders ... my ass was now clearly on display for him.

This is where my insecurity grew, the unknown territory for Brooke... a deal breaker. What if he hated this?

I heard the click of the tube of cream, then a bitingly cold sensation in my entrance as he pressed two fingers into me.

My toes curled as he sank his digits deep inside of me, distributing a thin layer of the lubricating cream through me. It was cold, but paired with my burning skin... it was needed.

"I must be doing something right," Brooke chuckled, "I've never seen you so quiet."

I blinked, glancing down to see him between my legs. This man was my fucking everything... the way he was looking at me, even in my least desirable of appearances, like I was the single most beautiful thing on this planet.

That was enough to bring me closer to cumming.

"Y-you're doing well," I grinned in return, "but I can't wait to have your massive fucking dick inside of me."

I watched as his eyes shifted, transforming into the embodiment of lust as he retrieved his fingers from inside of me and reached into his own trousers to retrieve his own manhood: rigid and ready... like he had been thinking about this for ages.

Brooke applied a generous amount of the gel to his hand, lubricating the shaft of his cock as he stared a burning lust into my eyes.

I wanted him more than I wanted oxygen. I needed him more than sleep.

My eyes locked onto his hand as it stroked his dick, slowly... gently. The sharp base of my teeth perched seductively on my lower lip, and my heart fluttered as Brooke lifted his hips, pulling me further down the seat in the same movement. I could feel the twitch of his cock against my balls, and he glanced down to angle his tip into my entrance.

A soft whimper slipped from my chest, guided by the arms of hope and desire. It filled Brooke's ears with the calls of my need, and in his eyes snapped to meet mine.

In that instant, he pressed himself into me, and I felt the world explode around me... like hell was I going to let him know that, though!

I returned that stubborn, hellbent stare into his eyes. As he sank into me, my knees bent until they were pressed flat against his shoulders. Fully submerged within me.

His lips twisted into a soft smirk, and he shuddered with pleasure. "You're so... fucking... tight," He whispered softly.

A compliment that I didn't expect to receive.

My cheeks dusted with a soft pink, but my own lips lifted into a smirk. "You like that?"

Clearly not immune to my teasing, he shuddered once more. "I'll like it more when you're moaning my name," The cheeky fucking git fired back.

"You think you're good enough for that?" I teased, pressing the tips of my manicured fingers to his chest, twisting the fabric of his black shirt in my hands.

Brooke's eyes darkened, and he slowly rolled his hips against mine. "I've got to be..." He pulled back, then slowly pushed until he had filled me once more. It took everything in me not to moan out.

"I can't believe we didn't do this sooner," He whispers, grabbing hold of my left knee as he grazed his teeth across the skin, following it with a soft kiss to where he had just nipped. His hips moved back slowly, generating a slow, but effective thrust that made me squirm.

My eyes fluttered shut, a soft tremble from building pleasure ramping up in my belly as he suddenly changed the rhythm, slamming into me roughly, but only once. The unexpected force triggered the softest, unintentional yelp of pleasure to fall from my lips, and he drank in that subtle sound.

"You're being stubborn, Baby," He whispers, hands falling to rest against my stomach so that he could gain more control.

I bit down on my lip with a seductive grin, "Maybe you should just try harder." The words fell from my lips like a challenge, a warning. "I thought you wanted me to scream your name."

He thrust harder into me, picking up a steady tempo. He knew he had me by now... he absolutely knew it...

"You're tense," He declared, one of his hands crawling from its place on my stomach to find itself nestled around my throat. "Be a good boy for me and let me fuck you," He tightened his grip.

The firm poker face that I had managed to maintain fizzled out, replaced by a desperate, hungry sparkle of my eyes. With every thrust, Brooke became more aggressive... his body perspired with salty, horny sweat that beaded along his forehead in tiny rivulets. His hand around my throat held me still, yet drew me in all at once.

Brooke had me right where he wanted me, and as I finally gave into him, I experienced every ounce of pleasure that sex had never been for me. He read my body, watched my cues. He respected my responses.

I could feel my prostate swelling, an overwhelming warmth in my gut and a buzz at the front of my head. "B-Brooke," I muttered.

"Yes, baby?" He hissed, his thumb pulsed against the side of my throat with his words and I trembled. His cock filled every last inch of me, and I could feel myself growing weak to the calls of an orgasm.

I clenched my teeth as a wave of pleasure buzzed through me, "F-fuck..." I whimpered, "Keep going, Darling... I am so fucking close," I trembled beneath him, feeling the rush of endorphins as he sped up his thrusts.

My head rolled back, but his hand followed, tightening his grasp. This pressure, the way he seemed to understand exactly what I needed... it was criminal.

"You're so fucking perfect, Ellis," He growled down at me, "Look at how well you take my fucking dick."

"Ah!" I whimpered, the feminine pitch of my voice sharpening the tone of the subsequent moans which followed. How the fuck was he doing this to me?

His hand which didn't presently hold my throat pulled to caress my hip, holding me still so that he could plow into me. "That's it, baby... fucking melt for me," He continued his growls, "Who is making you feel so good?"

"Y-you," I managed, breathless and dangerously close to a high.

"Who?"

"Y-you, Brooke..."

"Who do you belong to?"

I stuttered, the ring of pleasure growing in my ear. "F-fuck," I gasped.

He held his ground, "Who do you belong to, Ellis?"

"I-I'm yours!" I called, "Fucking... all yours, Brooke!"

My whole body convulsed as Brooke managed to strike in just the right place to send me over the edge.

"There you go, Baby... cum for me," He demanded in a husky tone, then he fucking watched as I did exactly that.

I called out, reaching above myself to grip onto the headrest as I came, my soul launched into another universe as Brooke continued his thrusting, though I could tell.... even in the delirium of this ecstasy, that the stutter in his tempo meant he was close. I wanted him to cum, to fill me with his seed. I wanted to feel his warmth deep inside of me.

"B-Brooke," I moaned, melting back into the seat in my own release, "Come on, Darling... fill me up," I begged, every thrust sent a warm rush through my body.

He closed his eyes tight, "You want me to cum inside of you?" He asked in a struggling query.

I nodded, "Yes, Darling... I want you to fucking breed me. Mark me... Make sure everyone knows who owns me!"

He struggled, dropping the dominant persona and trembling, "I-I'm going to cum, Ellis," He whimpered, then his thrusts became staggered, sharp, and his face twisted in release as he filled me with his cum.

For a moment, he hunched over me, panting and exhausted. The position in which he had been knelt in became obviously uncomfortable, and he struggled to pull from between my legs. Finally, he collapsed against the floorboard, head resting back against the dash with beads of sweat clinging to the ends of his curls.

He pulled his hands to his face, then pulled in a deep breath to try and soothe the panting that he was currently going through.

I ached from his ferocity, but not in the way that I usually did for rough clients. It was an ache which sent pulses of warmth through my veins. An ache which felt like passion.

"A...are you okay?" I asked softly, pushing myself to sit up. My eyes fell to his shirt, which was now blessed by a suspicious white stain.

Brooke glanced up at me, allowing his hands to slide down his face enough to reveal a buzzing smile. He laughed lightly, "Yeah, babe. I'm a bit too old for manoeuvring a car like this," He chuckled, "My back is going to kill tomorrow."

A blush lightened on my cheeks, and I grinned. "Sorry about that," I muttered.

He pushed himself forward, reaching a hand up to cup my

cheek as he pulled me down for a soft kiss. The sound echoed lightly in the cab, and his eyes opened to reveal a soft, sad expression.

The warmth in my chest was replaced with a dull throb of my own sadness.

It was time.

My face fell, eyes casting down to my lap, still bare. I sank to grab the puddle of boxers and joggers from the floorboards between us and pulled them back over my hips. After a moment of adjusting, I placed my face in my hands and sighed softly.

"I wish you told me sooner," I admitted. The jitters of pleasure still buzzed my spine as I parted my fingers to meet his gaze.

Brooke adjusted himself, now sitting criss-cross, though he was considerably squished. He reached to pull one of my hands from my face, stroking the skin of my forearm as he nodded slowly.

"I couldn't risk messing it up… if you didn't look terrified, they may have sensed something was off," Brooke explained, sending a gentle squeeze to his hand.

I sighed, reaching into the armrest to retrieve my ticket. The plane left at Two in the morning, and as I lifted my eyes to fall on the clock on the desk I felt my sadness deepen. Midnight.

"We gotta go in. Security takes ages in Atlanta," Brooke urged softly, brushing his knuckles against my knee. "Can you pass me the jacket in the back seat next to Rae's seat?"

The desire to revert to stubbornness boiled in my belly, and I glanced over my shoulder to the seat just behind me. My face pulled into a pout and I crossed my arms.

"You want to cover up all of my hard work?" I asked.

His eyes flickered, and a smirk lifted the corners of his lips. "Don't worry, I'll lick it clean later," he fired back.

Fucksake.

My face lit up in a deep crimson blush as my pout transformed into a cringe. "That's Gay," I said in a camp tease.

"Bisexual, actually," Brooke asserted,pointing to the jacket behind me, "Jacket?"

A sighed, resigned, then allowed the cross of my arms to fall so that I could retrieve the covering and toss it so that it covered his face. With him sufficiently covered, I grabbed the handle of the door and stepped out of the car into the silent and mostly empty parking garage.

The air was frigid despite the early springs of Atlanta being nice and warm. My feet tapped along the concrete as I slinked to the boot of the car to pull my duffle bag from inside.

By the time I had closed the lid, Brooke was at my side. Fully tucked away and dressed in a presentable manner. It was as though we hadn't just defiled this very car park with our deeds.

A stern pout twisted my face again as I met his eyes, "trying so hard to get rid of me," I whined.

He grinned, looping an arm around my waist to pull me closer as he gently kissed my forehead. "Actually, it is taking everything in me to hold myself together right now," Brooke admitted, pulling out his keys to lock the car as we started walking towards International Departures.

The echo of our footsteps in the concourse rattled through my mind, and I held a tight grip of my duffle bag's strap as my eyes followed along the floor.

A warm pressure softened against my forearm, the sensation of Brooke's hand gracing my skin as he gently pulled my fingers free of their death grip on my bag to intertwine with his own. He held our hands together between us as we approached a check in booth.

I checked in at the desk, then turned towards the TSA line… dread rushed through my shoulders, and I stopped dead in my tracks to glance at Brooke.

His eyes were distant, focusing on the far signage as he stopped alongside me.

"I guess this is see you later?" I asked softly, fidgeting with his fingers in my hand.

Brooke nodded softly, stepping closer to wrap his arms around me. He pressed his lips to my forehead and pulled in a slow breath.

I followed his actions, taking a deep breath of my own. This was fucking shit… here I was, leaving the only man who had ever actually even pretended to love me to follow my own dreams and escape my own nightmares… unsure if I'd ever actually see him again.

Tears filled my eyes, spilling down my cheeks as I trembled in a soft sob. My face fell into Brooke's shoulder as I clung to him. I didn't want him to let me go… not alone.

"Fuck," I choked out, "this is so… so fucking hard, Brooke."

He nodded, tightening his hug around me. For a moment, I felt the steam of his tears against my hair as he nuzzled into my skull.

"I love you, Ellis," he muttered, a hand gripping at my freshly dyed blonde hair.

I trembled, nodding softly. "I love you Brooke… I love you, and I wish I told you sooner…" I whimpered, "you… you better fucking come for me."

He chuckled, hooking a thumb under my jaw to angle my face towards his for a kiss. I sank against his lips in a hungry, morose embrace.

My heart ached in my chest as he pulled away slowly, both hands grasping to the flesh of my biceps.

"You be safe, okay? Find a way to contact me as soon as you can. Everything is going to be okay," He said, taking a defining step back.

The absence of his presence resonated within me like the dull buzz of a broken wire, an anxiety which manifested in intense dread and utter pain. My eyes fell, and I glanced back to the TSA line.

I needed to get myself together… there was no point in pussy footing around this. Brooke had given me an opportunity to escape, and I needed to grab it and fucking run before Lorenzo caught on that I hadn't been actually kidnapped.

My shoulders stiffened, and I returned my eyes to Brooke to flash him a bright, flamboyant smile. I fluttered my eyelashes and brightened my face with that artificial sweetener that I sprinkled over everyone I spoke to.

"Well, Darling… if you need anything…" I waggled my fingers to him sweetly, though my eyes conveyed a sadness that I couldn't verbalize in this moment. "Ask for Ellis!" I winked and blew him a final kiss before sashaying towards the TSA line.

I didn't look back.

I couldn't.

I just had to put one foot in front of the other, again and again, until I managed to disappear into the crowd.

When I finally drew the courage to spare a single glance

to where I had come from... Brooke was still there. His eyes cemented to me

A rush of energy surged through my veins, and I smiled... for real this time. I could do this... for Brooke.

What Good Is Love?

BROOKE

The sharp trill of my alarm sliced through the eaves of my gentle sleep. I opened my eyes, searching the dark corners of my room with a stiff groan as I pushed myself to sit up.

The bed was plush, comfortable but different than what I was used to.

To my side, Rae curled up sweetly against a pillow border that I had set up to prevent her from rolling off the edge of the bed.

Jet lag was fucking real… and England being five hours ahead of Georgia time meant that I was operating on the wrong time zone.

I gently ran a hand over Rae's back, then fluffed the tightly coiled brown curls on the top of her head. Thin but kinky hair that would more than likely soften in the coming years.

She squirmed lightly, squeaking as her little green eyes fluttered open with the sweetest squint. Her gaze searched the dim lighting of the room for me, tiny hands reaching beneath her to push herself upright.

It was September, now… the fact that I had a one-year-old was absolutely baffling to me. Rae had grown so much, and so quickly.

Rae spotted me, her eyes lighting up as she crawled from her spot to climb into my lap and snuggle against my chest. "Daddy!"

My face brightened, and I encircled my arms around her, "Good morning, my beautiful girl," I sang softly. With a gentle pull, I adjusted her so that her arms could circle around my neck. "You ready for a busy day?" I asked softly.

"Bee-see?" She asked in the cutest tone, pulling her head back to look at me.

I nodded, "yes. Super busy," I explained, leaning back against the headboard of this new bed. As my curls pressed against the wood, I pulled in a slow breath through my nose. The scent of old musk and dust. "We have to go get the keys to our home and then we have to buy you a bed so that you can sleep in your own big girl bed!"

She brightened, an excited look in her eyes.

It often surprised me how well she understood me, even if she didn't have access to all of the words to communicate back, she seemed to know exactly what I meant.

An excited bounce against my chest preceded a question which had been asked at an insane frequency as of late.

"Daddy, see Ellie?" She asked.

My heart raced in my chest, and I nibbled at my lip. "I hope so, baby," I kissed her forehead, pulling away so that I could let out a loud, boisterous, dad-yawn.

Rae pouted, "Miss Ellie," she said in a sad tone.

I smiled, nodding softly as I brushed my fingers through her hair, "I miss Ellie too, baby," I said softly, wrapping her up into a tight hug as I slowly stepped out of the bed.

With a twirl, I escorted Rae to where our suitcases were propped on a nearby table, then rested her on my hip while I rustled through the bags.

"What should we wear today, princess?" I asked, while snatching a rainbow coloured dress from the suitcase which held far more clothing of hers than my own.

After she was dressed, I set her down on her feet and handed her a doll which she had grown fond of. She clutched the toy to her chest and waddled over to a chair, climbing into the seat and snuggling the doll, a thumb in her mouth.

I grabbed the remote control to the small flat screen TV in her view and turned it on, flipping through the channels until I found CBeeBies, the children's network.

With Rae now thoroughly distracted, I took this time to dress myself and figure out the plan for the day.

My new job wanted me to come in for an induction, and they had arranged an on-site childminder to watch Rae for me… which was more than I could have ever asked for.

The jet lag still rocked me in my boots, though. A reminder of the fact that I had spent nearly twelve hours trapped in a plane with a toddler and two bags full of items that would have to supplement my life for the foreseeable future.

"Daddy," Rae called sweetly from her chair.

I glanced over at her, smiling softly as she pointed at the television screen.

"Ellie?" She asked.

The screen displayed a man with similar features and a strikingly similar accent, but it wasn't Ellis. A chuckle lifted to my lips, and I shook my head.

"No, baby. But he does *look* like Ellie a bit, doesn't he?"

She nodded certainly, pulling her thumb to her mouth as she snuggled her doll.

I smiled, returning to my original task. I brushed and tied my hair back... it was getting far too long, now... should have cut it before we flew. Then I grabbed the strap of Rae's bag, throwing it over my shoulder and stepping towards her to scoop her into my arms.

She snuggled close, eyes remaining on the bright, colourful images on the screen.

"Ready for an adventure?" I asked softly, smoothing down her hair.

Rae nodded, pulling her thumb from her mouth to wrap both arms around her doll.

I stepped out of the room, phone and key card in hand, then made my way from the hotel towards the hospital (Which... was within walking distance). The childminder met me in the lobby, and Rae reluctantly left my arms for this new person.

My induction lasted nearly six hours and consisted of paperwork, slide shows, team introductions, and being blatantly exhausted. Signing on as the manager for the dispatch call centre for one of the busiest Ambulance and police services in South London was a big deal... more so than I necessarily expected.

By the end of the workday, my head was spinning with all

of the things I wasn't quite sure about. Was I in over my head with this?

I couldn't exactly go back... not now.

As I made my way through the corridor towards the childcare reception, my phone buzzed in my pocket.

My heart leapt, and I quickly retrieved the device from my pocket. There was an understandable disappointment, though only brief, when I saw the name across my screen: Ginger.

I swiped to answer and pulled the phone to my ear.

"Hello!" I said in a hushed voice, aware of the presence of other people.

"Hiya, chicken!" The soft, feminine voice pulled through the speaker. "Seems you and the princess made a safe landing."

I grinned, pressing my back to the wall of the corridor behind me. "I'm struggling a bit with the time difference, but we are safe. I just finished here at the hospital and now I need to pick Rae up and get the keys to the flat," The more I spoke, the more I began to stress. There was so much to do...

A shrill, but calming laugh signalled from the other line. "Take a breath, hun. Are you coming tonight?"

Guilt burned in my chest, "I want to come, more than anything... but I don't have anyone to watch Rae, and I am worried it'll be too loud for her."

"Don't you dare," Ginger sang, "I know you're absolutely gagging to see our Ellis. We will arrange something for Rae."

My heart raced at the mention of his name. I hadn't been able to get through to him in the past few days because of how busy everything has been... I knew that has probably hurt him.

"Well?" Ginger asked.

I nodded, not that she could see me, "Yeah... okay. Give me the address, and I'll be there."

The energy on the call brightened significantly, and Ginger squealed, "Fantastic! He is going to be overjoyed," She said brightly, "I'll see you later, chicken, tu-rah!"

The call ended.

A familiar buzz rolled through me, like butterflies on a first date... I couldn't wait to see him.

After picking Rae up, I made my way to the lettings office that I was directed to, and the agent led me through the building to a door.

"This is you, Mr. Morris!" She sang in that same, chipper tone that Ellis always had.

I smiled, lifted the key to the lock and twisted it. The door opened, revealing a nice, modern apartment which came furnished. Relief fell over my shoulder, and I turned to the agent.

"Anything I need to know before I settle in?" I asked.

She smiled, "It has two bedrooms with a balcony, shower, and communal laundry facilities. Walking distance to shops and parks... a nice place for you and your bairn!"

Rae clung to my shirt, looking into the entryway of our home with a sweet gaze. I thanked the agent, then stepped inside. The little girl in my arms wriggled, wanting to be put down, and as I knelt to place her on the floor, she wrapped her hand tight around the fabric of my trousers.

"Do you like it, baby?" I asked, watching her curious gaze as she looked around.

She didn't respond, but walked away towards a couch in the lounge portion of the room. Rae placed her hands on the cushions, then glanced back at me with a sweet smile. She didn't know what was going on, but she was happy to be here. That was all that mattered to me.

I opened the doors to the bedrooms, breathing a soft sigh of relief that they had taken care of the bed situation. In the smaller room, there was a twin-sized daybed that would be perfect for Rae now that she was transitioning from her crib.

If anything gave me security, it was that Rae would be comfortable.

"Daddy!" She called to me, pushing her head between my knee and the frame of her bedroom door. "Fow Wae?" She asked, pointing at her bed.

I nodded, stooping to scoop her into my arms, "Yes, bug. This room is for Rae." I grinned and placed a kiss on her head. "We gotta go get our bags. Will you be a good girl and walk for Daddy?"

A pout pulled across her cheeks, but she looked resigned. Rae actually really enjoyed walking, she just didn't like people knowing that.

Together, we collected our belongings from the hotel and returned to the new apartment, where Rae lounged across the couch. Exhausted after all of her hard work and heavy lifting (of which meant carrying her doll the whole way... I know... dreadful, isn't it?)

I was just finishing filling Rae's drawers with her clothes when the alarm I had set on my phone went off from the lounge.

"Daddy!" Rae called, jumping down from the couch and grabbing my phone in her tiny hands. Her footsteps patter across the soft carpet as she ran into her room, where I was sitting criss-cross on the floor in front of her dresser. She held out my singing device with a bright, accomplished look on her tiny face.

"Ah! My hero!" I sang, collecting the phone from her hands and peppering her face in kisses, "Thank you so much, my pretty girl!"

She let out a few squeals, giggling sweetly to herself as she dodged my attempts to cuddle her.

"Go get your shoes, Rae. I'll help you put them on," I said as I pushed myself to stand.

The curly-top bundle of energy ran full speed towards a line of various shoes, choosing the little yellow rainboots with orang duck-bills on the toes and shiny black eyes. These were her absolute favourite thing to wear.

A smile lifted the corners of my lips as I knelt down beside her and helped guide her feet into the boots. When I finished, she clapped her hands excitedly and bent to poke the bills.

"Quack!" She sang.

I laughed, nodding. "Quack, indeed," I hummed stepped through the door to her room and grabbed a coat that lay across the simple white table in the dining room. "Ready to go?"

"Where go, Daddy?" Rae waddled over, her duckie rain boots clacking across the hardwood of the dining room.

A part of me debated on telling her the truth… I didn't want to get her hopes up, so I sank to collect her from the floor into my arms. She hugged my neck, and I nuzzled into her cheek, "We are gonna go see some friends, bug."

She seemed content with this explanation, so she snuggled close and I kissed the fluff of her hair atop her head. I queued up the maps for the venue and bundled Rae up for our walk.

Late September in England was significantly colder than Georgia's autumn, and though it made a nice change, my little one wasn't very fond of being cold.

Her little arms snuggled into my jacket, even though she was wearing quite a thick jacket already, and she buried her face in my shoulder.

The city life in England was different than the US, almost entirely. The architecture and overall attitude of the people were starkly different. Even the more built-up areas felt alive and intimate.

Occasionally, when I glanced down at Rae, I would see her eyes fixated by the bright lights, distracted by distant music of buskers. It felt safe... but it could just be because I had absolutely no clue what was going on or where I was outside of the little blue line I followed on Google Maps.

Soon, we approached the building where my digital guide came to an abrupt stop. It was a small dive bar with a bright pink neon sign bolted to the front, called *The Blue Lagoon*.

I glanced down at Rae, who met my eyes with an equally lost stare. We were here, in the middle of London, at some random bar that was meant to house the man of my dreams. This is what I had been waiting for since Ellis had to go months before.

"Hey, Chicken!" A familiar voice called from beside me.

I turned my gaze to meet the source. It was a woman whom I had never met before, and yet I recognized who she was in an instant.

"Hi, Ginger?" I asked cautiously, keeping my voice low.

This woman brightened, her blue eyes shimmering as she ran a hand through the bob of bright red hair on her head. Her large, full eyelashes fluttered as she looked me over and settled her own gaze on Rae.

"Is that our princess?" She asked in a thick cockney,

stepping closer. The bright yellow, designer dress fitting her figure in a beautiful, slinky silhouette. Her long, slender fingers outstretched to brush along Rae's cheek.

Rae smiled and pulled a hand from my collar to wave sweetly, "Hiya!" She said cutely.

My heart gushed, and Ginger melted.

"Hello, petal!" She sang, then turned her attention back to me. "Let's get you two inside before our bestie gets here. He is ALWAYS late, something I am hoping that your presence will fix in the near future." The woman hummed with a sassy sway of her hips as she moved towards the entrance of the bar.

I followed her inside, nuzzling into Rae's cheek as we entered the building. It was clearly not the classiest venue. The air smelled of alcohol and my shoes stuck to the tacky, sticky floor. This reminded me so much of the Midnight Raven that I nearly felt a pull of the anxiety back out the door, but Ginger sashayed onwards toward a double door which remained closed at present.

Ginger glanced back over her shoulder and winked, "Follow me, chicken. I don't bite!" She led us through what seemed like a backstage area to a dressing room.

Once inside, she locked the door and turned to face me and Rae. "Your Ellis has been a pain in my backside," she grinned, "He is always working. If he isn't working, he is in Drag. You'd think I didn't pay him a living wage!" She explained in a bubbly tone, skipping around the room.

Before I could speak, she was on again, "This is a private dressing room, the others are booked. I have requested for my sister to come in and sit with Rae while the show is on... she is a registered Childminder and she has just finished her levels in Early Years, so there is nothing to worry about!"

Levels?

Ginger was speaking blatant English to me, the language I had spoken my whole life... but I had no fucking clue what the hell a level was.

A knock sounded from the door, and Ginger sprinted to open it, poking her head out for a few seconds before opening the door and allowing a young woman who looked strikingly similar to her into the room.

This new woman smiled sweetly, long brown hair fell over her soft shoulders. She was modestly dressed, in a long blue dress and black tights. "I'm Kennah!" She said sweetly, "You must be Brooke." Her voice was softer than Ginger's, a smoother elegance that juxtaposed the redhead with a bob.

I chuckled, nodding, "Nice to meet you, Kennah."

Kennah grinned and looked at Rae. "Hello, gorgeous!" She sang sweetly, "I've brought so many fun things for us to do," The young woman stepped forwards to extend her arms. "Would you like to come with me so your Daddy can go see his friend?"

Reluctant, Rae pursed her lips, she looked up at me and narrowed her eyes as if I was withholding her from access to fun. I sent her a smile in return and pat her bottom.

"I'll bring you back a surprise," I said softly, "You play in here with Kennah, and I will bring you back a super cool surprise."

This seemed to persuade her, and Rae released her grip on me, outstretching her arms to this new stranger. Rae was a sociable toddler, one who seemed to do things without complaint.

I smiled as she sank into this new woman's arms and waved

to her before following Ginger back out of the room.

"You can see how much you love her. She is a very happy little girl," Ginger commented as we stepped through the corridor.

My face warmed with a smile, "Thank you, she is definitely one of the only things that keeps me going."

The redhead laughed softly, "I understand that. My son is my world, and I would burn this city down for him."

I lifted my eyes, noting that Ginger's blue eyes were settled on me. She had stopped walking.

"He has missed you so much... this is going to be so good for him, I am glad that you've asked for my help with surprising him." She said softly, then pressed her hand to the dining area door, "You sit in here. Front and centre. Ellis is always the opener, so you won't be away from Rae for too long. He performs three sets, but... tonight, I'm willing to let him go early. I can step in and fill his stilettos."

I tried to send her as much of a thankful expression as I could, the anxiety of what was to come building in my chest.

Ginger's eyes softened, and she extended her arms to pull me into a hug. Her shoulders were broad, a juxtaposition to his sister, and yet her lean arms enveloped me in a comforting hug. "It is all going to be so fun, just take a breath... get a drink on me. Show starts in half an hour."

As she pulled away, I felt the apprehension return, but I nodded, glancing down at my phone.

"Don't you dare tell him you're here," She grinned, then pushed me into the main dining area of the stage room, and closed the doors behind me.

I looked around, seeing quite a few other patrons inside. A few bachelorette parties were already in their seats, and a front row had a seat that seemed very strategically placed... I took the hint and found my seat.

The room buzzed with energy, and soon filled to the brim with chatting patrons. They all seemed to belong here, almost like they knew every other person in the room.

I held my phone anxiously, staring down at the screen. Switching to an English SIM meant that I could escape the barrage of calls and messages from my psychotic ex-wife. Even though she was currently in prison for attempted kidnapping and assault, the collect calls were frequent. It seemed that any time she gained access to the phones, she would spam my line.

The device buzzed in my hand as a message through WhatsApp pinged through. It was Ellis.

Ellis: Late to work, as usual. Ginge may kill me this time. Says there is a celebrity in the crowd tonight, lol. I miss you

xxx

My heart raced, and I smiled as I read the message over and over again. I quickly typed out my own response.

Me: I miss you too, better not let that celebrity sweep you off your feet.

Ellis: Well, can't make any promises. Ginger says he is well fit xxx

A grin covered my face, and I sank back against my seat... this was so fucking surreal.

Ellis: Jokes, Darling. I love you... I really miss you...

This broke my heart... it just reaffirmed that he really didn't know that I was just down the hall from him.

Me: I love you, Ellis. I'll be there soon, I promise.

Ellis: You better, I hear there is a fit celebrity outside.

Ellis: I'll give you a bell once I finish tonight. Gotta put my face on xxxxxxxx

Me: Have fun, speak soon <3

I settled in my chair, sinking back as Ginger emerged from backstage once more. This time, she had a bright red wig with a massive poof at the top of her head, a sparkling, slinky blue ballgown covered in rhinestones and heels that made her about half a foot taller than she had been before.

She stepped effortlessly to the middle of the stage and grabbed hold of the microphone. "Hello, my Darlings!" She sang into the crowd, silencing the room with her simple phrase. "I want to let you know that our lead act tonight may be disappearing after her first number, we have a super special guest in the crowd today that may be whisking our beloved Faye away. Don't you dare tell her, but her partner has arrived from America and this will be the first time they've seen each other for months. So, try not to cry, and lets enjoy our little kiki!"

A few whoops from the crowd, and some awing. I felt my cheeks warm as Ginger winked at me.

"Right you filthy slags, shall we get this fucking party started, then?" She called into the speakers. Music filled the room, and she continued to announce. As most shows go, discussions of consent and respect headed the actual show, and Ginger rattled off the script as though she had it scribbled behind her eyelids.

"And finally, most importantly, have a fucking ball, Darlings! Let's get this party started with our first fantastic bitch. My best friend, a West Midlands bumpkin with enough sass to single-handedly demolish the trees off a bigot, Faye Tality!" Ginger turned, pulling her hand back to motion to the doors behind her as the music shifted, a soft twinkle in the distance and the faintest rift of a guitar.

Then I heard him... I heard Ellis's voice take over the speakers around us.

My Dolled-Up Lunatic...

My heart raced in my chest, and I but down hard on my lip. For months I had longed to hear his voice... singing... to watch him in his element. The world mattered not when Ellis sang.

This band was his favourite. The Scarlet Opera.

"Life after love, I'm at the cinema. Where I pick apart the final feeling, the credits roll but I'm not leaving," two drum beats sound, and with that, the doors to the stage fly open to reveal... *Faye Tality*.

She had a blonde wig, voluminous with tightly wound ringlets that fluffed far beyond her face. A dress in cobalt blue hugged her features, slit from her hip to reveal the curve of her thighs... those thighs that drove me mad.

Her nails were long, a sharp, sparkling silver polish which complimented the rhinestones that dotted her cheeks. Deep crimson lips, darkly rouged cheeks... and those eyes.

Fuck me...

The stage lights framed her face enough to give me the most perfect view of those stunning brown eyes.

My face warmed, heart in my throat as I watched her. This was the love of my life, the fire to my soul.

And she didn't even know I was here.

Her hands gripped tight to a microphone as she launched into the chorus. Notes flew from her lips like silk as she belted the notes.

"What good is love?"

Her smoky-grey eyelids closed as she embraced the feeling

in the lyrics, sinking back to clutch a hand to her chest. I could feel the pain in her voice... had I done that to her?

She called the question out again, her eyes opening this time to scan the right side of the crowd, a hand outstretched to capture their attention.

The chorus finished, and Faye began to dance. As she lowered the microphone, I watched as her eyes scanned the back of the room, though I couldn't tell if she was actually seeing them.

"Rain on the phone," she galloped down from the stage, her silver heels clacking in sexy percussion against the floor as she stepped closer, unknowing. "You cry electrical!" Her free hand presses against a table as she leaned against it, throwing back her head in dramatic fashion.

"The powers out, I've lost your message... there's nothing left unsaid, I've said it!" Faye pushed from the table to sashay to a table directly opposite to her.

I revelled in the gust of wind that her movements sent in my direction, the faintest scent of vanilla laced with hairspray... familiar.

"Head over heels," she dipped to hook a finger under another man's chin, guiding his eyes up to meet hers for a millisecond, "I let the chaos take the wheel!" She pressed that hand to his chest to settle him back into his seat.

"A million miles from home and counting, the music stops and now I'm shouting..." Faye turned to face me head on, though her eyes fluttered closed as she belted out her question again.

"What good is love?"

I held my gaze on her, begging silently for her to open her eyes... to see me...

She outstretched her free hand to the ceiling. "What good is love?"

Her eyes opened once more, and as if by habit, she stepped forward, sinking into my lap and hooking an arm around my neck as she continued to sing, not even clocking where she was.

She was so warm… and I lifted my hand to brace against her lower back, pulsing a gentle squeeze that summoned a glare. In an instant… the glare shifted. Her voice cracked. She pulled the mic from her lips and slapped a hand over her mouth.

Faye stared at me as though she had seen a ghost. Her eyes locked onto mine, and the whole world faded away in that instant. The instrumental dissolved into the back of our senses, and the racing of my heart slowed to beat in heavy throbs.

The crowd around us cheered, clapping and hollering. Soon, the silence from Faye concluded, and she turned to place the microphone against her lips.

"Sorry, Darlings… this has just totally mind fucked me," she laughed into the speakers. She glanced back at me briefly, though the music has stopped now. "Did all of you know about this?" She pointed around us, a teasing, accusatory glare in her eyes as she peeled away from me.

The absence of Faye's warmth hit me like a ton of bricks, and she crossed her slender arms in a signature sassy stance as she looked down at me, "I'm so mad at you," she joked into the microphone, summoning a barrage of laughter from the crowd.

She lifted a finger to her eye, pretending to swipe away a tear as he dramatically cleared her throat, "Ehem… anyways..." she stepped back towards the stage, the fabric of her dress pulling tight against the plumpness of her ass as she lifted her legs one at a time to bound onto the platform.

With an elegant twirl, she faced the crowd again, "Right, you lot!" She fired a glare at Ginger, "I've got a bone to pick with my business partner, so I hope you enjoy the show..." just before she left the stage, she jabbed a finger in my direction.

"You," she snapped. "Backstage. Now."

The crowd erupted in laughter and vowel stretching, and the smirk that pulled across my face only partially masked the excitement that bubbled in my chest.

I pushed myself to stand, garnering a fair amount of applause myself as I stepped onto the stage and followed Faye out of the back-stage doors.

The instant the doors closed behind me, she spun around and pressed her hands to my shoulders to pin me against the near wall.

"You dick," She said, her voice dropping from the feminine pitch that it had embodied mere seconds before.

I stared up at her, towering above me with the support of her seven-inch platforms. The long, false eyelashes that framed her meticulously painted eyelids fluttered as she held onto my gaze.

"I wanted to surprise you," I muttered softly, my arms gently resting against her hips.

The touch softened the sass in her stance, and Faye melted away as she gathered her bottom lip with her teeth, biting down gently.

"Did Ginger help you?" She asked, the pin against the wall transitioning as she moved her hands to cup my face.

I nodded softly, "Will you stop being a diva and kiss me?" I asked.

She dipped down, pressing those crimson painted lips to mine. Electricity buzzed through me, warmth building on my cheeks. A hunger for everything that Faye was burned in my chest, and I melted against her touch.

"I knew you wouldn't be able to keep your hands off of him," Ginger's voice pulled through the echo of the hallway, and Faye pulled from me.

"You cheeky bitch," Faye fired to her friend, "you promised me a fit celebrity!"

Ginger smirked, glancing between us. "Listen, he is only short because you decided to wear fucking monster platforms! I bet he is a perfectly acceptable height when you don't have stilts on."

Faye stepped towards Ginger with a glare, arms crossed in a warning... but as the silence between them persisted, Faye softened and threw her arms around Ginger for a hug.

"Thank you," she whispered.

Ginger returned the embrace, placing a sweet kiss to Faye's cheek, "You deserve this, Darling... take this as your eviction notice."

Faye howled in laughter, "You're kicking me out?"

"Yes! I can't wait to have my dressing room back!" Ginger teased.

The laughed eased, and Faye glanced back at me, the buzz of excitement slowly fizzling out as she reached a hand back to me to beckon me closer.

"You two head on home... I've got tonight covered for you, Darling," Ginger placed a hand on Faye's shoulder with a gentle squeeze.

As I reached Faye's side, I extended my hand to lace our

fingers together. Her slender digits curled into mine, clasping tight on my hand as she nodded thankfully to her friend.

Without another word, Faye pulled me down the corridor towards a dressing room. "You wait here, the other Queens might not appreciate a guest."

"I will wait for you in this room," I pointed to the room where my daughter and the childminder waited for me.

She tilted her head, "Ginger told me that room was booked," she said softly.

I grinned, "it is. For me," I flipped my long curls over my shoulder, "How else was I supposed to look so good for you tonight?"

Faye smirked, stepping closer to steal a quick kiss before disappearing into the dressing room.

I relaxed, turning on my heels to enter the other room.

Rae was sat on a blanket on the floor next to Kennah, thoroughly distracted by a fibre optic sensory toy.

My shoulders eased, and I watched her tiny hands play with the nodes. She glanced up to notice me and her bright green eyes flashed with recognition.

"Daddy!" She squealed, pushing herself to stand slowly, then clumsily toddling to hug my leg.

A smile pulled across my face, and I crouched to ruffle her fluffy brown hair. "Hey, bug! Are you having fun?" I asked softly.

She pointed to the toy, grunting sweetly as it changed from blue to green.

"Gween!" She squealed happily, clapping her hands.

"That is Green!" I cheered, "isn't that neat?"

Rae giggled, nodding, "Neat!"

The woman who had been watching Rae smiled sweetly.

"Rae is such a good girl. We had a few tears when you first left, but she cheered up when we started playing," Kennah explained happily, tidying up the mess of toys, slowly putting them back in her bag.

"Thank you, she has always been a chill baby," I said softly, "haven't you, Rae-Rae?"

The toddler grinned brightly, toddling back to the fibre optic toy and stroking the fibres cutely.

The door behind me clicked as it opened, and Ellis entered. His face was still painted in his makeup from the stage, but he had removed Faye's wig and changed into an oversized hoodie, plain white tennis shoes, and sweatpants, a coat hooked over his arm.

My eyes widened, and I rose from my crouched position. Though I had held him moments before… it felt so real now that he was dressed naturally.

"Ellie!" Rae squealed, jumping up from her place on the blanket and running clumsily towards Ellis.

His eyes widened, and he hit his knees to catch her in a tight hug. "Oh my, Darling!" He called, scooping her into his arms as tears brimmed along his lower lash line, "you're walking now!"

My heart ached, and I had to hold my own composure at their reunion. Rae locked her arms around his neck and held tight to him, sinking into his chest.

Ellis braced her gently in his arms as he pushed himself to stand, one hand pulling gently through her hair, careful not to catch her skin with his nails. "I missed you so much, Babs," he covered her cheeks in soft kisses. The light imprint of his lipstick leaving pink pigment over her cheeks.

His gaze moved to meet mine, and he stepped closer.

"I'm taller, now." I hooked an arm around his waist as he grew close enough.

A pout pulled at his lips, "Barely," he fired back, sinking into my touch and allowing his eyes to close in contentment as his breathing steadied.

For a moment, I permitted this silence, sinking into his embrace just the same as I felt our energies burn together. The peace in our space felt immense, and I rested my cheek against his short blonde hair.

Natural blonde, not bleached. His frame felt firm, less sack of bones. He felt healthy. He felt strong.

My heart surged, and I breathed out a sigh of relief. My entire world was in my arms now.

"Can we go?" Ellis whispered, then moved his face to glance up at me, ear still pressed to my shoulder. "I need to be alone with you."

A chuckle lifted to my chest, and I nodded softly. "Let's go, then," I pressed a kiss to his temple and turned to Kennah.

"I don't have cash on me, but I will transfer Ginger some money to give you for watching Rae," I said softly.

Kennah laughed, shaking her head, "I did it as a favour. You two go on and get home, seems you've got lots to catch up on."

Gratitude burned on my face, and I nodded softly, moving to release my hold of Ellis and intertwining our fingers as I led him out of the building.

Ask For Ellis

BROOKE

Once outside, I pulled up the directions back home on my phone. This summoned a soft chuckle from Ellis, and he glanced at the maps.

"I've got it, you can put that away now. It may not seem dangerous, but people will nick your phone if you're not careful," he explained softly.

I listened, putting the phone into my pocket and following Ellis's lead.

Rae snuggled into him, whimpering.

"What is it, Darling? Are you cold?" Ellis asked sweetly, stroking her back as he pulled the breast of his coat open, tucking it around her tiny body to seal her within his embrace.

She settled, sinking into his chest with a sleepy grasp of his hoodie's collar.

His eyes softened, and he glanced over at me, the brown of his irises twinkling with the sweetest expressions. "My heart," he muttered.

I sent his hand a gentle squeeze, smiling in return.

Ellis guided me back towards the area of my new apartment, and when the buildings around me started to look familiar, I took over and led him to the complex and up through the elevator to the home which I had only just settled into myself.

As I pushed the door open, Ellis's eyes widened. "What? They've allocated this to you?" He asked as he stepped through the door.

I chuckled softly, locking the door behind us. "Yeah… it is temporary, of course. But it's ours for six months until we can find something else."

"Ours?" He asked softly, glancing back at me with a gentle smile.

My heart raced at the sight of him. Bundled up in warm clothes as he held Rae to his chest. A soft, loving expression on his face as he cradled her. My ever present silence continued, and my hands slipped into my pockets.

Ellis shifted, the smile on his face deepening as he fluttered his eyelashes. "You're staring, again," he said, tone dipping to a low whisper.

I blinked, shaking my head lightly to pull myself back into reality. "Sorry," I muttered.

"Don't be. I missed your awkwardness," Ellis grinned, then kissed Rae's forehead. She had fallen asleep against his chest, clinging tight to the fabric of his hoodie.

"Would you like me to take her?" I asked softly.

He sent me an offended glare, narrowing his eyes, "don't you dare," he warned, glancing around the room anxiously. "May I sit?"

I chuckled, rubbing my neck softly, "Baby, you don't have to ask to sit down," I said.

Ellis relaxed his shoulders, moving to sit down on the grey sofa, gently adjusting Rae in his arms as he sank into the cushions. He cooed to her in a hushed tone as his fingers gently pulled through her brown curls. Love burned in his eyes as he watched the sleeping girl.

Staring was an unbecoming trait of mine. Where words escaped me, I found solace in living in the moment and being able to experience the purity of these times.

"I like your new name," I said, my voice hushing to a whisper so as to avoid rousing Rae.

Ellis glanced over at me with a soft wink, "Life is about embracing the traumatic things," he whispered.

Trauma makes us who we are... and even though I wouldn't wish it on anyone or want to go through it again, it was important for my growth. And... I never would have explored this side of my romantic preferences had I not been burned.

The trauma didn't give me Ellis...Kelly didn't give me Ellis... the trauma gave the courage to face my discomfort and try something new... my something new just happened to be falling completely and totally in love with a man who had turned my entire life around. I didn't have the trauma to thank for where I was right now. Kelly wasn't to thank for that... I was.

He was so right. It is so... important to embrace the trauma, to use it to armour yourself.

I stepped closer. "Should we put Rae to bed?" I asked softly.

His eyes fell to her, staring into the peace and innocence that persisted in her aura. He nodded slowly, slowly getting up and following me to Rae's bedroom.

Ellis knelt down beside the daybed, tucking her into the blankets that I had laid out earlier on and pressing a kiss to her forehead as he pulled away.

A smile warmed my face, and I created a barrier wall along the edge of the bed with pillows. Rae was quite good at sleeping in her own bed, but it was protection for my own mind mostly.

As I stepped back, Ellis pressed into my chest, his head resting on my shoulder as he watched her sleep.

"She is so big now, Darling..." He whispered, sinking closer to me, "I missed so much..."

I nuzzled my nose into his hair, placing a kiss on his hair as slipped an arm around his waist. "She missed you. Every night she would ask about you."

His eyes glistened, and he hid his face in my chest. "Can we go sit?" He asked softly.

After checking on Rae one more time, I nodded and pulled him through to the lounge, leaving her door slightly ajar since I didn't have a baby monitor quite yet.

Ellis pulled from me. "I'm just gonna remove Faye," he said softly, motioning to his face as he stepped toward the bathroom and closed the door.

In the meantime, I sank into the couch. Today has been exhausting, and I wouldn't be entirely lying if I said that I was ready to crash.

But as the door to the bathroom opened, Ellis emerged in a

plain, cropped tank top and the sweats from before. He had removed his makeup, allowing the age on his face to show. He maintained the overall feminine shape of his face, but the more masculine features shine against his skin. Peachy patches from where he had scrubbed a bit more.

The second his eyes fell on me, the exhaustion zipped from my mind, and I allowed another relaxed sigh to roll off my chest.

Ellis stepped towards me, walking on the ball of his foot as though he was stuck in a pair of invisible heels. He sank into the seat beside me.

"There is a nice gym not too far from here," he said softly, leaning back against the seat as he smiled. "They do MMA classes. Maybe you can join?"

I chuckled, reaching to gently rest a hand on his thigh. "I might be up for that."

He hummed, reaching a hand up to pull through his hair. "I can't believe you didn't tell me anything," he said softly. There was a subtle disappointment on his face. One that I felt strike me in my soul.

Guilt burned in my chest, and I retrieved my hand from his thigh. This triggered a glare from him.

"I can be mad at you and still love you," he grumbled softly, "I can be mad and still be happy to see you."

I lifted an eyebrow, tilting my head as I slowly moved my gaze to meet his. His brown eyes soldered onto mine and I felt the breath vacate my lungs.

"Brooke," he said softly.

"Yes, Ellis?"

He sank closer to me, pressing a kiss to my jaw. "Thank you," he whispered, "For surprising me... I have been really struggling."

My heartbeat throbbed in my chest, and I moved to wrap my arms around Ellis's waist. "Do you need to talk about it?"

Ellis sighed, allowing his head to rest back against the couch.

"A week after I left… I got a message from one of my friends from the Raven," he said softly. "I don't know how she got my new number… but she did. She told me that she had fled the country with her partner as well…"

"That is a good thing, isn't it?" I asked softly.

He flashed his eyes over to mine, "I thought so… she told me that her partner had bombed Lorenzo's mansion in the hills."

"That… sounds even better," I said softly.

Ellis's eyes dulled. "I got a letter…" he muttered.

Apprehension grew in the energy of the room, and I tilted my head, waiting for him to continue.

"The letter was a summons to international court… He has put a hit on my head," Ellis muttered. "The case isn't supposed to start until twenty-twenty-seven… but I think he is going to do something before then."

"Why do you feel like that?" I asked.

He shifted uncomfortably, glancing around the room. "I think people are following me," he muttered softly.

That familiar feeling of dread rocked through my stomach, and I sighed. "Well… it seems I will be joining that gym," I said softly.

His eyes shifted, looking me up and down. "If they come for me, I don't want you to do anything, Brooke."

"Well that is stupid, I'm going to-"

"No," Ellis said decisively. "I will not let you risk Rae's

childhood."

I froze, taken completely and totally aback. Ellis was deadly serious.

"But… I could just be paranoid…" he muttered, "which… is also his fault because the drugs he used on me have that as a side effect," he sighed, balling his hand into a fist which he pressed to his temple. "So… let's just try to live life the way we intended to, okay?" I asked softly. "Let's… live out our fairytale…"

Fairytale.

I reached forward to press my hand along Ellis's jaw, pressing a soft kiss to his lips. "I promise I'll do what I can to make sure we have our fairytale," I said softly.

He pressed into my chest, stealing another kiss… this one was hungry, full of need.

A need which I planned to reciprocate.

As he kissed me, I pulled my fingertips along his skin, settling my grip around his throat.

A moan slipped from his lips, muffled by the pressure of our kiss. He tangled his fingers in my hair, one hand gripping hard at the mop of curls to peel my head away from him.

"I'm still mad at you," He muttered, trembling in desire.

My eyes narrowed in a seductive challenge as I sank to his ear, nibbling at the lobe as I whispered a sharp query, "What ever can I do to make it up to you?"

Ellis fluttered his eyelashes, returning an equally sultry gaze my direction as he slipped a hand along my chest to settle on my sternum. "Let me fuck you?" He asked in a husky tone.

My eyes widened, and a blush deepened on my cheeks. "Y-you want to fuck me?" I asked.

He nodded softly, "I'll be gentle… since it is your first time,"

He muttered, his eyes darkening with a deep, intense need. "Four months without you… I haven't even had a wank in months… I'm dying to sink myself into your virgin ass."

A shudder rolled across my skin, sending every hair on end as I bit down hard on my bottom lip. The silence seemed to unnerve Ellis, and he softened.

"Y-you don't have to," He muttered, "Not everyone likes being penetrated."

I lifted my eyes to his, sealing our gazes together, "No," I whispered, "I want to try."

The energy between us fizzled in an explosion of electricity, and Ellis's eyes glazed over with excitement. He tugged at my hair once more, forcing my head back as he pushed free from my hold of his neck to sink his teeth against the flesh of my neck.

He nibbled along the sensitive skin, pressing his free hand to my shoulder to push me to sit back against the couch as he swung a leg over my lap, straddling me.

"I need to run to the shop," Ellis whispered sharply in my ear. "Can I have your key?"

My heart raced, hands settling on the platform of his hips as I let out a groan. "Fuck, Ellis," I growled lowly, "Getting me fucking hard and everything just to tease me," I pressed my hips into his, hands holding him secure in his place.

I could feel the shudder of need pulse through him, but he shook his head, "I guarantee that you want actual lube for this, Darling," he hissed seductively, dragging his teeth lightly across my jaw as he pried my hands from his hips and slipped down from the couch.

The bulge in his sweatpants told me that I had succeeded in my own teases.

"Go have a shower, I'll be back before you even realize I'm gone," Ellis placed his hands on my knees as he bent to be eye level with me.

His hair fell messily into his eyes, but didn't hide them. Those brown orbs stared into my soul in a way that made every single atom in my body crave his touch.

I groaned, reaching up to circle my hand around his throat once more, pulling him close enough to steal a filthy kiss.

When I finally released him, Ellis swooned lightly, pulling back and facing away from me.

He swayed his hips in an expert way, no doubt a result of his profession. My eyes soldered to his ass as he disappeared into the bathroom for mere seconds to grab his hoodie from earlier.

When he emerged, still pulling his head through the hole at the top, he bent to grab the keys from the table near the door, glanced up at me to flash me his signature smile.

"Brooke," he said softly, reaching for the door handle.

"Yes, baby?" I asked.

Ellis's sultry features softened considerably, and he beamed at me. "I love you."

A familiar flutter rolled in my chest. He said these words far more often now... though I had only been able to hear them through the phone, read them on text. Hearing him say it in person sent chills through me every time.

"I love you, too." I replied, a bashful smile on my face.

He closed his eyes to send me a grin, then left through the front door.

Silence followed... the whole apartment felt cold in his absence. I could sense a familiar anxiety bubbling in my stomach as the thought of something so new filled my mind.

I had never even thought about Ellis wanting to top… but I wasn't against it.

I had learned so many amazing things from him… he'd never do anything to hurt me, and if you're going to have a first time with anyone… it helps that they know what they're doing, right?

Before heading for a shower, I stepped into Rae's room to make sure she was okay. She was curled up where Ellis had tucked her in, a hand gripping onto one of her brown ringlets. I stooped to place a kiss on her cheek, then fixed the wall of pillows on her side.

Once I was sure she was safe, I slipped back out of the room, pulling the door closed and making my way to the bathroom.

The vanity was wet. Splatters of dissolved pigment that had existed on Ellis's face before. My lips twisted into a soft smile as I wiped the water away, then turned on the shower.

Steam filled the room, and I slowly removed my clothes, dropping them on the floor before kicking them into a pile at the side of the room and stepping into the cubicle.

Warm water coated my skin, soothing the exhaustion and tension in my shoulders. Today had been so strenuous. I felt the waves of relief pill through my bones, and I think my whole body eased. The ultimate goal of today was to have Ellis back with me again… and that was attained.

I grabbed the tiny bottle of carry on luggage soap, lathering it across my whole body… every square inch. I left my hair untouched for now, not willing to deal with the backlash of my curls tonight.

When I stepped out of the shower, I grabbed a fluffy, folded towel from a platform above the toilet and thoroughly dried myself, tying it around my waist and pulling the door open.

The air in the main corridor was frigid against my bare, damp skin. My teeth chattered lightly as I stumbled towards the larger bedroom. It was just as simple as my bedroom back in the states had been: a king sized bed in fluffy white linen(which was currently home to my suitcase), and two small wardrobes on the far side of the wall.

The sound of the front door closing roused me from my fixation on how cold I was. My ears perked like a dog's as I peeked my head out into the corridor.

Ellis stood by the door, a thin plastic bag in his hands as he pulled his tennis shoes off, stowing them by the door. When he looked up, our eyes met, and he instantly smiled.

"You listened," he grinned.

"I'd listen to anything you told me to do," I admitted, stepping out to join him in the hallway.

His eyes fell to the towel around my hips. "Anything?" He asked in his menacing grin.

I lifted an eyebrow, crossing my arms in front of myself, "almost anything. I'm not into bodily waste," I said in a tease.

Ellis smirked, "Good, you couldn't pay me to do scat," he stepped towards me, throwing his arms around my neck. The bag of supplies clapped noisily against my back, and Ellis pressed our lips together for a kiss.

My hands moved to gently hold his hips, thumbs pressing into the bones that formed his pelvis so that I could seal our bodies together in this embrace. He softened, fingers resting in the crook of my neck for mere seconds before they slowly pulled down the outline of my spine and settled on my own hips. The skin in his wake burned with a sensitivity I hadn't ever felt.

Our kiss dissolved as Ellis pulled back from me, his brown

354

eyes fluttering to focus on the pink flesh that his own mouth had been poised against mere seconds before.

I felt a rush of anxiety in my belly, apprehension and fear… What if I didn't like it?

He seemed to sense this, the sharpness in his gaze smoothed to a cool, reassuring smile as he pressed our foreheads together.

"Do you have a safe word?" He asked softly, his voice hardly reaching above a whisper. I could feel the movement of his lips against my own.

I shook my head softly, the anxiety softening the grip that I possessed on his hips.

Ellis lifted a hand to rest gently against my sternum; the plastic bag which had slipped around his wrist now slid down to the middle of his forearm. His eyes fluttered closed as he pressed a kiss to my jaw. "Well, we should make one," He muttered, the sharp ends of his teeth grazing lightly along my skin. "It doesn't matter how much fun I am having, if you get uncomfortable… I will stop without question."

What the hell even was a safeword? What quantifies a safeword?

I pulled back slowly, scanning him… then the world around us. Searching for something… anything.

A chuckle fell from his lips, and he intertwined our fingers. "You're thinking far too hard about this, Darling," he turned, then nodded his head towards the couch. "What about *Chair?*" He asked.

"Chair?" I laughed wryly, then shook my head.

Ellis smiled, "Okay… how about something simple then?" He faced me once more, pulling me towards my… *our* bedroom.

Once inside, he pushed the door closed, dropped the bag on the edge of the bed, and turned to face me. His hands cupped either side of my face to pull me into another deep, hungry kiss. A kiss which I melted into, an overwhelming need to be kissed... to be held.

He perched himself at the edge of the bed, hands holding to each of mine as he pulled free from our kiss and stared up at me. "Green means?"

I tilted my head, "Go?"

A soft nod. "Amber means?"

"Amber?" I asked softly.

Ellis rolled his eyes with a smirk, "Sorry. Forgot you're an uncultured American. *Yellow* means?"

"Wait... you call yellow lights *amber?*" I asked.

"Brooke," Ellis said in a sultry, warning tone.

"Um... yellow means slow down?" I said with a soft blush burning across my cheeks.

His eyes flickered with something malevolent. "Red?"

"Red means stop," I said plainly.

Ellis chuckled, nodding. "If you're uncomfortable, say yellow... I'll slow down... but if it is too much..."

"Say red, and it stops," I finished his train of thought.

A smirk dotted his lips upward, and he nodded. "Remember how you told me earlier that you'd do *almost* anything I asked of you?" He hummed.

I nodded slowly, my gaze falling over him hungrily.

"Move the suitcase," he whispered sharply, nodding his head in the direction of the suitcase at his side.

My eyebrow raised as I grabbed the bag and placed it on the floor of our bedroom.

"Good boy," He smirked, "Lay down."

I absolutely could not... under any circumstances... let him know that those two words had sent electricity pulling through my veins, a throb ebbing in my cock. The demand he made of me filled my shoulders with lead, and I sank to sit on the edge of the mattress beside him.

In the blink of an eye, Ellis threw a leg over me, straddling my waist. "That isn't what I told you to do, Brooke," He said in a sharp, sultry tone that made me *want* to piss him off more. One of his hands pressed to my shoulder, urging me backwards until my spine rested against the mattress.

My eyes locked onto him, feeling the burn of need beneath my towel as it now sat pinned beneath Ellis's clothed pelvis. His eyes conveyed a knowing look.

"You're rock-fucking-solid, Darling," He hummed, a musical lilt to his words as he inched closer to kiss at my bare chest. "Sit there and let me fucking worship you like you worship me."

My chest warmed, a spreading heat of excitement as I bit down hard on my lip.

Ellis slipped down from my waist, sinking to his knees between my legs that still hung over the edge of the bed. His hands crawled beneath my towel, peeling back the covering to reveal my aching cock... I was already leaking needily.

His eyes flickered to meet mine, "So it's true," He whispered, his manicured fingers circled the shaft with the absolute perfect pressure. "Look how hard you get for me, Brooke."

The way he spoke struck a chord in my stomach, my cock twitching in his grasp. He moved his hand in slow strokes up and down my shaft. Every second that his hands touched my skin was a second I would thank whatever fucking higher power there was for.

My teeth pressed lightly along my lower lip as I stifled a moan, and Ellis pulled his hands away from my aching cock to run the point of his nails along my inner thighs.

"Put your legs over my shoulders," He ordered, and I did as told, allowing my knees to raise so that they rested on his shoulders.

Ellis smiled at me, biting hard on his bottom lip as he reached into the bag beside us and retrieved a small bottle of lube. Still on his knees, he covered one of his hands in the oily substance and positioned a finger at the base of my scrotum. There was a chill that surged through my body as he locked eyes with me.

"Isn't it kind of funny?" He asked softly, "Come out as bi, suddenly you're a virgin again."

My eyes fluttered softly as I nodded, "Y-yeah."

"Don't you worry, Darling... I'll take good care of you."

He rolled the tip of his finger along my entrance, allowing the lube to lather that area which had never seen the likes of this. I feared the effect of his nails on my poor internals... but I trusted him. Arguably... more than I trusted most people.

"Take a breath, relax. Just let me work my magic," Ellis placed his un-lubed hand on my stomach, just below my belly button. Then... his finger pressed into my entrance.

It wasn't a feeling that I think I really expected to ever find pleasurable... at least not yet. His finger slowly massaged my inner walls, pressing against an already swollen organ that I hadn't personally stimulated before.

"Your face," Ellis chuckled softly, pulling attention to the fact that I had twisted my face from the discomfort. "I promise... once I make you cum, you'll beg me to be inside of you all the time."

The idea of this sent shivers through my body, and I nodded softly.

He inserted another finger inside of me, and though they were slender... they were also long. Ellis worked with precision, massaging that focal point against my inner wall as much as he could, his other hand crawling down the few inches from my pelvis to wrap around my throbbing cock, stroking me again.

Now... that was a sensation that felt unreal. I think he knew exactly what the hell he was doing to me... because as I pulled a hand to cover my mouth, a smirk lifted to his lips.

"There you go," He urged softly, "Melt into my touch. Relax," Ellis turned his head to the side to kiss my knee that rested on his shoulder.

Soon, he removed his fingers from inside of me and pushed himself to stand, my legs following his movement to provide a blatant exposure of my asshole to him. He gazed down at me.

"Take deep breaths. It is going to hurt at first, but I promise you that I will listen. If you want me to stop... I will," He assured, a hand gently running the length of skin from my knee to my hip as he retrieved his cock from his sweatpants and pumped himself lightly with his oiled hand.

That familiar apprehension grew in my stomach as I felt his tip pressing against my entrance.

He pushed into me... slowly, his eyes fluttering closed as he moved his length deeper into me.

The pressure was immense, far more intense than it had been with just his fingers alone. There was a pain that cinched my eyes to a cringe as my body adjusted to his side. He didn't move.

"Use your words, Brooke," He muttered, restraint dripping from his words.

I trembled lightly, "Y-yellow," I muttered.

Ellis continued to push himself deeper, but he was slow with it. "Right, Darling. Just breathe and let yourself adjust... you're so fucking tight."

A nod was all I could muster as Ellis pulled back, slowly inching out... then back inside. Each slow stroke felt tantalizing.

He was right, I was starting to like this...

"G-Green," I whispered, flickering my eyes down just in time to catch the shift of Ellis's expression. His eyes were closed, but his teeth pulled at his bottom lip. My words seemed to trigger him as well, because I could feel the throb of his cock inside of me.

It was unreal.

He wasn't moving...

I fucking needed him to move.

"Ellis," I snapped, a gravel coating my tone.

He opened his eyes, gaze meeting mine as he smirked. "Yes, Darling?"

"Green," I repeated.

A chuckle left his chest, and he rolled his hips in a teasing half-movement. "You can't have adjusted so quickly," He said. "Or... do you just enjoy the pain?"

I trembled beneath him, shifting my hips slightly. "I thought you said you wanted to fuck me."

"I do."

"Then fucking prove it," I demanded.

The battle for power was intoxicating, because as much as I loved to dominate... Ellis was damn good at taking complete and total control without a single word.

His eyes darkened in a deep, mysterious lust, and he pulled from me. "You have to tell me when it gets too much," He muttered.

"Baby, shut the fuck up and fuck me," I ordered.

The lust in his gaze exploded into complete and total mischief, and he pushed himself deep inside of me… far faster than I was mentally prepared for. A stabbing pain pulled through my lower regions, but something about that pain fucking thrilled me.

I let out a groan, pressing my head back into the mattress as Ellis reeled back again, only to fill me once more to the brim with his throbbing cock.

"All big and bossy until I put my dick inside you," Ellis teased, "Look at you, melting on my cock. I knew you'd fucking love this."

The sound of his voice was hypnotic. I wanted him to hurt me… I needed it.

As he released a number of generous thrusts into me, I felt myself melting into his motions. Every single thrust pressed into the engorged flesh near my prostate, and I felt a searing burn in my forehead.

"F-fuck," I whimpered, hands reaching back to grip at the blanket above my head.

"Yeah?" Ellis moaned softly, the smack of his balls against the lubricated skin of my ass was a steady tempo that was pushing me closer and closer to the bring. "I have waited so fucking long to fuck you like this, Brooke… I want to fill you with my cum."

I flinched in pleasure, my back arching lightly as Ellis pounded me. What had once been painful and uncomfortable, now thrilled me. I could feel the buzz of a nearing orgasm in my fingers and toes, but I wasn't quite there yet. It seemed like the intensity was pushing me forward into this insanity of craving.

"H-Harder," I begged, gripping at the sheets.

Ellis wavered between my legs, but he obeyed, striking me harder. He sank his hands beneath my hips to angle me upwards... holy fucking shit he was rocking my entire world.

"Ellis!" I clamped a hand over my mouth and whimpered. How the hell did it feel like I was already cumming?

The precum leaked from my tip like crazy, and I wanted him to touch me so badly... but seeing as he was pre-occupied, I reached my own hand down to stroke myself.

Ellis groaned, a sound which only pushed me even further down the path towards complete and total self-destruction. I had never felt so amazing in my life.

"That's it, Darling. Touch yourself," Ellis whimpered, somehow adjusting himself so that every motion of his cock brushed against my sweet spot. "I'm gonna fill you up..."

I trembled, the sight of distant stars encroaching my vision. Before I even knew what was happening, the world exploded. My stomach tied into a tight knot, and a rope of cum spurt from my throbbing cock. This was the hardest I had ever fucking cum... and it felt so good that it sent aches through my entire body.

The second that I came, I felt Ellis's tempo stutter, and he emptied his own load inside of me. It wasn't something that I could feel. There was no great warmth or a feeling of wholeness... but the way the love of my life crumpled against me as he filled me to the brim was exquisite.

His body shook in unbridled pleasure, breathing deepening

into long, heavy gasps for air.

Then, I felt numb… like all at once, the pleasure had ripped through me and left without a trace.

Ellis retrieved himself from inside of me, collapsing onto the bed at my side. Only now did I feel the sensation of his cum leaking from within me.

It was fucking hot.

As we caught our breaths, Ellis reached over to place a hand on my chest. His face turned the opposite direction.

I reached to grasp that hand, my eyes falling on the back of his blonde hair…

"Baby," I muttered softly.

No response. Ellis's fingers twitched lightly in my grasp.

I rolled onto my side, sealing his hand against my chest as my other hand rested against his stomach. "Ellis," I tried again.

From this angle, I could see that his eyes were open, though they fluttered closed occasionally. He was avoiding my gaze.

My heart ached, anxiety returning as I rested my chin on his shoulder, "W-what's wrong?"

His chest rose and fell slowly, a steady rhythm that soothed only my concerns for him physically. Soon, his head turned to me, slowly meeting my gaze.

There were tears in his eyes.

Everything in the world froze, and I pushed myself to sit up, "Ellis, what is it?"

He sniffled softly, reaching up to swipe the gathered tears from his eyes. "S-sorry," He muttered at a volume just below a whisper. "I… I think I am still a bit scared," He admitted.

"Of what?" I asked, my eyes tracing up and down his body… I truly adored every inch of him.

Ellis whimpered, "I'm scared that I will wake up one day… and I'll never be able to experience what it feels like to actually *make love* to you again."

My heart sank, and I laid back down beside him, pulling his scrawny frame into my arms. I tangled my hand into his hair and pressed my lips into his forehead. "I promise you, Ellis… As long as I breathe on this earth, you will never have to worry about that."

He shook his head, "I know Lorenzo is going to come for me."

"If he ever fucking tries it, I'll rip his cock off and stuff it down his throat until his stomach acid devours it." I said flatly.

This triggered a soft chuckle from Ellis, and he shook his head lightly.

"Brooke," He muttered, pressing a hand flat against my broad chest.

"Hm?"

"Was that… okay?" He inquired.

A blush buzzed along my cheeks as I became keenly aware of a soft ache in my ass… but it would be an absolute lie to say I didn't enjoy it.

"It was amazing," I muttered, pressing a kiss to his hair.

From the other room, the soft sound of whimpers could be heard. My father-instincts shot upright like a post, and I quickly grabbed a pair of pajama pants, throwing them on and wiping my stomach clean of sweat as I rushed from the bedroom to check on Rae.

She was sat upright in her bed, soft tears on her cheeks as she looked at me with big, doe-eyes.

"What is it, baby?" I asked, the pitch of my voice raising as

I stepped closer to her.

Rae sniffled, her bottom lip jutting out as she pushed herself to stand, extending her arms to me. I scooped her up into my arms, but instead of settling, she looked up at me.

"Ellie?" She asked sweetly.

A chuckle fell from my lips as I pulled her close to me and walked back to our bedroom. "Are you decent?" I asked, a hand over Rae's eyes as I peeked through the door.

Ellis was sitting on the side of the bed, his sweatpants from before were back on and any evidence of our escapade had been done away with. He lifted his eyes to meet us, and I allowed my hand to fall from Rae's face.

"She asked for you," I smirked.

A grin pulled across his face, and the sadness from before seemed to disappear. "Of course she did!" He said in a bright tone, extending his arms to her.

As I grew closer, Rae practically leapt from my arms to Ellis. He welcomed her into his embrace without a second thought.

"I can't believe it. I have literally dedicated my entire life to raising her, and she wants YOU when she wakes up," I grumbled teasingly, climbing into the bed and slipping beneath the covers.

Ellis smiled, moving so that he was also beneath the covers, Rae snuggled sweetly into his chest. He moved closer, pressing himself against me. My arm wrapped lightly around his shoulder, and I smiled happily... this was my whole reason for living.

In a million lifetimes, a million universes, a million possibilities... in every single one... I would ask for this. I would ask for the peace... the love... this small family unit that we had scraped together from faltered funds and panic... I would ask for all of it.

But... I think, most importantly...

I would ask for Ellis.

The End...
Maybe...

Bonus Chapter: A Sky Full of Stars

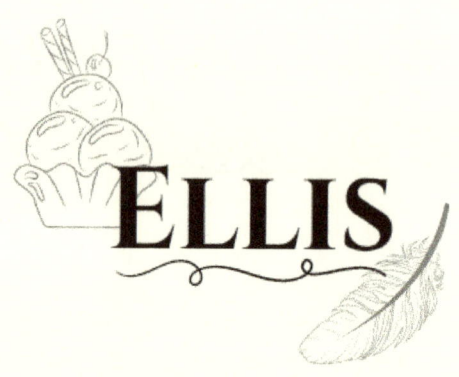

ELLIS

I think it must have been a year of us being here in England before Brooke and I finally managed to get away from the daily grind and set off on our own little adventure... and here we are, on the road towards the horn of Wales.

This had been a secret plan of my own since the day I stepped foot on the soil of my home country... I had scraped together every last spare pence that I could to surprise him with this trip.

Now, I am riding shotgun (as any good passenger princess knows, is the only way for a man of my calibre to ride), Brooke's hand rested firmly across my upper thigh in a firm grasp, his right hand on the steering wheel as he drove along the A55.

The radio of our family-sized sedan rang out with the soft music that I had expertly selected for our journey. Mixed hits from various time periods... but presently, it was playing a soft, jazzy tune by Ray Charles.

My eyes fluttered closed, head pressing against the pillar on my left side as I crawled my fingers to rest atop Brooke's hand.

"Tired?" He asked softly, though my eyes were closed, I could feel the softest warmth from his gaze as it briefly fell across my figure.

I pulled myself to sit upright, eyes opening to watch him. Warmth burned in my chest as a soft smile pulled across my face. "Not tired, just... at ease," I explained.

A soft chuckle left his lips, and he nodded. "You've been working yourself to the bone, El. You deserve the ease."

My grip on his hand tightened very slightly, and I watched him closely. His muscles were thick along his biceps, evidence of his efforts in the gym.

He was far too good to me.

"Darling," I muttered, leaning close to rest my head against his shoulder.

Brooke's head turned briefly to press a kiss to my hair, keeping his eyes forward.

"What's up baby?"

My chest ached, "I miss Rae... do you think she is okay?"

He chuckled, "I'm sure Ginger is having the time of her life with her, baby. We trust her, don't worry."

I nodded slowly, glancing over the driver's side on the right of the car to see the sea running along the side of the motorway.

Excitement burned in my mind as a smile lifted to my face. "It's been decades since I've been to the coast," I admitted, pulling myself to sit upright and retrieving my phone to take pictures.

Brooke smiled, "I don't think I've ever actually been to the coast."

"It is different here. Our beaches aren't big, sandy patches" I said softly, clicking another picture before I allowed my phone to fall into my lap. "They're rocky and frigid…"

A smirk pulled across his face, "I have dealt with rocky and frigid before, babes."

I laughed lightly, pressing back against my seat. The soft hum of the car, along with the comfort of the peace in the air, lulled me into a soft, slow blink… and when I opened my eyes, the car was pulled to a stop in the middle of an overgrown, grassy area.

My door opened, Brooke's head dipping under the arch as he grinned at me, "Damn. I was gonna carry you like a princess," he said.

I furled my eyebrows, rolling them in my own sassy rite as I pouted.

"Princess?"

His grin shifted, pulling one corner of his lips higher than the other to a smirk, and he placed his hands on either side of my headrest, pinning me to the seat.

Brooke's green eyes sparkled as he stared me up and down with that predatory desire.

"You're on holiday, so I didn't want to call you a Queen."

My heart fluttered in my chest, my teeth pinching at my bottom lip lightly. "Are we at the campsite?" I asked in a flustered tone.

He nodded, his curly hair shading his eyes lightly as he sank to be eye level with me.

"We are," Brooke whispered... I could taste his words against my lips. His eyes fluttered closed as he leaned in and kissed me.

His lips were soft, warm. The slightest bit of dry skin from his anxious habit of nibbling on his bottom lip didn't bother me, because it was an identifiable feature of his. I could recognize his kiss anywhere.

When he pulled away, his green eyes opened once more to hold their hypnotic gaze over me. A rush of adrenaline tickling the tips of my fingers as he withdrew from the car, extending his hand to help me out.

I accepted his gesture, nestling my manicured fingers around his palm as I remove my seatbelt and allowed his strong arms to guide me from the car.

The world around us was... hills. Green, rolling hills. There was a chill in the air, salted by a nearby ocean that we could see along the western horizon.

"The tent is up on that hill," Brooke advised, opening the back door to grab my rucksack from the seat and passing it to me.

I accepted the bag, a chorded fabric backpack with a nice maroon tint. A label along the top seam: *Sharpe Designs.*

"You head up and I'll grab the other bag, yeah?" The brunet at my side ushered sweetly, sparing me the slightest touch to the small of my back as he shut the back door and walked towards the boot.

At the top of the hill, stunning white canvas Bell-Tent stood in the rare bout of sunshine that Wales offered us.

A soft smile pulled across my face as I skipped up the hill

to pull the zipper of the tent open.

Inside was a double bed with a wooden frame, a unit at the footboard with a gas stove on top. Along the far side of the tent was a futon with a fluffy white blanket draped across it.

I placed my rucksack down beside the entrance, and… as one does, proceeded to rummage through every shelf to gather knowledge of the amenities.

Cups, plates, even frying pans. Everything we needed to exist for the three days in Ty Bugail.

From the entrance, a rustling sounded as Brooke dipped his head below the opening to step inside.

He brightened, some sense of relaxation pulling across his face as he set the larger bag beside mine and then collapsed against the bed.

"This is nice, baby. Good choice," he said, sinking into the comfort of a duvet which was covered with cute animal prints.

I stood from my crouched position in front of the unit, pressing my hands to the duck-egg blue wood of it as I stared at him.

Between the bed and this unit was a gold plated pole, wrapped in pretty fairy lights and leaves. It extended upwards to hold the tent upright.

"You gonna take a nap?" I asked, rapping my almond shaped nails against the wood.

He turned his head to glance up at me, the green of his eyes glittering lightly. "Are you gonna nap with me?"

I laughed, stepping around to sit on the edge of the bed. "I'm gonna make a quick run to see if I can secure us some tea. You've been driving all day, take some time for yourself," I placed a hand on the small of his back.

Exhaustion heated his skin, and I could feel him already slipping towards sleep as I pulled this hand along his spine to rub gentle circles into his shoulders.

He hummed, "are you gonna take the car?"

I shook my head, "nah, it's a small village so I am sure there is something within walking distance."

His eyes lulled closed, and he nodded. He kicked his shoes off, allowing them to fall to the floor beneath himself. Before I could say anything else, Brooke had dozed off.

I grinned and grabbed our bank card from the front pocket of my bag, and stepped out of the tent, pulling it zipped closed and pulling up Google Maps on my phone...

Maybe I should have brought the keys for the car...

What I thought would be a leisurely still turned into a twenty minute trek to a tiny petrol station called Premier. I guess I shouldn't have expected so much.

Luckily, this Premier was quite sufficiently stocked with plenty for us to have a decent tea.

Tea... not the kind you think. Tea is what English people call their evening meal. Dinner is what we call lunch... and supper... supper is an evening snack before bed!

It can get complicated.

I strolled through the aisles of this petrol station with an arm hooked through a basket's handles.

"Not from around here?" A man with a thick Welsh accent asked, a friendly smile on his fatherly face.

My own expression brightened at his question as I glanced down to this sticky old man standing in front of the milk fridges.

"Not this far West," I said, "Was born in the Midlands, but now I live with my partner and daughter in London."

The man nodded softly, his eyes looking up and down my tall, slender frame.

"You one of them Queens?" He asked.

A blush softened my cheeks, and I felt the anxiety of my appearance pulling into my consciousness. Suddenly remembering the pink shimmer that painted my eyelids.

"I am," I said, hesitation pulling at my words.

He nodded softly, "I can tell. You've got that shiny stuff on your face," he said, "Don't see many Drag Queens in Ty Bugail. Bit too rural for ya fancies?"

I laughed lightly, "See and here I was thinking that the queens would flock to the sea!"

This sweet old man chuckled, a hearty laugh that soothed my anxiety. "You staying at the campsite?"

"I am... it's a gift for my partner. He's never seen the stars properly."

His eyes brightened, "You came for the stars?"

I nodded softly, and the old man closed his eyes sweetly. "Sky is supposed to clear tonight. It's darkest at ten to eleven!"

This interaction had warmed my heart quite a lot, and I nodded, "thank you for letting me know."

"I'll let you off, then!" The old man pulled open the fridge to grab a pint of semi-skimmed milk, "you have a nice stay," he waved, then patterned away towards the tills.

At least I had something to tell Brooke about later on.

I grabbed a few drinks, then stepped around to the food section, where I grabbed chicken and potatoes... some tin foil, and red bell peppers.

As I turned back to the tills, I noticed a section dedicated to American sweets, and my heart swelled. A lot of things Brooke enjoyed weren't accessible here because of import taxes, and normally the American Sweet Shops never had the things he liked.

There was one particular sweet on the shelf that caught my attention. Brightly coloured lollies in the shapes of diamonds on the bands of a ring.

Ring pops!

I grabbed two, then paid and shoved the sweets into my pocket as I gripped the plastic bag and started my walk back towards the campsite. Another arduous twenty minutes on the side of a winding motorway with no path and poor visibility.

As I stepped up the hill towards the tent, I noticed Brooke was awake and sitting on a picnic bench outside of the tent.

He stared into the distance, taking in the hills and valleys in the distance as he nursed a cup of coffee.

"Hey," I called, growing closer.

Brooke glanced back, his face shifting visibly from that far away look to one of excitement.

God, I fucking love the way he looks at me.

"Hey, Gorgeous," he said softly, that sleepy huskiness coating his tone as he extended his arm to me. "You were gone a while."

I nodded softly, stepping closer enough for his extended hand to rest gently on my hip.

"I misjudged the distance, really. It is okay though, I have got us some drinks and food… and I made a friend," I laughed lightly.

"A friend?" He hummed, slipping his hand from my hip to the small of my back, which had developed a light arch over the years from my wearing of heels.

My head bobbed in a soft nod, "Just a curious old man.

He was a sweetheart, really. I'm sure I'll be the topic of conversation for the knitting circle later."

Brooke grinned, "You're not seducing old men, are you, Ellis?"

I threw a hand over my chest dramatically, "Me? Seducing old men? The cheek of you to even presume such tarty behaviour of me!"

His eyes fell closed in a gentle, sleepy chuckle, and his hand fell away from touching me so that he could grab hold of his coffee for another sip.

The gentleness in his movements made my heart race, and I sat down on the bench beside him.

"I got us some stuff to barbecue," I said softly, placing a hand on his knee. "Are you hungry?"

Brooke placed the mug back against the table and smiled softly, "I could eat. Wanna go get cozy and I'll set up the fire?"

My smile softened and I lifted my hand from his knee to rest against the center of his chest. "I am going to run up to the showers and wash up, I feel absolutely grubby after that walk to the shop."

He leaned in to kiss me, the whiskers of his moustache lightly tickling my nose as his lips pressed to mine. He tasted like coffee.

I like coffee.

A shudder ran through my spine and I gently pulled away, standing with a subtle wave of my hips.

A hand moved from the bench to slap my ass in a subtle tease, and I smirked down at him as I stepped back into the tent and placed the meats in an electric cooler, only to emerge once more to make my way to the showers, towel in hand.

Brooke was already hard at work setting up the fire pit.

He smiled at me as I walked by him and I sent him a wink, swaying my hips along the path towards the shower block.

As I stepped inside of the wet room, I felt a buzz of anxiety laced my chest, and I sank back against the door.

There was a reason I wanted to be alone with Brooke this weekend. Something I'd been planning for months now, that I never actually imagined would come to fruition

I placed my towel and clean clothes on the counter, then turned to start the shower. While it warmed, I stripped down... sweat soaked clothes sticking to my skin as I peeled them away.

After my shower, I made my way back to our Bell-Tent, and saw Brooke lounging back in a lawn chair behind the fire he had finished.

"Look at that!" I sang, stepping closer to Brooke and leaning to wrap my arms around his neck as I kissed him from above.

He leaned his head back and met the kiss.

"You smell nice," he said softly, lifting a hand to gently stroke my cheek "There is another chair in the tent."

I nodded, pulling back to re-enter the tent. Nothing the drop in temperature that came with the nearing if nighttime, I grabbed my fluffy jacket and pulled it over my shoulders.

There was a moment where I felt excitement buzz through me ... that moment only lasting insofar as my self-deprecating thoughts would permit, and the excitement quickly transitioned to anxiety.

With a deep breath, I smoothed the buttons of my jacket and went on to prepare our skewered chicken and veggies.

On my return, I possessed a tray full of kebabs and the folded lawn chair under my arm.

Brooke was lounging in his seat, staring peacefully into the distance.

His peace gave me such an intense feeling of pride. He worked his ass off and kept our lives together without a single complaint. I think that he deserved this more than anyone else.

When he noticed my approach, Brooke removed his feet from their lounged position on the bench at his side and stood to retrieve the tray from my hands.

"These look nice," he said, laying the tray out on the bench and placing the kebabs on the grill above the bonfire.

I set up my chair, sinking into the comfort of the seat a few inches from Brooke's seat.

He sank back into his chair and relaxed.

As the sun set, we cherished the time together and ate our food. And as the darkness of night took over the sky... I noticed that Brooke had grown silent.

When I looked at him in the firelight, I could see the orange glow on his face, the flames dancing in his eyes as his head leaned back to fixate his attention on the stars.

My mind flashed back to the night I had stormed out of the club... when Brooke told me he had feelings for me, and I kissed him... the memory brought forth a cascading sensation of butterflies across my skin, and my lips drew together to a soft purse.

This man...

He had saved me from evil, and saved himself from pain. We had moved here to start our lives fresh, to live as we must do.

To think that just over a year ago, I was refilling his glass of coke while he waited for someone else.

Now, we had our own place on the outskirts of London.

Brooke taught me to drive. We had a car and a bank account... and Rae was going to a good school!

Everything we could ever need or ever want has come true for us... for me.

A knot grew in my throat, and I patted the pocket of my oversized wooly jacket. There was a hard obstruction beneath the top layer of wool.

My eyes fixed themselves on the sky for a moment as I took in a slow, shaky breath and bit down on the edges of my tongue.

The stars were incredible...

Not a cloud in the sky, and we could see the faintest waves of the Milky Way above us.

"This is beautiful, El," Brooke said, his breath hitching on his whispers.

I nodded slowly, my eyes moving to fall back to Brooke.

His hair was down, allowing the brown curls to catch in the Welsh winds. The faintest of smiles painted his lips as he existed in this realm that was distant to all we had ever really known. This peace...

"B-Brooke," I stuttered out, feeling my heart flutter anxiously in my chest.

That stare into the sky broke, and Brooke turned his face so that he could look at me.

The warmth of his gaze burned far hotter than that of the bonfire, and I felt my cheeks darken with a nervous blush.

I reached one of my hands out towards him, a silent request for his touch which was accepted with little consideration.

Brooke's strong, thick fingers interlaced with my slender, almond tipped digits, and he twisted his face into a light grimace.

"Baby, how are you sweating? It's like three degrees out here!" He laughed lightly, though his hold on my hand remained strong.

His eyes danced over my face, studying me as he tended to do... and I watched the ease of his eyes drift at the analysis of my expression.

"What's wrong?"

I shook my head quickly, "No, Darling... nothing is wrong," I muttered, my free hand still resting firmly over my pocket as I fidgeted with the button which clasped it closed.

He nibbled his bottom lip, "You seem anxious... what's going on?"

This man knew me far too well. I smiled lightly and pushed

myself to stand, allowing his hand to fall from my own as I shoved my hands into my coat pockets, standing over the fire.

"Ellis, you're worrying me," Brooke said softly, the squeak of his chair from behind me alerted me to him standing.

A pressure began along my torso as Brooke slowly looped his arms through the gaps where my elbows sat, and I leaned back into his chest with my head falling to rest on his left shoulder. His arms held me tight, like he was scared I might run away.

I sank into his warmth, feeling the security wash over me as he held me.

"You know how we make that joke that neither of us are very good at picking who we want to marry?" I asked softly, the crackling of the fire before me filling my ears.

Brooke nuzzled his nose into my neck, placing a soft kiss against my flesh. I could feel his mouth shift to a grin as he nodded lightly.

"We aren't the best at making these decisions," He whispered calmly, maintaining his hold of me.

My fingers began to tremble, and I swallowed hard. "Brooke… do you ever regret meeting me?"

His grip lessened, if only slightly… but enough for me to absolutely notice. My heart raced in my chest as I waited his words.

"I wish you didn't have to ask that question," He said softly, and the embrace tightened once more. "Baby, there isn't a day that I exist on this earth that I'm not thankful for the day I met you."

My eyes fluttered closed, and I swallowed again, for some reason my throat felt tighter than it usually did… but Brooke

381

kept talking.

"Don't get me wrong... I never expected to love a man."

The racing of my heart seemed to stop in that instant. Those words... that statement...

"But holy fuck, like..." he removed one hand from me entirely, allowing his palm to press against my hip as he sank his lips to my shoulder. His caress set my heart racing again. "There is nobody on this planet that could make me feel so whole."

My breath hitched, and I opened my eyes to stare up at the sky. The stars captured my heart, thrusting me into a world of mystical serenity.

The streak of a brilliant white shooting star caught my attention and I bit down on my lip.

Say yes...

"Baby, you're shaking..." Brooke whispered, the hand on my hip rubbing soothing circles against my skin.

I absolutely fucking was.

"You love me, right?" I asked softly, pulling from him slightly so that I could turn to face him.

His arms fell, and the lack of contact sent an ache through my body as I stood, eye-to-eye with Brooke.

"You know that I love you, Ellis..." He muttered, an anxiety of his own gracing his expression. "Please tell me what is going on."

I pulled my hands from my pockets, placing my fingers against my face as I steadied myself.

"Brooke... what..." I paused, feeling my words catch in my throat.

He simply held me in his gaze, a gentle expression on his face.

Fucksake, I couldn't cope with all of this unrelenting emotional support.

"I know we have never talked about this," I muttered, peering at him through gaps in my fingers, "But.. I want this more than anything in the world."

His face shifted in confusion and concern, a twinkle in his eyes as the fire caught in the reflection of his irises.

I reached into my left pocket, gripping tight to the obstruction from before and pulling it free, without another word, I placed it in Brooke's hand and allowed my hands to cover my face yet again.

Silence persisted for an ungodly amount of time, only to be broken by a soft chuckle.

"A Ring Pop?" He asked.

My heart stopped.

A...

Fucking...

What?!?!?!?

I opened my eyes and glanced down at Brooke's hand. There, in the centre of his palm... was a bloody strawberry flavoured Ring Pop!

My brow wrinkled in an annoyed and confused expression, and my cheeks darkened.

Of course I'd mess something like this up.

I patted myself down, and found that the item I actually intended to hand him was in my RIGHT pocket.

The embarrassment washed over me in waves, and as I lifted my eyes to meet Brooke's, a grin was plastered across his face.

"Is this revenge for the pirate outfit?" He asked softly, opening the packet and retrieving the sweet from inside.

"The… what?"

"You know," he chuckled, slipping the ring onto his finger and bringing it to his lips. They surrounded the red gemstone, and he sucked at the sugary snack for a few seconds. When he pulled away, his mischief shone in his smile, "My crappy Party City pirate outfit."

That mischief permeated the very anxiety which held me in situ, and I burst into a soft laughter.

He had my whole heart.

"Why would this be revenge?" I asked in a light tease.

He chuckled, "I don't know. You're the one sitting here, shitting your pants over giving me a Rig Pop."

"I'm not shitting my pants over the fucking sweet," I admitted, "Though… I might be now."

He extended his hand to me, presenting the lolly to my lips. His eyes were light, amused.

I glanced down, the soft scent of strawberry now pungent in my senses as I locked my eyes on Brooke's and sank my lips around the gemstone myself. My lips graced his knuckles, and a soft moan slipped from me as I pulled back and rolled my tongue across the top of the lolly.

His eyes flickered, and his other hand moved to stroke my face. "I want you to suck me like that."

That anxiety which had burned within me mere seconds before was replaced with desire, and I pointed to his chair.

"Right, then. Sit."

He glanced back, taking in the chair for a moment before flashing me a sky smirk. He stepped back and sank into this chair.

Without hesitation, I sank to my knees between his legs… one of them at least. My other knee, I rested against as

I reached back into my pockets and retrieved what I had intended to grab earlier.

I lifted my eyes to meet his as I fidgeted with the velvet item in my hand.

"You know you're my whole world, right? You and Rae are my life…"

"You're being weird again, El," he chuckled lightly.

I scowled, if only for a second. "You know that, though … right?" I asked sternly.

The playful expression on his face softened and he nodded softly, "Yeah, baby… I know."

"Then…"

Say yes…

I lifted the box in my hands, extending it anxiously in front of myself as the trembling once more took over my body.

Please say yes…

"Brooke… will you marry me?"

The noise of the world around us ceased to exist, ripped from my awareness by the tides of fear that ripped at my senses.

My eyes met Brooke's, and the throb of my heart burned in my throat as he stared back at me.

Usually, I treasured his stare… but today… right now… I felt sick.

In my hands, the tiny velvet box stood, open. Perched in the very centre of the box was a simple titanium band with Rae's initials and birthdate engraved into the metal. The box shook with the tremble of my hands, and every second of silence felt deafening.

Brooke softened, "You're right… we didn't talk about this," He muttered, eyes glancing down at the box in my hands.

He's hesitating...

"Is this why you've been working so much lately?" He asked.

I felt the sting of tears behind my eyes, my knee wavering as I let it fall to meet the other against the ground.

"I... I wanted it to be special," I whispered, feeling the sharpness of my voice as it contorted against the worry explicitly stated in the air.

Brooke pulled my chin up, "Ellis, why do you look like your heart is breaking?"

I sniffled, "Y...you didn't answer..."

His eyes widened, and he looked down at my hands, which had fallen to my lap. "Oh, baby..." he moved forward in his chair and placed a soft kiss on my forehead, "I'm so sorry... I think... I just wasn't expecting-"

"It's fine," I cut him off. My eyes closed, and I shut the box. The chill of night soaked through my body like a raging wave, dousing my flame.

He was quiet for a few seconds, then leaned in to press his lips to mine.

"Sorry... I've already said yes a million times in my head," he whispered against my lips.

The meaning of his words took a few seconds to reach my comprehension, but as they did... I opened my eyes wide.

"What?"

He laughed, "I want to marry you, Ellis."

"You..." I sat straight, face warning considerably as I stared up at him. "You do?"

Brooke smiled, "I mean... you asked," he said in a cheeky tease.

My brain finally connected with the rest of my body, and I shot up, throwing my arms around his neck to hug him tight.

My heart raced in my chest, and the tears which had once gathered from fear now poured down my cheeks in elation.

He placed kisses along my cheek, pulling me to sit in his lap.

When I pulled back, Brooke's hand rested against my chest while the other found a place on my knee.

"You looked terrified, El," he grinned, placing a kiss against my jaw.

A rush pulled through my body and I nibbled at my bottom lip. "I don't think I would have recovered from your rejection," I admitted, pulling the edges of my nails along the front panel of his flannel shirt.

"Rejection?" He smirked, shaking his head, "I'd never fucking risk rejecting you. That would be the stupidest decision I ever made."

A blush dusted my cheeks, "Really?'

Brooke laughed, nuzzling his nose into my neck gently. His lips pressed lightly into my collarbone, "Ellis, you are about as far out of my league as someone could get," he said softly, a hand rubbing along my knee.

He turned his head, pulling the trail of kisses up the side of my neck until his lips formed a suction just behind my ear.

I shuddered, pulling my nails up to rest against one side of his throat.

"Mm," he hummed, the hand on my knees trailing up my thigh to rest against the crevice where my legs met. His fingers pressed between them to spread my legs and permit him access to squeezing my inner thigh. The strawberry lolly still perched on his pointer finger.

My blood ran from my head, leaving dizziness in its wake as I pressed myself into his touch.

"You should probably take your Ring Pop off," I whispered guiding his face in my direction.

His lips spread in a soft smirk and he shook his head, "Not until you put my new one in my finger."

I glanced down to the box in my hand, my heart raced light as I pulled it open and removed the new band from the velvet case.

He removed his hand from between my thighs, lifting his ring to my lips once more. "Use your sexy fucking lips," he whispered sharply.

In my trousers, my cock twitched in anticipation. I sank my lips around the diamond shaped sweet, flickering my eyes dangerously to meet Brooke's.

He bit down on his bottom lip, and I pulled the ring down his finger, then hooked my pointer finger through the loop and extracted it from my mouth with a sultry *pop.*

Brooke grunted, his eyes glazing with that sultry silence. I could sense him undressing me with his eyes.

I reached back to place the sweet on the bench behind me. When I turned back, I grabbed hold of Brooke's left hand and slipped his new band over his ring finger.

Electricity buzzed in the air between us, and he instantly brightened, a soft blush burning across his cheeks.

"Why are you so bashful?" I teased, peppering his face with kisses.

He chuckled, "I... have never been proposed to before," he said softly.

"I have," I retorted. "It was shit," a grin pulled across my face to mask the absolutely raging terror and anxiety that are me up from the inside.

"Do you... like it?" I asked anxiously.

388

His eyes softened, "I would have said yes if you had actually proposed with the Ring Pop, babe." He rubbed our noses together. "It is gorgeous... thank you for this. For everything."

My face brightened considerably, then I smirked. "I knew you'd love it!" I cheered, pushing myself from his lap to stand.

A gust of stronger wind blew through the hills around us, knocking a chill through my bones.

Brooke pushed himself from the chair and winked at me, "Should we head inside? I'll knock the fire out, you go warm up the bed."

I nodded lightly, grabbing the chairs and carrying them back inside the tent. The walls lit up in a brilliantly warm light, and a small space heater had significantly warmed the abode.

Stepping on the heel of my converse, I pulled my foot free from my shoes and tucked them neatly against the end of the bed, then climbed into the soft sheets of our bed.

Soon, Brooke entered the tent and zipped it closed, stalking towards me with a massive grin on his face.

"What's got you so smiley?" I asked in a sassy chirp, pulling the blanket around my body.

He grinned, grasping at the corner of the blanket and pulling it off of me. His eyes scanned me briefly before settling in my face.

"Nothing much, just excited to see my fiance."

My heart raced at the title, and a blush crept across my cheeks, "Oh? Your fiance?" I asked in a feigned pout.

"Yes, just the most beautiful man on this earth," Brooke teased, sitting on the edge of the bed and placing his hand on my stomach.

I flickered my eyes down to his hand and nibbles my lip,

"Beautiful?"

A stern, sure nod bounced Brooke's curls, "Absolutely."

His hand slipped down the front of my boxers, cold fingers gracing my flaccid dick as the irises of his eyes sparkled lightly.

I wanted to taste his lust.

"You aren't even a little bit excited?" He asked in husky whisper, retrieving his hand. "I can fix that."

In an instant, Brooke threw a leg over me to straddle my waist, hands pinning me to the mattress as he began to grind against me.

If I hadn't been hard before... I was now.

A smirk danced across his face, and Brooke leaned down to place a filthy fucking kiss against my lips. His tongue pushed my mouth open so that he could explore, and I sucked on his tongue.

A soft groan of pleasure left his chest, and he pulled away slowly so that he could sit straight. He grabbed the hem of his shirt and pulled it off over his head.

As he did so, the muscles in his arms bulged and contracted.

I watched on in need, my hands moving to press to his abs. His skin was warm, and I wanted that warmth.

"Your so hot," I said softly, looking up and down his body to inspect him. The pressure against my pelvis was enough to drive me mad.

He grinned, rolling his hips against mine with just enough force to set a gentle moan from my lips.

"Fuck," I muttered, "I love you."

His eyes flashed with recognition, and he lowered himself once more so that he could press out foreheads together, "I love you, Ellis."

The mischief took over, and I knew that it was my turn to take the reigns of this session. I hooked a thumb under his jaw, pulling him closer to me so that I could kiss him.

This time, I was the filthy one. I grabbed his hip with my free hand and pushed him to roll, immediately taking the high ground of straddling him.

A gruff chuckle left his lips as Brooke reached to circle his hand around my throat, peeling away from my lips so that he could smirk up at me.

"You like being on top?" He asked in a low grumble.

Lust burned behind my eyes, and I nodded. "Fuck yes, I like to be on top," I hissed in return.

His grasp of my neck tightened as he pulled me closer, "You better make good on your promise to suck me like you did that ring," he demanded lightly.

"You want me to suck your dick?" I asked a hand trailing down his bare chest to fidget with the buckle of his belt.

He grinned, releasing my throat with a soft grin as he tapped his fingers in a gentle slap against my cheek, "Fuck yes, I do."

A race of chills burned over my skin and I sank back, undoing his belt and throwing it to the side. I made quick work if his trousers, undoing the button and urging his hard cock from their confines.

Fucking hell, I loved his cock.

My hand circled around his length, and I started to pump him lightly. Eyes flickering up to stare into his eyes.

Brooke watched my with that extreme precision that drove me nuts, his pupils following the pattern of my hand.

"If I suck your dick right now, you have to let me fill your ass with cum," I bargained, my tongue falling free of my lips to drag slowly along the thick veins at the base of his shaft.

He shuddered, "You do a good job and I'll let you cum inside of me every day for a week."

"A week?" I hummed in a sultry tone.

"A week," he reaffirmed.

I fluttered my eyelashes at him and nodded, "you've got yourself a deal, Mr. Unlucky."

With that, I pressed my tongue to his tip, lapping up the precum that had already begun to leak for me.

He tasted of salt, in the best of ways.

My lips circled around this bulb, and I started to take him in. Slow, deep strokes that would cost along the roof of my mouth.

Brooke's head rolled back, and I felt the twitch of his dick as I took him all the way to my throat.

He loved feeling my throat from the inside.

"Fuck," he muttered, reaching a hand back to grip onto the pillows.

I hummed, allowing the vibration to tease him as I began to increase the tempo, taking him as deep as I possibly could.

If I had to die today, I would die in peace knowing that it was from choking on his massive fucking cock.

The sex-worker deep inside of me reared his head, and I let loose.

But this is when Brooke flipped the switch on me.

"Fuck yes, Ellis," He muttered, "You're so fucking perfect."

My heart raced, and the ferocity at which I sucked him off began to decrease.

"Oh my god, you take my dick so well!" His eyes fluttered closed, "such a good boy."

My own cock ached behind the restraint of my trousers,

and I moaned against his shaft.

This fucking man knew exactly how to make me melt.

"I want to worship you, Ellis," Brooke said.

I glanced up at him, my heart racing as I allowed his cock to slip from my mouth. My breathing was heavy, and a few beads of sweat had gathered on my brow.

His eyes locked onto mine, and a hand outstretched to brush a strand of my hair from my face.

Brooke sat upright, pinching beneath my chin to guide me closer.

I could still taste his precum on my tongue, and as Brooke pressed his lips to mine, I couldn't help but force my tongue past his teeth so he could taste himself as well.

His free hand moved to grip at my hair, and he sucked on my tongue as he pulled back, the tips of his teeth gracing my flesh as he did.

"Pants off. Give me your ass," He demanded in a husky tone.

Warmth covered my body, and I fluttered my eyelashes as I slipped off the bed.

I grabbed my phone from the unit at the base of our bed and swiped through my playlists until I found Feeling Good, by Michael Bublé.

As the music began, I flashed Brooke a sultry smirk, then started to dance for him.

First to go was the long-sleeved shirt which concealed my pale skin, I tossed it to the ground and reached to grab his hands, placing them against my chest.

His teeth pressed against his bottom lip as his hands explored my skin to the music.

I dipped to administer a filthy kiss to his lips, only pulling away once I felt his hands move to the waistband of my trousers.

With a sway of my hips, I pushed my trousers down and stepped free from them, coaxing Brooke to sit on the edge of the bed so that I could give him a lap dance.

His dick stood rigid, twitching occasionally as he watching me lustfully.

"I love when you dance for me," he whispered in a husky tone.

I spun around to press my ass into his lap, grinding back against him.

He allowed a subtle moan to escape his lips, his hand lifting to clasp around my throat as he pulled my back against his chest and sank his teeth into the soft flesh of my shoulder.

"Ah!" I whimpered, melting into his touch.

Brooke released my shoulder from his bite, trailing soft kisses and love bites up to my neck where he knew I was the most sensitive.

The hand which didn't presently retrain my throat slipped into my boxers to stroke me.

Fucking hell, this man was perfect.

"I- I thought you promised I co-could cum inside you," I muttered.

Brooke turned his head, nipping at the bottom of my ear lobe, "You can, just shut the fuck up and let me worship you."

My heart fluttered, and I whimpered in pleasure as Brooke coaxed my boxers down. My own manhood stood erect, throbbing.

He pulled me from his lap with his grip around my throat and pushed me face down into the bed, then his fingers released from around my neck, slipping down the length of my body seductively as he stood behind me.

"Fucking hell, Ellis," he growled, "Look at how perfect your body is." He gripped my waist, hoisting my hips aloft as he pressed kisses down my spine.

I whimpered, a burning blush pulling across my cheeks. It spread down my chest, along my spine.

"You like my body?" I asked in a sultry whisper.

He reeled a hand back to deliver a solid smack to my ass, "Hell yes."

The slap sent shivers over my body, and I pressed my hips back so that I was closer to him.

He sank to his knee, hands on either side of my ass to spread me apart. My heart raced as he slipped his tongue into my entrance.

My whole body reacted to this sensation. This was something that Brooke had only very recently discovered that he enjoyed doing, but that meant that it was a frequent addition to our bedroom play.

"Nnn," I gripped onto the duvet beneath me as Brooke ate me out like I was fucking dinner. Moans slipped from my lips, and I whimpered with pleasure.

Suddenly, he flipped me again, a hand pushing my hip to roll me into my back as he transitioned to leaving light kisses all over my balls.

I placed my legs on his shoulders, and he slipped a finger into my entrance as he kissed every square inch of flesh that he could kiss.

Brooke licked that space of flesh where my scrotum ended, sending a wave of pleasure through my body as he continued to finger me.

My hand circled my dick, pulling in slow motions along

with his movements inside of me. The flesh in my face burned with excitement.

Soon, he pulled from inside of me and stood, walking to one of our bags and grabbing a bottle of lube. He tossed it onto the bed and smirked down at me.

"I want to watch you cover your cock in lube," he said, dropping his boxers the rest of the way and grabbing hold of his rigid shaft as he stared down at me, stroking in slow, long strokes.

His demands thrilled me. I relished the fact that he felt comfortable with bossing me around now. There was a period of our relationship where he was subdued and only occasionally asked for what he wanted... now he was relentless, and it was fucking hot.

I grabbed the bottle of lube and poured some of the slick gel onto my palm, then coated my length in the substance, locking eyes with him as we each stroked our cocks in unison.

He groaned lightly, stepping closer to me and climbing back onto the bed in a high straddle of my waist.

He wanted to fucking ride me.

This knobhead knew that this was the way he could stay in control and still give me what I wanted.

Brooke reached behind himself to take hold of my cock, gently guiding me towards his entrance. With a slow, taunting movement, he sank down until I had filled him up.

We moaned in unison, and he flickered his eyes down to meet mine.

"You're so fucking perfect," he whispered, his eyes glazing over as he began to move up and down.

He was tight, tight enough to push me just that very little bit further towards absolutely filling him up with my cum. I craved this sensation.

"Yeah, Darling... that's it," I whispered sharply, "Ride my fucking cock!"

As Brooke adjusted to my size, he placed his hands on my shoulders to control the roll of his hips. His face darkened with need and I felt my stomach knotting.

I reached down to stroke him as well, matching his pace. He twitched, leaking precum over my stomach as the pair of us dissolved into a complete mess of moans.

"F-fuck, Baby..." Brooke groaned, changing his tempo to increase the speed.

My hips ached under his weight, but I craved that fucking burn. With his new tempo, the knot in my stomach grew bigger. I whimpered.

"B-Brooke," I muttered, the call causing a stutter in his movements as he bounced faster.

I rolled my head back, "Fuck. I'm so close, Darling!" I called out, ready to burst.

He smirked, swirling his hips as he bounced. My entire body swelled with pleasure, and my toes curled.

I thrust my hips up against his movement, hitting him harder. The swell of his prostate was obvious, and as I moaned out for my final release, Brooke stopped his bounces to allow me to fill him as deep as I possibly could.

Trembling, buzzing with need, I whimpered as he pulled free from me and collapsed on the bed at my side.

No.

That is wrong.

He hadn't cum.

Though the exhaustion pulled at my senses, I reached to grab his cock once more.

"Y-you don't have to," he whispered, trembling from his own pleasure.

Like fuck was I gonna listen to that.

I moved into my hands and knees beside him, taking his cock into my mouth and giving him the best head I could muster in that moment.

He was so fucking close, I could feel it in the twitch of his cock, and I could taste it in his tip.

By now, I fucking NEEDED him to cum. I would be an absolute savage for him until he had.

"E-Ellis," he moaned out, "F-fuck, baby... yes... let me cum in your mouth!"

I moaned around his throbbing length, taking him all the way to the very end of the line until he came, a trembling mess of moans as his body convulsed and I swallowed that hot load.

Once he had taken a breath, I collapsed beside him on the bed. His arms encircled me, pulling my close as he pressed out foreheads together and gently pulled his fingers through my hair.

"I love you so much," he whispered softly.

"I love you too, Darling," I replied with a soft kiss to his nose.

Later that night, we dressed in our cozy pajamas and dressing gowns and stepped outside once more to have a look at the stars.

In the darkness, Brooke stood with his arms around himself as he stared up at the sky full of light.

My heart was so full...

I stepped closer to him, wrapping my arms around his waist.

He opened his arms to me and pressed a kiss to my temple, holding me against him as we stared together at these stars.

Maybe I hadn't fully escaped Lorenzo… maybe the things of my past were dreadful… but here I am free to be myself.

Who could ever ask for more?

COMING
Soon

The Importance of Loving Ernest

A TALE FROM THE MIDNIGHT RAVEN

Fall into Fall

HarperCollins*Publishers*
1 London Bridge Street
London SE1 9GF

www.harpercollins.co.uk

HarperCollins*Publishers*
Macken House, 39/40 Mayor Street Upper
Dublin 1, D01 C9W8, Ireland

First published by HarperCollins*Publishers* 2025
13 5 7 9 10 8 6 4 2
© Pesala Bandara 2025.
Recipes by Heather Thomas
Design by Hart Studio

A catalogue record of this book is available from the British Library
ISBN 978-0-00-876618-4

Printed and bound by PNB Latvia

**When using kitchen appliances please always follow the manufacturer's instructions.
Use extreme care when handling knives and do not allow children to use knives
without adult supervision.**

Fall into Fall

The Unofficial Guide
to Cozy Season for Every
Gilmore Girls Obsessive

Pesala Bandara

HarperCollins*Publishers*

Contents

Introduction

Introduction

La – la, la – la, la la la-a-a-a-a a-a-a, la la laaaaa.

At the first hint of gold and crimson on the trees or the smell of woodsmoke in the air, the true *Gilmore Girls'* fan feels a familiar tug on the heart that draws them back to Stars Hollow. It's a town that seems designed for fall – the gazebo bedecked with garlands of red, orange and yellow, the storybook streets lined with pumpkin-adorned porches.

In *Gilmore Girls* we find a sanctuary, watching Lorelai and Rory banter over steaming mugs at Luke's while the world around them turns into a kaleidoscope of beautiful fall colors. All we need to do is slip on our favorite knitwear, drape a cozy blanket across our knees, brew a strong coffee, and, as we hit the play button and the familiar theme tune begins, it feels like slipping into a warm bath. In a world where so much is changing too quickly, what could be more comforting than the time capsule of Stars Hollow?

For many of us, *Gilmore Girls* embodies the essence of the season and a rewatch is an essential as we wave goodbye to those 'lazy-hazy-crazy days of summer'. The changing seasons are at the heart of the show's rhythm – back-to-school meetings, the warm glow of fairy lights in the town square, and hayrides at the town's Harvest Festival. These provide an anchor for characters and viewers alike in the simple, vital beats of life.

Watching *Gilmore Girls* is a reminder to us all to slow down, appreciate the sound of leaves crunching beneath our feet and the sweet taste of cinnamon-sprinkled pasties. It also reminds us of what's important, like heartfelt conversations with those we love and sharing our time and energy with our communities.

This book invites you to fall even more deeply in love with fall, with *Gilmore-Girls*-inspired ideas of ways to embrace the season. Whether it's baking up a treat in the kitchen to make Sookie proud, tips on cozy home décor that wouldn't look out of place at the Dragonfly Inn, or a long reading list from Rory that you can lose yourself in, you'll welcome the new season in with *Gilmore-Girls* style.

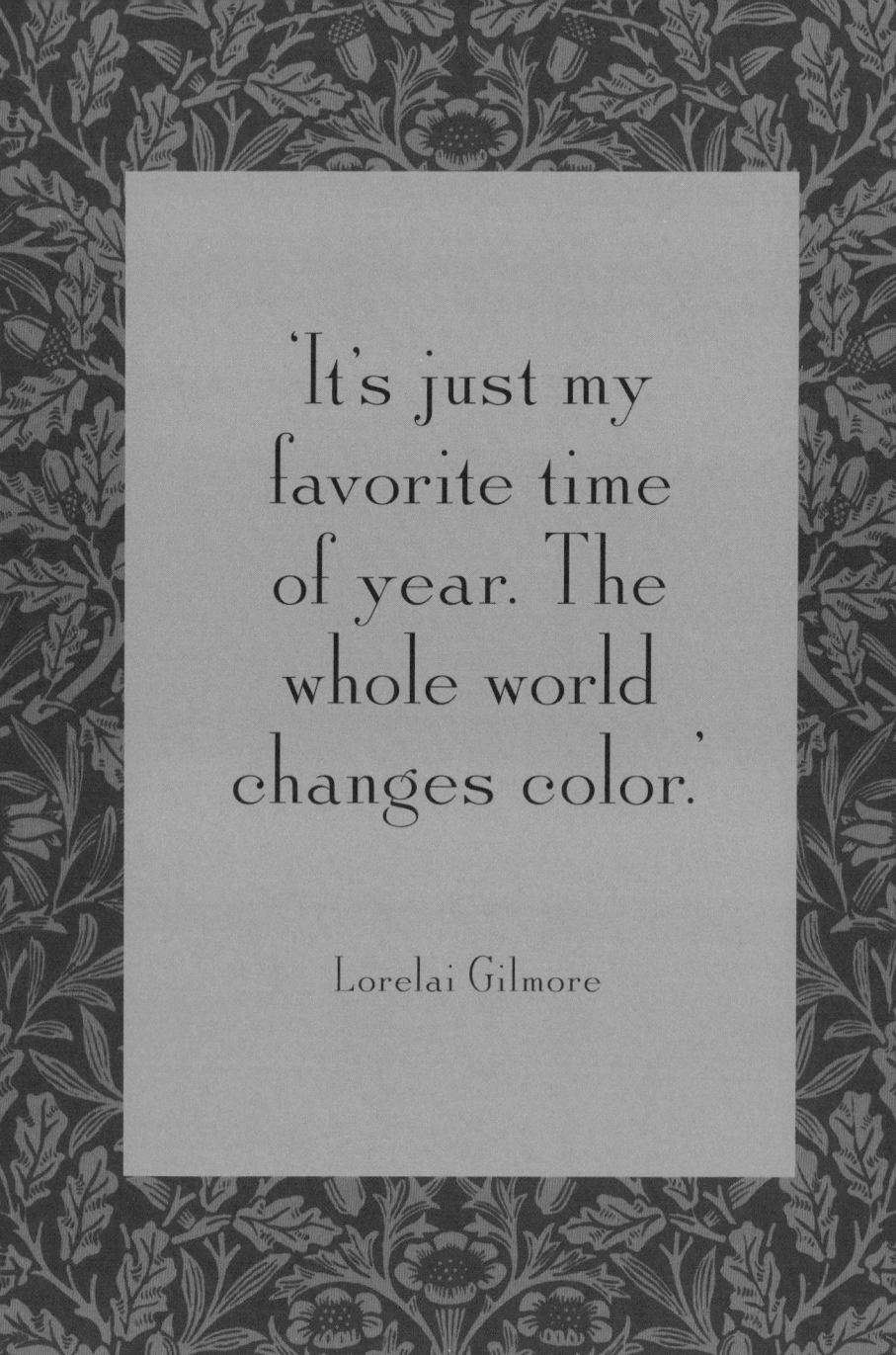

'It's just my favorite time of year. The whole world changes color.'

Lorelai Gilmore

Seasonal Recipes

Seasonal recipes

Gilmore Girls isn't just a show about a fast-talking mother-and-daughter duo in an idyllic New England small town; it's also a show about food. And for Lorelai and Rory, food is much more than sustenance – it's pure joy, especially when the weather turns crisp and the vibrant colors of autumn envelop Stars Hollow.

Fall in Stars Hollow means daily trips to Luke's Diner for pancakes and steaming mugs of coffee to keep the cold at bay (endless coffee, because Lorelai is '90 per cent water and 10 per cent caffeine'). It also means warm cookies baked to perfection by Sookie, and pie of every imaginable kind: apple, peach, and even muffin-bottomed. It's a season of cozy indulgence, when ordering copious amounts of Chinese takeout on a frosty autumn night becomes a ritual, and leftovers stretch for days. It's the time of year when Lorelai and Rory somehow manage to eat four separate Thanksgiving meals in one day, all in the spirit of celebration.

Watching *Gilmore Girls* in the fall feels like a permission slip to lean into all your cravings. The warm glow of autumn makes every bite of food feel like it's laced with nostalgia. It calls for sipping hot cider and eating pie straight from the pan. Even coffee somehow seems to taste better in the fall – richer, cozier, and more comforting.

In this chapter, we'll celebrate fall in all its glory with hearty bakes and warming drinks: cinnamon shortbread, spiced hot cider, a seasonal homemade apple pie, the ultimate Stars Hollow hot chocolate, as well as pumpkin-spice-flavored pancakes and French toast. So go ahead and immerse yourself in the taste of fall, one glorious bite at a time.

Autumn's secret ingredient: Pumpkin spice

When the leaves start falling, it's almost like you can smell the unmistakable aroma of pumpkin spice in the air. Nothing captures the essence of autumn (otherwise known as Gilmore season) quite like the warm, inviting aroma of pumpkin spice.

These recipes for a homemade pumpkin-spice blend and pumpkin purée serve as the foundation for the fall-inspired French toast, pancakes, apple pie, and ultimate Stars Hollow hot chocolate featured in this chapter. While you can easily pick up a pre-made version of pumpkin spice and purée, the fresh, sweet-smelling goodness of homemade recipes cannot be beaten. Making these yourself will also fill your kitchen with the signature scent of fall.

There's something magical about stepping into a home that smells like autumn. It's as if you've walked straight into a hug.

Homemade Pumpkin Spice

Makes: about 3 tbsp | Prep: 5 minutes

Make sure your ground spices are as fresh as possible for maximum
potency and flavor, and not near to or past their expiry date.

6 tsp ground
  cinnamon
2 tsp ground (or finely
  grated) nutmeg
2 tsp ground ginger
1 tsp ground cloves

Variations

· Add ½ teaspoon
  ground allspice
  to the mix.
· Add ½ teaspoon
  ground cardamom.
· For a more pungent
  spice mix, add a
  pinch of ground
  black pepper.
· Add a pinch of
  ground mace
  or star anise.

1. Put all the ingredients in a small bowl and mix
   together well. The ginger sometimes has a tendency
   to clump, but using a wire whisk and then sifting the
   mixture through a fine sieve will prevent this.

2. Transfer to an airtight screw-top glass jar (you can use a
   funnel to fill the jar) and store in a cool, dry, dark place.
   It will keep for up to 12 months.

Tips:
· If you are a big fan of
pumpkin spice, just double or
quadruple the quantity and store
it in a larger jar for a delightful fall
centerpiece in your kitchen.
· You can stir the pumpkin spice
mix into a jar of caster (superfine)
sugar and use it in drinks
or for sprinkling over
pies and cakes.

Pumpkin Purée

Makes: about 1–1.5kg (2¼–3¼lb/4–6 cups) purée
Prep: 10 minutes | Cook: 40–60 minutes

1 small pumpkin
(about 1.8–3kg/
4–6¾lb)

1. Preheat the oven to 200°C (180°C fan)/400°F/gas 6. Line a large baking tray with baking parchment.

2. Cut the pumpkin in half and scoop out and discard all the seeds and any stringy flesh. Place the two halves, cut-side down, on the lined baking tray. Bake for 40–60 minutes, or until you can easily pierce the outer skin with a skewer and the flesh is soft and tender and coming away from the skin. Remove from the oven and set aside to cool.

3. When the pumpkin is cool enough to handle, peel away the skin and transfer the flesh to a food processor. Blitz until you have a really smooth purée. Check the texture – it should not be watery. You want it to be similar to that of tinned pumpkin purée. If it's too watery, just spoon it into a fine-mesh sieve (strainer) lined with some muslin (cheesecloth) and set it over a large bowl to catch any excess water.

4. Transfer the purée to a sealed container and keep in the fridge for up to 7 days. It also freezes really well, so you can always have a supply of your delicious homemade version to hand (store in the freezer for up to 3 months).

Tip: If you don't have a food processor, you can make the purée in batches with a hand blender.

Pumpkin Spice French Toast

Serves: 4 | Prep: 5 minutes | Cook: 12–18 minutes

Luke's Four-Slice French Toast has been a staple on the specials board at his
diner ever since Rory can remember. It's a dish so beloved by her that she
is beside herself when Luke replaces it on the menu with an omelet!
In this recipe, Rory's favorite French toast is given a sweet, fall-infused twist,
elevating it with the warm, comforting flavors of pumpkin spice and purée.
For best results don't use fresh bread, which will soak up the batter
and go soggy. Instead, cut the slices from a firm day-old loaf.

3 medium free-
  range eggs
120ml (4fl oz/
  ½ cup) milk
50g (2oz/¼ cup)
  Pumpkin Purée
  (see page 20)
1½ tsp Pumpkin Spice
  (see page 18)
1 tsp granulated sugar
Pinch of sea salt
2 tbsp unsalted butter
8 thick slices of
  bread or brioche
Maple syrup, for
  drizzling
Icing (confectioners')
  sugar, for dusting
Crispy bacon or
  pancetta, to
  serve (optional)

Variations
· Use plant-based
  milk instead of dairy

1. Beat together the eggs and milk in a bowl. Add the
   pumpkin purée, pumpkin-spice mix, sugar and salt
   and whisk until well combined.

2. Melt half the butter in a large non-stick frying pan
   (skillet) over a medium heat.

3. Dip the slices of bread, one at a time, into the batter,
   soaking it for a few seconds to absorb the liquid.
   Let any excess batter drip off the bread and back
   into the bowl.

4. Add the bread to the hot pan, in batches (depending
   on how many slices the pan can hold), and cook for 2–3
   minutes, or until golden brown and crisp underneath,
   then turn and cook the other side for 2–3 minutes.
   Remove from the pan and cook the remaining bread
   in the same way, adding more butter, as required.

5. Serve the French toast immediately, drizzled with
   maple syrup and dusted with icing sugar, with some
   crispy bacon or pancetta on the side, if desired.

Pumpkin Spice Breakfast Pancakes

Makes: 8–10 pancakes | Prep: 10 minutes | Cook: 25–30 minutes

Lorelai likes her pancakes with a side of pancakes. And who could blame her? A batch of these warmly spiced, fluffy pancakes, drizzled with maple syrup will give you all the fall feels. Adding pumpkin spice and purée transforms the batter into something truly special. It's the ultimate cozy breakfast to whip up while bingeing *Gilmore Girls*. Top tip: 'Ted Koppel's Big Night Out' (Season 4, Episode 9) – which features Luke's memorable pumpkin pancakes – is the perfect *Gilmore Girls* episode to watch while making this recipe.

2 large eggs

200ml (7fl oz/ scant 1 cup) milk

115g (4oz/½ cup) Pumpkin Purée (see page 20)

1 tsp vanilla extract

5 tbsp vegetable oil, plus extra for brushing

200g (7oz/2 cups) plain (all-purpose) flour

2 tsp baking powder

3 tbsp caster (superfine) sugar

2 tsp Pumpkin Spice mix (see page 18)

½ tsp sea salt

Maple syrup, for drizzling

Variations

· Substitute buttermilk for the milk.

1. In a bowl, beat the eggs, milk, pumpkin purée, vanilla extract and oil until well blended.

2. Sift the flour and baking powder into a large bowl and stir in the sugar, pumpkin-spice mix and salt. Make a well in the center and pour in the beaten-egg mixture.

3. Stir gently until everything is well combined but be careful not to overmix. Transfer to a measuring jug.

4. Set a large frying pan (skillet) over a medium to high heat and lightly brush with oil. When it's really hot, add a small ladle of the batter to the pan. When bubbles appear on the surface and the edges start to brown after 1–2 minutes, flip the pancake over and cook for a further 1–2 minutes until set and browned underneath. Remove and keep warm while you make the rest of the pancakes in the same way.

5. Serve the pancakes piping hot and drizzled with maple syrup to finish.

Tip: You could use two frying pans to cut the cooking time.

Spiced Apple Pie

Serves: 6 | Prep: 20 minutes | Chill: 30 minutes | Cook: 50 minutes

In Lorelai's world, there's nothing more important than education, family – and, of course, pie! All *Gilmore Girls* fans know that Lorelai's love affair with pie runs deep, and it's no surprise as to why. Pie is the quintessential autumn dessert, embodying comfort, tradition, and sweet, sweet nostalgia. This crisp apple pie, brimming with juicy fruit and infused with warm pumpkin spice, is so delicious that Lorelai would be inspired to write songs about it. Whether you're baking this pie for a family gathering or simply indulging in a slice on a cozy night in, this is sure to become your new fall tradition. And don't forget to brew a pot of strong coffee to pair with your pie for the true *Gilmore Girls* experience.

For the shortcrust pastry (pie crust)

350g (12oz/3½ cups) plain (all-purpose) flour, plus extra for rolling

Pinch of sea salt

175g (6oz/¾ cup) chilled butter, diced, plus extra for greasing

2–3 tbsp cold water

1. Make the shortcrust pastry: sift the flour and salt into a mixing bowl. Rub in the butter with your fingertips until the mixture resembles breadcrumbs. Stir in enough cold water with a palette knife for the mixture to come together and form a dough. Use your hands to mould it into a ball, then wrap in cling film (plastic wrap) and chill in the fridge for at least 30 minutes.

2. Preheat the oven to 190°C (170°C fan)/375°F/gas 5. Place a baking tray in the oven to heat up. Lightly butter a 20cm (8 inch) loose-bottomed tart tin (pan).

3. Roll out about two-thirds of the pastry on a lightly floured surface and use to line the tart tin, pressing it into the fluted sides. Don't worry about any overhanging pastry.

continues over the page

900g (2lb)
cooking apples
(green apples,
e.g. Bramley),
peeled, cored,
and quartered

150g (5oz/¾ cup)
caster (superfine)
sugar

1 tsp Pumpkin Spice
(see page 18)

Juice of 1 lemon

1 tbsp chilled
butter, diced

1 egg white, beaten

Variations

· Use brown sugar
with the apples for
a caramel flavor.

4. In a bowl, toss the apples in 125g (4½oz/generous ½ cup) of the sugar and the pumpkin-spice mix. Transfer to the pastry case and sprinkle with the lemon juice and diced butter.

5. Roll out the remaining pastry and cut into a circle large enough to cover the top of the pie. Fold the overhanging pastry from the base over the edge and press together to seal. Brush the top with egg white and sprinkle with the remaining sugar.

6. If wished, decorate the edge by pressing down lightly with a fork. Make two small incisions in the top to allow the steam to escape.

7. Place the pie on the hot baking tray and bake for 20 minutes, then reduce the temperature to 170°C (150°C fan)/325°F/gas 3 for 30 minutes, or until the pastry is golden. Serve hot or cold with custard, cream, or ice cream.

Ultimate Stars Hollow Hot Chocolate

Serves: 2 | Prep: 5 minutes | Cook: 5 minutes

There's nothing quite like a comforting mug of hot chocolate (or 'hocho,' as Lorelai likes to call it) to ward off the fall chill. While hot chocolate is often seen as a strictly winter indulgence, this fall-inspired twist infuses all the best flavors of the season into a classic, soothing beverage. With pumpkin purée and a blend of spices, this is a cozy, sweet, and ever so slightly spicy treat. And for an extra touch of indulgence, you can add a dash of whisky or cognac.

120ml (4fl oz/½ cup) milk

85ml (3fl oz/generous ¼ cup) double (heavy) cream

45g (1½oz/¼ cup) dark (bittersweet) chocolate chips

1 tsp unsweetened cocoa powder

1–2 tbsp Pumpkin Purée (see page 20)

½ tsp Pumpkin Spice (see page 18)

½ tsp vanilla extract

Whipped cream and grated or shaved chocolate, to serve

Variations

· Dust with pumpkin-spice mix, grated nutmeg or ground cinnamon.

· Substitute white or milk chocolate chips for dark.

1. Put the milk, cream, chocolate chips, and cocoa powder in a saucepan over a low to medium heat. Whisk until the chocolate melts and the mixture is well blended and smooth.

2. Add 1 tablespoon pumpkin purée and then the pumpkin-spice mix and stir well. Taste and add more pumpkin purée if you prefer a more intense flavor. Stir in the vanilla extract.

3. When the chocolate mixture is hot (but not boiling), pour it into two small mugs or heatproof glasses. Top with whipped cream and sprinkle over some grated chocolate. Serve immediately.

Cinnamon Shortbread

Serves: 8 | Prep: 35 minutes | Cook 20–25 minutes

This buttery, melt-in-the-mouth cinnamon shortbread is the perfect autumnal treat to cozy up with. You can also double the quantity and wrap in pretty packaging and ribbons for delicious, edible fall gifts for friends and family.

200g (7oz/2 cups) plain (all-purpose) flour

100g (3½oz/⅔ cup) rice flour

100g (3½oz/scant ½ cup) caster (superfine) sugar, plus extra for sprinkling

200g (7oz/scant 1 cup) butter, diced, plus extra for greasing

1 tsp ground cinnamon, plus extra for sprinkling

Grated zest of 1 orange

Variations

· Add some chocolate chips to the shortbread mixture.

1. Preheat the oven to 180°C (160°C fan)/350°F/gas 4. Lightly butter a 20 × 20cm (8 × 8 inch) cake tin (pan).

2. Mix the flour, rice flour, and sugar in a large bowl. Add the butter and rub together with your fingertips until the mixture resembles fine breadcrumbs. Stir in the cinnamon and orange zest.

3. Bring everything together to form a soft dough. Transfer to a bowl or work surface and work with your hands into a smooth ball.

4. Transfer to the prepared cake tin and press the mixture down firmly, levelling the top. Prick the surface several times with a fork and then bake in the preheated oven for 20–25 minutes or until pale golden.

5. Set aside to cool in the tin before cutting into squares. Mix a little caster sugar with a large pinch of cinnamon and sprinkle over the shortbread. Store in an airtight container for up to 2 weeks.

Tip: You can blitz the butter and sugar for the shortbread in a food processor, then add the flours and pulse until the mixture resembles breadcrumbs.

S'mores Salted Caramel Pots

Serves: 4 | Prep: 25 minutes | Chill: 30 minutes

There's something about s'mores that feels quintessentially autumn.
These salted caramel s'mores pots are a delicious dream come true (just like Sookie's
glorious dark chocolate s'mores wedding cake!), offering a unique and indulgent twist on
the classic campfire treat: instead of sandwiching the marshmallows and salted caramel
between graham crackers, we've layered them here in elegant glasses with creamy
chocolate and topped them with a fluffy marshmallow meringue.

8 digestive biscuits (graham crackers)

4 heaped tbsp Salted Caramel Sauce (see page 36)

150ml (¼ pint/¾ cup) double (heavy) cream

115g (4oz) dark (bittersweet) chocolate (70% cocoa solids), broken into squares

2 medium free-range egg whites

85g (3oz/⅓ cup) caster (superfine) sugar

¼ tsp cream of tartar

Variations

· Use crushed gingernut biscuits (cookies) or Oreos instead of digestives.

1. Put the biscuits in a Ziplock bag and bash into crumbs with a rolling pin. Divide them among four heatproof glasses and top with a spoonful of the salted caramel.

2. Put the cream in a saucepan over a medium heat and bring to the boil. As soon as it is boiling, remove from the heat and add the chocolate. Leave until the chocolate has melted, stirring occasionally, then whisk until smooth and glossy. Spoon the chocolate cream mixture over the salted caramel in the glasses and chill in the fridge for at least 30 minutes.

3. With a hand-held electric whisk, beat the egg whites, sugar and cream of tartar in a heatproof bowl suspended over a pan of simmering water until the meringue triples in volume and is white and glossy. Remove the bowl from the heat and whisk for a few more minutes until the meringue stands in stiff peaks.

4. Pile the meringue on top of the chocolate cream in the glasses and either use a blowtorch to brown it or place under a preheated hot grill until toasted.

Salted Caramel Sauce

Makes: approx. 250g (9oz/1 cup) | Prep: 15 minutes | Cook: 10 minutes

This is a classic salted caramel sauce – the only one you'll ever need
for serving with desserts and pouring or drizzling over ice cream,
sundaes, pancakes, waffles, crêpes, French toast, cookies, and crumbles.

200g (7oz/1 cup)
caster (superfine)
or granulated sugar

120ml (4fl oz/½ cup)
water

100g (3½oz/½ cup)
salted butter, at
room temperature,
diced

120ml (4fl oz/½ cup)
double (heavy)
cream, at room
temperature

1 tsp sea salt flakes

Variations

· Substitute full-fat
crème fraîche
for the cream.

· Add 2–3 drops
of vanilla extract.

1. Put the sugar and water in a wide, heavy-based
saucepan (not non-stick) over a low heat. Tilt the
pan so the water covers and dampens the sugar.

2. Watch the pan carefully as the sugar dissolves, stirring
occasionally, then turn up the heat and boil for about
10 minutes, or until it starts to brown, before turning a
golden amber in color. As soon as this happens, remove
the pan from the heat. Do this immediately or the
caramel will catch and burn. You want it to be as dark
as possible without burning.

3. Add the butter and whisk it in (this is best done with an
electric hand-held whisk, if you have one), until it melts
into the caramel. If it separates, just keep whisking –
it will come back together.

4. Gradually, stir in the cream, then the sea salt. If you're
not using the sauce immediately, set aside to cool in
the pan for 10 minutes before transferring to a screw-
top jar. It will keep well in the fridge for up to 3 weeks.

5. To rewarm the sauce, stand the jar in a pan of hot
water or reheat in the microwave.

Tip: It's very important
to keep a close eye on
the pan while making the
caramel. If you miss seeing it
turn amber and don't remove
it from the heat immediately,
it will catch and burn.

Hot Buttered Apple Cider

This is the ultimate fall hug in a mug! With its warm, spiced apple flavors and a rich, buttery taste, it's the kind of drink we can easily imagine Stars Hollow's Cider Mill serving up on chilly autumn days. Brew a batch of this delightful cider to fill your kitchen with the comforting scents of apple and cinnamon. Drink it from a mug or take a thermos of it to sip as you stroll through the crisp autumn air. This drink requires a spiced buttered batter, using nothing more than sugar, butter, a hint of sweetener, and a variety of warming spices. Make the batter and let it rest in the fridge for at least an hour (although the flavors meld far better after 24 hours). If you want to store it for longer, put your seasoned butter 'log' in the freezer, then let it thaw before using it.

Buttered Batter

Serves: 12 | Prep: 5 minutes

....

150g (5½oz/⅔ cup)
  brown sugar

115g (4oz/¾ cup)
  unsalted butter, at
  room temperature

60g (2oz/¼ cup)
  agave nectar

½ tsp ground cinnamon

¼ tsp ground allspice

¼ tsp ground cloves

¼ tsp ground nutmeg

Pinch of sea salt

1. Combine all the ingredients in a small bowl, stirring until well incorporated. Form the batter into a log and wrap in cling film (plastic wrap), then refrigerate for 1–24 hours, or freeze for up to 3 months.

Hot Buttered Apple Cider

Serves: 1 | Prep: 2 minutes

....

30ml (2 tbsp) Buttered
  Batter (see above)

60ml (2fl oz/¼ cup)
  apple cider

90–120ml (3–4fl oz/
  ⅓–½ cup) hot (not
  boiling) water

1 cinnamon stick,
  to garnish

Variations

· Add a shot of
  zero-proof rum or
  whisky along with
  the batter before
  adding the liquid.

1. When ready to build the drink, place a dollop of the Buttered Batter in a mug, then add the apple cider and top with hot water. Garnish with the cinnamon stick.

Tip: For extra flavor, brew a black tea and use instead of water.

How to order cocktails like a Gilmore

Want to sip your way through Stars Hollow like one of the Gilmores? Here's a guide to our characters' favorite drinks.

Rory Gilmore: Shirley Temple
Rory orders this mocktail at Lorelai's bachelorette party before her wedding to Max. Named after the famous child actress of the 1930s, a Shirley Temple is the classic combination of ginger ale, grenadine, and a cherry.

Emily Gilmore: Gimlet
'Richard! I need a gimlet!' has become one of Emily Gilmore's most iconic lines. A gimlet is a simple yet sophisticated cocktail made with gin (or vodka) and lime juice, and served with a twist of lime. This no-nonsense drink is as refined as Emily herself.

Luke Danes: Beer
While Emily raised an eyebrow at Luke's beer order during Friday night dinner, it perfectly encapsulates his down-to-earth nature. Simple, no-frills, and reliable, Luke is the kind of guy who's content with a cold beer after a long shift at the diner.

Lorelai Gilmore: Gin Martini with an Olive
When she's not drinking her body weight in coffee, Lorelai considers a gin martini with an olive her go-to cocktail order. In fact, Lorelai gets annoyed when Emily dares to ask her if she takes her martini with vodka and a twist. A martini is a classic cocktail typically made with gin and dry vermouth, known for its crisp, clean flavor.

Richard Gilmore: Scotch

Who can't picture Richard Gilmore pouring himself a glass of scotch before Friday night dinner? Whether it's a smoky single malt or a smooth blend, Richard's drink of choice is traditional and reliable, just like him.

Takeout options if you're feeling lazy this fall

On a chilly autumn day, sometimes cooking feels like too much effort. The simple joy of having your favorite food delivered to your door – no cooking, no dirty dishes – is one of the most indulgent ways to embrace the season. And no one understands the comfort of takeout better than Lorelai and Rory Gilmore! Here are some of the girls' signature takeout orders to inspire your next delivery.

- **Chinese.** Lorelai and Rory are known to order lots and lots of Chinese takeout from Al's Pancake World – far too much food for two people in Richard's opinion. Some of Lorelai's favorite dishes include egg rolls, Kung Pao chicken, Moo Shu pork, and garlic chicken.

- **Indian.** When Rory has the house to herself in Season 2, she orders Indian food from Sandeep's, including garlic naan, samosas, and vindaloo.

- **Pizza.** Lorelai considers pizza to be one of the four major food groups. When Dean comes over for his first Gilmore movie night, Lorelai orders a pizza with everything on it – including pineapple, pepper, tomato, and onion.

- **Luke's Diner.** As Luke notes, Lorelai and Rory regularly order a double cheeseburger and fries as takeout from his diner. According to Rory and Jess, it's fast-food gospel that French fries should be eaten with hot sauce and a salt-and-pepper dip.

- **Tacos.** Tacos are another classic Gilmore Girls takeout order. Rory's advice is that you order three tacos per person, because two is never enough. Gilmore tip: Coffee and tater tots both go great with tacos.

Home Is Where The Crafts Are

Home is where the crafts are

Fall doesn't need to just be happening outside your window. It is something you can welcome into your home through smells, décor, and craft projects. Creating the right space for your cozy hibernation, dressing your home in autumn's finest, are key to relaxing the mind and soothing the spirit.

Whether your home is full of soft furnishings (like Lorelei and Rory's), expensive antiques (like Richard and Emily's), or perhaps even antlers and singing fish (as in the uber-masculine makeover Sookie's house underwent before Jackson moved in), the key to any home is that it's where you feel comfortable. And what could be more comforting than the gorgeous warm reds, soft oranges, and glowing golds of fall? From your door to your dining table, there are plenty of ways to let autumn take center-stage across your home. Whether you embrace crafting by hand or simply rearranging what you have, it takes less work than you'd think to turn your home into a seasonal haven.

This chapter is full of fun and practical ideas designed to create the right atmosphere for you to linger, relax, and savor the season, getting yourself in the perfect mood for your annual *Gilmore Girls* rewatch, without needing to resort to a pilgrim costume or hayride. Leave any troubles at the door and let's get crafting!

> Dressing your home in autumn's finest is key to relaxing the mind and soothing the spirit.

A quick guide to fall flowers and foliage

Many of the ideas for decorations in this chapter suggest using foliage or flowers. Of course, when decorating for autumn you can use any flowers that take your fancy, as there are plenty that have the signature hues of the season, but here are some of my favorites.

Fresh flowers

Dahlias | Roses | Cyrsanthemums | Sunflowers | Hydrangeas
Asters | Cosmos | Phlox | Crocosmia | Japanese anemones
Sedum | Hesperantha | Sea lavenders | Gypsophila

Dried flowers

Amaranthus | Pampas grass | Phalaris | Wild fennel | Achillea Parker
Mimosa | Poppy heads | Lunaria | Gypsophila | Nigella

Foliage

Oak leaves | Peony leaves | Eucalyptus | Rosemary | Corn
Wheat | Chasmanthium grass

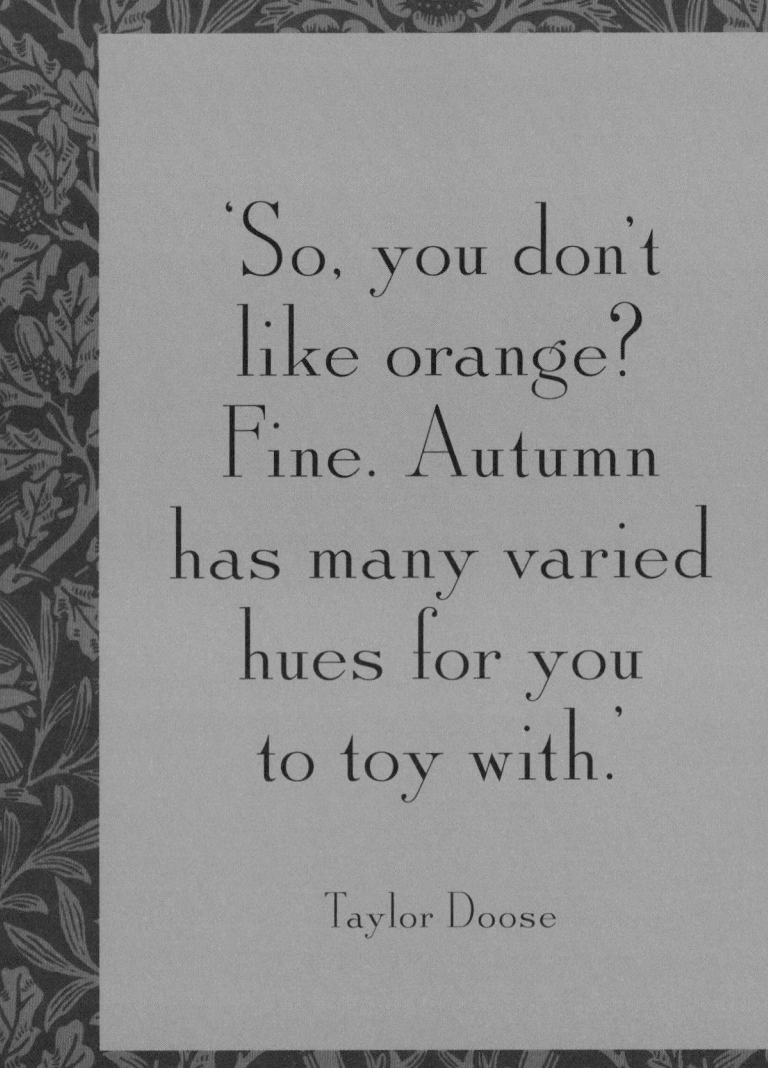

'So, you don't
like orange?
Fine. Autumn
has many varied
hues for you
to toy with.'

Taylor Doose

Making a natural autumnal wreath

A beautiful wreath hanging on your front door is the perfect way to set the tone for visitors, while also welcoming you home after a long day. Nothing could make you feel more like you're living on Peach, Plum, or Orange Street (or one of the other fruit-named streets in Stars Hollow) than a ring of joy adorning your entranceway.

If you've been put off making your own autumn wreath in the past, perhaps because you don't see yourself as crafty or find you are always short on time, I'm here to reassure you that these can be incredibly quick and simple to put together. A wreath can also be very inexpensive, especially if you source most of the elements from your garden or an obliging nearby wood.

The most important thing to bear in mind for your wreath is that anything goes! There is no wrong or right way to decorate yours. They don't have to be symmetrical; you could just focus your decorations on just one part of the wreath if you want to. You could opt for authentic objects from the natural world or go for store-bought items, so you can use the wreath year after year. Or it could be a mix of the two. You can also choose whether to go for something big and dramatic, or more delicate and pretty. Not sure what you want? Try trawling the internet for suggestions. Or you could just try gathering some materials and having a go. What could really go wrong?

You will need:
- *Foliage, such as parsley fern (optional)*
- *A base wreath (rattan, willow, straw, vine, etc.)*
- *Fresh flowers*
- *Scissors*
- *Florist wire*
- *Strong glue (a hot-glue gun or extra-strength glue dots)*
- *Your choice of autumnal paraphernalia (pinecones, leaves, flowers, tiny pumpkins, dried orange slices, etc.)*
- *Ribbon or rustic twine*

Steps:

1. Lay out all your elements so they are ready to use: flower and foliage stems should be around 10cm (4 inches) long.

2. If using foliage, add this first. Gather little bunches together, then snip sections of florist wire long enough to wind one around each bunch with a couple of centimeters (an inch) remaining. Add the bunches one at a time by feeding the bit of remaining wire through your wreath and using that to secure the bunch tightly. Continue to add these in a zigzag formation, so each new bunch covers the stems of the last, until the wreath is covered.

3. If using fresh flowers, add these now by threading the stems through gaps in the wreath. They may not need to be secured if the gaps are close enough, but wire can be used where needed.

4. Now add your autumnal accoutrements with strong glue. Find or create gaps in your wreath, so you're securing these directly to the base.

5. Finally, add your ribbon or twine to secure the wreath to your door. Wrap this around the top of your wreath and tie in a bow. You can decide how much space to leave it to hang, depending on how much of a feature you want to make the ribbon.

Tip: Dried-flower wreaths are a great way to reuse and recycle a bouquet on its last legs. Simply hang the flowers upside down in a dark room until they're ready to use, then add them last to your wreath, as they can be delicate and break more easily.

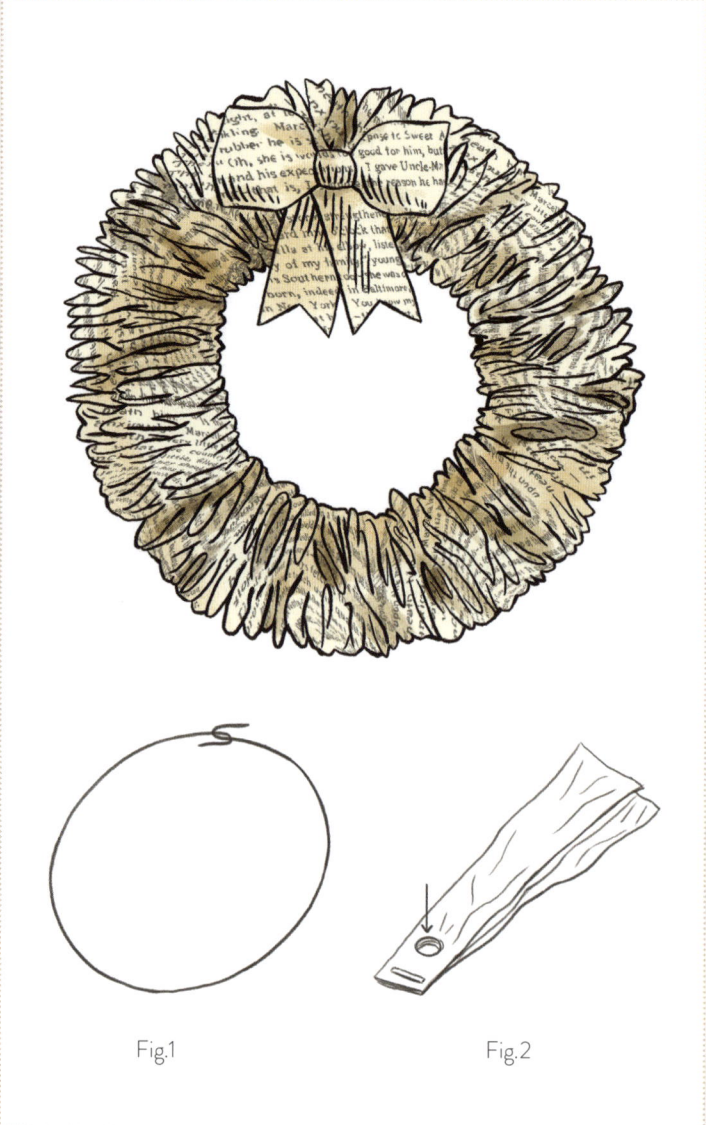

Fig.1   Fig.2

DIY book-paper wreath

If you're anything like Rory, you'll have plenty of books that have been read so many times they're now on their last legs and ready for their next life. If not, you can source books from libraries (just ask if they have a stack ready to be chucked out) or second-hand bookshops. This wreath is perfect for book lovers looking for something a bit different, although as it would be ruined by the rain, it's best to hang it indoors or in a covered porch.

You will need:
- *A large metal wreath hoop (no specific size; with a clasp, if available)*
- *Wire cutters/pliers*
- *Book pages (lots of them)*
- *A stapler*
- *A hole punch*
- *A hot-glue gun/superglue*

Steps:
1. If you're lucky enough to have found a hoop with a clasp, great! If not, clip your wire hoop and use your pliers/cutters to curl the ends, so that they can clasp shut (see Fig. 1).

2. Take your book pages and cut them in half, lengthways. Scrunch them up, straighten them out again, and then fold them twice, along their length. Staple each piece at the bottom, then punch a hole just above where you've stapled (see Fig. 2).

3. Thread the pages onto the hoop, slipping them on through the punched holes. You should stagger them slightly, placing them at different angles, and use your glue gun/superglue to stick them to the ring. Add a little glue between the pages, too, so they'll remain stuck to each other. Keep going, until your hoop is well packed with pages.

Design a festive
and welcoming porch

Whether you're lucky enough to have a wide-open porch like Lorelai's (the termite issue aside), or you live in an apartment with an indoor front door, you can always find ways of creating a beautiful entry point. You may need to adjust some of these ideas depending on the space available to you, but here are some suggestions for creating a charming extension of your indoor autumn décor, blending the natural world with the cozy comforts of home on your doorstep.

- **Pumpkin arrangements.** Line steps or either side of your doorway with pumpkins in varying sizes, colors, and textures. Mix classic orange with white and green, using real pumpkins or even artificial velvet ones for a modern twist.

- **Hay bales or crates.** Use small hay bales or wooden crates to create levels for displaying pumpkins, gourds, or potted chrysanthemums. Not enough space for a whole hay bale but love the effect? Tying small bunches of wheat and propping them up on the floor by your door, or tying them to hang on either side, brings the same quaint farmyard vibes.

- **Lanterns and candles.** Place lanterns filled with candles or fairy lights outside your door for a soft, inviting glow in the evenings. Tall lanterns standing sentinel on either side of your doorway can give particularly effective results.

- **Seasonal plants.** Add potted chrysanthemums, ornamental cabbages, or asters in rustic planters to bring vibrant fall colors to your porch or entryway.

- **Plaid/tartan and cozy fabrics.** Drape a plaid throw or blanket over a chair or bench for a pop of seasonal pattern and texture. This will create the perfect space to sit and watch the leaves fall.

- **Scarecrow or figurines.** Place a small scarecrow, wicker baskets, or even whimsical gnomes on the porch for a touch of fun.

Make your own doormat

A seasonal doormat is a perfect way to greet guests and makes for a very simple craft project (it's an especially great one for people who don't think of themselves as very crafty). You can go for whatever design you like. How about a greeting such as 'Hello, fall!' or 'Hey there, pumpkin', or a lovely autumn-leaf design. Or to really enter the fandom, why not go full *Gilmore Girls* with something like 'I'd rather be in Stars Hollow', 'Where you lead, I will follow' or 'I smell snow'.

You will need:
- *A plain coir doormat*
- *A printable stencil (you can find many images and fonts online)*
- *Freezer paper and iron/adhesive vinyl*
- *A computer and printer*
- *A Cricut/craft knife*
- *A stiff paintbrush*
- *Flex Seal or outdoor paint in color of your choice*
- *Sealant, such as Flex Seal Spray*

Steps:
1. Choose the pattern or words you want to appear on your doormat and sketch out how you want these arranged (the dimensions will depend on the size of your doormat and the number of letters in any phrase you choose).

2. Once you know the dimensions of each of your letters or icons, you can size them on your printable stencils accordingly (Google will give you many options in all sorts of fonts). Using Word or a similar application, fit as many letters and icons as you can on each page to eliminate waste when you print them.

3. Cut the freezer paper/vinyl to letter size (29.7 x 21cm/ 8.27 x 11.67 inches), place it in the printer and print onto the matt side. Cut out using a Cricut, if you have one, or a craft knife. Scissors also work, but will be more fiddly.

4. Position the stencils on the doormat, ensuring it all lines up perfectly. If you're using freezer paper you should iron this on, or peel off the backing paper if using vinyl.

5. Use a stiff paintbrush to dab paint to form the letters, taking care to push it straight down around the edges to keep them neat. Make sure you apply a thick coat, so none of the original doormat color shows through. This may require another layer or touch-ups.

6. Once dry, remove the stencil and apply a sealant to fix the design. Leave for at least a day before using.

Seasonal centerpieces
for your table

You don't need Emily's budget for glass apples to create a beautiful centerpiece, creating a focal point that can feel festive, yet refined. There are many, many ways you can do this, but here are some ideas (and feel free to customize them as you see fit).

- **A simple flower arrangement.** This can either be in a simple vase or – if you really want to up the autumn ante – in a hollowed-out white pumpkin. For the latter, simply cut a disk from the top of your pumpkin, scoop out the innards, line with a plastic bag (ensuring there are no holes!), then fill with water and a selection of flowers in your favorite autumnal hues.

- **A pumpkin and gourd display.** Not just for Halloween, these are perfect for a centerpiece, especially when using small ones in a variety of colors: oranges, yellows, whites, and greens. It's best to display them on a wooden tray or wire basket so they can be moved more easily, and they also look great combined with candles and sprigs of eucalyptus or wheat.

- **Harvest-themed fruit bowl.** A fruit bowl is a great table centerpiece all year round, but in fall it presents the perfect opportunity to celebrate all the bounty of the season. Think juicy apples, luscious pears, ripe figs, and vibrant persimmons. Pick a bowl with rustic appeal, keeping the focus squarely on the colors of the fruit you've selected, arranging them artfully with bigger fruits at the bottom.

- **Simple fall leaves centerpiece.** For this very cheap but also very effective option, simply gather branches with autumn leaves aplenty and arrange in a vase of your choice (clear glass is often the most effective). They shouldn't need water but will need to be swapped out for new ones if they start to wilt. Fortunately, you shouldn't be short on branches to replace them with.

- **Glorious golden array.** It's easy to create a luxurious display with some glitzy spray paint in gold and copper tones. This is easiest with a spray-paint gun (you can pick one up in most hobby-crafting stores), but you can also use a paintbrush. Just grab some leaves with twigs, pinecones, and pumpkins and spray to your heart's content. They look great arranged in a white box-tray.

Decorating mantels
or console tables

These ideas are great for surfaces you want to make a feature of. Garlands and displays can bring life and texture to your décor, adding a touch of seasonal whimsy – and are very Dragonfly Inn. They're all adaptable to the space you have available and the level of decoration you're looking to achieve, while being equally stunning, all creating the desired effect of increased cozy vibes and contentment!

- **Dramatic floral display.** These are a lot easier to make than you'd imagine. All you need is a block of floral foam with a tray and a selection of your favorite foliage and flowers. Before you start to assemble your arrangement, fill a sink with water and place your floral foam on the surface. Let it sink down on its own (don't force it) and, when it has completely submerged, remove it from the water and let it sit on a towel for a few minutes. Start adding your foliage by cutting stems at a 45-degree angle (this makes them easier to insert), then start slotting them into the foam. Next, add bigger, more dramatic flowers, followed by smaller, more delicate ones, spacing these out until you're happy with the overall look.

- **Simple hanging garland.** Very simple but effective, this can be hung on the wall above your mantel or suspended from either end so it hangs down beneath it. All you need is a long piece of jute string (length is dependent on the area you're working with) and whatever autumnal elements you'd like to string along it: dried orange slices, small pinecones, leaves, etc. Cut or drill holes in the elements you're using and slide them onto the string, spacing them out as you wish. Alternatively, you could try cutting felt leaves in a variety of reds, yellows, and oranges. To finish, just tie knots on either end and you're ready to hang it!

- **Woodland log slice display.** What could be a better celebration of fall than using little tree stumps as podiums to champion wonderful natural elements? Select log slices of different heights (these can be cut with a chainsaw or bought online) and arrange them along your mantel, varying the heights but with the highest in the middle. Then display seasonal elements on them, including candles, little pumpkins and gourds, diffusers, small plant pots, flowers, or pinecones. You could also include the pumpkin flower vase on page 62.

- **Wood slice painting.** Instead of using your log slices as little podiums, you could paint cheery little images or messages on them to celebrate the season: perhaps a pumpkin, pinecone, or sunflower; or how about 'Fall into fall', 'Hello, autumn', or four slices that spell out 'F-A-L-L'. Prop these upright or lay them flat along your mantel. You may wish to combine this with another mantel decoration from this section, or just intersperse with some foliage.

- **Simple added touches.** If a big display isn't for you, why not just bring autumn into your home in a softer way, by adding bowls of chestnuts or pinecones, candles, vases of branches, or posies of dried flowers to surfaces around your home.

Tip: Any of these displays can be elevated with the simple addition of some delicate fairy lights.

Fig.1   Fig.2

DIY book-page garland

Another perfect way to breathe new life into old books is to make a beautiful garland with their pages. These look great in any season but are well suited to fall when the paper is stained in beautiful autumnal colors. And if you can find an old, falling-apart copy of one of Rory's favorites (see pages 107–110), what could be more perfect?

This garland can be as long or as short as you choose, which is why the instructions are not too specific (but to create one long enough for a standard mantelpiece, you may need an entire book).

You will need:

- *Book pages (many)*
- *Orange/red/yellow paint (watercolor)*
- *A sponge*
- *A stapler with lots of staples*

Steps:

1. Mix a small amount of each paint color with water (you can vary this depending on how strong you want the colors to be or how much of the text on the pages you want to come through) and, using your sponge, brush the pages lightly (if they are too wet, they may tear). Then either leave or hang the pages to dry or put them in the oven on a low heat (this will only take a few minutes, but you should do just a few in one go).

2. Take the pages, one at a time, and loosely fold them into a fan shape (without pressing along the folds), stapling at the base of each fan (see Fig. 1). Some fans should be tighter and some looser (the lack of uniformity adds to the finished effect).

continues over the page

3. Once you have done a few, start stapling them together, joining the bases in a line (see Fig. 2). This will take a lot of staples to secure but, don't worry, no one will see them. Just be very careful not to accidentally staple your fingers.

4. Keep going until you are happy with the length (or you have run out of pages), then display in your place of choice (taking care to position your garland so the staples are out of sight).

'Oh, I read a lot.
Do you read?'

Rory Gilmore

DIY bunting

Another lovely way to welcome the season is with bunting made from dictionary paper. You could make this short (simply 'F-A-L-L') or a longer message, such as 'IN OMNIA PARATUS'. These can either be kept on white paper, or stained with paint in fall colors, as on page 71.

You will need:
- *An old dictionary where a large, centered capital letter appears at the start of a section/printed pages found online*
- *A scanner and printer/photocopier*
- *Card*
- *A ruler and pencil*
- *Scissors*
- *A length of ribbon*

Steps:

1. First, you need to decide what you want your bunting to say. And unless you have countless dictionaries to cut up, the best thing would be to scan copies of the relevant book pages and print them out onto card, ensuring you have all the letters you'll need. Alternatively, it is possible to find scans online.

2. Use a ruler and pencil to measure out triangular bunting shapes on each of your pages, all the same size, with the letter centered at the top (see Fig. 1). The size you make them will depend on how big you want the bunting to be and how many letters you're trying to fit on. Cut these out. If doing multiple words on the same piece of ribbon, you could make a blank triangle on your card to go between the words, to make them easier to read.

3. Make an incision on either side of each triangle at the top, ensuring they are level with one another.

4. Starting with the first letter in your word, pass the ribbon through each of the holes (see Fig. 2). Continue with each subsequent letter, until your word/words are complete, ensuring you have enough ribbon on either side to hang the bunting.

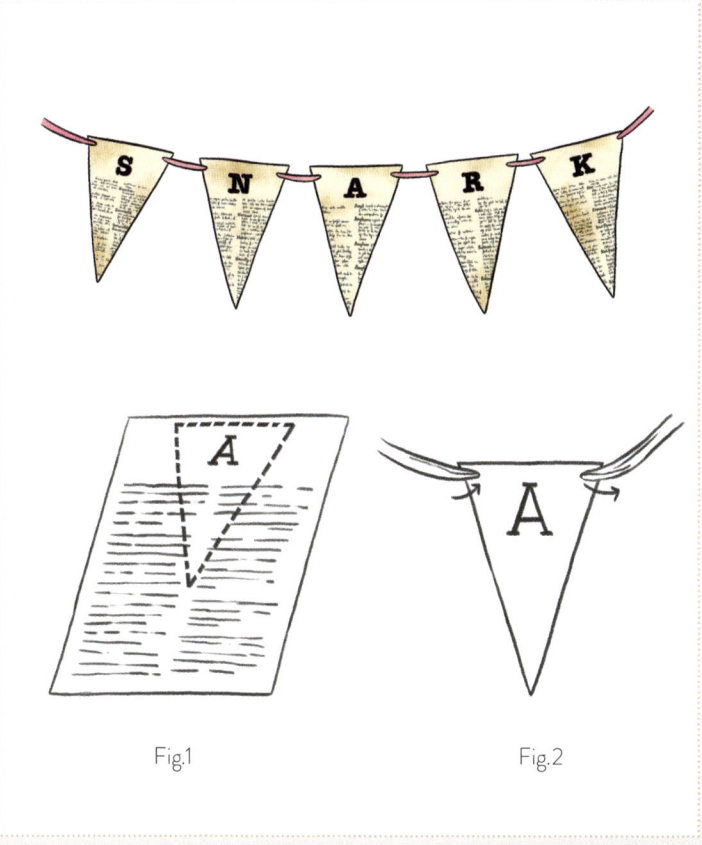

Fig.1   Fig.2

Making your home smell like fall

There's something magical about stepping into a home that smells like autumn. It's as if you've walked straight into a hug. Fall scents don't just fill a room – they create a mood, evoke memories, and transport you to pumpkin patches, cozy coffee shops, and woodland walks; or, for me, the Dragonfly Inn. There's no place I'd rather spend a lazy afternoon! Whether it's the warm spice of cinnamon or the fresh crispness of apple, these aromas turn your home into a sanctuary of seasonal charm.

Scent is one of the fastest ways to transform your space and your mindset. A flicker of a candle, catching an aroma as you pass a diffuser, or a simmering pot of spices on the stove can instantly make everything feel more soothing. You can layer scents as you would blankets, combining subtle hints that blend together, wrapping your home in the essence of autumn.

Here's a short guide to some of my favorite autumnal scents that not only smell incredible but also stir feelings of warmth, nostalgia, and joy.

- **Cinnamon and clove.** Just like the comfort of freshly baked cookies (and what could be more *Gilmore Girls* than the spice Babette's cat was named after), these two scents blend together beautifully, feeling cozy, welcoming, and familiar. Perfect for evenings spent curled up with a book and, for this reason, they're perfect for your bedroom or in snugs where you like to relax, too.

- **Vanilla and nutmeg.** These create a creamy, indulgent aroma, engendering a luxurious and calming feel – like wrapping yourself in your favorite oversized jumper.

- **Apple and pear.** These bring a crisp, fresh sweetness that can balance out heavier scents. They can be invigorating and playful, like a brisk walk through an orchard, and are particularly well placed in the kitchen.

- **Pumpkin spice.** A quintessential fall blend that combines spice and sweetness in perfect harmony. It's whimsical and celebratory, evoking images of pumpkin patches and Halloween fun.

- **Cedarwood and sandalwood.** These impart depth and earthiness, grounding your space in natural, woodsy tones. They will leave you feeling relaxed and serene, like a stroll through the forest with leaves crunching underfoot.

- **Orange and ginger.** Another great blend for the kitchen, these scents provide a bright, zesty twist that's both energizing and spicy. Uplifting and lively, the scent gives you a bit of a buzz, like the feeling of being at a bustling fall market.

- **Smoky birch or fireplace embers.** These scents will mimic those of a cozy, crackling fire. Perfect if you don't have a fireplace! Intimate and nostalgic, these are great for the living room on chilly nights, especially if you're having friends over for a relaxed evening of conversation.

How to infuse your fall scents

Here are some suggested ways of infusing your fall scents, depending on time and budget. Whichever you choose, they will all have your home smelling gorgeous in no time!

- **Simmering pots on the stove.** Many scents can be created by going directly to the source. Take foods you like the smell of – such as orange peel, vanilla, cloves, cinnamon sticks, apples, or berries – and boil them up in a pan of water. Once boiled, leave them to simmer, topping up the water as needed. If you keep topping them up, they can be gently simmering on and off for a few days, before you need to swap out the ingredients for new ones. And as an added bonus, this will humidify the air as it scents.

- **Candles and wax melts.** These will enable you to create different scents in different rooms, for contrasting vibes across your home.

- **Essential-oil diffusers.** A low-effort way of keeping your rooms smelling autumnal, these can also help you to sleep or relax. Just research the particular properties of your favorite scents and find the ones that best fit your needs. The great thing about this option is you can experiment with different oil combinations, like cedarwood and vanilla or orange and clove.

- **DIY sachets.** Fill small cloth bags with dried herbs, spices, and even pinecones to tuck into drawers or hang in closets.

- **Delicious baking.** Nothing beats the smell of spiced apple or pumpkin wafting from the oven – air fresheners at their finest! It's no surprise that the oldest trick in the book when showing a home is to have an apple pie baking in the oven. And the obvious added benefit? You have something delicious to eat as an end product. See Chapter One for plenty of ideas to fill your home with mouth-watering fall aromas.

10 ways to bring the magic of fairy lights into your home

It's hard to think of Stars Hollow decor without also thinking of fairy lights – shimmering quietly in the background during town festivals or draped across porches on crisp fall nights. In the world of *Gilmore Girls*, these twinkly lights aren't just decorations – they're part of the mood. Here are some suggestions for how you can bring the magic of fairy lights into your home and bottle a little bit of that charm.

1. **Drape them over your headboard**. Create a soft, dreamy glow around your bed to help soothe you into dreams of Paul Anka (the real one, not the dog one).

2. **Weave them through your bookshelf.** Nestle lights between stacks of books and trinkets for a Rory-inspired reading nook that glows.

3. **Wrap them around a window frame.** A lovely way to frame the view of falling leaves or softly falling snow.

4. **Tuck them into a mason jar or glass vase.** Instant lantern! Perfect for centerpieces or a nightstand glow.

5. **Outline a mirror.** Adds charm to your morning and evening rituals, with just enough sparkle – and who doesn't love some soft illumination that doubles as a ring-light?

6. **Wind a string around a bed canopy or curtain rod.** Turn your bedroom into a Stars Hollow B&B moment.

7. **Create a 'photo wall' with pegs and prints.** Hang fairy lights across a wall and clip on Polaroids, postcards, or GG quotes.

8. **Highlight a workspace or study nook.** Keep it cozy while you journal, write, or work – with just enough ambient light.

9. **Line a hallway or stair banister.** Guide your way like a trail of magic – especially enchanting on darker evenings.

10. **Hang in a canopy tent or reading corner.** Make yourself a soft, glowy retreat – perfect for rewatching *Gilmore Girls* or escaping into a book.

Slowing Down
The Pace

Slowing down the pace

There's a particular kind of magic in fall that whispers, slow down. It's the unhurried journey a leaf takes as it flutters to the ground . . . the way that twilight lingers a little longer . . . the crisper evening air encouraging us to start a mini hibernation. Autumn is not a season for rushing. Rather, it's a time to pause, to breathe and to savor.

In Stars Hollow, where the world's longest traffic light and crosswalk mimic life's pace for those lucky enough to call it home, it's a lesson well learned. We can all take a leaf out of the town's oldest living resident, Mrs Lanahan's book, as she makes her leisurely way from one side of the street to the other. The characters understand the joy of a relaxed gossip over coffee at Luke's, an evening spent discussing inane matters in a town meeting, or a few hours spent browsing in the local bookstore.

This chapter is an invitation to not only take a break from the rush of everyday life but also to create space to truly be. Autumn is not so much about doing, it's about experiencing and introspection – lingering in the moments we enjoy and finding ourselves within them. Fall gives us permission to watch the clouds roll by, to lose ourselves in a good book (or seven), and to indulge in the kind of stillness that makes a *Gilmore Girls* binge-watch feel like a warm embrace. It's not just about pressing play on your favorite episodes; it's about preparing yourself, mind and body, to fully immerse in the cozy, whimsical world of Stars Hollow.

Here you will find tips and tricks to help you slow down and make the most of this magical season.

Leaning into hibernation

When Richard Gilmore takes a break from Rory's wild sixteenth birthday party, preferring to sit on the porch with some choice reading material (provided by Rory), he is prompted by a Cosmo quiz to determine what season he is. 'I am an autumn', he pronounces solemnly. His actions at the party certainly confirm this statement. Although he has attended his granddaughter's birthday party (likely at Emily's insistence, but certainly to bring pleasure to Rory), he chooses to step away from the wildness of a party he is very unlikely to enjoy, opting to sit, read, and observe instead.

Autumn, for many, is a time for solitude or close intimacy with a select few, and if you, like Richard Gilmore, welcome time spent on reflection, here are some tips on how to approach social events in the slow season:

Be selective. You don't have to attend every event or say yes to every invitation, and while this doesn't mean hibernating completely, you can give yourself permission to actively choose how you spend your time.

Practice saying 'no'. It's not always easy to decline an invitation, so prepare in advance how you want to approach it. It's ok to be honest, even though it's tempting to invent excuses. A true friend will understand that you need a break and are taking some time to slow down.

Be mindful of the rhythms of your week or month. When choosing social events, be careful not to 'bunch book' them, or you may find you have two weeks at home, then four nights out in a row, which would certainly be a shock to the system. Be mindful of how your plans fit into your week or month as a whole, and don't be afraid to reschedule catch-ups with friends for a more convenient time.

Choose social activities that give you what you need. Perhaps a friend invites you to a big gathering or an activity that you know you won't enjoy? It's always possible to respond with an alternative plan that better suits your autumnal temperament. See pages 139–141 for inspiration for some fall-friendly social activities that will get you outdoors and celebrating nature in its fall finery, or Chapter One for recipes you could bake with friends (surely the most delicious way to bond with others). Or if you fancy a cozy night in, see Chapter Four for suggestions for the ultimate movie night or reading recommendations if you fancy starting a book club. And then, of course, there's the ultimate fall social activity: a *Gilmore Girls* marathon with your bestie.

Embrace your local community. While the more draining social activities may feel off the table in the season of hibernation, this is a great time to connect to our own natures as community-seeking humans. Stars Hollow residents certainly know the importance of coming together to achieve something for the greater good, raising money for town causes like rebuilding a bridge or fixing the church roof. Whether you're leading or just participating, it's amazing to feel a part of your community, so look out for events or festivals in your local area that you could volunteer to be a part of.

'Tis the season for self-care

It's not uncommon to find that your mood is a little more unstable in the colder and darker months, so it's important to regularly check in on yourself, performing small acts of self-care and embracing rituals that nurture both body and mind. Autumn reminds us of the beauty in transitions, urging us to let go of what no longer serves us, just as trees shed their leaves. It's a season of balance, where rest feels restorative and small acts of self-kindness carry the magic of renewal.

Caring for yourself comes in many forms, some of which will be entirely personal to you and your interests, but here are some ideas:

A bath. It's a classic for a reason. A bath with candlelight and relaxing music or a podcast is the perfect way to bring the heart rate down, soothe your senses, and wash away the stresses of the day.

Retail therapy. This is something Lorelai certainly knows the benefit of, although she would caution strongly against window-shopping when you're broke!

Pamper night. Remember April's birthday party, when Lorelai took them all to Stars Hollow Beauty Supply to buy whatever they wanted, then they spent the evening doing makeovers and facemasks and generally pampering themselves? It's wonderful to enjoy putting make-up on purely for the fun of it (Vicious Trollope lip shade, anyone?) and a great way to experiment with new looks.

Writing to-do lists. Not the first thing you might consider when thinking of 'self-care', but this is straight out of the Rory Gilmore survival handbook. When your emotions are uncertain and you're off balance, a to-do list you can steadily work through helps to add structure to the chaos and will leave you feeling calmer, assuming you put achievable tasks on there.

Spa day. A more expensive but very effective option, even if you're tricked into it by your mother who insists, as Emily Gilmore once did to her daughter, on having side-by-side treatments. Whether you're getting a massage, a mud bath, or a cleansing facial, the focus on you and on relaxation is an incredible way to center yourself and find stillness.

Animal therapy. Although this is much easier to achieve if you have your own pet (named after a 1950s' crooner?), it's never too hard to find a way to spend time with a furry, feathered, or scaly therapist. Whether you like dogs, cats, or horses – or something far more unusual – studies have found that spending time with animals will reduce stress (lowering cortisol), improve your mood (increasing oxytocin), help with feelings of loneliness, and even make you feel more confident and capable. And if it's an animal that gets you out of doors and active, you'll likely find your sleep improving, too.

Unplugging from technology. Just because you don't have a Luke Danes around to shout at you until you hang up the phone, that doesn't mean you can't self-enforce time spent away from technology. Try leaving your phone in another room, or at the bottom of your bag when you're with friends, or even, heaven forbid, at home when you go out for a walk. You might just find you feel a little bit lighter for being able to disconnect from the social pressure of always being available to others and that you can focus on simply enjoying the moment.

Positive affirmations

As the world slows down, and you start being more introspective, it's easy to get caught up in more negative thought processes. Put simply, more time spent thinking can become too much time spent overthinking. Break the pattern by starting the day with these *Gilmore-Girls*-inspired affirmations, to be spoken aloud three times, ideally while looking at yourself in a mirror.

'I am strong enough for this.' The Gilmore Girls have their wobbles, too. Can Lorelai handle opening her own inn when the costs and decisions build up? Can Rory cope with the immense academic pressure of Yale after Mitchum Huntzberger tells her she's not cut out to be a journalist? As both women find, no one else can tell you your worth or where your strengths lie. You are strong enough to cope with anything if you put enough faith in yourself.

'I can lean on my loved ones.' It's easy to get caught up in a dangerous mindset that we have to do things on our own, so it can help to remind ourselves regularly that it's ok to ask for help. In the immortal words of Rory, 'I cannot do this alone. I need my mommy, and dammit, I don't care who knows it.'

'The things that make me different are what make me special.' Stars Hollow certainly knows how to embrace a little eccentricity and weirdness, and it's what makes the characters so lovable and popular with audiences. Indeed, when Tristan says to Rory, 'You're very odd, you know that?' her response is to thank him. Don't shy away from your weirdnesses. Embrace them!

'I might feel scared, but I'm going to jump anyway!' Take a leaf from the book of the Life and Death Brigade. And while jumping, just imagine you're holding Logan Huntzberger's hand, and everything is sure to turn out fine. In Omnia Paratus!

'I always learn from my mistakes.' As Lorelai wisely says, 'Yeah, everybody screws up, Lane. That's what happens. It's what you do with the screw-ups, it's how you handle the experience, that's what you should judge yourself by.'

'I am kayak, hear me roar.' When Lorelai says this, it's in response to Emily's appreciation of her independence. While she is very much part of her community, she makes it clear she does not need a romantic partner to get by, or someone else to take care of her. This is the perfect battle cry for anyone needing a little bit more faith in their own abilities.

'I want to win and I'm going to win.' So says Rory's long-term frenemy. Because sometimes we just need to channel a little Paris-Geller confidence!

'Oy with the poodles already!' I'm not sure if this is an accurate interpretation of the quote, but I see it as a reminder to shake off the things that don't matter. And, of course, to have some fun (this phrase features two words that Lorelai considers the funniest in the world).

'I'm so hot, I may hit on myself tonight.' Now that's Lorelai levels of confidence we could all do with more of.

'I am a pro, not a con.' Remind yourself regularly of your own worth.

'I'm in. I'm all in.' The words of Luke Danes when committing himself to Lorelai are the perfect motivation to start your day. It is a reminder to bring your whole heart to the table when you're approaching the things that really matter.

Guided meditations

Guided meditations are a powerful tool for nurturing your mental and emotional well-being. Whether you're new to meditation, or looking to deepen your practice, structured sessions offer step-by-step guidance to help you relax, focus, and find clarity. If Paris Geller and Doyle could find the benefit in yoga and meditation, imagine what these practices could do for you!

You can find apps, podcasts, or online platforms that are tailored to your specific need, whether it's reducing stress, improving sleep, enhancing focus, or cultivating gratitude. Many sessions include visualizations, breathing exercises, or affirmations to center your thoughts and anchor you in the present moment.

Here is an example of a guided meditation that invites you to embrace the fall. You could try reading it aloud, giving yourself time after each section to close your eyes and visualize the scene suggested, or ask someone to read it for you. Just find a quiet, calm space where you feel comfortable. By incorporating guided meditations into your routine, you can create a sacred space for yourself, fostering mindfulness, resilience, and inner peace.

Autumn is not so much about
doing, it's about experiencing
and introspection.

Guided meditation:
Embracing autumn's transformation

Find a comfortable position, either seated or lying down. Close your eyes and take a deep breath in, imagining yourself outdoors (if you're not), the crispness of the air filling your lungs. Exhale slowly, letting go of any tension in your body. Allow yourself to settle into this moment, surrounded by the essence of autumn.

Step 1: Grounding with the earth

Imagine yourself in a forest in the heart of autumn. Visualize the ground beneath you, blanketed with fallen leaves in hues of gold, amber, and crimson. Feel the connection between your body and the earth, as though you are rooted like the sturdy trees around you. With each breath, draw strength from the ground, anchoring yourself in the present moment.

Step 2: Acknowledging change

Take a moment to notice the gentle breeze brushing against your face. It carries the scent of woodsmoke and fallen leaves. As the breeze moves, imagine it carrying away anything that no longer serves you – worries, fears, or habits you're ready to release. With each exhale, let go of whatever is weighing you down, just as the trees let go of their leaves.

Step 3: Embracing the harvest

Now, shift your focus to the abundance around you. Picture the vibrant colors of the leaves, the warmth of autumn sunlight filtering through the trees, and the richness of the season's harvest. Reflect on the gifts in your life, the seeds you planted earlier in the year that have now come to fruition. Breathe deeply, and silently express gratitude for these blessings.

Step 4: Preparing for rest

Feel the forest quietening around you, preparing for winter's stillness. Allow yourself to mirror this natural rhythm. Visualize a warm, glowing light surrounding you, symbolizing peace and preparation for a restful period. This light wraps you in comfort, reminding you that rest is as vital as growth.

Step 5: Closing with intention

When you're ready, begin to bring your awareness back to the room. Wiggle your fingers and toes, take a final deep breath in and exhale slowly. Before opening your eyes, set a gentle intention to carry the lessons of autumn with you: to embrace change, express gratitude, and honor the cycles of rest and renewal in your life.

When you're ready, open your eyes and take a moment to reorient yourself. Carry the peace of this meditation with you into your day.

Take yourself back to Stars Hollow

And the ultimate gift in self-care? If you're reading this book, you're likely already aware of how a *Gilmore Girls* rewatch makes you feel, but there is actual science to prove that watching a favorite show multiple times brings immense emotional support. You know how things are going to turn out, so there is no real jeopardy, the characters feel like old friends you're reconnecting with, and (especially if it's a show you liked as a kid) there's nostalgia that can release oxytocin and make you feel all warm and happy inside. Ellen Hendriksen, a clinical psychologist and assistant professor at Boston University, has described how rewatching a favorite show can be a healthy coping mechanism for stressful times. She calls it a 'certainty anchor' for when 'predictability or certainty is missing from your life, or if we're reflecting on the larger political landscape, or environmental uncertainty'.[1]

This is especially true of *Gilmore Girls*, a show where there's no violence (a couple of pretty funny, very unserious punch-ups aside) and nothing truly awful or insurmountable happens. Fans have described how *Gilmore Girls* got them through break-ups, bereavements, or other times of huge upheaval, providing an anchor that they can come back to whenever times get hard.

It is also not surprising that viewing figures are so much higher in the fall, the season when people traditionally connect with friends on a deeper level and are more introspective. Stars Hollow is a town where everyone knows one another and so much of their lives is built around their community. Rewatching *Gilmore Girls* makes us feel part of that community, connected deeply to the characters we've loved for so long; and watching it is like the ultimate comfort food and a true act of self-care.

Cozy Cultural Fixes

Cozy cultural fixes

One of *Gilmore Girls'* most endearing traits is its deep obsession with pop culture. There is nothing our fast-talking girls love more than a good pop-culture reference. As they hug steaming mugs of coffee, Rory and Lorelai's conversations brim with lightning-quick allusions to movies, books, and music.

Many episodes of the show promote the kind of cozy behaviors and cultural pursuits we naturally gravitate toward as fall arrives with its cooler weather, gently nudging us indoors. Every *Gilmore Girls* fan has dreamed of being invited to one of Rory and Lorelai's epic movie nights, where classic films are binged, mountains of junk food devoured, and everyone nestles into the Gilmores' impossibly cozy couch (arguably the comfiest in TV history). Meanwhile, Rory stands as a champion for bookworms everywhere. Whether savoring the smell of the pages of a novel or reading in the Chilton dining hall, Rory is the poster-girl for the joy of curling up with a good book. Even the quirky town of Stars Hollow, with its annual Movie Night in the Square and resident music aficionado, Lane Kim, celebrates and cherishes cultural pursuits in a way that feels both charming and familiar.

Lorelai and Rory understand that it is sometimes the simplest pleasures – reading a great novel or settling in for a movie marathon – that bring the most comfort and warmth, especially during the autumn months. In this chapter, we'll dive into some of the literary and pop-culture references in *Gilmore Girls* and encourage you to create your own traditions, whether it's hosting cozy movie nights or embracing your inner bookworm. And all while savoring the magic of fall.

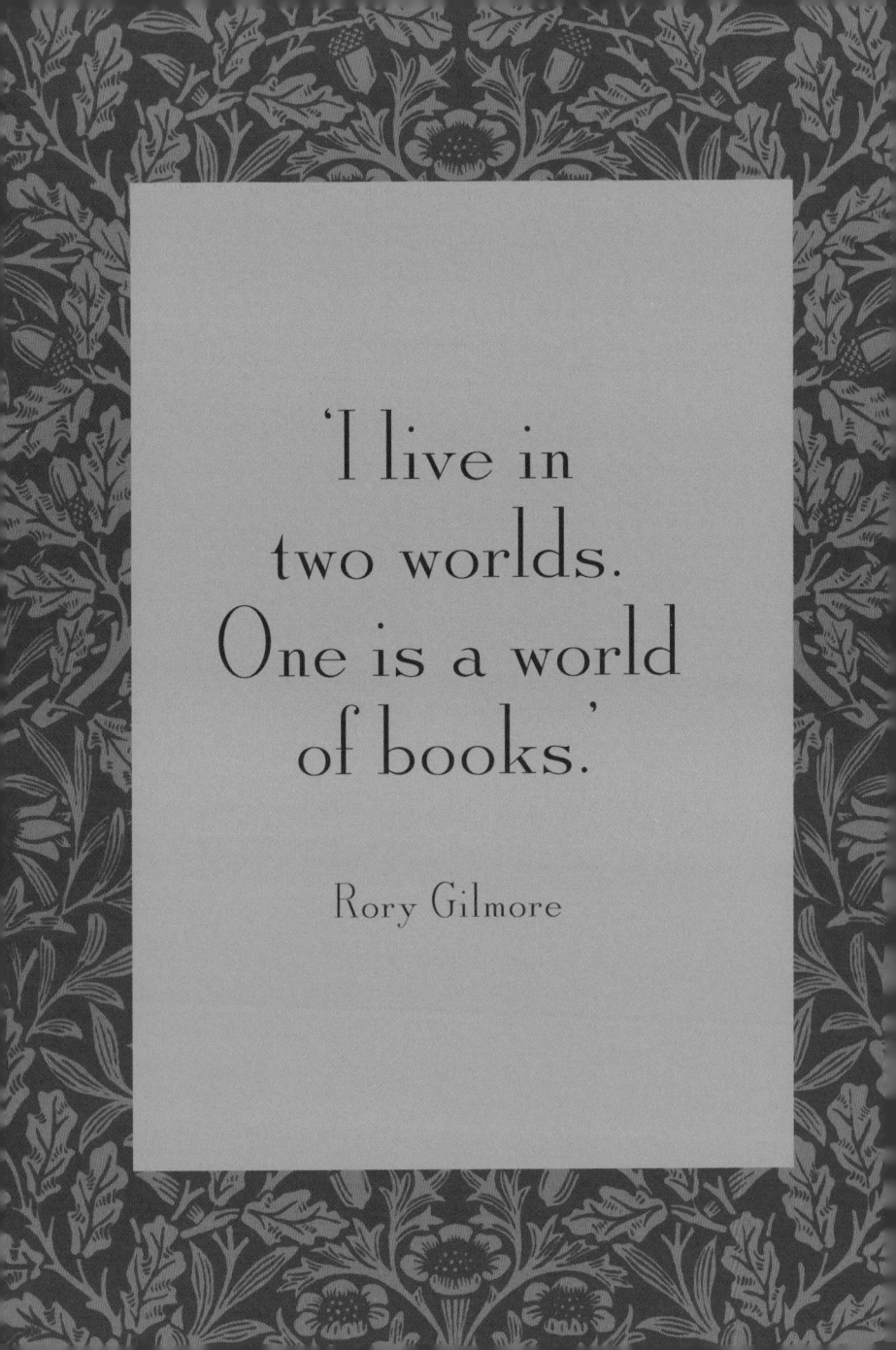

'I live in
two worlds.
One is a world
of books.'

Rory Gilmore

Reading

Rory famously brings a book with her wherever she goes. Her reading list spans classics, contemporary literature, and obscure titles. Fall is the perfect season for page-turners. So if you're in search of a good book for autumn, here are some of Rory's best cozy reads.

Rory's fall reading list

Howl and Other Poems by Allen Ginsberg

This is the book that Rory and Jess first bond over. In a romantic gesture, Jess swipes *Howl* from Rory's room after they first meet and returns it to her later with notes in the margins (Jess has read it forty times). Allen Ginsberg's landmark poetry collection came to define the Beat generation in the post-World-War-II era with its raw, unflinching exploration of sexuality, counterculture, and societal rebellion. Its title poem, 'Howl', captures the disillusionment and frustration of a generation struggling against the pressures and demands of society and conformity. No wonder our favorite bad boy, Jess, loved it!

Anna Karenina by Leo Tolstoy

This is one of Rory's favorite books, although Dean describes it as 'depressing' (an early hint that their relationship was doomed). *Anna Karenina* by Leo Tolstoy is a sweeping Russian novel centered on the fated adulterous affair between Anna and Count Vronsky. Considered a classic novel for its richly detailed storytelling, complex characters, and exploration of love and social constraints, it's the perfect fall read.

Atonement by Ian McEwan

Rory is seen reading *Atonement* when she first starts at Yale University. The story follows young Briony Tallis, whose false accusation alters the lives of her sister, Cecilia, and her lover, Robbie, unfolding across the backdrop of World War II. *Atonement* is a powerful novel that explores themes of love, guilt, and the far-reaching consequences of a single lie.

The Year of Magical Thinking by Joan Didion

Rory reads this when she goes to stay at Logan's family home on Martha's Vineyard. *The Year of Magical Thinking* is a memoir by Joan Didion, chronicling the author's journey following the sudden death of her husband, John Gregory Dunne, in 2003. This deeply personal portrait of what it means to navigate life after unimaginable tragedy has become a classic.

Franny and Zooey by J. D. Salinger

In Season 2, Lorelai catches Jess snooping around Rory's book collection. Jess wants to see if Rory has a copy of *Franny and Zooey* by J. D. Salinger. And she does! Salinger's novella follows Franny and Zooey, two siblings of the intellectual Glass family, as they deal with spiritual and emotional struggles. The plot centers on Franny, who questions the world's superficiality and spirals into disillusionment, and Zooey's attempt to help her find peace. It's no surprise that Rory and Jess, both bookish and drawn to complex, introspective characters, would appreciate Salinger's work.

The Bell Jar by Sylvia Path

Rory and Lorelai mention *The Bell Jar* twice during the course of *Gilmore Girls*. It tells the story of Esther Greenwood, a young woman who battles mental illness and feels trapped by the expectations of society. Drawing heavily on Plath's own experiences, the novel is a poignant and powerful exploration of identity. Rory is clearly a fan of Plath's writing; she is also seen reading *The Unabridged Journals of Sylvia Plath*.

Madame Bovary by Gustave Flaubert

Madame Bovary is the one of the first novels that Dean sees Rory reading. Rory's 'unbelievable concentration' while reading the book is what first attracts Dean to her in the pilot episode of *Gilmore Girls*. Gustave Flaubert's 1857 debut is a renowned literary classic. It follows Emma Bovary, a young, beautiful woman who is dissatisfied with her dull marriage. Encouraged by reading romance novels, she seeks excitement through extramarital affairs, leading to devastating consequences. This theme of infidelity mirrors the tensions in Rory's and Dean's relationship first hinted at in the pilot.

Leaves of Grass by Walt Whitman

Leaves of Grass is a groundbreaking poetry collection by Walt Whitman, celebrating the beauty of the individual, nature, and democracy, and it is often regarded as one of the most influential works in American literature. Upon returning from his second honeymoon with Emily, Richard gives Rory a 100-year-old copy of *Leaves of Grass* in Greek, and she gushes over the thoughtful gift. These bookish moments highlight the warm, loving bond between Rory and her grandfather and the deep love of literature they share.

The Fountainhead by Ayn Rand

Ayn Rand's *The Fountainhead* is a philosophical novel that explores the life of uncompromising architect Howard Roark, who battles against conventional standards to maintain his artistic vision. Rory describes *The Fountainhead* as a 'classic novel' to Jess and says that no author could 'write a forty-page monologue' the way that Rand could. *The Fountainhead* reflects Rand's views that the individual is more valuable than the collective, and the importance of personal integrity over societal pressures.

The Portable Dorothy Parker by Dorothy Parker

Rory takes *The Portable Dorothy Parker* to the formal dance at Chilton – because she takes a book everywhere, of course! Dorothy Parker was a sharp-witted American writer, poet, and critic known for her satirical humor and insightful commentary on society, love, and relationships. *The Portable Dorothy Parker* is a collection of her best works, including poetry, short stories, and essays, showcasing her biting humor and keen observations of human nature. This book is essential for Parker fans like Rory. *Gilmore Girls* creator Amy Sherman-Palladino shares this admiration for the writer, and her production company is named 'Dorothy Parker Drank Here', with the logo appearing at the end of each episode of our favorite fall show.

Other Rory-approved book recommendations:

- *Emma* by Jane Austen

- *Moby Dick* by Herman Melville

- *Letters to a Young Poet* by Rainer Maria Rilke

- *Mrs Dalloway* by Virgina Woolf

- *A Heartbreaking Work of Staggering Genius* by Dave Eggers

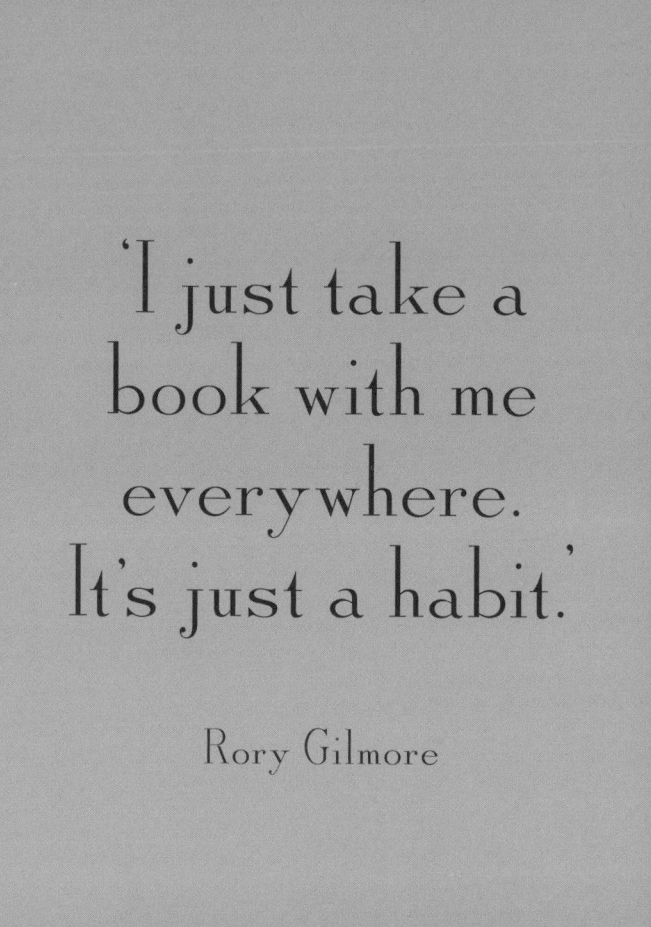

'I just take a
book with me
everywhere.
It's just a habit.'

Rory Gilmore

Pumpkin spice and plot twists: How to embrace reading in the fall season

This fall season, do yourself a favor and lose yourself in a good book. Here's how to make reading your autumn obsession, Rory-Gilmore style.

Create your cozy reading haven. Autumn is the perfect time to transform reading into a self-care ritual. Create a cozy corner in your home where you can fully immerse yourself in a book. Think soft blankets and warm cups of freshly brewed coffee. As the leaves turn, let this chillier season, with its shorter days and longer nights, be a reminder to slow down. Embrace these calmer moments and let classic books take you on adventures instead.

Carry a book wherever you go. Whether she's taking a book to the school dance or sneaking a chapter on a bus ride, Rory's love for books isn't limited to occasional moments. Instead, reading is a constant in her life. Embrace this habit and bring a book with you everywhere, too. Whether it's a few pages between errands or an entire chapter while waiting in line, reading on the go is the ideal way to fit more stories into your life. You just never know when the perfect quiet moment will appear to get lost in a book.

Share the magic of reading. One of the most delightful parts of Rory's reading life is how she shares books with the people she cares about, like lending novels to Dean and talking about literature with her grandfather, Richard. Share your love of reading with those around you by recommending your favorite novels to friends and family. Sharing books is a beautiful way to create bonds.

Explore libraries and bookstores. As Rory will tell you, there's something magical about the smell of books. There's no smell like it! Why not make time to explore old libraries and visit bookstores this fall? Head to your local independent bookstore, take in the atmosphere, get lost in the aisles, browsing novels, and find your next great read.

'This was
supposed to be
a simple night,
watch a movie,
eat junk, go to
bed feeling sick.'

Rory Gilmore

Film

Lorelai's and Rory's love of movies is a cornerstone of their bond. The cozy image of the mother-and-daughter duo bingeing classic movies while snuggled on the couch makes movie nights feel like the ultimate fall activity.

Lorelai's top movie-night picks

From cult classics to romantic masterpieces, here are a few of Lorelai's must-watch films for you to explore this season.

Casablanca (1942)

Casablanca is the movie that Lorelai shows Luke on his first introduction to a Gilmore movie night. She classifies *Casablanca* as a true classic: a tier far above 'a guilty pleasure' or a 'nothing-else-on' movie. Set during World War II, *Casablanca* follows the story of American nightclub owner Rick Blaine who is torn between his love for Ilsa Lund and helping her and her fugitive husband escape the Nazis in French Morocco. With iconic lines and career-defining performances from Humphrey Bogart and Ingrid Bergman, *Casablanca* is an unforgettable tale of love and the true meaning of fighting for a noble cause.

Love Story (1970)

After Rory splits up with Dean, Lorelai advises her to get over her first break-up by watching a really sad movie like *Love Story* and having a good, long cry. *Love Story* is the heartfelt tale of a boy and girl who fall in love despite their different backgrounds – but then tragedy strikes. Considered one of the most romantic films ever made, *Love Story* is the perfect movie to watch for a cathartic cry. Keep a box of tissues at the ready!

An Affair to Remember (1957)

Another perfect tearjerker of a movie, recommended by both Lorelai and Rory for anyone going through heartbreak. *An Affair to Remember* stars Cary Grant and Deborah Kerr as strangers who fall in love during a transatlantic cruise. They agree to meet at the Empire State Building six months later, but a tragic accident jeopardizes their reunion. So grab a pint of ice cream and get ready for a movie that remains one of cinema's most beloved romances.

Willly Wonka & the Chocolate Factory (1971)

Willly Wonka & the Chocolate Factory is the movie Rory watches with Dean on their first 'hang-out' (with Lorelai in tow, of course). Rory and Lorelai are also known to often rewatch this movie as they indulge in every junk food imaginable. Based on Roald Dahl's classic children's book, this musical fantasy tells the story about a poor boy called Charlie who wins a golden ticket to tour the eccentric Willy Wonka's magical chocolate factory. Delightfully quirky, this movie features memorable songs and an iconic performance by the enigmatic Gene Wilder as Willy Wonka.

The Way We Were (1973)

A film that gets frequent mentions in *Gilmore Girls* is *The Way We Were* – a 1973 romance starring Barbra Streisand and Robert Redford. The film clearly resonates with Lorelai and, during a moment of turmoil in her relationship with Luke, she finds herself drawn to it once more. *The Way We Were* follows the complex love story between a passionate activist and a carefree writer. The movie has had enduring popularity for its universal themes of love and loss. It also features an unforgettable theme sung by Streisand.

The Breakfast Club (1985)

Mentioned in *Gilmore Girls* numerous times, *The Breakfast Club* is clearly a film that has stuck with Lorelai. She even credits watching the coming-of-age teen drama with helping to shape Rory's language skills. Directed by John Hughes, *The Breakfast Club* is set in a high-school detention, where five seemingly very different students bond over their shared experiences. This cult classic remains one of the most influential movies of the 1980s.

Jerry Maguire (1996)

This romantic comedy is mentioned by both Lorelai and Emily, who describes it as 'delightful.' *Jerry Maguire* stars Tom Cruise as an ambitious sports agent who gets fired after experiencing a crisis of conscience. He then starts his own management firm with single mother Dorothy Boyd, played by Renée Zellweger. This heartfelt and charming movie is packed with life lessons about love, loyalty, and personal redemption.

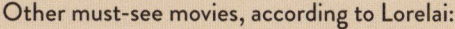

Other must-see movies, according to Lorelai:

For Keeps (1988)

Lorelai says she learned everything she knows about raising a child from this coming-of-age drama, which bears a resemblance to her own life. It stars Molly Ringwald as a clever high-school student whose life takes an abrupt turn when she becomes unexpectedly pregnant by her boyfriend.

A Star is Born (1937, 1954, and 1976)

Lorelai rents all three versions of this tragic romance (starring Janet Gaynor, Judy Garland, and Barbra Streisand) via Netflix (back when Netflix mailed out DVD rentals). *A Star is Born* is one of Hollywood's most remade stories. Each adaptation revolves around an aging male celebrity who mentors and falls in love with a younger female star. As she rises to fame, her success comes at the cost of their relationship.

Showgirls (1995)

An erotic drama which tells the story of an ambitious young woman who hitches a ride to Las Vegas to follow her dream of becoming a professional dancer. Although it was critically panned when it was released, *Showgirls* has gone on to become a hate-watch classic and has acquired a huge fanbase. Lorelai is one of the movie's many dedicated fans and is known to regularly rewatch it, sometimes with an accompanying drinking game.

Cool Hand Luke (1967)

Lorelai and Rory plan to watch this prison drama at the local Black & White & Read Bookstore and movie theater with Dean and Luke. Paul Newman stars as the unbreakable petty criminal Luke Jackson who becomes an inspiration to other prisoners by refusing to play to the sadistic guards' rules.

Lorelai's movie rules:

'No talking during the movie. No exceptions during a true classic. And minimize distraction. You know, no shifting around a lot, no phone calls, nothing. No going to the bathroom. If you go, you miss the movie because we're not pausing the movie.'

Lights, camera, cozy!
How to fall into a movie night

Lorelai's movie nights are nothing short of legendary. With a couch full of pillows, a pile of takeout containers, and Rory by her side, these evenings are a masterclass in an autumn evening done right.

Here's how to turn your living room into a Stars-Hollow-approved sanctuary and throw a *Gilmore-Girls*-inspired movie night at home.

Build your comfy-couch paradise. What is at the center of every *Gilmore Girls* movie night? A couch so comfy it practically hugs you – Lorelai and Rory's plush and inviting one is basically a character in its own right. To make your couch the comfiest spot in the world for a movie marathon, pile up your seating area with plenty of soft blankets and cushions, regardless of whether they match or not. (In fact, the quirkier the mix, the better!) Go for unusual patterns or anything that looks like it's been nabbed from an eclectic Stars Hollow boutique. Soft lighting is key: dim the lamps and add some candles, like Lorelai does, to give the room a cozy glow.

Serve snacks worthy of a Gilmore feast. No *Gilmore-Girls*-inspired movie night is complete without a spread that's borderline outrageous. Lorelai and Rory never skimp on a variety of snacks and takeout, and neither should you. It's part of the movie-night experience. When it comes to selecting snacks, the more sugary and salty, the better. (Although Lorelai once added carrots to the movie-night snack spread because she was worried Rory wasn't eating healthily at Yale!)

Skip the dining table. Instead, park the snacks right in the middle of the coffee table. Gilmore rules say it's not a proper movie night if you're not reaching over someone to grab a slice of pizza or a handful of Red Vines. And don't forget to stock up on tiny side tables within arm's reach for coffee mugs, bowls of sweets, and any last-minute snack emergencies.

Lorelai and Rory-approved snacks:

- Marshmallows

- Skittles

- Raw cookie dough

- Crisps

- Chocolate chips

- Popcorn

- Cheese puffs

- Red Vines

- A tub of peanut butter (with spoons, so people can dig straight in)

- Takeout (Chinese, pizza, or, ideally, both – see page 44 for the best takeout options)

- Cheeseburgers

Embrace the 'sit-however-you-want' rule. A set-up that invites everyone to sit, stretch, or sprawl across the couch, as they wish, the sit-however-you-want rule is crucial (formal seating arrangements have no place at movie night). Whether you curl up with your legs tucked under you, lie flat across the cushions, or end up on the floor with a blanket, the goal here is comfort for the ultimate viewing experience.

Let the debate begin: choose the movie. No Gilmore movie night is complete without a little spirited debate. Channel your inner Lorelai and Rory and argue over which movie to watch first. It doesn't matter who wins – half the fun is in the banter. Playfully insisting that your choice is superior while defending your reasoning with humor is practically a Gilmore tradition.

No cell phones! According to Lorelai's movie-night rules, no phone calls are allowed. 'Shifting around' and 'distractions' are also banned. The only thing that matters is that everyone focuses on the classic movie being shown. Part of the irresistible charm of *Gilmore Girls* is down to the distinct lack of cell phones in the show. The characters live fully in the moment, making even simple activities like movie nights feel magical. So, for a movie night inspired by the show, ditch the phones and focus on creating an atmosphere that encourages connection.

When you're ready, grab your snacks, hit play, and soak up the charm of a Gilmore-style movie night.

Watching *Gilmore Girls* in the fall feels like a permission slip to lean into all your cravings.

Music

The leaves are falling, and music is calling!

In her graduation speech, Rory fondly remembers how Lorelai filled their house 'with love and fun and books, and music.' Throughout the series, *Gilmore Girls* regularly showcases the characters' appreciation for a wide array of musical artists. Here are some of Lorelai's and Rory's favorites.

The Bangles

The Bangles are an American pop rock band formed in 1981, known for their harmonious sound and hits like 'Eternal Flame' and 'Manic Monday'. Their music blends 60s-inspired pop with 80s' rock. Lorelai makes numerous Bangles references throughout the series. She tells Max she loves them so much that she dreams of being a band member. The girls even go to a Bangles concert together and Lorelai mentions that she almost named Rory after lead singer, Susanna Hoffs.

The Shins

The Shins are an indie rock band known for their catchy melodies, introspective lyrics, and vocalist James Mercer's distinct falsetto. They gained popularity with hits like 'New Slang' (2001) and have remained influential in the indie music scene ever since. The Shins make an appearance performing at a Florida club where Rory and Paris spend spring break.

The Go-Go's

The Go-Go's are an all-female rock band, formed in Los Angeles in 1978 and known for their catchy pop-punk sound and hits like 'We Got the Beat' and 'Our Lips Are Sealed'. They were one of the most successful and influential female bands of the early 80s, breaking barriers for women in rock music. While Jess and Rory are looking at records in New York, Rory finds a Go-Go's album signed by the band's lead vocalist, Belinda Carlisle, which she knows Lorelai would love.

David Bowie

David Bowie was an iconic British musician and actor known for his ever-evolving sound, blending rock, pop, and experimental music with theatrical performances. He was revealed as the best-selling vinyl artist of the twenty-first century. Lorelai's, Rory's, and Lane's shared love of Bowie is clear early on in *Gilmore Girls*. In one episode, Lorelai sings the opening words of 'Space Oddity', while Bowie's song 'The Man who sold the World' memorably plays during Lane's first kiss with her boyfriend, Dave.

Belle and Sebastian

Belle and Sebastian are a Scottish indie pop band formed in 1996, known for their literary lyrics and whimsical music. In the early years of the band's existence, Belle and Sebastian were known for performing in unusual and small venues, including church halls, private homes, and libraries. In Season 2, Rory has Kirk and Michel help in an (adorable) top-secret operation to get Lane the newest Belle and Sebastian single on CD without her strict mother knowing.

A fall *Gilmore-Girls*-inspired playlist:

- 'Eternal Flame', The Bangles

- 'I Try', Macy Gray

- 'New Slang', The Shins

- 'Space Oddity', David Bowie

- 'Shadow Dancing', Andy Gibbs

- 'This Town', The Go-Go's

- 'The Boy with the Arab Strap', Belle and Sebastian

- 'The Man Who Sold the World', David Bowie

- 'There She Goes', The La's

- 'Mona Lisa', Grant-Lee Phillips

- 'Reflecting Light', Sam Phillips

- 'My Little Corner of the World', Yo La Tengo

TV shows to watch after *Gilmore Girls*

Every autumnal *Gilmore Girls* binge-watch must eventually (and sadly) come to an end. But don't fear, here are some more super-cozy tv shows to fill that stars hollow-shaped hole in your heart!

The Marvellous Mrs Maisel
Every *Gilmore Girls* fan needs to watch Amy Sherman-Palladino's other hit TV show, *The Marvellous Mrs Maisel*. It revolves around a 1950s housewife who accidentally becomes a stand-up comic, discovering a wild new life on and off stage. Expect more fast-talking comedy gold from the actors as well as some stunning vintage fashion.

Dawson's Creek
Love, heartbreak, and sharp banter in a small town full of witty characters. Sound familiar? *Dawson's Creek* may just be the ultimate TV series to get stuck into after *Gilmore Girls*. The show, about teenage friends growing up in the fictional town of Capeside, Massachusetts, aired at the same time as *Gilmore Girls* and has a similar close-knit feeling of community. The deep conversations, iconic love triangles, and early-2000s nostalgia hit just right.

Parenthood
Obviously, no show can ever truly replace *Gilmore Girls*, but Lauren Graham's follow-up *Parenthood*, comes surprisingly close. She plays a single mother raising her rebellious teenage daughter and sensitive younger son after breaking up with their rockstar father. It's heartfelt, funny, and packed with all the messy, beautiful moments that make family life feel real. With 100 episodes to binge and all the Lauren Graham you could ever want, this is instant comfort!

Hart of Dixie

In this charming show, new york doctor Zoe Hart accepts an offer from a stranger, Dr Harley Wilkes, to work in a medical practice in the fictional town of Bluebell, Alabama. Zoe finds herself tangled up in small-town traditions, complicated love triangles, eccentric characters, and unexpected friendships. *Hart of Dixie* is basically *Gilmore Girls* with a southern twang. And the similarities don't stop there. If you think the town of Bluebell looks a lot like Stars Hollow, that's because the two shows share the same film set!

Sweet Magnolias

Set in the picturesque, fictional small town of Serenity, South Carolina, this show follows lifelong friends Maddie, Helen, and Dana Sue, who call themselves the 'Sweet Magnolias'. Watch as these lovable friends lift each other up while juggling relationships, family, and careers with lots of margaritas and emotional chats on the porch. *Sweet Magnolias* is the perfect follow-up show, balancing cozy with emotional depth, just like *Gilmore Girls* did.

Friday Night Lights

Set in a rural Texan town, this heartfelt drama centers around high-school football coach Eric Taylor, his wife Tami, and the lives of the misfit players in the Dillion Panthers. Warm, wholesome, and full of small-town authenticity, there's a reason why *Friday Night Lights* has become a cult favorite among TV fans. While football is the backdrop of the show, the real focus is the emotional highs and lows of small-town life – love, family, growing up, and finding your path.

Schitt's Creek

This hilarious and heartwarming comedy follows a wealthy family who lose everything and wind up living in the tiny town of Schitt's Creek that they once bought as a joke. With witty writing and lovable, quirky characters, *Schitt's Creek* is the definition of a comfort show that you can watch over and over again – just like *Gilmore Girls*!

Virgin River

Seeking a fresh start, nurse practitioner Mel Monroe moves to the remote town of Virgin River. But small-town life comes with unexpected challenges, emotional entanglements, and a brooding local bar owner who might just mend her heart. If you're looking for another glorious show with cozy feels, quirky townspeople, and a romance to root for, *Virgin River* is the show for you. The soothing scenery, heartfelt stories, and slower pace are perfect for post-Gilmore winding down.

Anne With an E

This reimagined adaptation of the beloved *Anne of Green Gables* novels follows Anne Shirley-Cuthbert, an imaginative, fiery-haired orphan who's mistakenly sent to live with aging siblings Marilla and Matthew Cuthbert in the quiet village of Avonlea. *Anne with an E* is a coming-of-age period drama full of heart, and bookish Anne is basically Rory Gilmore if Rory were a redhead in puffed sleeves. So, wrap up in a blanket this fall and feel all the feelings.

Fall gives us permission to watch the clouds roll by, to lose ourselves in a good book (or seven), and to indulge in the kind of stillness that makes a *Gilmore Girls* binge-watch feel like a warm embrace.

The Great Outdoors

The great outdoors

Your favorite fall activity is very likely watching *Gilmore Girls* under a blanket, surrounded by candles, and drinking a steaming mug of coffee. But you're going to need to get some fresh air in between episodes. And getting out into the beautiful natural world is only going to enhance your appreciation of this wonderful season.

This chapter offers you plenty of ideas for activities that will get you off the sofa and out of your front door, whether for a solitary ramble or a catch-up with friends.

Fall-friendly social activities

Fall festival outings. Don't expect them to be quite the standard of Stars Hollow, but it's always worth checking out local harvest festivals or fairs, featuring live music, crafts, and seasonal treats. This is an ideal way to soak up the spirit of autumn with plenty of activities to enjoy together.

A forest or woodland walk. What could beat a walk with a friend among the falling leaves? Whether you head out to catch the early-morning crispness or the late-afternoon sun, you'll look like you've stepped straight out of a Hallmark movie montage. Try staging a competition to catch the most leaves before they hit the ground? Bring a flask of coffee or soup for sustenance to keep you going? You may just find yourself making a habit of nice, long strolls throughout the season.

Coffee in the park. Whether you have a perfectly situated café, a strategically placed gazebo, or simply a favorite bench you can bring your own cup to, it's the perfect time of year to sit with a friend and watch the world go by. Just make sure to wrap up warm (and if you haven't already got a pair of heated socks, now is the time seek one out).

Pumpkin-patch outing. Gather friends or family for a trip to a local pumpkin patch. Spend time picking the perfect specimens; it's completely up to you which color you choose and whether you go for smooth or gnarled (although the latter is harder to carve – see pages 169–171 for tips on pumpkin carving.). Enjoy hayrides and sipping on warm cider. It's a fun way to embrace the season while supporting local farms.

Apple-picking adventure. Visit a public orchard or apple farm and spend the day picking apples. It's a great group activity that ends with a delicious reward – fresh fruit to bake pies, make cider, or simply enjoy, as nature intended. See page 27 for a fantastic spiced apple pie recipe.

Farmers' market trips. While a local farmers' market is great to visit all year round, a fall trip just hits differently. Stock up on seasonal produce (great for your autumn baking), fresh flowers for a wreath or centerpiece (see Chapter Two), and handmade goods for your home. It's a lovely, relaxing way to connect with others and stock your cupboards with fall essentials.

Bike ride. Remember Lorelai's new-found love of her commute to the Dragonfly Inn when the truck gives up the ghost? A bike ride down winding country lanes or smooth woodland paths will set your soul singing. It may also be the perfect way to journey to your chosen pumpkin patch or orchard (see above), assuming you have a big enough basket to bring the goodies home in.

Hay-bale maze. If you're lucky enough to find a hay-bale maze in your local area, it's an attraction that simply can't be missed. Although the residents of Stars Hollow are initially skeptical when they realize Taylor has spent the entire fall-festival budget on an enormous maze, they quickly change their tune once they see it.

- **Bonfire gatherings.** Host a bonfire night with friends for an evening of marshmallow roasting and storytelling. The crisp autumn air makes the fire's warmth even more enjoyable. As Rachel, Luke's former girlfriend once commented, 'The firelight really changes people. Makes them seem happier, freer, all the troubles of the world completely gone.' But make sure you learn from the annual mistake at the Stars Hollow Firelight Festival and actually bring some matches to light it with! See page 35 for a next-level s'mores recipe.

Stargazing. Legend and Miss Patty tell us that Stars Hollow was founded in the spot where two lovers met, brought together by following a trail of stars that magically appeared in the sky. It is the reason the Firelight Festival is celebrated each year. And there is truly nothing that can put things in perspective more than gazing up at the stars above, their very existence reminding us that all our problems are smaller than a speck in the history of the universe – a very freeing thought and one that is perfect for the season of self-reflection.

Outdoor movie night. The nights might be drawing in, but that can make it even cozier to host an outdoor movie night, as long as you have plenty of blankets, warm socks, and maybe even a fire pit for added atmosphere. Brew up some hot chocolate (see page 31) or hot buttered cider (see page 39) and grab a classic fall movie. As long as it's only a private viewing and not a ticketed event, you won't be restricted on choice and end up with only *The Yearling* to watch – Stars Hollow's go-to film.

Autumn outfits inspired by Stars Hollow

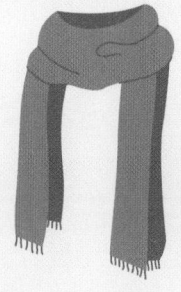

The ultimate lookbook for leaf-crunching strolls, impromptu town meetings, and endless coffee runs:

Statement tee + corduroy jacket

Whether it's her 'heavy metal rules' top or 'knit or go home' top, Lorelai loves a statement tee. It's a fall staple in her book. Throw a fun statement tee on under a warm jacket and then add jeans, sneakers, and a touch of sarcasm, obviously.

Oversized scarf + ankle boots

The unofficial uniform of a Stars Hollow autumn. A cozy, oversized scarf is basically a portable blanket – and Lorelai would never say no to fashion that doubles as comfort. Pair with slim jeans or a skirt and ankle boots and you've got instant small-town style.

Chunky jumper + shorts + tights

Rory knows a good chunky jumper when she sees one. Think Rory's iconic white fisherman sweater from the pilot episode – oversized, cozy, and completely timeless. While she paired it with jeans, you can elevate the look with denim shorts and opaque tights for a modern twist.

Leather blazer + knee-high boots

This is Lorelai's 'I'm going to be professional but make it fun' fall outfit. A leather or faux-leather blazer thrown over a knit dress adds an autumnal edge. Pair with knee-high boots and you're ready for a business meeting with Michel and Sookie.

Turtleneck + plaid mini skirt

A fitted turtleneck tucked into a plaid mini skirt is a Rory-at-yale signature outfit. It's giving academic-chic-meets-cozy-autumn energy.

Oversized cardigan + coffee-stained jeans

A sumptuously soft, oversized cardigan is perfect for those chilly mornings when coffee is the only thing keeping you going. If there's a little coffee stain on your denim, then you're doing it right.

Classic trench coat + book bag

When you're striding to the library in a rush, a trench coat over a cable knit sweater is a perfect fall look. Add a structured book bag for Rory-core perfection.

'Let's walk arm-in-arm like window-shopping ladies do in movies.'
Lorelai Gilmore

Gardening for spring

One of the best ways of embracing nature in fall is to literally get your hands dirty, planting bulbs to get a head start on your spring garden. Just as in other areas of your life, fall is the perfect time for good intentions to start to germinate and take root, ahead of the new life and energy that will come in springtime. And if you don't have a garden? Why not get some pots on your balcony, plant up a window box, help out a neighbour, or find spaces in your local area that might welcome some green fingers to breathe new life into them.

After the heat of summer, autumn is ideal for planting, when the cooler air is easier on your plants but the ground isn't too cold, so roots will still be able to grow. You can also move plants more easily (less chance of heat stress), taking cuttings and dividing overgrown clumps. It's also the time when garden centers often sell off their summer stock, so you can get yourself a bargain. Here are some great options to look out for.

Bulbs. This is peak time for planting spring-blooming bulbs, such as daffodils, tulips, crocuses, hyacinths, and alliums. Buy varieties with a range of flowering periods, so you can enjoy the blooms throughout spring. Bury them with the pointed ends facing upwards (the general rule is the depth should be about three times their diameter). It's best to plant a cluster together, rather than single bulbs too spaced out, as this is much more impactful. But don't do a Lorelai – remember when Babette bought her some bulbs to distract her from the emptiness in her life, but she left them in the garage to go mouldy?

Annuals for the cooler season. Plants like violas, pansies, snapdragons, lobelias, and cornflowers are perfect to plant in autumn, to bring an infusion of color to tired-looking post-summer gardens. They can put on a fantastic show during the colder months, easily surviving the frostier evenings. For ease, you can buy bedding plants from a garden center and plant them directly into your soil as soon as they become available.

Trees and shrubs. It's a great time of year to plant many of these as the cooler temperatures will be much easier on them. Also, the air temperature being cooler than the soil means the top-growth slows, allowing the plant's energy to be focused on root development. Great trees and shrubs to plant at this time of year include burning bush, witch hazel, rhododendrons, azaleas, camellias, and viburnums. Aim to plant them earlier in fall, ideally six weeks before you're expecting frost, covering the garden beds with a few inches of mulch to keep the soil even warmer.

Fall vegetables. The start of autumn can be a great time to sow vegetable seeds for winter, as the warm soil at this time of year will help them to germinate quickly. The growing season may continue for several weeks if the weather is mild enough, but a greenhouse or polytunnel will extend this. Great options for your fall planting include:

Radishes – with extremely fast-growing times, these will be ready four weeks from planting, so are a very popular option for vegetable gardeners in fall.

Carrots – a staple for autumnal roasts, casseroles, stews, and soups, these are pretty hardy and can tolerate colder temperatures very well. Plant as early as possible in fall and keep them protected for a gorgeous crop in the winter.

Spring onions (scallions) – don't let the name fool you, as these are a great option to grow in fall. Plant early and you'll have a plentiful harvest about eight weeks later.

Turnips – plant in early autumn and these beauties will be ready for picking in winter.

Kale – this leafy green is surprisingly easy to grow and very hardy. Sow in early September and after about fifty days you'll find the plant has matured and you'll be eating it for months.

Spinach – This will do great in autumn and through winter, continually growing after you pick its leaves. But ensure you remove the flowers, or it will go to seed.

'Just you wait until spring. You're gonna wake up one morning, walk out and *pow*: color coming out of your ying-yang.'

Babette Dell

All Hollow's Eve

All Hollow's Eve

Fall isn't just about cozy sweaters and apple pie. The season also has another side – a darker, spooky side: a Halloween side! It's a time for costumes and candy, pumpkins and decorations, ghosts and ghouls, and all the delightful little moments that make October 31 so enchanting.

Few shows capture the essence of autumn and its Halloween vibes like *Gilmore Girls*. As Ellen Gutoskey writes for *Mental Floss*, the cultural lore of *Gilmore Girls* implies that the show's backdrop, Stars Hollow, is a perpetual 'Halloweentown' but 'without all the monsters.'[2] In *Gilmore Girls*, you often see the picturesque streets of Stars Hollow decked out with pumpkins, scarecrows, and hay bales – every corner just radiating small-town Halloween magic.

The show even gives us glimpses of how the characters embrace the spooky spirit of Halloween. There's the time when Lorelai tries to compete with Babette's and Morey's Halloween decorations, making plans for a scary skit involving Luke and link sausages. And who can forget when Rory goes to a costume party as *Kill Bill*'s Gogo Yubari, or when she and Lane dress up as pilgrims? And of course, there is Kirk's unsettlingly bizarre short film screened during annual Stars Hollow Movie Festival – a genius David-Lynchesque creation that feels like a nod to the scary movies we love to watch in October.

In this chapter, we'll inspire you to bring the same Halloween charm of Stars Hollow into your own home. From how to make a stylish jack-o'-lantern carving to DIY sweet jars and gourd candles, you'll find plenty of decorative ideas to embrace Halloween with charming flair. We'll even show you how to make a 'Luke' scarecrow to watch over your fall festivities (and keep any pesky customers at bay).

A Luke scarecrow

With his signature plaid shirt, backward baseball cap, and endearingly grumpy charm, Luke Danes is the perfect cranky character to greet trick-or-treaters. This creation is inspired by the scarecrows that often line the streets of Stars Hollow during fall festivals and is guaranteed to make your Halloween decorations stand out. Prop your Luke scarecrow by your front door or in your garden to supervise the spooky festivities just like he runs his diner.

You will need:

- *Wooden stakes or PVC pipes to build the frame*
- *A plaid shirt (flannel works best)*
- *Straw, old clothes, or newspaper for stuffing*
- *Twine, zip ties, or strong tape to secure everything*
- *A pair of jeans or work pants*
- *A pillowcase or cloth bag*
- *Markers or paint for the face*
- *A baseball cap*
- *An old pair of shoes*
- *A coffee mug or mini coffee pot, for a prop*
- *An apron and a small sign that reads 'No Cell Phones' (optional)*

Steps:

1. Build the frame for your Luke scarecrow. Start by creating a simple 'T' shape, using wooden stakes or PVC pipes. The vertical piece will form Luke's spine, while the horizontal piece becomes his shoulders. Secure the frame firmly in the ground where the Luke scarecrow will stand.

continues over the page

2. Once you have made the frame, it's time to stuff the scarecrow's body. Grab the plaid shirt and fill it with straw, old clothes, or crumpled newspaper, until it's solid. Button the shirt and tie off the cuffs and waist with twine to keep the stuffing inside. Repeat the process with the jeans or work pants, ensuring they're just as sturdy.

3. Assemble the scarecrow by sliding the shirt over the shoulders of the frame and securing it with zip ties or twine . To make it easier to slide the shirt on, you can unbutton the top few buttons and gently drape it over the frame. Attach the pants to the bottom of the shirt, tying them securely, so they won't budge.

4. Create the head of the scarecrow by filling the pillowcase or cloth bag with straw or stuffing. Use markers or paint to draw a grumpy expression (think furrowed brows and a frown in true Luke style). You can also add some stubble to Luke's face, if you like.

5. Once complete, secure the head to the top of the frame and tuck the shirt collar neatly around the base.

6. Now it's time to add Luke's signature look to your scarecrow. Place the baseball cap backward on his head and add the shoes onto the bottom of the pants.

Tip: For an extra touch, tie an apron around your Luke scarecrows waist, give him a coffee mug to hold or prop up a small sign near by that reads 'No Cell Phones' as a cheeky nod to his diner rules.

Trick-or-treating costumes, Gilmore Girls-style

Stuck for something to wear this Halloween? Look no further than *Gilmore Girls* for costume ideas. Over the years, Rory Gilmore has rocked some unforgettable fancy-dress outfits that are perfect for spooky season. Whether it's channelling Tarantino cool or rocking wartime fashion, there's a Rory-inspired outfit for every trick-or-treater. So get your Gilmore on this Halloween!

'I'm going to hand out candy, which is the entire point of Halloween.'
Lorelai Gilmore

Tarantino chic

In Season 5, Rory and Logan attend a party where guests come dressed as characters from Quentin Tarantino movies. Rory dresses up as the innocent-looking (but murderous) schoolgirl Gogo Yubari in Kill Bill, while Logan sports Bruce Willis's iconic yellow boxing robe from Pulp Fiction. Tarantino's characters are full of Halloween-costume potential. Imagine dressing up as Pulp Fiction's Mia Wallace, with her sleek bob and crisp white shirt; or rocking the Bride's signature yellow jumpsuit in Kill Bill.

What you'll need for Gogo Yubari: *A navy blazer, plaid skirt, white knee-high socks, a red bow tie (and a plastic toy chain weapon for extra authenticity).*

Wartime glamor

Rory has a soft spot for 1940s' fashion, as seen in her clothing choices for the Stars Hollow twenty-four-hour Dance Marathon and Emily's World-War-II-themed DAR bash. From elegant tea dresses to USO Worker chic, the wartime era brought stylish practicality to the forefront. Think cinched waists, bold red lipstick, and perfectly coiffed hair. Even during wartime rationing, women still found ways to look fabulous.

What you'll need for 1940s' glam: *A vintage-style tea dress or tailored skirt suit, low-heeled pumps, and accessories like a turban, or a wartime-style hat. Don't forget to curl your hair into victory rolls and swipe on that red lipstick for the finishing touch.*

Steampunk dreams

In *Gilmore Girls: A Year in the Life*, Rory joins Logan, Colin, Finn, and Robert on a wild night out in Stars Hollow with the Life and Death Brigade. They spend the evening gallivanting and tango dancing through Stars Hollow in Steampunk-inspired outfits. (Steampunk is a fantasy esthetic set in an alternate reality where man never progressed past steam power. It fuses Victorian clothing with more futuristic pieces.) Rory and Logan are both seen wearing top hats, waistcoats, and long Victorian-style coats.

What you'll need for Steampunk style: *To embrace the Steampunk look, think Victorian clothing staples like corsets, waistcoats, military jackets, and top hats. Add modern twists with metallic details, such as goggles or a prop cane to channel the adventurous spirit of the style.*

Dazzle like a debutante

In Season 2, Rory attends a debutante ball and formally comes out to society as a favor to Emily. She arrives at the event, wearing a truly stunning white debutante dress with long white evening gloves. With its classic silhouette, the outfit captures the timeless charm of old-world sophistication. Later, in Season 5, Richard and Emily throw a stylish party so Rory can find a suitable boyfriend. Rory turns up in a long black evening gown and a tiara fit for a princess! Why not be the belle of the ball like Rory this Halloween?

What you'll need for debutante chic: *A white evening gown, long white gloves, a pearl necklace, a tiara (and Dean on your arm, in a tux).*

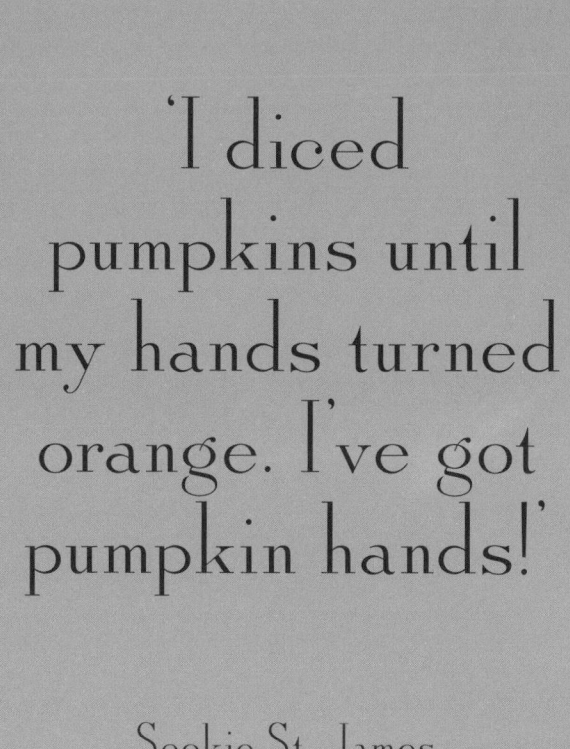

'I diced
pumpkins until
my hands turned
orange. I've got
pumpkin hands!'

Sookie St. James

DIY spooky sweet jars

These DIY spooky sweet jars are inspired by Lorelai and Rory's insatiable sweet tooth. With colorful candy inside and marshmallow ghosts adorning the rim, these jars are deliciously fun to make and ideal for gifting or as indoor Halloween decorations. They're the perfect mix of spooky and sweet, just like a cozy Stars Hollow Halloween.

You will need:
- *Clear glass jars (Mason, or any others you have at home)*
- *Marshmallows (regular size work best)*
- *Edible food markers, including black, for eyes and mouth*
- *Frosting or melted white chocolate, to attach the marshmallows*
- *Candy for filling the jars (such as jelly beans and foil-wrapped chocolates)*
- *Ribbon, twine, and gift tags, for decoration (optional)*

Steps:
1. Start by preparing your jars. Wash and dry them thoroughly to ensure they're clean and ready to showcase your Halloween treats.

2. Decorate the marshmallows to look like ghosts: using the edible food markers, add two black eyes and a circular black mouth.

3. Spread a thin layer of frosting or melted white chocolate around the rim of the jar, then gently press each marshmallow onto the frosting, arranging them so the ghost faces peek outward. Let them set for a few minutes until they're securely attached.

4. Once the marshmallow ghosts are in place, fill the jars with your favorite Halloween-themed candy. You can layer bright colors like jelly beans or mix in foil-wrapped chocolates.

5. Add a finishing touch by tying a ribbon or some twine around the neck of the jar. Orange and black ribbons look particularly festive. If you're gifting, you can also add a small tag to your DIY sweet jar with a Halloween message like 'Boo!' or 'Trick or Treat!'

6. Display or gift your sweet jars. Place them on a table as festive decorations or give them as treats to friends and family.

How to make a stylish Jack-o'-lantern for Halloween

Jack-o'-lantern carvings are the quintessential Halloween decoration, bringing festive charm to any doorstep. With a little creativity, you can transform an ordinary pumpkin into a glowing masterpiece that perfectly captures the spirit of spooky season. Best of all, it's a fun, hands-on activity to enjoy with friends – get ready for messy hands and plenty of pumpkin guts!

You will need:

- *A large pumpkin (choose one with a smooth, symmetrical surface, if possible)*
- *A pumpkin-carving kit (including a scooper, knives, and a poking tool)*
- *A pencil or washable marker for sketching your design*
- *Battery-powered LED tea lights or fairy lights*
- *Metallic paint and eco-friendly glitter to decorate the pumpkin's exterior for added flair (optional)*

Steps:

1. Head to your local patch or store and pick out a large pumpkin that's smooth, even, and free of blemishes. This will make it easier to carve clean, stylish lines and patterns.

2. To prepare your pumpkin, very carefully cut a lid around the stem using a serrated knife. Make sure to angle the cut slightly inward, so the lid doesn't fall through when replaced. Scoop out all the seeds and stringy bits inside, leaving the walls about an inch thick. This ensures your design will shine brightly without weakening the structure.

continues over the page

3. Use a pencil or washable marker to draw your chosen design onto the pumpkin. For complex patterns, you could make a template on a piece of paper, tape it to your pumpkin, and poke along the lines to transfer the design.

4. Use the appropriate tools from your carving kit to carefully cut out your design. Work slowly, especially on intricate patterns, and remove each piece gently to avoid breaking delicate sections. If you're creating a pattern with holes or dots, use a drill or poking tool for a clean finish.

5. Once you have carved your design, place battery-powered LED tea lights or fairy lights inside your pumpkin (these are safer than candles and allow you to adjust the brightness for the perfect effect). If you wish you can also use metallic paint and glitter to add a festive touch to the pumpkin's exterior. Apply the paint first, then sprinkle glitter on top while the paint is still wet for a shiny, sparkly finish. Let it dry completely before displaying.

6. Place your stylish jack-o'-lantern on your porch, mantel, or table as a centerpiece.

Some design ideas

Floral motifs. Create a blooming flower or delicate vine design for a chic and elegant effect.

Celestial themes. Carve out stars, moons, and constellations for a dreamy, night-sky vibe.

Minimalist faces. Think simple dots for eyes and a single line for the mouth – stylish and understated.

Words. To make your pumpkin truly unique, try a personalized touch, such as carving your name or a word into it. If you're feeling particularly adventurous, you could carve the logo for Luke's Diner.

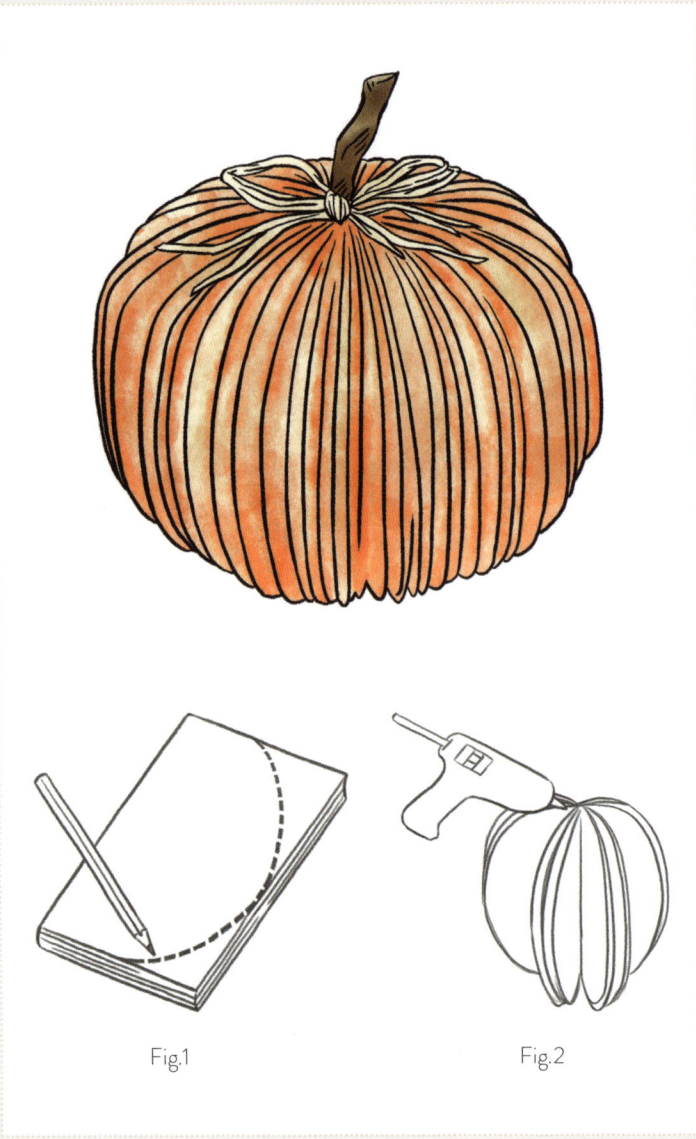

Fig.1   Fig.2

A DIY pumpkin made from a book

Real pumpkins are great, but this is another one for you to showcase your bookworm tendencies, as well as your love for a simple craft. And the best part is that this will never go moldy or smelly.

You will need:
- *A craft knife*
- *An old paperback book*
- *A pencil*
- *A hot-glue gun*
- *Orange spray paint*
- *A small stick*
- *Natural raffia ribbon*

Steps:

1. Use a craft knife to remove the book's cover.

2. Draw a semi-circle with the pencil on the top-most page, with the spine of the book as the long, straight edge (see Fig. 1). It doesn't need to be perfect.

3. Use the craft knife again to cut into the semi-circle you've drawn, cutting a few pages at a time, until you have cut through the entire block. Again, perfection is not the goal; some rough edges will add to the effect of the end product.

4. Bend the spine of the book back to make it pliable and start fanning the pages out.

continues over the page

5. Use the hot-glue gun to apply glue to the spine and the first and last pages. Carefully bring those pages together and hold them until they've stuck. Fan out the pages to make your pumpkin nice and full.

6. Spray paint the book pumpkin, preferably outdoors, making sure you have even coverage.

7. Use the hot-glue gun to attach your stick to the top of your pumpkin, nestling it into the gap in the spine.

8. Tie some natural raffia ribbon to the base of the stick to finish off the look.

Tip: It may be time-consuming, but for best results, put a spot of glue between each of the pages in the gutter, to help keep them separated (see Fig. 2).

Gilmore ghouls: Spooky films loved by Lorelai and Rory

The Witches of Eastwick (1987)

The Witches of Eastwick is a 1987 dark-comedy film starring Jack Nicholson, Cher, Susan Sarandon, and Michelle Pfeiffer. It follows three women who discover their magical powers after becoming involved with a mysterious and sinister man called Daryl Van Horne. Lorelai compares herself and Rory to the characters in this movie.

Carrie (1976)

Carrie is a 1976 horror film based on Stephen King's novel. The film stars Sissy Spacek as Carrie White, a shy high-school student with telekinetic powers, who seeks revenge on her classmates after being humiliated at her prom. Rory references a classic scene in Carrie before her own prom.

Edward Scissorhands (1990)

Directed by Tim Burton and starring Johnny Depp, this movie follows an artificial man with scissors for hands, who is taken in by a suburban family. As he navigates love and loneliness, his unique abilities spark both admiration and fear. Rory loves this film so much as a child that she wants to marry Edward Scissorhands. With its gothic charm and themes of otherness, it's a wonderful Halloween watch.

Psycho (1960)

The movie follows Marion Crane, who steals money and checks into Bates Motel, where she encounters the mysterious and unsettling Patrick Bates. Known for its shocking twists and the classic shower scene, *Psycho* is considered one of the greatest and most influential horror films of all time. Lorelai and Rory mention this classic several times throughout the show.

Gourd candles

Gourd candles add a touch of fall magic to Halloween. Each one is charmingly unique and gives out rustic autumnal vibes. Plus, crafting them is a delightfully hands-on experience – think scooping, melting, and turning an everyday gourd into a flickering work of art.

You will need:

- *A knife or pumpkin-carving tools*
- *Small gourds or pumpkins (choose small, sturdy ones with solid bases to stand on; their size will determine how large your candles can be)*
- *A small scoop or a spoon or melon baller*
- *A drill or screwdriver (for drainage holes)*
- *Battery-operated tea light candles*

Steps:

1. Using a knife, very carefully cut a circular opening around the stem of each gourd and slice off the tops. Think of these like the lid of a jack-o'-lantern (keep them for later to cover the candles, if desired).

2. Use a spoon or melon baller to scoop out the flesh and seeds inside the gourds, just as you would with a pumpkin. Make sure you leave enough thickness for the shells to support the candles.

3. For safety, create draining holes in your gourds. Drill or poke a small hole in the bottom of each one. This allows heat to escape and prevents the candles from overheating.

4. Place the battery-operated tea lights inside the gourds, ensuring they fit securely. If you've kept the lids place them back on top.

5. Arrange your gourd candles around your home or on your Halloween display. Turn them on, and let the gentle flickers set the mood for your spooky celebration!

Preparing for winter the *Gilmore Girls* way

As the last leaves fall and your final pumpkin spice latte cools, winter makes its dramatic entrance and you might just be able to smell snow . . . This is your guide to surviving (and thriving) through the colder months like a Gilmore. Because when the temperatures drop, the layers go up and the snacks inevitably multiply.

Stockpile coffee like it's a blizzard essential. As Lorelai says, 'Nothing says coffee like 6 a.m. in the morning' ... or any freezing cold moment! In the depths of winter, coffee becomes both comfort and survival. So, stock up like you're bracing for a snowstorm – bags of beans, boxes of pods, and instant ground coffee (no judgement here). When the chill hits, let the aroma of fresh coffee work its magic. Bonus points for a novelty mug shaped like a snowman or a reindeer.

Master the art of layering. Stars Hollow winters aren't for amateurs, so stay warm like a pro: scarf over a jumper, under a coat, under a blanket for good measure. Add fingerless gloves (for book-holding or grabbing takeout coffee from Luke's). And, of course, with the change in seasons comes the return of the cozy hats beloved by Lorelai – think all varieties of knitted, fuzzy, pom-pommed, and floral.

Schedule at least one snow-in movie marathon. Snow day = movie day. Instead of letting snow days catch you off guard, prep a cozy movie lineup in advance – old Hollywood classics, feel-good musicals and those so-bad-they're-great films. (If you need some inspiration you can find some of Lorelai's top picks on pages 117–121.) Pyjamas are highly recommended and snacks should be kept within arm's reach.

Prepare for first snow drama. Start practicing your best Lorelai 'I smell snow' gasp in the mirror. *Gilmore Girls* was all about romanticizing life's small, magical moments and nothing says 'seasonal main character' like the first snowfall. When those flakes start to fall, it's your cue to dash outside in pyjamas and slippers, breathe in that icy air, and soak up the moment like you're standing in the middle of Stars Hollow.

Make weekly calls a cozy ritual. As the nights get longer, swap your scroll time for phone calls with your best friend or your mom (ideally while wrapped in a blanket and sipping coffee on the couch). Bonus points if it turns into a three-hour conversation about nothing and everything, à la Lorelai and Rory.

Decorate like a town square ceremony is imminent. Twinkling fairy lights aren't just for trees – they're for bookshelves, windows, and headboards (see pages 80–81 for more ideas). Break out the pine-scented candles, hang garlands in places that make no sense, and don't forget the mini wreath for your coffee maker.

Make a seasonal photo diary. Start capturing winter the *Gilmore Girls* way – one whimsical, blink-and-you'll-miss-it moment at a time. Take pictures of every tiny winter moment: the first snowflake on your sleeve, your dog in a ridiculous jumper, your coffee steam against the cold window. Keep your photos in a folder called 'Stars Hollow Winter' or go wild and put them in a scrapbook like it's 2002.

'Everything's magical when it snows.
Everything looks pretty. The clothes
are great – coats, gloves, scarves, hats.'
Lorelai Gilmore

Autumn with *Gilmore Girls*: Every fall episode

This book should have prepared you heart, body, and mind to get the most out of your *Gilmore Girls* rewatch!

While it is traditional to watch from start to finish, you may very well want to get falling into fall right away, in which case, here is a list of every fall episode in the *Gilmore Girls'* cannon, so you can dive straight in. Enjoy and savor each moment. There truly is nothing like spending time with the Gilmore Girls.

Season 1, Episode 2: The Lorelais' First Day at Chilton
Season 1, Episode 5: Cinnamon's Wake
Season 1, Episode 6: Rory's Birthday Parties
Season 1, Episode 7: Kiss and Tell

Season 2, Episode 4: The Road to Harvard
Season 2, Episode 5: Nick & Nora/Sid & Nancy
Season 2, Episode 6: Presenting Lorelai Gilmore
Season 2, Episode 7: Like Mother, Like Daughter
Season 2, Episode 8: The In and Outs of Inns
Season 2, Episode 10: The Bracebridge Dinner

Season 3, Episode 5: Eight O'Clock at the Oasis
Season 3, Episode 6: Take the Deviled Eggs
Season 3, Episode 7: They Shoot Gilmores, Don't They?
Season 3, Episode 8: Let the Games Begin
Season 3, Episode 9: A Deep-Fried Korean Thanksgiving

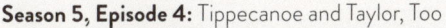

Season 4, Episode 4: Chicken or Beef?
Season 4, Episode 5: The Fundamental Things Apply
Season 4, Episode 6: An Affair to Remember
Season 4, Episode 7: The Festival of Living Art
Season 4, Episode 8: Die, Jerk
Season 4, Episode 9: Ted Koppel's Big Night Out

Season 5, Episode 4: Tippecanoe and Taylor, Too
Season 5, Episode 5: We Got Us a Pippi Virgin
Season 5, Episode 6: Norman Mailer, I'm Pregnant!
Season 5, Episode 7: You Jump, I Jump, Jack
Season 5, Episode 8: The Party's Over
Season 5, Episode 9: Emily Says Hello
Season 5, Episode 10: But Not as Cute as Pushkin

Season 6, Episode 5: We've Got Magic to Do
Season 6, Episode 6: Welcome to the Dollhouse
Season 6, Episode 7: Twenty-One Is the Loneliest Number
Season 6, Episode 8: Let Me Hear Your Balalaikas Ringing Out
Season 6, Episode 9: The Prodigal Daughter Returns
Season 6, Episode 10: He's Slippin' 'Em Bread . . . Dig?

Season 7, Episode 4: 'S Wonderful, 'S Marvelous
Season 7, Episode 5: The Great Stink
Season 7, Episode 6: Go, Bulldogs!
Season 7, Episode 7: French Twist
Season 7, Episode 8: Introducing Lorelai Planetarium
Season 7, Episode 9: Knit, People, Knit!

***Gilmore Girls: a Year in the Life*, Episode 4:** Fall

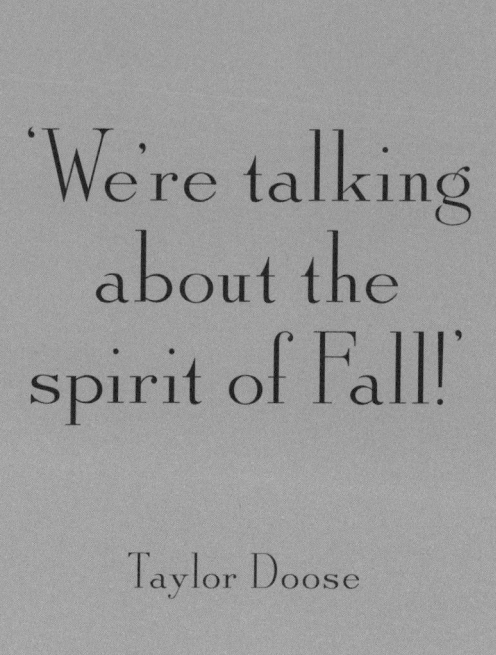

'We're talking
about the
spirit of Fall!'

Taylor Doose

Acknowledgments

Thank you to everyone who made *Gilmore Girls*, indisputably the best television show in history. You have given us fans endless joy and succour from all the difficult things in the world.

Thanks to the team at HarperCollins for allowing me to write this book: Harriet Prideaux, for commissioning it; George Atsiaris for managing the process; Abi Hartshorne for the most beautiful cover and design; and Amelia Deacon for the illustrations.

Endnotes

1 Delkic, Melina '"Gilmore Girls" Is an Endless Buffet of TV Comfort Food,' *New York Times* (www.nytimes.com/2024/01/31/arts/television/gilmore-girls-netflix-rewatch.html)

2 Gutosky, Ellen 'Smells Like Stars Hollow: How Much of "Gilmore Girls" is Set in the Fall?' Mental Floss (www.mentalfloss.com/posts/gilmore-girls-fall-tv-show)

Picture credits

pp. 6, 12, 46, 61, 82, 101, 102, 136, 152, 156, 161, 162, 163, 164 © Amelia Deacon
p. 8 Denis Tangney Jr/Getty Images
p. 11 Neal Pritchard Photography
pp. 14, 29 DEEPOL by plainpicture
p. 16 Ekaterrina Fedulyeva/Getty Images
pp. 19, 21, 22 © Sophie Fox Photography
p. 25 Vladislav Nosick/500px/Getty Images
p. 26 Howard Oates/Getty Images
p. 38 Anne DEL SOCORRO/Getty Images
pp. 40–41 Mariana Medvedeva on Unsplash
p. 43 Daniel on Unsplash
p. 45 Polina Lebed/500px/Getty Images
p. 48 Stania Kasula/Alamy Stock Photo
pp. 56, 70, 75, 174 © Ollie Mann
p. 66 Ronnie George on Unsplash
p. 69 plainpicture/Narratives/Rachel Whiting
p. 72 Gulfiya Mukhamatdinova/Getty Images
p. 76 Alan Majchrowicz/Getty Images
p. 81 Shashi Chaturvedula on Unsplash
p. 84 Denys Bilytskyi / Alamy Stock Photo
pp. 88–89 Alisa Anton on Unsplash

p. 90 EyeEm Mobile/Getty Images
p. 93 Allison Christine on Unsplash
p. 96 Vira Petrunina/Alamy Stock Photo
p. 99 Jenifoto/Getty Images
pp. 112–113 Budhi Siswanto/500px/Getty Images
p. 119 Svetikd/Getty Images
p. 127 Stephen Knowles Photography/Getty Images
pp. 142–143 Lucas Larsson on Unsplash
p. 144 Kate Glotova on Unsplash
p. 148 VICUSCHKA/Getty Images
p. 154 Education Images/Getty Images
p. 159 Brian Jannsen/Alamy Stock Photo
p. 167 Eli Asenova/Getty Images
p. 171 Catherine Falls Commercial/Getty Images
pp. 172–173 Craig Dimmick on Unsplash
p. 178 Daniela Baumann/Alamy Stock Photo
p. 180 Svitlana on Unsplash
pp. 184–185 Alex Albert on Unsplash
p. 188 Pinkybird/Getty Images
p. 191 Elena Popova/Getty Images
All other images: Shutterstock.com